P9-CDA-665

BEYOND RECOGNITION

Also by Ridley Pearson

Chain of Evidence

No Witnesses

The Angel Maker

Hard Fall

Probable Cause

Undercurrents

Hidden Charges

Blood of the Albatross

Never Look Back

BEYOND RECOGNITION

RIDLEY PEARSON

NEW YORK

This is a work of fiction. All characters are works of the author's imagination; no similarity to persons living or dead is intended. Any factual mistakes or liberties taken are the author's responsibility—I offer my apologies, up front, for any such errors.

Library of Congress Cataloging-in-Publication Data

Pearson, Ridley.
    Beyond recognition / by Ridley Pearson. — 1st ed.
        p.   cm.
    ISBN 0-7868-6240-8
    I. Title.
    PS3566.E234B4   1997
    813'.54—dc20   96-21125
                            CIP

Book design by Gloria Adelson

FIRST EDITION

10 9 8 7 6 5 4 3 2 1

Beyond Recognition is dedicated to my parents, Betsy and Bob Pearson, for all the great years, past, present, and future, and to my wife, Marcelle, for her love and guidance.

Special thanks are due to:

Brian DeFiore, editor

Bob Pearson	Pete Conrad
Richard Hart	Andrew Hamilton
Lynette Westendorf	Donald Reay
Karen Oswalt	C.D. and Hap Happle
Barge Levy	Norm Prins
Walt Femling	Christian Harris
Jerry Femling	Royal McClure
Fletcher Brock	Donald Cameron
Callie Huttar	Bill Dietz
Steven Garman	Paul Witt
Emily Dreyfuss	Chris Wrede
Ben Dreyfuss	Robert Gilson
Nexis-Lexis	Mary K. Peterson
William Martin	Nancy Luff
Maida Spaulding	Albert Zuckerman
Michael Youngblood	

BEYOND RECOGNITION

The world, an entity out of everything, was created by neither gods nor men, but was, is, and will be eternally living fire, regularly becoming ignited and regularly becoming extinguished.

—Heraclitus, *The Cosmic Fragments*, no. 20 (c. 480 B.C.)

We all live in a house on fire, no fire department to call; no way out, just the upstairs window to look out of while the fire burns the house down with us trapped, locked in it.

—Tennessee Williams, *The Milk Train Doesn't Stop Here Anymore* (1963)

1

T H E fire began at sunset.

It filled the house like a hot putrid breath, alive. It ran like a liquid through the place, stopping at nothing, feeding on everything in its path, irreverent and unforgiving. It raced like a phantom, room to room, eating the drapes, the rugs, the towels, sheets, and linens, the clothes, the shoes, and blankets in the closets, removing any and all evidence of things human. It invaded the various rooms like an unchecked virus raiding neighboring cells, contaminating, infecting, consuming. It devoured the wood of the doorjambs, swarmed the walls, fed off the paint, and blistered the ceiling. Lightbulbs vaporized, sounding like a string of Black Cat firecrackers. This was no simple fire.

It vaporized the small furniture, chairs, tables, dressers, all dissolving in its wake. It refinished and then devoured the desk she had bought at a weekend flea market, a desk she had stripped of its ugly green paint and lovingly resurfaced with a transparent plastic coating guaranteed by the manufacturer to last thirty years.

Longer than she lasted.

For Dorothy Enwright, it was more like a camera's flash popping in the dark. It began long before any clothes or rooms were claimed. It began as a strange growling sound deep within the walls. At first she imagined an earthquake. This was dispelled by the quick and surprisingly chilling spark on the far side of her eyelids. To her it began not as heat but as a flash of bone-numbing cold.

It burned off her hair, the skin on her face—and she went over backward, her throat seared, unable to scream. In a series of popping sounds, her bones exploded, brittle and fast, like pine needles dumped on a fire.

The toilets and sinks melted, a sudden flow of bubbling porcelain, running like lava.

Dorothy Enwright was dead within the first twenty seconds of the burn. But before she died she visited hell, a place that Dorothy Enwright did not belong. She had no business there, this woman. No business, given that a member of the fire department had received a threat eleven hours earlier, and the person receiving that threat had failed to act upon it.

By the time the fire hoses were through, little existed for Seattle's Marshal Five fire inspector to discover or collect as evidence. Little existed of the truth. The truth, like the home of Dorothy Enwright and Dorothy herself, had gone up in smoke, destroyed beyond recognition.

2

THE Boldts' home phone rang at six-forty in the evening, September tenth, a Tuesday. Elizabeth, who would be forty in March, passed her husband the receiver and released a huge sigh to make a point of her disgust at the way his police work interfered with their lives.

Boldt croaked out a hello. He felt bone tired. He didn't want Liz thrown into a mood.

They had seen their precious Sarah to sleep only moments before and had stretched out on their bed to take a fifteen-minute break. Miles was occupied by a set of blocks in the corner.

The bedding smelled of Liz, and he wished that the phone hadn't rung because he hated to see her angry. She had every right to be angry because she'd been complaining about the phone being on her side of the bed for the past four *years*, and Boldt had never done a thing about it. He didn't understand exactly *why* he hadn't done anything about it; she mentioned it all the time, and replacing the phone cord with something longer wasn't the most technically challenging job in the world. He reached over to touch her shoulder in apology, but caught himself and returned his hand to his side. No sense in making things worse.

Cupping the phone, he explained to her: "A fire." Boldt was homicide, so it had to be a serious fire.

She sighed again, which meant she didn't care much about the content of the phone call, only its duration.

"Keep your voice down," Liz cautioned wisely. Sarah was a light sleeper, and the crib was only a few feet away, against the bedroom wall where Boldt's dresser had once been.

The baby's crying began immediately, as if on Liz's cue. Boldt thought it was her mother's voice that triggered it, not his, but he wasn't about to argue the point.

Boldt took down the address and hung up.

Liz walked over to the crib and Boldt admired her. She kept herself trim and fit. The second time around, that had been a challenge. She looked ten years younger than other mothers the same age. As the cradled baby came eagerly to her mother's breast, Lou Boldt felt his throat tighten with loving envy. There were unexpected moments in his life that would remain with him forever, seared into his consciousness like photographs, and this was one of them. He nearly forgot about the phone call.

Liz talked quietly to the baby. She glanced over at her husband. "I'm sorry I snapped at you," she said.

"I'll move the phone," Boldt promised her.

"Sometime this decade would be nice," she said. They grinned at each other, and their smiles widened, and Lou Boldt thought himself lucky to share his life with her, and he told her so, and she blushed. She lay back on the bed with the child at her breast. Miles was into creating the second story of his block fort. Maybe he'd grow up to be an architect, Boldt thought. Anything but a cop.

Lou Boldt smelled the fire before he ever reached it. Its ghost, spilled out like entrails, blanketed most of Wallingford, settling down onto Lake Union as a thin, wispy fog. It didn't smell of death, more like wet charcoal. But if, as a sergeant of Crimes

Against Persons, Boldt was being called to a fire, it was because a person or persons had perished and Marshal Five had already made a call of suspicious origin. Someone had torched a building. Someone else was dead.

There were a lot of fires in Seattle in any given year. Not so many homicides, not by national standards. The two seldom mixed, and when they did it was always—*always*, he emphasized to himself silently—one or more firefighters. The Pang fire had been the most recent and the worst: four firemen dead in an arson fire. Four years in the past, it was still vivid in the collective mind of the city. Boldt had worked that case as well. He didn't want another one.

He had been off-duty at the time of the call. Rightfully speaking, the investigation belonged to a detective other than himself. Yet there he was, a little overweight, a little gray at the temples, feeling a little anxious, speeding the department-issue beat-up Chevy toward the address he had scribbled on a sheet of notepaper torn from a pad given to him as a Christmas stocking present. Duty bound is what he was. As the department's "most veteran" homicide cop—a pleasant way of saying he was a little too old for the job—Boldt was assigned more than his fair share of the tough cases. In his line of work, success was its own penalty.

Many times he had considered the thought that Lieutenant Phil Shoswitz assigned him those more difficult cases in an effort to persuade him to apply for, and accept, a lieutenant's desk. But Boldt was not easily moved from his position. He preferred people to paperwork.

Fire scenes instilled fear in him, even from a respectable distance. It wasn't the flashing lights; he was long since accustomed to those. It wasn't the tangle of the hoses, or the wet, glistening pavement, or the supernatural look of the behemoth firemen in their turnout gear, helmeted and masked. It was the damp musk smell, the smudged filth that accompanied any fire, and Boldt's own active imagination that too easily invented a claustrophobic room entirely engulfed in flames and he, a fireman, smack in the middle of it, aiming a fire hose in revenge: the burning ceiling giving out, the floor breaking away underneath, a wall coming down. To die in fire had to be the worst.

Battalion Chief Witt, clad in his turnouts, met Boldt as the sergeant approached one of the pumpers, where the crew was busy packing up the rig. Witt had a florid face and bloodshot eyes. He reminded Boldt of an Irish drinker, the kind of guy to come across in a Boston pub. He shook hands firmly. "Marshal Five's in there," he said, indicating what remained of the house—precious little.

The September air was a pleasant temperature, even without the heat still radiating from the site. Boldt wore a khaki windbreaker, a cotton sweater, and khaki pants. He carried his hands in his pockets, but not to keep them warm. His posture reflected a tension, a tightness; the cables in his neck showed as his jaw muscles flexed into hard nuts.

"He called it in to our arson boys," Boldt informed him. "Must have been mention of a body, because they called me."

"No body found so far," Witt explained. "A neighbor says he saw her in there, though. Saw her just a couple minutes before the flash." He repeated, "Flash, *not* explosion," as if this should hold significance for the sergeant. Boldt experienced a sinking feeling. He had a lot to learn, and all catch-up at that.

"Your department," Boldt said honestly. "Or Marshal Five's. My concern is the body."

"If we ever find her."

"Will we?" Boldt had to shout above the sound of the trucks' mechanicals, the bark of the radios, and the shouting between firefighters still on the site. "Find her?" he finished.

Witt answered obliquely. "ME's on the way."

Dr. Ronald Dixon, one of Boldt's closest friends and a fellow jazz enthusiast, was King County's chief medical examiner. Boldt welcomed his participation.

Boldt asked, "What's that mean? Is there a body or not?"

"This baby was one hot sucker, Sergeant. What started in there and what ended up in there are two different things, ya know? Two different animals." Witt, too, shouted to be heard. "If she's in there, there's not much left. That's what I'm saying. Hot,'' he repeated ominously. "Like nothing I ever seen. Like nothing I want to see again, ya know? A real showy son-of-a-bitch, this one was.''

"Marshal Five called it?'' Boldt asked, seeking to verify that the cause of the fire had been ruled of suspicious origin. Witt's eyes darted to and from the site. He seemed to be keeping something to himself. It troubled Boldt.

"I'm assuming so,'' the chief answered. "Else why would you be here? Am I right?'' He added, "Listen, Sergeant, we put the wet stuff on the red stuff. Marshal Five handles the rest.''

"Something bothering you?'' Boldt asked bluntly.

"It flashed; it didn't blow—that's if you trust the witness. It burned real hot. Only thing close is Blackstock or Pang. We shoot for a four- to six-minute response time. We were six, maybe eight on this baby. Not bad, not our best. But she was ripping long before we got here. Ripping mean, is what I'm saying. Ripping hot, right up through the center of the structure; a weird burn is what it was. You check air traffic control, Sergeant. That's what you do. My guess is six, seven hundred, maybe a thousand feet in the first thirty seconds. Something on that order. Something big. Bigger than stink. You've been in this as long as I have and that shit scares you, that's all. It scares you.'' He walked off, leaving Boldt with water seeping in through the soles of his shoes and the taste of charcoal in his mouth and nostrils.

It was the taste that confirmed it. A taste that wouldn't go away completely for two or three days—he knew as much the moment it rolled over his tongue. As foul a taste as a person could experience.

A dead body. No question about it.

3

"GET out of here. Go upstairs, or watch TV or something."

Ben had never seen the man with this particular girl before, but she wasn't much different from any of the others—a waitress, maybe, or just a girl from the bar: big boobs and tight jeans—not much different.

The guy, who called himself Ben's father but wasn't, drew closer. "You listening to me, kid?" Definitely the bar. He smelled of it: cigarettes and beer. He blinked a pair of glassy eyes, unable to focus. Pot too, probably, Ben thought. He smoked a lot of the stuff. Weekends he started smoking pot with his first cup of coffee, around noon.

The man's name was Jack Santori, and Ben owned that same last name, but not by birth. He hated the man, though hate was too soft a word.

"You told me to clean up the kitchen," Ben protested, reminding Jack of the earlier order. He felt confused and angry. Bone tired. He wished he were eighteen instead of twelve; he wished he could walk right out the door and never come back—the same way his mother had. He missed his mother something fierce. "I washed the sheets," he said, hoping to pick up some credit. He had been told to wash the sheets *before* starting in on the kitchen, and that's just what he had done, so maybe the bastard would cut him some slack.

"Upstairs," Jack ordered, walking unsteadily toward the fridge and rummaging on the shelves for a pair of beers. He asked the girl, "Brew?" and as she nodded her boobs jiggled. She cast a sympathetic look in Ben's direction, but it wouldn't help because she was new around here. She didn't know Jack. If she lasted more than one or two nights it would be a record. Ben knew what went on down there at night; Jack was rough with them. Same way he was rough with Ben. Best thing about seeing him this drunk was he'd sleep until noon. Best thing about the girl being with him was he probably wouldn't hit Ben in front of her. Jack tried to make out like they were friends. The man had lying down to a science.

He had married Ben's mother when Ben was five and she was out of money. She cut hair for a living, but she had been fired. She had explained it all to Ben; she had apologized. "Jack's a pretty nice guy, and he can provide for us." She was proved wrong on both counts, but she was gone now, so what did it matter? Ben was stuck with the guy.

"Upstairs. Now!" Jack shouted. The girl stiffened with that tone of voice, and her boobs stuck straight out. Ben had heard that same slurred anger too often to fear it, and besides, he knew the guy wouldn't hit him in front of her. Not the first night.

Ben turned off the water, dried his hands, and glanced at the girl. Her shirt wasn't buttoned right. Her hair was toussled. Her lipstick was smeared, deforming her mouth. It repulsed him. He knew what they did down there in that room. He washed the sheets, after all. Every now and then he saw one of the girls walking around naked in the morning—the only good thing about them coming over. But that meant he saw the bruises too, and he knew only too well where they came from. Jack liked to pretend how he was so tough. He didn't know that Ben occasionally heard him crying down there when he was all alone. Sobbing like a baby. If

Ben hadn't feared him so much, he might have found room to pity him.

Jack and his blond bar girl went at it most of that night, Ben unable to sleep for all the noise. He was just drifting off when the headboard started slapping the wall again like someone beating a drum, and the girl with her moaning, and everything got faster until the headboard sounded like it was going to beat a hole in the wall. She cried out like he was killing her, and then it stopped, and Ben wondered if maybe he *had* killed her. He seemed capable of it. There wasn't much that Ben would put past Jack.

When morning finally showed its mercy by allowing the sun to rise, Ben got dressed and got the hell out of there before the trouble began. Trouble came with pain in that house. It was to be avoided at all costs.

The southeast neighborhood where he lived was mostly black and poor. The houses were old and beat up, the cars parked outside them, not much different. He and his mom had lived better before Jack came along, though Ben didn't remember much about those days anymore. He'd never met his real father.

The roadside gutters were littered with soggy trash, and there was a smell like garbage because the stray dogs got into the black plastic bags every trash day, which was Wednesday. Most of the houses showed chipped paint and carried moss-covered roofs half-rotten from the long wet winters. Occasionally a building was condemned, its residents evicted. It seemed to happen pretty much at random. He wasn't sure where those people went, didn't know what would happen if Jack's house was condemned. He couldn't think about it. He didn't like to think beyond tomorrow or the day after. Next week seemed an eternity away.

He climbed up the hill, the growling sound of a jet overhead, a hum of traffic from Martin Luther King Boulevard. The gangs were about the only thing Ben feared. They shot each other over stupid stuff. Ben kept to himself and walked fast. Once a kid had tried to recruit him to be a drug runner, and it was only through clever thinking that Ben had avoided the job without getting beat up for refusing. He had pulled out his glass eye, his left eye, and, holding it in the palm of his hand, had explained that with only one good eye he couldn't see who was coming from his left, so he made an easy target. A real gross-out, the eye trick worked every time.

The glass eye was the result of a birth defect—Peter's anomaly—and though Ben wished he had two eyes like everyone else, the trick of popping out his glass eye came in handy every now and then. Like with girls. They screamed and ran the other way, which was just fine with him. Who needed girls?

Except Emily. She didn't count as a girl, even if she was one, technically speaking. She lived at 115A 21st Avenue East, a small purple house with dark blue trim. There was a six-foot-high metal globe of the world on her lawn, along with a plastic pink flamingo and a miniature Negro painted whiteface and holding a sign that read FORTUNES $10—TAROT—ASTROLOGY. There was a blue neon sign in the window that read YOUR FUTURE, YOUR PAST—AT LAST! There were white stars and pale blue moons painted on the purple siding. There was a flagstone path that Ben followed to the front door. He knocked twice rather than ring the bell. There was no car parked in the drive, so he assumed she didn't have a customer.

"Come in, Ben." Emily always knew it was him. Just how, he wasn't sure. People doubted her powers, talked about her behind her back, but Ben knew better. Emily possessed a gift, and the gift was *real*.

"I didn't see a car," he explained. Not all of Emily's customers arrived by car, which was why he had knocked. If she had not answered, he would not have knocked for a second time; he would have either waited up the cedar tree alongside her driveway or sneaked in the back door.

"Business will pick up," she promised. Emily was rarely wrong about anything. She had rich brown hair, kind blue eyes, and was probably about the same age as his mother, which was old—somewhere around thirty. She wore a flowered dress with a red plastic belt, pink stockings, and red high-top sneakers. The house smelled like maple syrup. She left the door for him to shut and led the way to the kitchen, the pair of them moving with a comfortable familiarity, like mother and son—which was how Ben liked to think of it.

On the way to the kitchen they passed through the room in which she told fortunes. The ceiling was draped in parachute cloth dyed sky blue, the sheer fabric gathered around a white globe ceiling fixture that was on a dimmer always set low. Below the light was a round table with a black tablecloth and two ladderback cane-seat chairs with round black pillows for cushions. On the table was a leaded glass candle holder for a single red candle that burned at eye height so it partially blinded the customer when he or she ventured a look at the hostess. A thumb-worn deck of tarot cards was set to the left of Emily's place, and below the lip of the table were three switches that allowed her to control the mood of the room. The most impressive special effect in her limited arsenal was the ability to project a good rendition of the summer night sky onto the parachute cloth, which she utilized as atmosphere in the event a customer wanted an astrological reading. The small gray box taped to the underside of the table alongside these switches controlled the radio-transmitter earpiece insert that Emily wore. The walls of the room were painted in a confused assortment of fat Buddhas sitting with partially clad vixens in Hindu-inspired postures and a bad rendition of Zeus with a lightning bolt, all colored in a psychedelic assortment of yellow, blue, and red.

It was the bare-breasted women that kept Ben from suggesting to Emily that she repaint the room.

"How was he last night?" she asked him, once they were into the kitchen through the swinging door.

"The same. A new girl."

"Drunk?"

"Both of them."

"He hit you?"

"No, not with a new girl, he wouldn't do that." He considered this. "Though he hit *her*, I think. Sounded like he did, the way she was screaming. I don't know," he said, not wanting to work her anger into a lather, pretending to reconsider. "It might have just been . . . you know, that they were . . . you know." He felt himself blush. He tried to avoid mentioning the sex that went on in that room, because Emily said it was wrong of the guy to allow Ben to hear them going at it, but with walls and floors like paper there wasn't much choice.

"I'm working on it," she promised, as she fixed the tea. She let him drink the real thing—caffeine tea. Milk. Sugar.

"I know you are," he answered her.

"I'm trying."

"I know," Ben said. He knew what she was up to. She wanted them to be together. He also knew she wouldn't push him. She needed evidence against Jack if she was to have any chance of breaking Ben free of him. And Ben didn't feel like giving evidence. He didn't feel like talking to a social worker about it; he wouldn't allow Emily to take pictures of his bruises. He had his reasons. If he offered evidence, if Jack was questioned by the police—or whoever did that kind of thing—and for some reason Emily failed, the guy would beat him senseless, maybe even kill him. Ben knew this, deep down inside himself, where he hid the pain inflicted on him and the mountain of fear that made him question his every move, his every word. Better not to try at all than to try and fail—this he knew, no matter what arguments she threw at him. This was a matter of survival. This was not something up for discussion.

They drank the tea in relative quiet; Emily used silence to punish Ben. He was used to it. She had pleaded; she had cried. Recently she had turned to this nudging, expecting Ben to make some offer and sulking when he refused to take the hint. He didn't want to play along, and yet he loved Emily and didn't want to let her down. He heard himself say, "I'm not ready."

"They can protect you," she said.

"No," he answered. "You don't know him." He could have said Jack needed him. He could have explained that the guy cried alone in the dark. He could have tried to express how utterly convinced he was that Jack would not let him leave under any circumstances—and how he would come looking if he lost Ben to a bunch of social workers. "You don't know him," Ben repeated with a dry throat. She hadn't brought this up in a long time; he wondered why she bothered to try again. She knew perfectly well how he felt.

He was saved from further discussion by the sound of a car in the gravel drive. They both heard it.

"I told you," Emily said with loving eyes.

Ben smiled at her. They were a team again. They had work to do.

Ben grabbed the hand-held device. Emily tucked the clear plastic earpiece under her dark hair and into her ear. "Check," he said, into the device, and Emily nodded. He slipped out the back door as Emily went off to answer the doorbell. Midday on a Saturday could mean either a man or a woman. The same time of day during the week would have meant a woman for sure. He moved down the concrete steps and over to the corner of the house, where he edged his eye out just far enough to see down the driveway to the beater yellow Ford Pinto wagon.

"They're paying me to tell them what they want to hear," Emily had explained to him a long time ago. "The more we learn, the more we know about them, the closer we come to telling them what they want to hear, the happier they are, the more they keep coming back." It made sense to Ben. He had no problem with spying on them. To him it was a game. It was fun. And he knew he was good at it, and it pleased him to be good—really good—at something. Emily said that someday he would make one hell of a cop.

He heard the front door thump shut and went right to work. He walked briskly to the car, glanced once at the front door to make sure the driver was indeed inside for a reading, and began his assessment. The sticker on the windshield was an employee parking permit for the U. There were three of them, all different colors, different years. Looking through the passenger's side window he spotted a Victoria's Secret catalog addressed to a Wendy

Davis at a street address that placed her about a mile north of Green Lake. On the floor were two mashed candy boxes for Sour-Boys. In the back seat, a baby's safety seat was strapped in facing backward, looking at a rusted dog guard wire wall that sequestered the empty rear area from the front of the car.

He glanced again at the house, lifted the walkie-talkie, carefully checking the volume knob, and, bringing his lips close, spoke the woman's name clearly—"Wendy Davis"—followed by a description of the cluttered condition of the car's interior, the fact that it was an old beat-up Ford, the presence of a child's seat, and the existence of candy boxes indicating the likelihood of an older child as well. "Hold it," he said, noticing the newspaper wedged between the plastic median and the driver's seat. He came around the vehicle quickly. The paper was folded open to the want ads. A number of apartment rentals were circled. He reported this important find. "She's house hunting. It's yesterday's paper." He wouldn't open the car door, no matter how tempted; that was against the law and could get Emily into serious trouble, which would ruin everything. He wondered if some of the employment want ads were circled as well, but he would never know.

Bingo! he thought, as he caught sight of the two passport-size color photos stuck into the plastic by the car's speedometer. One was of a baby boy, the other of an older boy, perhaps five years old. He reported this, as well as the fact that the woman smoked Marlboro Lights and drank cans of decaffeinated Diet Coke. "Maybe religious," he added, noticing the small black cross that hung from the rearview mirror. He chastised himself for not noticing this right away. Sometimes he missed the obvious stuff in his determination to see absolutely everything. The challenge was to build a life out of a car's interior. Some people made it easier than others.

This had been a pretty good haul. He returned by the back door into the kitchen. Soft New Age music purred from the other room, played in part to cover any chance of a customer hearing the earpiece: xylophone, flute, and guitar. A far cry from the Springsteen that Jack played when he was working the girls in his bedroom. "Born to Run" was what he always started with. If he was really drunk, he played air guitar along with the record and shouted his tone-deaf melodies, believing he was actually singing. Ben hated him. He had never hated anything or anyone before Jack's arrival on the scene.

He heard Emily's voice cut through the soft patter of the music as she told her customer, "I'm getting an image of a problem . . . a worry . . . a decision, perhaps. . . ."

"Yes!" the unseen woman gasped in astonishment.

"And one . . . no, two boys. Children."

"Oh, my God!" the woman exclaimed.

"Your children?"

"Yeah! I can't believe—"

"An infant . . ."

"Charles. Charlie," Wendy Davis said.

"And the other is older—what?—four or five?"

"Harry! Just turned five."

"You're concerned for them," the fortuneteller said.

"Yeah."

"I see suitcases . . . cardboard boxes. . . . Moving, are we?"

The customer released an audible gasp. "Oh, my gosh," she said. "You're for real!" She chuckled, sounding giddy. "I'm sorry. Of *course* you're for real. I only meant that . . . I don't know . . . it's just that—" she laughed again—"I mean, a psychic and all. . . . Oh, my gosh. How did you . . . ? But of course . . . I can't believe this!"

"Looking for a new place to live," Emily said patiently. "Concerned for the children over the move. You live near a lake—"

"Green Lake," the woman shouted—*shouted!*—enthusiastically. "Yes! Yes!" she continued, sounding like one of the guy's bedroom partners on the way to a high-pitched scream. "I can't believe this!"

Ben felt proud that he had done such a good job. Sometimes the car turned out to be borrowed and the session a complete disaster; those customers rarely returned. But this one would be back, he felt certain of it. Emily would be thrilled, and he lived for her praise.

The customer stayed longer than the fifteen minutes promised her for her ten dollars. This upped Emily's fee to twenty, but there weren't any complaints. Judging by her expression as she left, Ben believed Wendy Davis was noticeably happier, which made him feel good. This was Emily's stated goal. She only added her ominous warnings at the end of the session to keep the customer returning. "I see something darker in the near future" was her typical line. Something about work, or the family, or health—those were the real showstoppers, the live worm on the end of the hook that proved irresistible. And like a hairdresser or a doctor, Emily kept an appointment book. She could "fit you in" if you were lucky. Every one of her customers was lucky.

"You need something to eat," she announced, as she entered the kitchen. One of Emily's passions was food; she seemed to him to always be around the refrigerator, inspecting its contents. "You're far too skinny."

"I'm twelve years old," Ben declared. He used this argument on Jack, but to mixed results.

"Too skinny," she repeated. "I've got some pork loin for you," she exclaimed. "My Aunt Bernice's recipe. Marinated in lemon juice, oregano, salt, and pepper. . . . Do you like garlic? Yeah, you do," she answered rhetorically. "Olive oil." She pulled the thing out of the refrigerator and set it on the counter. It was just a tube of pink meat with soggy green specks all over it. It looked disgusting. "Don't worry," she said, catching his expression, "it's better than it looks."

An hour later they were eating lunch at her kitchen table. He liked the mashed potatoes most of all. "We can have the leftovers for dinner," she said, talking with her mouth full of food. If he did it she screamed at him, but she did it all the time. He liked Emily—loved her, maybe—but he didn't understand her. Not completely.

He was glad she mentioned dinner, because it meant he didn't have to think about going *there*. Jack would leave for the bar by seven; it would be safe to go back then. If he was lucky, Emily would ask him to sleep over. She let him do this about twice a week. Not once had Jack asked him about where he went or where he stayed—his only complaint would be if a chore didn't get done, and those complaints were often of the physical variety, so Ben kept up on the chores.

"It's even better as a leftover," she promised. She drank pink wine that she poured from a paper box in the fridge. After lunch they did the dishes together. Emily put on some more lipstick and said she was going outside to "feed the cat." The cat would have been more correctly named Marlboro, but she pretended Ben didn't know this.

She made Ben read to her as she sat in her favorite chair, and she fell asleep with a smile on her face. The nap lasted about twenty minutes, at which point Ben heard a car pull in the driveway.

"Another one," he said, gently shaking her by the upper arm. She was softer than anything, anyone, he had ever touched. She was magical. Special. He'd seen her know things that no one could ever possibly know. It didn't happen all the time, but when it did there was no explaining it. She had a power. "A gift," she called it. But it was more than that. It was a vision, an ability to see ahead, like a dream but real. Magic.

"A gal's got to earn a living," she said, coming out of the chair and stroking the wrinkles out of her clothes. She patted Ben on the head affectionately. "Your reading's getting better," she said. "You might work out after all," she teased. "I might keep you yet."

Ben waited for the car to pull up and the engine to go quiet. Then he slipped out back, prepared to do his job.

4

"WOULD you like a cup of coffee?" The young kid turned red in the face and corrected himself. "Tea?"

"No, thanks." Lou Boldt, embarrassed by the offer, felt sorry for the young patrolman. He had been put up to this by someone—probably John LaMoia, who was constantly working the rookies—breaking them in, he called it. Boldt, senior homicide sergeant, was often singled out as the target of such errand running. There was no obligation for a rookie to play the role of a personal servant. Boldt's tolerance level for LaMoia's rites of initiation was far above that of Lieutenant Phil Shoswitz, whose nervous disposition and bug eyes resembled a miniature pinscher. If you knew what was good for you, you left Shoswitz in his glassed-in office.

Boldt could think of several ways to turn this stunt back around on LaMoia, but it would mean using this rookie as the go-between, and that seemed manipulative and unfair. "I'm fine," Boldt told the kid. "Thanks anyway."

He remembered what it was like to be in uniform and on the fifth floor for the first time: the pounding heart, the prickling skin. Homicide was viewed by most rookies as the top—the pinnacle of a career. Boldt thought back to those feelings and wondered how such myths were started. It was true that homicide dealt with life and death, as opposed to traffic tickets or jaywalkers, but that came with a price of insomnia, guilt, and frustration. Homicide was no cakewalk.

The forty-two-year-old man sitting in the chair today—graying hair cut close to his scalp, his rounding face reflecting the thirty pounds he couldn't shake, the fingers of his thick hands gnarled from broken knuckles of decades past—was a far cry from the fit, bright-eyed, enthusiastic rookie who had once been tricked into using the chief's private toilet, a liberty that had cost him two months of walking a beat in the International District.

He could no longer see the Space Needle from the Public Safety Building's fifth floor. Real estate development in the eighties had taken care of that. It had also choked the roads and interstates, crowded the ferries, and sent real estate appraisals soaring right along with the crime rate. Other than that, newcomers were welcome in Seattle, as far as Boldt was concerned.

He was feeling tired. Miles, his three-year-old son, and Sarah, his eight-month-old beauty named after Sarah Vaughan, had taken turns complaining through the night, leaving both him and Liz exhausted and in foul moods. When Liz got tired, Boldt steered clear, if possible, but a morning encounter in the kitchen—which had something to do with the yoke of a soft-boiled egg not being right—had erupted into a tirade about how Boldt was allowing himself to be absorbed by the job again, an unfair charge in his opinion, given that he had beaten her home four of the last five nights. Commercial banking was definitely more time-consuming than police work. He had said something like that to her, which did not score big points, except on the Richter scale. At the moment he was suffering through a dull headache.

He carried that headache with him to the medical examiner's office in the basement of Harborview Medical Center, where Dr. Ronald Dixon awaited him.

Harborview, perennially under construction, sat atop Pill Hill with a sweeping view of Elliott Bay and the Port Authority's towering cranes, feeding and unloading the container ships. Parking anywhere near Harborview was impossible. Boldt took one of two open spots reserved for the ME and placed his OFFICIAL POLICE BUSI-NESS card on the dash. The September air was in the high 60s. Boldt squinted under the glare of sunshine. A college coed wearing a bikini top sped through the Alder-Broadway intersection on a pair of roller blades. A few of the construction workers stopped to take notice. She wore blue jean shorts with holes in them. To Boldt, she looked too young to be in college.

Dixie's round face looked Asian in certain expressions, his eyes wide-set, his nose flattened by a college intramural football game. There was a look of intelligence in his eyes. One sensed a formidable presence, a busy mind, just looking at the man. He came out from behind his desk and sat at a small conference table, using a jeweler's screwdriver to clean his impeccably clean nails. He grimaced a smile at Boldt and indicated a plastic evidence bag left on the table.

On the wall was a framed poster for a performance of Shakespeare's *Two Gentlemen of Verona* by the Seattle Repertory Theater and a black-and-white time exposure showing lightning strikes hitting the Space Needle at night. Boldt always found himself mesmerized by that photo, by the power of nature. There was also a pair of pen-and-inks of western subjects—horses and cabins—that reminded Boldt of Zane Grey.

Boldt examined the contents of the bag, a blackened bone three inches by three inches. Dixie said, "From that fire the other night." Several days had passed since the Dorothy Enwright arson. Until that moment, Boldt had not known which of his squad's cases were involved. He took a deep breath and reminded himself that he had a lot to learn about fires.

"Is this all?" the sergeant asked.

"All that's worth anything," Dixie replied, working the screwdriver under his thumbnail. "It's fairly common in burns for the spine and pelvis to go last. That's a piece of the pelvic bone. Pelvis gives us sex. Spine gives us age. Do you see the calcification on the inside edge?" he asked. Boldt pointed. "Right. That indicates some aging. This wasn't a teenager. Probably wasn't even in her twenties."

"Her?" Boldt inquired, his own spine tingling. He had yet to see any paperwork confirming Witt's mention of an eyewitness.

"What we can tell you is that it was most probably a female. Beyond that, I'm afraid. . . ." His voice trailed off. "We sifted the site thoroughly. So did Marshal Five and the other inspectors who helped him out. I would have expected to see more than this," he admitted, sensing correctly that it was to have been Boldt's next question. "Fingers, toes, ankles, wrists, they can go pretty quickly." He made it sound like a grocery list. Boldt held a vision of a woman burning to death. He trusted that eyewitness, paperwork or not. "But the femur, the spine, the pelvis . . . depending on how she fell, they take awhile to cook, even longer to reduce to ash."

"Time or heat?" Boldt asked.

"The rate of destruction is a product of both."

"This was hot," Boldt informed him. As suggested, he had spoken with air traffic control. The initial spike of flame had stretched eleven hundred feet into the night sky. No house fire had ever caused such a phenomenon. It was the kind of record setting of which Boldt wanted no part.

"We're hoping for some bone frags to come out of the lab work. We sent off a garbage can of ash and debris. Some metals hold up pretty well in fire. We might get something there. Quite honestly, it's unusual to come away with only that." He indicated the contents of the plastic evidence bag. "Highly unusual, one might even say. If an assistant had performed the site work for us, I'd send him or her back to try again. But I did this one myself, Lou. There just wasn't anything to work with." He paused. "You okay?"

"I wouldn't want to die like that."

"No." Dixie added, "You wouldn't like the autopsy either. Toasters and floaters, the two worst bodies in the business."

"So I'm working a homicide," Boldt confirmed.

" 'Circumstances of discovery raise a suspicion that this was a violent death.' That's how I'll write it up. Are there circumstances of disappearance? That's your bailiwick."

"There are," Boldt confirmed. "One Dorothy Elaine Enwright went missing the night of the fire. An eyewitness saw a woman fitting Enwright's description in the house just prior to the fire."

"Well, there you are," Dixie said.

"There I am," Boldt replied.

The medical examiner's determination of a body present in the rubble threw the investigation into high gear and even higher profile. Local news agencies clamored for information. Boldt assigned two of his squad's detectives to the investigation, John LaMoia and Bobbie Gaynes, to be joined by two probationary firemen, Sidney Fidler and Neil Bahan, loaned to the Seattle Police Department as arson investigators. Boldt would act as case supervisor, reporting, as always, directly to Phil Shoswitz.

A coordinating meeting, arranged for the SPD fifth floor conference room, came off on time, as scheduled on Monday at 10 A.M., six days after the Enwright fire. It included Boldt's team and four members of the King County Arson Task Force, an alliance formed of Marshal Five fire inspectors representing various fire districts within the county.

Boldt had never been fond of meetings involving more than three people; to him, they seemed exercises in tongue wagging. But this meeting went differently. The four fire inspectors worked well with their brethren assigned to police duty, Fidler and Bahan. Boldt, LaMoia, and Gaynes participated primarily as onlookers while the technical details of the fire were discussed. A burn pattern on wood known as "alligatoring" had steered the inspectors toward the center of the structure, where destruction was so severe there was literally no evidence to be gathered. The area of origin—an essential starting point for any arson investigation—was therefore impossible to pinpoint.

The longer the meeting went, the more anxious Boldt became. Reading between the spoken words, he experienced a sinking feeling that the fire's intense heat had destroyed any and all indication of its origin. Worse, all six experts seemed both intimidated and surprised by the severity of the heat.

With everyone still present, Neil Bahan summed up the discussion for the sake of Boldt and his detectives. "It goes like this, Sergeant. We have the initial plume reported as a flash. *Not* an explosion. That's worrisome, because it excludes a hell of a lot of known accelerants. Add to that the eyewitness reports of the height of the plume, and the flame itself being a distinct purple in color, and we figure we're looking at liquid accelerants. We could make some guesses, but we're not going to. The prudent thing to do is send our samples off to the state crime lab and test for hydrocarbons. That will point us to the specific fuel used, which in turn may give John and Bobbie a retail or wholesale source to check out." LaMoia and Gaynes nodded. Gaynes scribbled down a note. "As it is, we'll put it out to every snitch we got. This guy brags about it—as they love to do—and we nip him. Meanwhile, we go about trying to make sense of the rest of the evidence."

"Which is?" Boldt questioned.

Bahan eye-checked his buddies and said, "I would rather wait and see what the lab tells us, but the deal is this: We've got some popcorn in the foundation's concrete, some spalling. Fire suppression washed a lot of this evidence away and may have affected the rest of it, but what we *don't* have is slag or heavy metals—both of which we would expect to see with liquid accelerants. But added to that we have some blue concrete right beneath the center of the house—quite possibly the area of origin. That's bad shit, blue concrete. That's something we *don't* want to find, because it means this thing went off somewhere above two thousand degrees. If that's right, it lops off another whole shitload of known accelerants and, quite frankly, gets out of our area of expertise."

"ATF, maybe," another of the fire inspectors suggested.

Bahan agreed. "Yeah, maybe we bring in the Feds or send some of the stuff down to Chestnut Grove, their Sacramento lab. See what they have to say."

"So what you're saying," Boldt suggested, "is that the origin of the fire is unusual."

Two of the Marshal Fives laughed aloud.

Bahan said, "You could say that, yes."

"And you're suggesting that we stick by the ruling of suspicious origin."

"Most definitely. This sucker was torched, Sergeant."

"We're checking out her ex-husband, any boyfriends, employer, insurance policies, neighbors," Boldt informed the visitors. "We'll turn up a suspect, and when we do, maybe we send one of you guys into his garage to have a look-see at his workbench?"

"No shortage of volunteers for that assignment," Bahan answered for the others. "This guy is good," he explained. The others nodded.

Boldt bristled at the idea of an arsonist being considered talented. "She was a mom. Did you know? Seven-year-old boy."

"He was in the fire?" one of the fire inspectors gasped, his face draining of color. It wasn't difficult to spot the parents in this group.

"No. Home with his father, thank God," Boldt answered. He imagined his own son Miles in a fire like that. "Thank God," he muttered again.

Bahan said, "We turn it over to the lab and we see what we see. It's really too early to make a decent appraisal. For the time being, it's in the hands of the chemists."

"We'll continue the questioning," Boldt told them. "Maybe something shakes out."

The members of the Arson Task Force nodded, but Boldt's own detective, John LaMoia, did not looked impressed. "John?" Boldt asked, wondering if he wanted to contribute.

"Nothing," LaMoia replied.

It wasn't nothing, and Boldt knew it. A feeling of impending dread accompanied him on his return to his office, where a blanket of telephone messages had collected like the falling leaves outside.

"Lieutenant Boldt?" a deep male voice asked at the door, mis-quoting his rank.

"Enough with the jokes," Boldt complained, assuming LaMoia had put another rookie to work.

It wasn't another rookie he faced. It was one of the four Mar-shal Fives from the meeting. He didn't remember the name. He was a tall, handsome man with wide shoulders and dark brown eyes. He wore a full beard. He had big teeth. Scandinavian, Boldt decided. The sergeant came out of his chair and corrected his rank. The two shook hands. The other's right hand was hard and cal-loused. He wore his visitor's badge crooked, clipped on hastily. A pager hung at his belt, and his boots were heavy leather. His hair was cut short, his sleeves rolled up. He reintroduced himself as Steven Garman.

"What district are you with?" Boldt asked.

Garman answered, "Battalion Four: Ballard, Greenwood."

"I thought the meeting went well," Boldt said.

"Yeah, I suppose," Garman replied anxiously.

"Not for you?" Boldt attempted to clarify.

"Listen, Sergeant," the other man said, leaning on the word, "we're overworked and underpaid. Sound familiar? Sometimes we connect the dots, sometimes we don't."

Boldt wasn't enjoying this. He wanted Garman to go away. "Paint by numbers," Boldt said. "Those kind of dots."

"Exactly."

"So we don't see the right picture."

"I knew you'd understand. We see a picture but not the right one." Garman was a huge man. Boldt was uncomfortable with him standing.

The sergeant borrowed a rolling chair from a nearby cubicle and pulled it up to his desk. He offered it to Garman, who viewed it suspiciously and said, "Maybe someplace a little quieter, a little more private."

Boldt allowed, "If this is an attempt to put me at ease, it isn't working."

He had wanted to break the ice, but his visitor wasn't amused. Garman looked around, searching for privacy.

"Come on," Boldt said. He led him into B, a small interrogation room next to A, the Box, the interrogation room of choice. Boldt closed the acoustically insulated door. They took seats at a bare Formica table rimmed with short brown cigarette burns. "Let's talk about those dots," Boldt said.

"Everyone says you're the go-to guy around here," Garman said.

Boldt countered modestly. "I'm the old man around here, if that's what you mean."

"I'm told you're willing to play hunches now and then."

"My own hunches, yeah," Boldt agreed. Boldt was currently in the doghouse with his lieutenant for playing a hunch. He didn't need another. He had taken on an investigation that lay outside his department's jurisdiction—defined by the incorporated city's boundaries. A thirty-five-year-old man had been found dead and decomposing in the middle of the national forest not far from Renton. That in itself might not have been too unusual, except that this particular man was clad in SCUBA gear, head to toe, flippers to mask. The nearest lake was seven miles away.

Boldt had taken the job based on its unusual nature—though he was quick to point out to Lieutenant Shoswitz that he had not used one hour of SPD time on the investigation. Shoswitz's argument was that by accepting the case Boldt had set a precedent. SPD was allowed to *advise* outside its jurisdiction, but Boldt had *taken* the case, assuming the position of lead detective, and this violated regulations.

"I'm pretty careful about playing hunches," Boldt said.

That Boldt had solved the case in five phone calls was never discussed. Nor that, had Shoswitz added up the sergeant's time—off-duty time—spent on the case, it would have amounted to less than one work day. Regulations were regulations.

The solution was simple. A forest fire had raged several months earlier. Firefighters had fought the blaze on the ground, planes had dumped chemicals from the air, and helicopters had worked the spot fires. The victim had been diving in a mountain lake. Accidentally scooped up by a helicopter grabbing water to fight a spot fire, he had been dumped into the fire's center from a hundred feet up. Case solved. Nonetheless, Shoswitz remained upset about Boldt's violation of the regulations.

"Unless I'm wrong, the first couple were just vacant structures," Garman said. He didn't strike Boldt as the kind of guy to be wrong. He exuded a quiet confidence once he got talking. "Listen, in this city, even a piece of ground the size of a postage stamp is worth ten grand, but not necessarily the structure on it." He explained, "Property valued at ten grand or higher—that's when Marshal Five is called in to investigate. Suspicious fire. Known arson. Any of those three. But truthfully, the way it works is that the IC—the incident commander—makes an early call on a fire and determines whether Marshal Five should investigate. We usually speak by phone. I'm apprised of the situation. If it's cut and dried, some photos are shot, some sketches maybe, and the next day I look it all over. Ten times out of ten I agree with the call. It keeps us from investigating every fire there is."

He was working up to something and taking his sweet time about it. Boldt's time also. Garman was an animal with his nose to the ground, carefully approaching the scent.

Boldt felt like asking Garman why he had waited. Why hadn't he brought up whatever it was at the meeting? Why be secretive and demand privacy and talk *around* it? Running out of patience, he said, "Maybe you should just tell me whatever it is."

"They fit some of this," Garman replied. "Vacant structures, all of them, until now. Teardowns, over in Battalion Five, mostly. The land has all the value, the building nothing. We look at them— Marshal Five—because although they don't fit the ten grand requirement, they obviously aren't the result of a lightning strike. But ten times out of ten we have bigger fish to fry. Most of them are the work of JDs, kids out for kicks. We're not going to catch them anyway. We shoot for a witness, but if we can't scare one up they go in the back of the file cabinet with a heck of a lot of company. It wouldn't be the same for you. I'm not talking dead bodies;

I'm talking worthless shacks, garages, condemned buildings. Just kicks. A kid with a match and nothing to do.''

"You're making me uncomfortable, Mr. Garman. I'm viewing all this with a jaundiced eye.''

"Six of them. Maybe as many as fourteen. Maybe more if I dig around. Battalion Five is not my turf, but we trade around, you know, and I've worked a few of them. I remember two that appeared to me to have burned especially hot: heavy alligatoring, some spalling, just like we were talking about.''

"What exactly is spalling?'' Boldt asked.

"The concrete gets so hot so fast that the little moisture that's trapped inside it boils and explodes the surface. You've seen it on sidewalks in winter, maybe. Looks just the same. Like bad acne. Liquid accelerants, ten times out of ten. That's okay in a shack because these kids typically use gasoline or some close relative— gas and diesel, diesel and acetone. Readily available stuff. But the two I'm talking about burned hotter than a big dog. Never seen gas do that. I wasn't thinking in terms of a pro, because who's going to bother with a little shack? But after we were talking just now, it occurred to me who *might* bother: Someone testing out his stuff. Let me tell ya, Sergeant. Every fire has a personality. I'm no expert when it comes to understanding everything about fire, even though that's my job; no one knows everything. But as corny as it sounds, I do know that every fire tells its own story. Studied long enough, it reveals its secrets. To the ordinary eye it produces destruction and chaos, but to those of us who live and die with the beast, it speaks volumes. It will tell you when, where, and how the dragon was born and chronicles its growth to the raging inferno it becomes. Fire respects nothing. No one. But for everything it consumes, it leaves evidence, the telltale marks of who or what created it. It takes on the personality of its creator, just as offspring do their parents: some dull and uneventful; others creative and imaginative.

"I walked the Enwright fire,'' he continued. "I had met its little sister, its little brother, these stick burns I'm talking about. They're all in the same family. To bring it up in the meeting, I embarrass my buddy; I make it look like he should have made more of those stick fires than he did. Monday morning quarter-backing. But it scares the fool out of me, the way those fires feel the same. And if that's right, then they were warm-ups—pardon the pun. He wanted it just right for Enwright. Made sure he knew exactly what to expect: amount of fuel, speed of burn, degree of destruction."

"You're giving me gooseflesh, Mr. Garman," Boldt said.

"Scares the fool out of me," he repeated. "Want to know why? Lemme ask you this: Does a guy light off two, three, four test fires—does he take all that risk—just to get Dorothy Enwright perfect?"

"Does he?"

"No way. It's too risky. One fire, maybe. But four? Six?"

"What exactly are you saying?"

Garman reached into his shirt pocket and withdrew an opened envelope. He placed it before Boldt, who elected not to touch it. The address, written in blue ballpoint ink, was scripted in poorly formed block letters.

"You've handled this?" Boldt asked.

"Yes."

"Anyone else?"

"No. I've haven't shown it to anyone."

Boldt found a pencil and expertly maneuvered the envelope to face him, curious but at the same time reluctant. "Why me? Why now?" he asked.

Hearing the question clearly troubled Garman, and Boldt sensed he had prepared himself for the answer ahead of time. "How many of these do we all get? You get them, I get them. Quacks. Freaks. Tripsters. Former squirrels we're not using any longer. Most of them end up in the can. I got a whole series from a woman once, following a TV interview I did. First one was a sexy letter. Second one was another letter and a photo. Third, was a letter and another photo, this time with her shirt off. By the fifth, she was stark naked on a bed, and I mean rude. The sixth, there wasn't any letter, just a video. That was the last one. They stopped coming after that." Garman wiped some perspiration off his upper lip. It wasn't hot on the fifth floor, not compared to summer. "So, something like this comes, you file it under freak. But it arrived the day of the Enwright fire—addressed to my home, not my office."

"You brought it with you today to the meeting but elected not to show it," Boldt reminded the man. "Why?"

"I'm showing it to you now." Garman had naturally red cheeks and a big smile when he allowed it.

"Why show it to me and not your colleagues?" Boldt asked.

"Those guys? I'm *one* of those guys. I know how they think. We investigate fires, Sergeant. They would have laughed me out of that room. This," he said, indicating the envelope, "maybe it's something, maybe it's not. But it's your thing, not mine, not those guys. If it means anything at all, you're the guy for it."

"Am I really?" Boldt didn't want the letter. He didn't want the case any longer. Too many guys between him and the evidence, too much he didn't know about and would have to learn. He realized that if the body was subtracted from the case, it wasn't his. He briefly resented Dorothy Elaine Enwright.

Seeming to sense this, Garman said, "Listen, it's just a bunch of nonsense. That's the other reason. It's not a threat or anything. But it's off the wall. Some plastic and a poem. So what? And then I'm thinking maybe it means something. Those stains on the envelope? I threw the thing out. It was in the trash for three days. I only fished it out this morning before the meeting, because it occurred to me the dates were the same."

"It's mailed from Capitol Hill," Boldt said.

"Yeah, I saw that too."

Using a pencil's eraser, Boldt carefully opened the back flap. He hoisted the envelope with the pencil and dumped out its contents. An unremarkable blob of what appeared to be melted green plastic slid out onto the desk's surface. It was about the size of a poker chip.

Using a second pencil, Boldt extracted and unfolded the note. His eyes fell to the crude drawing of a small headless man climbing a ladder. Boldt could imagine the figure a fireman. The fact that it lacked a head would require the interpretation of the department's psychologist, Daphne Matthews. Alongside, in the same undeveloped handwriting as on the envelope, was written, *He has half the deed done, who has made a beginning.*

After an excruciating silence, Boldt looked up at the big man sitting next to him and said dryly, "I don't like this."

"No," said the other. "I know what you mean."

5

THE psych profile was ready on Friday.

Daphne Matthews, the department's psychologist, notified Boldt by leaving a message on a piece of notepaper, accompanied by her trademark doodle of a smiling bird.

Sight of her still stopped Boldt's breath. Some things never changed. He wondered if it was because of her thick mane of chestnut-brown hair or the narrow face with the sharp features. Perhaps the slender body, the dark skin, and long fingers. She was a woman who could play a set a tennis, talk a suicide out of a window, or hold a press conference where no one shouted. Maybe it was those lips, red, pouty, that just had to taste sweet, had to be softer than warm butter. Her clothes helped. She wore smart clothes, not high fashion. On the morning of September twentieth, it was khakis, a hunter-green plaid shirt that she filled out deliciously, and a silver necklace with a jumping porpoise leaping below her collarbone.

On her desk, a small plastic Charlie Brown held a sign that read THE DOCTOR IS IN—5 CENTS. A teapot with a twisting vine of soft blue flowers sat on a coaster next to a pile of multicolored file folders. Her ninth-floor office was the only one in the entire building that didn't smell of commercial disinfectant and didn't feel like something built by a city government. She had real curtains covering her window, and the poster art on the walls reflected her love of English landscapes and Impressionists. She had a red ceramic lamp with brass handles on the opposite corner from the phone. Vivaldi played from a small boom box on the shelf behind her. She turned down the music, pivoting in her chair, and smiled. The room seemed a little brighter.

In the small stack of files were problems common to the department: the officer-involved drunken brawl at a downtown hotel that erupted after two of the men had entered the hotel pool, after hours and stark naked; the attempted suicide by a narcotics officer that followed the near fatal beating of his ex-wife; the evaluations of several officers in drug and alcohol rehab; a few repeat offenders; a few who couldn't sleep anymore; and some others who slept too much, burdened by depression.

Daphne Matthews was referred to as the staff shrink. She attempted to paste back together the cops who fell apart. She listened to those who needed an ear. She created psychological profiles of suspects based on whatever she could find.

She poured him tea without asking, putting in one sugar and enough milk to make it blond. She stirred it and handed it across the desk. She didn't ask why he was here—there were too many years between them for such formalities. "The green plastic in the envelope mailed to Steven Garman? I don't know what it means. Money? Jealousy? Death? None of the above?"

"The verse?" he asked.

"*He has half the deed done, who has made a beginning*. It's from a poem by Horace. Quintus Horatius Flaccus. Born in the century before Christ. Major influence on English poetry. One of the greatest lyric poets. Heady stuff. Our boy knows his literature. College educated, maybe a master's. It's either a cry for help or a threat."

"Our boy?" Boldt asked. "The killer? You think so?"

"We play it that way, don't we?" she said. "At least until you hand me someone different. The sketch is of a headless fireman going up a ladder. It talks about a deed being done."

"A confession?" Boldt asked, his heart beating strongly in his chest.

"More of a warning, I think. He warned Steven Garman; it allows him to disassociate from the consequences of the fire."

"It's Garman's fault," he proposed.

"Exactly. Perhaps Garman is the headless fireman in the sketch—the guy up the ladder." She explained, "I have to caution you that the handwriting, the block letters, the inconsistent spacing, contradicts the notion of a well-educated individual. I'm not sure how to interpret that. He may be young, Lou. Let me run some numbers by you." She picked up a sheet of paper on her desk. "Sixty-six percent of arson arrests are people under twenty-five years old. Juveniles account for forty-nine percent of those." Her face tightened while reading.

He asked, "What is it?"

"Just a number."

"Daffy?"

"Nationally the clearance rate is only fifteen percent."

Boldt sagged, literally and emotionally. *Eighty-five percent* of arsonists got away with it. "I don't like those odds," he admitted.

Attempting a more upbeat note, she said, "This blob of green plastic is symbolic to him. Though without knowing what that symbolism is, we're at a bit of a loss."

"If it's significant, we run with it."

She asked, "Have you thought about testing the plastic to find out what it was before it was melted?"

"That's an interesting idea," he admitted.

"It would sure help me to know what it was."

"What about a fireman?" Boldt asked, stating what he believed an obvious question.

"Certainly near the top of our list," Daphne answered. "A disenchanted fireman. Someone turned down by the department. Discharged. Denied a promotion." She clarified this. "It works for the sending of the note, but not for killing Dorothy Enwright. Why kill an innocent woman if you're venting anger? You'd kill a fireman or fire inspector, wouldn't you?"

Boldt nodded but didn't speak. He heard it in her voice, her words: This was bigger than Dorothy Enwright, bigger than anyone had foreseen.

"We need the connection," Daphne said. "The spark, if you will. The motive. It may be something as eclectic as the architecture of the house. It may tie in directly to Dorothy Enwright or Steven Garman."

Boldt experienced it as a dryness in his throat, a knife blade in his stomach. He didn't want to ask the question of the psychologist because he feared her answer. Nonetheless, it had to be asked. "It isn't over, is it?"

She met his eyes; hers were filled with sympathy. "The note tells us that: *He has half the deed done, who has made a beginning.*" She asked rhetorically, "So what comes next?"

6

NOTHING much changed. If Ben had one complaint in life, this was it. He felt powerless to change things himself, and, left to grown-ups, things remained too much the same. School was school; home was home. He felt pressure from Emily to give the social workers the evidence they needed, but he wasn't about to give in, so in the end he blamed himself for his situation, and it hurt.

He had *Monday Night Football* to thank for keeping Jack Santori away. His stepfather wouldn't come home from work but, instead, would head directly to the bar for the game. He wouldn't come home from the bar until late, because he placed bets on football and he drank heavily, win or lose. Sometime around midnight he would stumble in downstairs, bang around, and find his way to bed—if he was lucky—or more likely end up passed out on the couch with TV fuzz hissing back at him. By that same time, Ben would be safe, locked behind his bedroom door, having spent the late afternoon and evening with Emily.

There had probably been a time when he had been afraid of the dark, though it had long since passed. He had other things he feared more. Jack had a way, with his eyes and voice, of terrifying Ben so that his legs suddenly went to Jell-O and his thoughts became tangled and confused. There were times when for no reason at all he would press Ben to the floor and, holding a pillow against Ben's back, would beat him, hammering away with his drunken, reckless fists so that the bruises ended up buried deep inside Ben's flesh, not on the surface where they might show. Ben's pee stung for days in a row and his poo was tar black. "You're going to do as I say, right?" Jack would ask, as he carried out this punishment. And if Ben was stupid enough to answer, stupid enough to open his mouth, the punishment continued until Jack grew physically tired or lost interest. For Ben to cry aloud was unthinkable.

Ben liked Seattle in September. Less people than in the summer, fewer cars on the streets. Ben had heard it called a transition neighborhood: blacks, mostly; very few whites. Ben knew which streets to avoid, which hangouts to circumvent. Most of this he had learned the hard way, although being shoved around by a bunch of zit-faced bullies was nothing compared to things at home. Fear was like water: it sought its own level. For Ben, it took some kind of threat to make him afraid, discounting the effect of Jack calling upstairs, "You going to do as I say or not?" That was an entirely different kind of fear. One of these days, the guy would go too far. Emily kept warning of that.

The neon sign in Emily's window was lighted—YOUR FUTURE, YOUR PAST: AT LAST!—which meant she was home and open for business. She got a lot of customers in the evening. Her business was both repeats and drop-ins.

There was a car parked out front, so Ben didn't disturb her. He recognized the car as Denise's, an Emily regular. He went quietly around back and tried the kitchen door and, finding it locked, sat down in the cool September evening and waited. The city hummed. Somewhere out there was his mom. He wondered for the thousandth time why she had left without taking him with her. Fear. He had Jack Santori to thank for that.

After a few minutes he got lonely and bored and decided to climb the cedar tree. From the hastily erected platform high in the tree, he could see the traffic over on Martin Luther King. He saw the blinking lights of planes crisscrossing the sky. The downtown skyscrapers rose dramatically, creating a city skyline he knew by heart. He could point to and identify the various buildings like an astronomer with constellations.

When the car below him started up and pulled out of the drive, he realized he had been daydreaming. He hurried down through a pattern of limbs he knew by heart: down, down, down. Monkey man, Emily called him.

She greeted him as if she hadn't seen him in months, when in fact it had only been a couple of days. She gave him a huge hug, told him how good it was to see him, and immediately insisted that he eat something. She was warming up some lasagna in the microwave when the doorbell sounded.

"You go ahead and eat," she said. "You don't need to help me tonight."

"I want to," he protested, jumping up and pulling open the drawer that contained their wireless radio system.

She didn't stop him. He tested the system by speaking softly into the walkie-talkie. She nodded at him that it was working. She checked her appearance in a mirror, pinched her cheeks, and headed out to answer the door. Ben slipped out the back.

The vehicle parked in Emily's short driveway was a beat-up blue pickup truck with a dented and chipped white camper shell. It had a cracked windshield and a broken outside mirror on the passenger side. Ben went around to the driver's window, because from here he couldn't be seen from the front door, allowing him to hide if the customer unexpectedly came outside. On the back bumper was a Good Sam Club cartoon of a stupid-looking guy with a halo over his head. Through the driver's window he saw a pair of sunglasses on the dash, and a cardboard cutout of a nude woman hanging by a thread from the rearview mirror. A man, he decided. Light from the street penetrated the cab, but it wasn't as if it were daytime; he couldn't see much of the floor—and there was a lot of stuff down there, probably trash. The ashtray was filled with butts. "He smokes," he said into the walkie-talkie. "Parking sticker on the windshield for Chief Joseph Air Force Base." He strained to see the dash. "Nice music system, considering the condition of the truck. He's into music." How badly Ben wanted to open the door or, even more tempting, check to see if the camper shell was unlocked, but Emily had her rules. He was breaking no laws by simply observing. To enter the vehicle was a different story.

There wasn't much more to see. He stepped back, studying the camper shell. He mentioned the Good Sam Club to her, because maybe it would tell her something about the kind of person he was. He noticed the camper had a rooftop skylight that was partially open, and he could picture himself slipping down inside and finding out everything there was to know about the guy. He *wanted* to know everything there was to know. He wanted to give Emily something worthwhile. One of the lower limbs of the cedar tree went out just above the camper shell, and he debated climbing out on this limb and trying to see down into the shell, but the skylight didn't look like it was open far enough, and everything was too dark.

He circled the vehicle once more and then crept quietly into the kitchen, taking up his favorite spot at a peephole that Emily had put into the wall just for this purpose. She liked to leave the room every now and then and spy on her customers to see what they did when she was gone; she claimed this could tell her a lot about a person. Ben placed his one good eye to the wall, blinked repeatedly, watched, and listened, his heart racing, his skin tingling.

The guy was built solid, with wide shoulders, thick arms, hard features, and pinpoint eyes. His hair was buzz-cut down to nothing, blond maybe, and his jaw was square as if sawed off at the chin. Ben looked first to the man's face and then at his right hand, which was ugly and hard not to look at. His last three fingers were fused together with pink, shiny skin so they looked like a small flipper. Ben, because of his glass eye, knew what it was like to be a freak, and rather than wince at the sight of this hand, he felt empathy toward the man. That hand would be a tough thing to live with.

"Are you sure?" Emily asked her customer.

"Yes, ma'am. Just October second. That's all. Wednesday, the second. Just whether or not that's a good day for me—you know, as far as the astrology stuff goes."

"Just that one day."

"That's all. Whether or not it's a good day for me to do some business."

"I'll need to do a chart and then make a reading. It's not something I can do just like that."

He said, "I understand. A girl I know is into the stars. How long?"

"Four or five days. You'll have to come back."

"That's okay. I can get up to the city, no problem."

"I charge fifty dollars for a chart. But once it's done," she added quickly, "it's just ten dollars a reading from then on—if you wanted more readings."

"I might." He added, "The money's all right. The fifty bucks."

Ben thought the man looked nervous, and he wondered if it had to do with that hand, if this guy always felt uncomfortable, always thought people were staring at it. Ben knew that feeling. He had worn dark glasses for the first year after the operation, but the glasses had attracted more attention than the fake eye. He wondered what was so important about October second. He learned things hanging around Emily. Watching her work. People wanted someone to tell them what to do, and when to do it. They would gladly shell out ten or twenty dollars just to hear it. Emily said her customers were sheep desperate for a shepherd. She drummed a single message into him constantly: Believe in yourself.

"Fifty for the chart, ten for the reading," Emily clarified, ever the businesswoman.

"That's okay."

"Good. I need your birth date, time of day, and the location—"

"Time of day?" he asked, interrupting.

"It's important, yes."

"I don't know what time of day I was born. Who knows that?"

"Could you call your mother?"

"No!" he said sharply. He seemed to grow larger. "There's no one."

Ben felt a chill run from his toes to his scalp. The words swirled in his head. They might have been his words if he hadn't had Emily. *No one.* They had more than a disfigurement in common.

"I have my birth certificate," the man said. "Is it on there?"

"Very likely."

"Then I can get it for you. No problem. Can I call you or something?"

"That would work."

Suddenly irritable, he said, "Shouldn't a person like you *know* these things?"

"You think I don't know about you?" she asked.

He squinted back at her, like Jack when he was drunk and trying to concentrate.

"You're a military man," she informed him. He looked shocked. Ben swelled with pride. "Air Force. You live by yourself. You're considerate of others, the type of man to help someone out who needs a hand. Money is a little tight right now, but things are looking up. There's a deal on the horizon. . . ."

His eyes were the size of saucers, though he tried to contain his shock. He rubbed his hands together briskly, although the flipper stayed out of it, as if the knuckles didn't bend. He glanced up at Emily and said, "Okay, so I'm impressed. So what?" He waited briefly and asked, "How could you know any of that?"

"It's my gift," she said.

Pride surged through Ben, warming him. He'd done a good job out at the truck. Emily needed him. They were a team.

7

HOMICIDES were about victims. The way a victim had lived often told more about his or her death than the way a victim died.

Boldt was scheduled to meet with Dorothy Enwright's mother and sister. It was an interview that he would have rather pawned off onto a detective, but he did not. He wanted to know what kind of life the dead woman had lived, her friends, her enemies. Something, somewhere in Dorothy Enwright's past, had ensured her untimely death. She had most likely been robbed, caught in some act, or loved the wrong person. It was Boldt's job—his duty—to identify that individual and bring him or her to the courts with enough incriminating evidence to win a conviction. A deputy prosecuting attorney would accept nothing less.

Lou Boldt would accept nothing less. From the moment that Dixie had confirmed the existence of a bone in the rubble—a body—Boldt's central focus was to see a person or persons brought to justice, to force Enwright's murderer to capitulate and repay society for the victim's undeserved and unwarranted death.

Arson investigator Sidney Fidler showed up at Boldt's office cubicle just in time to delay the sergeant's departure for the interview with Enwright's relatives. Boldt felt like thanking him.

Fidler was anxiously thin and prematurely bald. He wore clothes that didn't match, and he always looked half asleep, though he had one of the finest minds of anyone Boldt had worked with in years. It was too bad that Fidler was a fireman on rotation to SPD rather than a permanent member of Boldt's homicide squad. In terms of ability, there weren't many Sidney Fidlers out there. Single and a loner, he looked and acted about sixty. He was somewhere in his early thirties.

"I thought I might interpret this lab report for you, Sergeant." Despite his diminutive size, he had a deep, rich voice. He looked Boldt directly in the eye. "And to bring you up to date on some of the particulars." He didn't wait for Boldt's reply but continued on, confidently, passing Boldt the report. "It's a preliminary report in the form of a memo, to give us an idea of what we'll receive." Boldt adjusted himself in his seat. Such memos were courtesy of the Washington State Patrol Crime Lab, typically offered only on cases where the information was so hot as to ensure it would leak. The memos gave investigating officers a head start on the findings and were themselves rarely leaked to the press. But the existence of a memo told Boldt that the lab findings were significant enough to *expect* a leak. Not good news.

"Sure thing," Boldt said.

"Bahan and I had a parley with a couple of the task force boys—"

"Was Garman there?" Boldt interrupted.

"As a matter of fact, he was. You know him?"

"Not well," Boldt answered. "Go on."

"These Marshal Five guys are older by a few years, but they're wiser too. There's five thousand firefighters in this city, assigned to forty-two stationhouses. There are only seven Marshal Fives, okay? Between them they've got maybe two hundred years' experience on the line. I say this for your own education, Sergeant. Forgive me if I'm telling you something you already know."

"No, no," Boldt corrected. "I appreciate it. Go on," he repeated. He felt anxious about these findings. Fidler's setup had left him guessing.

"A fire inspector, a Marshal Five, follows a burn to its area of origin, hoping to lift samples of the accelerant for the chemists. As you know, the Enwright fire was a bastard because the area of origin was nearly entirely destroyed. Maybe that explains it, and maybe not, but the guys on the task force think not. The thing of it is, Sergeant, the lab report is going to come back negative for hydrocarbons. That's about the gist of it. I imagine in your area of expertise it would be like finding a drowned body with no water in the lungs. Quite frankly, it's baffling."

"What's it mean?" Boldt asked.

"Honestly? Not much. But it won't look good. Our best defense to the press is that we didn't locate a good pour, so the analysis came back negative. It also happens to be the truth. But we *did* locate the spalling and the blue concrete, and that sure as hell should test positive for accelerant, and that's the baffling part, if you ask me. Why no hydrocarbons, no petroleum products whatsoever? This is not the end of the story, not by any means. The collective wisdom of the Marshal Five boys is that we repackage some new samples and send them off to Chestnut Grove, the ATF lab. They're good guys, great chemists. And Chestnut Grove specializes in arson and bombs. We ask for a rush, maybe we hear back in a couple of weeks. Most likely they pick up what we missed."

Fidler paused, training his rich brown eyes on the sergeant, allowing a moment for his words to be absorbed. He then said, "You asked what it means. There had to be one hell of an accelerant in that fire. You don't go to eleven hundred feet and turn concrete blue with only a match set to the two-by-fours. We could have missed it for any number of reasons. Best bet is to send it to the Feds and try again. They'll scare up something."

"Hydrocarbons," Boldt provided for him. "They'll find hydrocarbons."

"It would certainly surprise me if they didn't."

"And if they don't?" Boldt inquired.

"Let's take it one square at a time."

Boldt didn't like the sound of that. "Maybe you should brief me, just in case."

"Clutter your mind with worthless facts? What kind of person does that?"

"Ignorance is bliss?" Boldt asked. He suddenly felt uncomfortable with Fidler. Was he trying to hide something?

"If you want to take a master's in pyrotechnic chemistry, that's your business, Sergeant. Me? I like waiting for the lab reports and learning what it is I need to know for that particular burn. How were you in organic chemistry?"

"Next question," said Boldt. He didn't want to admit that as a junior in high school he had taken the senior chemistry course and earned one of two A's given out for the year. It would mark him as a nerd. His comment caused Fidler to grin; the man needed some dentistry. Boldt said, "Blue cement and negative lab reports. Is that about the sum of it?" He paused. "Tell me, Sid, what do you think of the stuff that Garman received? Related or not?"

"The timing's good. Weird note. Don't know about the plastic."

"I sent it all downstairs for analysis."

"What's your opinion?" Fidler asked.

"We would give it weight in a straight homicide, especially if the victim had received it."

"But if *you* had received it?"

Boldt answered, "Yeah, I suppose if I'd received it I might give it weight too."

"So it's Garman getting it that bugs you."

"He's on the arson task force, I understand that. But Enwright's home isn't in his district."

"His battalion," Fidler corrected.

"Whatever. So if it's legitimate, why did the torch send it to a different Marshal Five? I mean, if he knows so much about the internal structure of fire investigations, why send it to the wrong guy?"

Fidler's face screwed up into a knot and his lips pursed. "Hadn't thought about it that way."

"It bothers me," Boldt said.

"Yeah, right. You're right," Fidler agreed, "he screwed up."

"People screw up for two reasons, Sid. Either they make a mistake or you make a mistake in *thinking* that they made a mistake."

"Accidentally or intentionally."

"Exactly. And if it's intentional, it isn't their mistake at all, it's only yours for reading it that way."

"So if it wasn't a mistake?" Fidler tested. "If he meant to send it to Garman?"

"Why Garman?" Boldt asked. "You see?" He could watch Fidler's thought processes displayed across his face. "It may narrow down the search for us. Someone Garman put away? Someone he knows, works with?"

"Shit," Fidler gasped. "That complicates things. It takes us away from the woman—"

"First things first," Boldt replied, interrupting. "I start with getting to know Dorothy Enwright, post facto. Things are rarely as complicated as they appear at first glance."

"And me?" Fidler asked.

"I'll tell you what: Why don't you get to know Steven Garman?" Boldt instructed, adding, as an afterthought, "Just in case."

The two Enwright women, mother and sister, had refused Boldt's efforts for a meeting in the mother's home, a condominium in Redmond. Despite the drive, Boldt had wanted the mother on relaxed ground, a place she wouldn't be afraid to cry, a place she might be more open and honest. But the victim's sister worked downtown, and Boldt's attempts to separate the two women into different interviews failed, and in the end he agreed to meet them at four o'clock in the Garden Court of the Four Seasons Olympic hotel. He asked them both to bring photographs.

Located on Seattle's fashionable 5th Avenue, the Olympic was one of the country's few remaining grand hotels, ornate, opulent, and spacious, restored lovingly and sparing no expense. The lobby was glorious, the service impeccable. Boldt was no stranger to the place. His love of a formal tea service brought him there several times a year, in spite of the fourteen-dollar price tag. It was one of the few treats he allowed himself. His colleagues spent their money on Scotch and ball games. When he could afford it, Boldt preferred tea at the Four Seasons or dinner and a show at Jazz Alley.

But he knew the hotel well and welcomed the soothing ambiance of the ficus trees, the gentle sound of the running water, the thirty-foot ceilings, and the classical piano. The room was open, in three tiers, and smelled of a flower garden. The women servers all wore shimmering gold dress uniforms, while the waiters wore white jackets. The hum of active conversation was muted by the plush carpet. Boldt gave the attractive receptionist, an Asian woman in her twenties, the name Magpeace, Dorothy Enwright's maiden name. She seated him on the second level near the waterfall on a love seat in front of a table with starched linen and bone china.

Mrs. Harriet Magpeace and her thirty-year-old daughter, Claudia, entered ten minutes later, wearing grim faces to the table. They shook hands all around. Boldt held the chair for Harriet. His notebook lay open on the table. It seemed odd to order tea and scones and cucumber sandwiches on the edge of discussing a young woman's brutal murder, but he knew from experience that people seek comfort in extremely individual ways at such times. He'd gone on a long walk once with the husband of one murder victim, the man claiming he had barely stopped walking since the death: all hours of day and night, any destination, it didn't matter. Two weeks later, Boldt had arrested him for the murder.

Harriet Magpeace kept her graying hair short over her ears. She had Irish coloring and a long elegant neck, around which she had fastened a string of pearls. She was dressed in gabardine slacks and a black cotton sweater, nice but not showy. Her daughter, who had inherited her mother's Irish green eyes, was wonderful to look at. She wore a modest gray suit, appropriate for her job in a downtown advertising firm. If Dorothy had looked anything like her sister, she had been a beauty.

The mother removed a small group of photos from a Coach purse and slid them disdainfully across the linen toward Boldt, as if not wanting to see them herself. "I'm sorry I couldn't meet you at the police station or my home," she apologized, glancing around. "This is better." She did not look comfortable.

"We do want to thank Detective Matthews for telling us about the arson before the press got hold of it," the daughter said meekly. Matthews was not a detective; she was the departmental psychologist, a lieutenant, but Boldt did not correct the woman.

"Obviously it's a shock," the mother said. She tensed, and Boldt worried that she wouldn't hold up.

A violent death was more than a shock; he understood this well. It was an invasive event that pried open the victim's life in a sterile, analytical way that was like shining too much light onto a face or into a room. It bared all. It left the victim defenseless to explain the hidden bottles of vodka, the nude videos, the love letters, the stash of crisp hundred-dollar bills. It rolled the rock off the dark places of a private life. He hated to do this to Dorothy Enwright.

Boldt explained, "This is a lousy job at times. This is one of those times. I have to ask questions that imply I don't trust the quality of Dorothy's character. I want you to know right off that that is not the case. I would love to approach this a different way, but I'm afraid the truth is often more elusive than any of us would believe. What my experience has taught me is that none of us want to be here, and that by getting to the point we get it over more quickly, which is what we all want. Again, I do this only for the sake of getting to the truth, not because I've formed any advance opinions of Dorothy."

"I think we understand," the dark beauty said. Her mother nodded.

Boldt said, "If she was murdered"—at which point Harriet Magpeace twitched violently—"then we start first with looking at people close to her: a husband, a lover, a co-worker. Since the house may or may not be involved, itself a victim, we might want to look at repairmen, contractors, service providers. What I need from you is a snapshot of Dorothy's life, including, but not limited to, the events that led up to the day of the fire."

The older woman stared at Boldt sadly. "Yours is a morbid life, isn't it, Sergeant?"

Boldt winced. He didn't appreciate his work—his life—being reduced to such a statement, hated it all the more for the truth of it. Death was a way of life for him, it was true; but for Boldt it was seen as a means to an end, the only acceptable end being justice and the imprisonment of the party responsible. An investigator who relied upon the victim to tell the story—a man who even lectured on the subject—Boldt understood the intricacy of the relationship between victim and killer. That he exploited this relationship was nothing he tried to hide or make light of. That it often bordered on the grotesque was inescapable.

"I'm sure my mother means that sympathetically," Claudia interjected, attempting to lessen the blow and come to her mother's aid. "We certainly appreciate all you're doing to find Doro's killer—if that's actually what happened. I have to tell you, the whole thing is a little fantastic. Arson? Murder? Doro? I mean, come on!"

Boldt was prepared for disbelief. He hesitated to tell them that no one—no one!—ever anticipated murder, except on television. Even the parents of known drug dealers were stunned with surprise to learn of their child's death. Boldt said the few words he would rather have not said. "Can you tell me a little bit about Dorothy?"

The mother blinked rapidly. This was where business and the nature of that business collided. Claudia filled in quickly. "Doro was divorced two years ago. Bob's an architect. Doro writes— wrote—for garden magazines and a few of the food magazines as well. She . . . it was Doro's fault—the divorce."

"It wasn't her fault!" the mother snapped.

"She fell in love with another man, Mother. It certainly *was* her fault." To Boldt, Claudia said, "The boyfriend died of cancer a few months after the separation; she lost him. It was awful. For every-one," she added. "Dorothy lost the child in the divorce. She only got visitation rights. It was miserable."

"*She* was miserable," corrected the mother.

"But there was no hostility on her part. She understood the judge's ruling, as much as she hated it. We talked about it. It's not like she threatened Bob or anything."

"She was a lovely girl," the mother mumbled.

"You spend all those years with someone," the sister said, "and you just expect them to be around. And then they're not. There are so many things I want to tell her."

Boldt nodded. This, too, he had heard a hundred different times.

Claudia said, "I know what you're looking for, Sergeant. At least I think I do. But I just don't see it. Bob would never, ever, do such a thing. Not a chance." She hesitated, studied Boldt, and then rattled off Bob Enwright's office and home phone numbers, know-ing Boldt would want to talk with him. She was right.

The sergeant asked, "Did she own the house?"

"A rental," the sister replied. The mother looked lost. Claudia said, "You were thinking insurance, weren't you? She burned it for the insurance and got caught in the fire? No chance."

"We consider every possibility," Boldt said.

The mother said, "Someone murder Dorothy? Why?"

"That's why the sergeant's here," Claudia said perfunctorily.

"Don't patronize me, dear. I'm your mother. I know perfectly well what we're trying to do: to give someone a reason to kill Doro-thy. It's absurd, don't you see?" she directed the question to Boldt.

"The child had last visited the mother—"

"The day before," Harriet answered.

"Two days," Claudia said in disagreement.

That also was to be expected, Boldt thought. Take down five eyewitness reports of the same crime and be prepared for five dif-ferent stories—occasionally, completely different stories.

Claudia said firmly, "It was two days before. Remember din-ner, Mother?"

The mother squinted, considered this, displayed an expression of self-disappointment. "Two, you're right."

"The father picked up the child?" Boldt asked.

"Not typically. I would doubt it."

The mother said, "No. Dorothy dropped him off."

Claudia explained, "Doro was the more flexible of the two."

If given half a chance, if at all average, they would lie to get custody of the child; they would be eager to conspire against the former husband. Boldt had come prepared to see through this. When they failed to make any such attempt, Boldt felt somewhat disappointed. Could Dorothy Enwright have committed suicide? he wondered. Watching out for the sister, he said, "Dorothy was a gardener. Obviously a good one. One would assume she stored fertilizer, used various fertilizers in her work."

"In the shed, not the basement." Claudia added, "She wasn't in the habit of making bombs, if that's what you're driving at. Whatever happened to 'innocent until proven guilty'?"

"Making bombs?" the mother inquired.

The daughter answered, "You can make a bomb out of fertilizer and gasoline, Mother. The detective is implying—"

"Nothing," Boldt interrupted, cutting her off. "I'm not implying anything. Asking questions is all. It might be easier for everyone if we could just deal with the questions rather than jump to conclusions."

"I see where you're headed with this," the victim's sister cautioned, ignoring his suggestion.

"I don't," the mother interjected.

"He thinks maybe Doro was plotting something sinister. He's a policeman, Mother. They're all suspicious by nature."

"Not by nature, by occupation," Boldt corrected, meeting the daughter's eye. "I think we're off to a bad start," he said. He directed the next question to the mother, hoping to avoid the sister for a moment. The mother glanced at her daughter disapprovingly. "Do you know of any work being done on the house? By the landlord, perhaps?" Boldt asked.

Harriet replied, "No. Not that I'm aware of. She was quite happy there."

Wanting this over, Boldt asked Claudia, "Any boyfriends out of her past? Anybody you think I might want to speak with?"

"I know you're only doing your job, Sergeant. I respect that. I apologize. I just don't think there's anything to tell you. Doro was a wonderful, loving person. She didn't deserve this."

"We don't know, do we," the mother asked, "that it was my Dorothy? In the fire, I mean. You people haven't confirmed that, have you?"

This was the sticking point Boldt had hoped to avoid. The tea and scones were delivered, sparing him an answer. The pit in his stomach had deepened, changing to an ache. The room had lost its glitter; the waitresses had lost a step. The piano sounded a little out of tune on the low end. The glue that held his world together had softened. He felt tawdry, cheap, a gumshoe who lacked empathy and compassion. A woman was dead. No one wanted to talk about it—or even admit it, for that matter. She had had a sad life of late and a sad death and Lou Boldt understood damn well that all the investigating in the world wasn't going to bring her back. The mother would go on living with her hope that it had been someone else in that fire. The sister would go on defending where no defense was necessary. Boldt would go on with his questions. The victim ruled all his investigations, but ultimately it was not about the victim, it was about the killer, about balance.

Boldt had seen a dead cat by the side of the road earlier in the day, and it had overwhelmed him with a sense of tragic loss. In his mind he transferred Dorothy Enwright, the woman in the photographs before him, to that same place on the side of the road— naked, face down, struck dead. He sat there with his notebook, his pencil, and a haunting determination to find the person responsible. Death made people give up; it made Lou Boldt *sit* up. He felt bad about that; he didn't like himself. Dorothy Enwright had no obvious enemies. Boldt could create a dozen scenarios accounting for that fire and that woman in it, but only because he did so day in and day out; his job was to create such situations and pursue them to their outcome, to turn a woman like Enwright into something he could work with.

"You're not eating," the mother told him.

"No."

"You don't like it?"

Did she mean the scones or the investigation? he wondered, realizing quickly that it didn't matter; he had the same answer on the tip of his tongue. "No," said Boldt. With the victim's finances, correspondence, and paperwork lost in the fire, Boldt requested permission to contact Dorothy's banks and auditors and look over the accounts. The mother saw nothing wrong with that and agreed.

"I have an image of Doro out in her garden," said the sister. "You know? The sunlight slanting across her face. She was quite beautiful. Hands working the soil. Weeding, planting. She laughed a lot, Doro did. Used to," she added. "The last two years took a lot out of her. But I think of her as laughing nonetheless. You know, I have this image, and I don't even know if it's real or something I made up to remember her by. And the funny thing is, it doesn't matter, does it? It's the image I'm left with. The smile. The contentment at being outdoors and working with plants. The joy of being a mother. She loved little Kenny."

"It broke her heart when the judge took Kenny away," the mother said. "I don't think she ever fully recovered."

"Was she depressed, drinking, anything like that in the days before the fire?"

Claudia cautioned, "She did *not* kill herself, Detective. Not intentionally, not accidentally. She kept her gardening supplies in the back shed. You're out of line."

"Is that a yes or no to the depression?" Boldt asked, irritated. He kept seeing the cat by the side of the road, then Dorothy Enwright. If there was one thing he had learned early as a homicide investigator, it was how fragile life was, how easily lost. Men stepping out into traffic. Kids playing on the rocks in the hills. Women going home at night to an empty house. One day here, the next day gone. And if the death came with questions attached, it was Lou Boldt's job to answer them, or to help others to answer them for him. All he needed was a few answers. He couldn't picture the woman setting fire to a rental house. People did not use fire as a method toward suicide. But he had other problems with Dorothy Enwright. Of chief concern to him was why she had not run from the house when it caught fire; it had not exploded. She had been seen walking inside the house, presumably of her own volition, moments before the blaze. He thought she must have had an opportunity to escape, given the way the fire had burned from a central core outward. It had not trapped her by sealing the doors. Why then had she not escaped?

Had there been someone else in the building with her?

"Dorothy was having problems," her mother told him, "but she was surprisingly cheerful, wouldn't you say, dear?"

"Absolutely," Claudia agreed. "She was a remarkable woman, Detective. She had a great attitude."

"Who would want to kill her?" the mother blurted out, too loudly for the soft buzz of conversation in the Garden Court. Heads turned. Fortunately, only Boldt saw this.

The two women who sat with him did not see. Their eyes were filled with tears.

8

OCTOBER second came and nearly went without Ben's taking any notice of it. Had it not been for Emily, he might have failed to remember its significance. But when he arrived at Emily's late on the afternoon of the third, she sent him by bus all the way up to Steven's Broadway News on the corner of Olive and Broadway, where he used the money she gave him to buy copies of the *Seattle Times*, the *Intelligencer*, the *Tacoma News Tribune*, and the *Everett Herald*.

Back at her purple house, the two of them read headlines and lead paragraphs, back and forth, until Ben asked, "What exactly are we doing?"

"The military man," she said. "Do you remember him? May thirteenth, 1968."

"Who?"

"The bad hand."

Ben remembered the hand.

She said, "He came back for his reading about a week later. You must have been in school. I told him that the stars looked good for a business deal on October second. He was real nervous about it, and I got the feeling his business wasn't exactly legitimate.''

"So we're looking for something he might have did.''

"Might have *done*,'' she corrected. "Yes. He'll be back, that one. Very superstitious. I'd like to know what it was he did.''

"And you think we may find something in the papers, something about what he did?''

"If it was criminal, we might.''

"You think he's a criminal!'' Ben felt a pang of excitement in his chest. He didn't know any criminals.

Turning a page she said, "He had something going on the second. I tested if it had anything to do with love and got nothing back from him. I tested money and got a definite reaction—lots of body language, discomfort. He's selling something or buying something, and it wasn't anything he wanted to talk about. If I identify it, and he walks back in here and I can tell him about it, I'll have a customer for life. That's the way it works, you know, Ben. You give people what they want, and they're yours forever. He wants me to be able to see his past *and* his future.''

Ben read more carefully. Each article that dealt with any kind of crime he read aloud. Together, they cut the articles out of the paper with scissors and put them in a pile. The papers were full of various crimes. Ben said, "Nothing much good.''

"No. Nothing very good.'' She pushed the papers aside and looked at Ben and said, "Tell me what you remember about him, Ben.''

This was a test. She did this every now and then—made him exercise his memory skills. She claimed it would make him smarter. He reeled off all that he could recall about the beat-up pickup truck, the camper shell, the contents of the front seat. He told her how he had been tempted to get a look inside the camper through the skylight. He gave her a detailed description of what he had seen through the peephole: buzz-cut hair, pinpoint eyes, the fingers on his right hand.

"How old did he look?'' she asked.

Ben knew exactly how to answer this. It took him a moment to subtract the numbers. "Twenty-eight," he answered, using the birth date she had already supplied.

She reached over and rubbed the top of his head, messing his hair, which was Emily's way of saying how much she cared about him.

She said, "He wore black military boots. He had a faint red stamp on the back of his left hand that read COPY—probably from a bar or nightclub. When he paid me, he pulled out his wallet. He carried a pass to the PX, a discount shopping center on the base, which means he's either active or works there. His driver's license was from Kansas; I couldn't make out the town or city. He had a ticket to the Seahawks in with his money."

"He wore a big silver buckle," Ben remembered. "Like a rodeo guy."

"Very good!" she exclaimed. "Yes. That caught my eye as well. And did you catch it when he turned to leave?"

"Something on his back? I don't remember," he answered.

"His belt," she said. "It had a first name stamped into the leather. Nick."

"The guy's name is Nick?"

"Yes. He's twenty-eight, a long way from home, working on one of the bases, a football fan, hits the bars at night, rode a horse at some point in his life, or had a relative who did. He's got business dealings that worry him to the point he's having his chart read. The deal is worth a lot more than sixty bucks, or he wouldn't be willing to shell out that kind of money."

"We know a lot about him," Ben said, impressed.

"Yes, we do," she answered. "But not what he's up to." She went through the small pile of articles they had clipped. "And I have a feeling that's his biggest secret of all."

WHEN Liz voluntarily took the kids with her to the cabin for the weekend, Boldt knew he had trouble. Typically, she found the cabin too remote, too far from a doctor should the kids need one, and was bothered by being too far from the city and all its weekend treasures. Her more common complaint about the cabin was how cold it was, and in early October it was likely to deliver on that front. She had not called him at work, but instead had left him a note he couldn't possibly receive until she and the kids were well on their way, the decision beyond discussion. That struck him as odd, completely unlike her—until he reached the part in the note where she suggested he "come up if you can get free." Then he realized it was a test, a conspiracy, and it made all the sense in the world. He had a choice: his family or his job.

Liz knew that when he sank his teeth into something like this arson case there was no letting go. These cases only came around once every two years or so, but she resented them more than when he had six domestic battery investigations running simultaneously, taking him away from home fifteen hours a day. It was almost as if she were jealous of these larger investigations, as if it stole something personal from her when he dove in like this.

What really hurt was that he was going to fail the test. There was no way he could get up to the cabin for the weekend. Sunday night was going to be pins and needles on the home front. She would be angry, but with a smile pasted onto her face. He would feel guilty, but act casual and confident. He couldn't wait.

On the plus side, he had the house to himself. It didn't happen that often, and when it did he felt as if she had handed him the greatest gift of all. The thought bubbled up then that perhaps she had gone to the cabin in sacrifice, knowing perfectly well how he valued quiet time during a difficult investigation. This made him feel all the worse because his first thoughts had been so negative. He reread her note one more time, hoping to find clarity there, but to no avail. Marriage was many things; easy was not one of them.

He switched off the front porch light and put on an Oscar Peterson album. He sat down at the piano and played for the first time in several months, wondering why the great things in life were always the first to be sacrificed. He played roughly through the opening, reset the tone arm, and tried again.

After twenty minutes with Oscar, Boldt went through his investigation notes, reading every line carefully.

Boldt had good ears. A car pulled past his drive, slowed, and stopped. He went to the curtain and peered out: Daphne's red sports car. She climbed out carrying her briefcase, not a good sign.

He raced around, trying to pick up. A moment later he heard her footsteps on the back porch and opened the door for her.

"You not answering your phone?"

"Liz turns the ringers off—Sarah's a light sleeper. Sorry."

"Your pager? Your cellphone?"

"In the bedroom, along with my piece. I've had the music kinda loud," he aplogized. "Nothing intentional. Come on in."

"Liz?" She seemed hesitant to enter.

"Took the kids to the cabin. It's all right." He motioned her inside.

"It's *not* all right," she corrected, stepping inside, already down to business. "Today's press conference was a disaster. Shoswitz talks too much! And then there's *this*." She reached into her briefcase and handed him a photocopy. "The original's with the lab," she informed him.

Minutes later she was sitting across from him at the kitchen table, sipping from a glass of red wine. Boldt had a glass of juice. He reread the note silently another time before finally speaking. *"Suddenly a flash of understanding, a spark that leaps across to the soul."* Several minutes had passed. "Sent to Garman?"

She nodded gravely. "It's Plato. Our boy is something of a scholar."

"Just now you're on your way home?" he asked, dodging the issue a moment while he considered the consequences of the note. "It's late for you."

"Garman delivered it unopened," she informed him. "He knew what it was. He said he wanted to protect it as evidence." She let him digest this a moment before saying, "I offered to bring it over."

"Yeah, thanks," Boldt said. He added, "I hate this, you know? I really hate it."

"Yes."

In her eyes he saw a deep-seated sympathy. They both understood perfectly well what this meant, but Boldt had no desire to voice it, as if by doing so might give it more weight. Nonetheless, his imagination fixed on the thought of another Dorothy Enwright out there, at home, minding her own business, about to come face to face with the gates of Hell. They had recovered only a single bone of her body. It seemed all but impossible.

"Why?" Boldt asked Daphne, still withholding any mention of what this second note represented—another fire, another victim.

"The fire or the note?" she asked.

"Is there a difference?"

"You bet there is." She sipped the wine, though she didn't seem to enjoy its taste. She looked a little less pretty all of a sudden, tired and under the same relentless pressure that Boldt found himself. Investigating a violent crime was one thing; anticipating and stopping such a crime, another thing entirely. With the arrival of the second note, their charge was to prevent a death. It was an undeserved burden—unwarranted in many ways—but inescapable. They had been here before, the two of them, and this went unmentioned as well, for lives had been lost; other lives changed forever, not the least of them their own.

She continued, "The first note, as we discussed, could have been anything from a cry for help to a poorly timed coincidence. This note changes all that. Remember," she cautioned, "this is only an opinion, an educated guess."

"I'm with you."

"These quotations are warnings, Lou." Boldt felt a chill. "Forget the cry for help. He's going to strike for a second time. By mailing them, he dated both poems, don't forget. If I'm right, that means the fire is today or tonight. It's immediate. He's not giving Garman any time to figure this out. He warns; he strikes—which means that by the time the card arrives, he has already targeted his victim, perhaps even rigged the house to burn."

"Jesus!" Boldt expelled his breath. "With only one victim, we hardly have what could be considered a pattern."

"It's premeditated, and he's enjoying it. But his intended victim may not be the resident, don't forget," she warned. "May not even be human. He may be after the work of a particular architect, the structure itself that he's trying to 'kill.' More likely, it could be Garman he's after. The pressure you're feeling—that I'm feeling, for that matter—may be solely intended for Garman. He's a fire inspector, Lou. His evidence puts arsonists in jail. Revenge is potent motivation."

"Fidler is checking out Garman."

"Well, that will help," she said, knowing Fidler's reputation for detail.

"I've got Bahan working the technical end, the chemistry of the arsons." He sensed her unease. "What's up?"

"Firemen," she answered. "Fidler, Bahan, Garman, all of them. Cops are one step away from being the bad guys—we've discussed this before—far too many of us are in it for the power.

Present company excepted, of course. Firemen are no better. Put-ting out a fire is only one step away from setting it. In fact, as we both know, firemen set structure fires all the time to train the new boys. They love torching places." She met his skeptical expression. "I'm generalizing, admittedly, but I don't think even the firemen would argue this point too hard. My point being, if we're looking for an arsonist, we might not have to look very far."

Boldt said inquisitively, "Who better than a fire inspector to go torching places and sending himself notes? Is that what you're saying?"

"Anyone in turnouts, Lou. They all have the bug. How busy has this fire season been? How much budgetary pressure is on the department to start cutting costs? These things have to be an-swered. Who goes first if the cuts are made? He or she could be our torch."

"She?" Boldt asked.

"Poison and fire, a girl's best friends."

"Prior convictions and current firemen. Quite a list. Anyone else?" Boldt felt an impending urgency; the second note was like a fuse burning inside him. "What about victims? How do we stop a second death?"

"How do we stop potential copycat fires?" she asked, avoid-ing an answer. Arsons were notorious for spawning copycats; it was something they all knew but no one wanted to discuss. "How do we ask the press to hold off to stop the chances of a copycat?" she asked rhetorically. "It can't be done, Lou. Let's hope we've got it wrong. Maybe there is no second fire. Maybe that first note wasn't tied to Enwright. Who knows?" She added, "And if there *is* a second fire, a second victim, we don't collapse under the weight, we don't allow the city—or even the brass, for that mat-ter—to run the investigation. It's your case, Lou. Everyone should be grateful for that."

Pep talks and compliments, they traded them often. She seemed to sense when he most needed them. Their friendship had started that way. That it had developed into a single night of frantic sex six years earlier was their business and theirs alone. He had a line of sarcasm on the tip of his tongue, but he withheld it—she meant well enough. But just the fact that she would attempt to pump him up troubled him. It meant she was as scared about a second fire, a second victim, as was he.

She added, in a frail voice that confirmed his concern, "No one wants a second victim. I'm not suggesting that."

Boldt had dealt with a peer of Daphne's, a forensic psychiatrist from the East brought in to profile an earlier case. The man had once told Boldt, "The more they kill, the more we learn, the greater the chance we'll catch them." It had been one of those hard pieces of truth that Boldt wanted nothing to do with, yet it had lingered in the back of his mind. The psychiatrist was a strange man, but his message simple: An investigator could not afford to allow an increasing body count to kill the investigation over guilt and grief; he had to rise to the challenge and gather as much additional evidence as possible. He had to persevere.

"We can put the fire department on alert," Boldt suggested, trying to find something to do other than sit around and wait for another body to burn. "We can contact the Marshal Fives—the Arson Task Force—and ask them to pump their sources for information. This guy isn't operating in a void."

She offered, "We've had a few calls from psychics wanting to sell us information. I haven't followed up, but I'd like to."

Boldt winced. He had no room for psychics in his cases. "Not for me," he reminded her.

"I'd like to run with them. At least a follow-up."

"Your stuff, not mine."

"Don't start with me," she cautioned. "They may have something to offer. We take tips from *junkies*, Lou! Are you trying to tell me a psychic is less believable than a junkie?"

"You handle the psychics," he quipped. "I'll take the junkies."

She fumed, exhaling heavily. Daphne rarely lost her cool. They sat in silence.

She focused on the glass of wine, her long fingers running up and down the stem. She changed the subject, asking, "Did you

10

THE brunette with the thin waist and the tight skirt was in the kitchen cleaning up from the popcorn, and Ben knew that she had to come through the living room to reach Jack, who was already waiting in the bedroom. She was a new one, brown hair pulled back with a hair band, less makeup than the others, thinner than most of the women he dragged back with him. Ben liked her. She had rented the video with him in mind. The movie was a little sappy, but Ben enjoyed what passed as a normal evening at home. Typically, the only normal things in his life were school and—after school—Emily.

He wondered what better way to welcome her than to share his cherished death pose with her. He didn't let just anybody see it.

He positioned himself in the guy's favorite chair, one of the ones with a handle that leaned way back and lifted your knees, and he hung his head over the arm, so that he stretched his neck and the blood ran into his face, turning it a bright red. Then he popped out his glass eye, carefully cupped it in his hand, and opened both his eyes in a deadman's stare that he fixed on the bookshelf across the room.

catch the sound bite they ran in the news. Shoswitz threatening the arsonist?''

"I caught it. They ran it on PLU." Shoswitz was the lieutenant. He was terrible with the press, but there was no stopping him.

"He may have baited him, Lou: 'Madman . . . nut case.' He even mentioned you by name."

"Lead detectives are often mentioned," he reminded her, unconcerned.

"In ongoing cases? It's wrong. I wish he wouldn't do that."

"The lieutenant dances to his own drums."

Boldt's pager sounded. He and Daphne exchanged looks. There was danger in hers. They both knew it was a fire before Boldt ever made the phone call.

A minute later he heard the water stop and her footsteps approaching, and he spread his arms out so they were floppy, and he held in his breath so that his chest stopped moving.

Her scream was loud enough that a neighbor called the police, and to make matters worse she peed in her pants, making a big dark stain in the crotch of her jeans. Jack had hold of Ben before Ben could settle her down, and all at once there was that unmistakable sound of his belt singing out of the loops, and Ben felt his world invert and then the belt started connecting with his butt and he thought maybe he'd be sick to his stomach. The girl, Jane? June? April?—Ben suddenly couldn't remember—screamed even louder for the guy to stop, but that belt kept coming like a whip, and when the girl ran from the house the guy turned the belt around so that the buckle became part of the punishment. Somewhere in the ensuing nightmare, Ben threw up on the fancy chair, which only brought the belt down harder.

When he had satisfied himself, Jack dropped Ben into the chair like a sack of potatoes, pushed his face into the vomit, and told him to clean up the mess or "face worse." Ben was solid tears, but he hadn't let out a peep—that was one of the rules.

Maybe the cops saved his life—he thought later—because the knock on the door, followed by the strong voices announcing themselves, forced Jack to send Ben to his room rather than let Ben be seen. He pulled the boy by the hair to where his sweating face nearly touched Ben's tearstained cheeks, and he spoke in a dry, forced whisper. "Out of here. And not a sound!"

Ben could barely move, his butt was so raw, but he flew up those stairs nonetheless. He heard one of the cops say something about a complaint from a neighbor; the cops wanted a look around. "We gotta check something like this out," the unfamiliar voice explained.

Ben understood his situation clear as day. One, in his condition he couldn't let himself be discovered by the cops; Jack could get in big trouble, which would only mean more beatings. Two, the guy was sure to kill him once the cops were gone.

He opened his window and went out the familiar route, along

the roof—quietly!—over to the tree off the kitchen, and down through the limbs. His butt was a source of blinding, nauseating pain. With a deep inhale of the cool night air, he felt free—the most amazing, most welcome feeling of all.

For the walk to Emily's, Ben, slow on his feet and unable to run even if he had wanted to, stayed off Martin Luther King, sticking to back streets. He did not think of Seattle as a dangerous place, and he was not afraid of the dark, but his temporary disability from the whipping, and his blind eye, left him with an acute sense of vulnerability and uneasiness.

The air smelled faintly of the sea and strongly of bus fumes. The sky glowed vividly from the brightness of downtown. The constant hum of engines and the whine of tire rubber played out like a chorus of summer insects. A ferry horn bellowed. The city. The Seattle he would have known even blindfolded.

Emily's house was dark, the neon window sign switched off, and he was loath to roust her, loath to admit on any level that his existence with the guy was untenable, that the time to offer evidence against the guy had long since passed. That the time had come. His fear was not of pain or reprimand but of being alone. Not of loneliness but aloneness. He felt sorry for himself. She had told him that for a time he would be in the care of the state, and nothing scared him more. She had told him she would rescue him from their care and provide for him and nourish him and love him, and though he trusted her intentions he remained skeptical of the process. Of the system. He feared desertion. His mother had run away without a word.

Briefly, the truth clanged inside his chest, as it did on occasion: His mother would never have left him behind.

He climbed the cedar tree, past the sitting limb, and up to the platform—six boards nailed between two old boughs, each capable of supporting a car. He had a more complete tree fort behind his own house, but this platform at Emily's was a safer refuge given the trouble he'd caused. He lay down on the platform keenly aware of his wounds and curled himself into a ball, where he hugged himself until he fell fast asleep, pulled down into the drowsiness of a body and mind in need of repair. Of escape. Sucked down into a dream that turned nightmare: his own inescapable existence.

11

BEHIND the incessant pulse of emergency vehicle lights, Boldt and arson investigator Neil Bahan waited for the site to cool enough for them to walk it. Boldt had a borrowed helmet and turnout jacket. He wore his waterproof hiking boots.

They had been waiting four hours by the time the Marshal Five inspector entered the remains of 876 57th Street North. Accompanying him was Steven Garman, who had arrived by the second of the four alarms.

The ground was soggy beneath Boldt's boots. The air smelled bitter, a mixture of the wet, smoldering materials and a taste of charcoal. Neil Bahan led Boldt through a gaping hole in the side of the building, saying, "Keep a close eye on your footing. I'll keep watch overhead. If I tell you to duck or jump, don't hesitate, just do it. That's why you want to be looking down—you need to pick a good spot to move to."

Both Bahan and Boldt carried strong flashlights, illuminating the wreckage. Boldt was surprised at how unrecognizable it was and said so. "There's not much left to look at," he commented, pointing down into the basement area where the two Marshal Fives were already at work.

"It was overhauled," Bahan explained, sounding disappointed. "The firefighters basically tear the structure apart to be sure all the fire is caught. It's good fire fighting, but we encourage the IC to hold off on any overhaul in suspicious fires, because it hurts the investigation. Thing is, a fire this hot, it creeps into all kinds of hidden spots. To make it safe, to keep it out, you basically have to overhaul it; it's simply a matter of timing. We—the inspectors—would rather the overhaul came later. Let us in when it's still hot but under control. Investigators have to look at everything before it moves, to stand much of a chance. By the time Marshal Five is through with this, they'll have it cleaned down to the cellar's slab pour. You could eat a meal off it, swear to God."

The structure was a tangle of charred and smoldering lumber, bent aluminum window frames, toppled furniture, soggy carpet, and broken glass. Bahan and Boldt carefully dodged their way through the maze. Well over half the house was missing, a gaping round hole open to the sky above and the basement below, where Garman and the other Marshal Five rummaged through the remains. The fire had run like a pillar through this center section and had chewed whole sections of walls toward the back of the building. Bahan mumbled, "Never seen anything like this." He added, reconsidering, "Except in the Enwright pictures."

"Worse than most?" Boldt attempted to clarify.

"Not even close. Worse by a long shot."

"What exactly should I look for?" Boldt asked.

"Most of it will probably be down there," Bahan answered. "The cellar catches most of the debris. It falls into it like a cup: lumber, glass, tile, electrical conduit, insulation." He shined his flashlight into the hole. Garman glanced up at them and went on about his work. "You see what's missing?" Bahan asked Boldt. Pointing, he said, "Sinks. Toilets. Where are they? Same as Enwright. I'll tell you where: They're down there, melted flat, which means we're looking at temps in excess of two or three thousand degrees Fahrenheit, which basically puts this baby into a class by itself. Add to that the fact that the adjacent structures did not catch fire—because the thing burned so frigging fast—and you have one confused fire inspector."

"So the evidence is down there?" Boldt questioned.

"And not much of it at that. Most everything in this center core was vaporized." Bahan repeated for the sake of emphasis, "Vaporized."

A news helicopter flew overhead, training a blinding spotlight onto the structure. Bahan's face was dirt-smudged and his eyes were bloodshot. The air smelled suddenly different, yet familiar, and Boldt glanced around anxiously.

"What is it?" Bahan asked, sensing Boldt's agitation.

"It's a body," Boldt answered solemnly.

There was traffic noise and ambient two-way radio sounds and the occasional shudder of helicopter thunder. An angry dog barked in the distance.

Bahan dragged his forearm across his face, mopping sweat and smudging himself. "You sure about that?"

"I'm sure," Boldt answered. Panic gripped him. The neighbors who had been interviewed could not swear that anyone had been inside at the time of the fire. "Maybe a pet. Maybe not a human." Though he suspected it was. It was wafting up from below. Did only homicide cops know that smell? he wondered. He had no desire to be on hand when a cooked body was found. He'd seen one in autopsy. Once was enough.

He reached for Bahan's arm and caught the man, saying, "If it's all the same with you, someone should conduct a perimeter search before we lose it to contamination. Gum wrappers, popsicle sticks, bottle caps, toothpicks, pieces of clothing—"

"I'm with you." He pointed down. "The action is all down there, anyway. Area of origin was right in the center of the structure. They don't want us in their way. It'll be another hour or two at least."

"We'll each take a side and then swap." Boldt felt on familiar ground as they cleared the structure and reached dirt and mud. "Eyes to the ground," he instructed. "Eyes wide open."

Understanding what Boldt was after, Bahan said, "Anything this close to the structure went up with the fire. Not gonna be any gum wrappers on the ground."

Boldt appealed to the man. "Humor me."

"Hey, gladly," Bahan replied. "Beats wandering the charcoal waiting for Marshal Five to move his sorry butt."

Boldt winced and glanced down into the black pit where Garman and the other inspector searched the rubble. He thought everything was too far burned to find a body, and without a body there was no homicide. No investigation. His squad had a knifing up on Pill Hill to work, an apparent drowning near Shilshole. His nose knew what eyes could not confirm. Perhaps the body he had smelled would never be found.

The grass surrounding the structure's foundation was charred black from the heat and the ground beneath it soaked to a spongy mud by water from the fire hoses. Boldt looked for bottle caps, cigarette butts—anything at all that might tie in to a suspect. As he moved around the concrete foundation of the burned-out home, he attempted to reconstruct the crime. There were mythic stories of cops able to "see" a crime—to visualize a killing. Boldt possessed no such prescience. But on occasion he could reconstruct the methodology of a homicide based on the observable facts. On rare occasions, his imagination overpowered him, ran away from him, leaving him a spectator as the crime played out before him. That night in early October was just such an occurrence.

He looked up, and suddenly the *unburned* house stood before him, a house he had never seen. It had brown shingles and chipped white paint trim around the windows. It was a simple saltbox, two-story. No chimney, only an old TV antenna, bent and rusting, long out of service to the cable system. He saw a ladder leaning against the side of the house and the back of a man climbing up this ladder.

A siren sounded behind him, and Boldt lost the image. He looked around, taking his bearings, like a person just coming awake. These hallucinations were never shared with anyone, not even Liz. Part of his reluctance arose from the potential for embarrassment, part from superstition—he didn't want to do anything that might jinx his ability to occasionally transcend.

He knew enough from past experience not to move from this location. He knew from his discussions with Daphne that such moments of vivid "imagination" were typically triggered by an observation, a sound, a smell; that such stimuli imprinted themselves subconsciously. He understood that the trigger was probably close by or just past. He listened first for any sounds in the air. Then he paid attention to the burn smells overpowering him. All the while he visually scanned his surroundings.

The answer lay at his feet, not in the smells or sounds. Twin impressions in the mud. Two rectangular indentations in the black grass. Next to the right-hand dent were some blue flecks in the mud. He crouched and studied the area, disappointed as he identified them as ladder impressions. Firemen, he thought. The legs of the ladder had sunk about two inches into the turf and mud, leaving a distinctive stamped imprint of chevrons.

Boldt immediately sketched what he saw, after which he looked up to see Bahan standing alongside.

"Got something?" Bahan asked.

Boldt pointed, "I take it the fire crew used ladders fighting this one?"

"No way. Too hot for that. Besides," he said, pointing to the area in front of the impressions. "There was no wall there at all; the fire destroyed it. A little hard to lean a ladder against that."

Again Boldt glanced up into the air where the wall should have been, and again he was overcome with the image of a man climbing a ladder. He took time to mark the area with police tape before continuing around the foundation. By the time they had finished, only the ladder impressions were of interest to him.

Boldt telephoned the office and requested Bernie Lofgrin, the senior Identification Tech, to send someone out to cast and photograph the impressions and take samples of the colored flecks alongside. Excitement welled inside him. Crime-scene evidence, any evidence at all, is paramount in a case. Two fires too many, he thought. No more, he promised himself.

• • •

It was only as Boldt stepped inside his house later that night that another piece of crime-scene evidence revealed itself. He had stayed on-site for hours, overseeing the collection of the ladder evidence, and had been on hand for the grotesque discovery of the charred partial remains of a body discovered in the basement, trapped underneath an overturned bathtub. The removal of the remains had been conducted carefully. Dixie had showed up personally to help, something Boldt appreciated. The sex and age of the victim remained undetermined. More would be revealed in autopsy the following day.

But it was back at his house that Boldt stumbled—literally stumbled—onto that additional evidence, for his boots stuck to the kitchen floor as he stepped inside. They stuck, and Boldt fell forward and tumbled like a drunkard after a long night out.

He pulled them off and almost touched the melting rubber sole before thinking better of it. Whatever could disintegrate a Vibram sole was nothing to mess with. He wondered if any of the others had experienced the same phenomenon. Or had he been the only one wearing civilian shoes?

He called Bernie Lofgrin, awakened him, described the soles of his boots, and was told to wrap them thoroughly in aluminum foil and bring them into the lab in the morning.

"What's it mean, Bernie?" Boldt asked his friend, when the man was through with the instructions.

"A strong base or acid," Lofgrin replied, his voice puzzled. "But what that's doing in a fire is anybody's guess."

BEHIND his Coke-bottle glasses, Bernie Lofgrin's eyes looked like hardboiled eggs cut in half. Lofgrin stood five feet five inches off the ground. He was balding and overweight. He wore baggy khakis and a button-down blue oxford with no tie. There weren't many stars in any city government department, including the police, but Lofgrin stood out despite his diminutive size. As senior identification technician, Lofgrin had two decades of experience and a nose for evidence collection and analysis. Rookies observing him at a crime scene for the first time would say he possessed a sixth sense. But it had nothing to do with paranormal ability; it was a trained eye. Lofgrin knew his stuff.

He and Boldt and Dixie shared a love for their work. Perhaps, Boldt thought, this was what made them such close friends and allies. A common interest in bebop jazz brought them together, but it was dedication to the job that fixed the bond. When Lofgrin was definite about an opinion, Boldt ran with it and placed his faith in it, no matter how tempted to do the opposite.

There were only a few people on the department who would travel across town on a Saturday morning to sit around a kitchen table and talk shop. Bernie Lofgrin was one of them. Boldt fixed him a pot of coffee, put on a Scott Hamilton album, and cut open a cantaloupe. He cleaned out the seeds and cut off the rind and served them on a plate. Lofgrin dug right in. He spoke with his mouth full. "I came to get those shoes of yours."

"Have you been up all night?" Boldt asked.

"I went in at five and worked these impressions, and not because I love you. Your obsequious captain put me up to it. The shit is flying now that there's a second victim. The media is blaming a serial arsonist. The match has been dubbed the Scholar." He grimaced. Lofgrin, a civilian employee of SPD, was constantly put off by politics. He said, "You know how many ladders are sold in and around this city in any given year?"

"No idea," Boldt replied, thinking: Too many.

"Me neither." The little man laughed, and when he did he squinted his eyes closed and shook his head as might a man about to sneeze. There was only one Bernie Lofgrin.

Boldt bit into a slice of melon and waited for him to get to the point. Lofgrin had a way of taking his time.

"You wouldn't have noticed it, neither did I, but the width between the pads on the ladder's feet is significant. And we got good impressions of those pads, which serve as good strong fingerprints for us. Retail extension ladders, the kind you buy in hardware stores and discount houses, come in a variety of widths. Some manufacturers use twenty-four inches, some twenty-five or twenty-five and a half, depending on the tensile strength of the materials used—commonly aluminum or an aluminum alloy. All retail extension ladders are required by OSHA to have small pads, or feet, that grip the ground-level surface and help keep the base of the ladder from slipping. Each company goes with a slightly different grip pattern for those bottom pads, like tire treads in tire companies. What we're looking at is a Werner ladder. And that's significant, because it's not your weekend chores ladder, your honey-do around-the-house kind of ladder. Werner manufactures wooden, aluminum, and fiberglass lines. The imprints you found are from the high end of their fiberglass line, considered a professional line: electricians, painters, that sort of work."

"Firemen?" Boldt asked.

"Not fiberglass, no. It's flammable. Aluminum is the ladder of choice for firefighting, steel alloy for the hook-and-ladders."

"And do we have a particular model we're looking at?" Boldt asked. He knew Bernie well enough to know that he wouldn't come with his gun half loaded; the man was just taking his time giving Boldt the good news.

"It's a Werner twenty-four-foot fiberglass extension ladder," Lofgrin said proudly. "Manufactured between July '93 and August '94. Sold, probably, into '95. They changed the tread pattern and grip material in September '94."

"Do we have any idea how many Werner twenty-four footers were sold in this area?"

"Not a hard figure to get," Lofgrin answered. "That's your job." He added, "It wasn't many. It's the top of their line, and in '94–'95 they only had one wholesaler in western Washington."

"Good stuff, Bernie," Boldt said.

Training his bulging eyes onto the sergeant and slipping a curve of melon into his hungry mouth, Lofgrin said, "What, you think that's all I've got?" Feigning a wounded air, he crossed his arms and leaned back in his chair. "O ye of little faith."

He passed Boldt a black-and-white Polaroid of the cast impressions made at the fire site.

"Impressions are their own science," he explained, elevating his own importance, as he did whenever possible, "and it's anything but exact, I'm sorry to say. But, that said, we can make certain educated assumptions, given soil-compression ratios and water content. It takes a specific weight to effect a specific depth of impression."

"Are you telling me you can guess the weight of the person who climbed the ladder?"

"Estimate," Lofgrin corrected sternly. "*You* guess, *I* estimate. Let's get that right, Lou. We measure, we test, we simulate, we analyze, we scrutinize. Guess? What do you think they pay me for?''

Boldt held his tongue.

"Soil compression is difficult to re-create, to measure, and I've only had a few hours, don't forget. But give me a few days and I'll have a minimum and maximum weight for your ladder climber, and with that we can estimate his height. For the cloth fibers—and that's what they are, by the way—give me the better part of a week."

"Can you memo me the Werner ladder info?" Boldt asked. "I want to get LaMoia on it."

Lofgrin passed Boldt a handwritten note containing the details. "Consider it done," he said. "And don't call me, I'll call you."

Boldt reacted physically to the information, a knot forming in the center of his chest. He retrieved his damaged shoes, already ensconced in aluminum foil.

Lofgrin took the last piece of melon, stood, and left. "Thanks for the coffee," he said.

Boldt followed the man with his eyes, out the door, down the drive, still chewing the fruit. Court cases relied so much on physical evidence that Bernie Lofgrin was arguably the most influential person on the force. A civilian with an attitude and a good ear for bebop trumpet.

Boldt held the memo in his hand: hard evidence at last.

BEN awakened in Emily's cedar tree to
the sound of a car pulling into her driveway below. Collecting his
bearings, he realized he was lucky not to have rolled off the platform, for he was precariously close to the edge, lying face down,
one arm dangling off into space. As he sat up, he winced with pain
and recalled the whipping that sleep had kept him from thinking
about. He wondered if it was time to give Emily the evidence
against his stepfather that she requested, time to do something, but
he shuddered with the thought, terrified of what would become of
him if the guy ever found out.

He heard the car door open below him and looked down to
see not a car but a blue truck with a white camper shell, and his
heart raced in his chest as the man with the buzz-cut hair climbed
out and headed for Emily's front door. Ben remembered the man
with the fused fingers. She had said his name was Nick and had
called him a criminal; her powers of observation had filled in a
dozen details about him.

The camper's skylight window was open.

Ben moved around the trunk of the tree and lowered himself

to the next branch, telling himself he was just climbing down, but feeling his curiosity getting the better of him. Two sides of his thought process entered into competition, as if both arms, fully outstretched, were being tugged on at the same time, threatening to pull his joints apart. He didn't want to descend and go wait in the kitchen, eye trained to the peephole; he wanted a look inside that camper shell.

The excitement grew inside him as he worked his way down through the branches. It was not an excitement inspired by a chance to see Emily; it was not the thrill of being in a tree—it was that open skylight immediately below him, for, as he paused and looked down through it and into the camper, he saw a dark steel tube that just had to be the barrel of a gun.

His decision was made.

Ben moved through the tree fluidly, lowering himself from limb to limb nearly as effortlessly as a monkey. He was completely at ease in a tree, regardless of height. He trusted the live branches and avoided the dead. If he went well out on a limb, he made sure to keep a strong hold on the limb overhead and to balance his weight between the two as evenly as possible. He made just such a move, inching his way out over the camper shell, the truck parked immediately below, hands overhead, fingers laced, dividing his weight between hands and feet. The farther out he went, the more the branch bowed under him, bending down and pointing toward the camper like an invitation. If he could have rolled a ball down the limb it would have bounced off the roof of the camper. He was incredibly close.

He fixed his full attention on his position and the decreasing support offered by the limbs over and under him. He needed to walk another three feet to reach the edge of the camper shell—two or three steps—and it began to feel like walking the plank. The limb below him sagged drastically. He hoisted himself into a pull-up and distributed as much weight as possible to the overhead limb, but it too was sagging. He glanced down, realizing he faced a fall of ten or twelve feet over gravel if the limbs snapped. It wouldn't kill him, but it wouldn't be fun. He could easily break something. Worse, he could draw attention to himself and his intentions, and that could get Emily in trouble as well.

He tested the next step and both limbs drooped tremendously, and he realized he had reached the extreme limit. His only hope of making it to the camper was to take the overhead limb and jump out and off the limb he stood on, using the flex in the overhead branch to swing him onto the shell. Again, he checked the ground below—it suddenly seemed much farther away. He slid his hands out on the overhead limb, held his breath, and jumped.

The sensation of being carried through the air, of being lowered by the bending limb, immediately reminded Ben of an elevator. He swung out, the limb sagged, and Ben's sneakers caught and grabbed the edge of the camper. He timed it perfectly, letting go of the limb just before it arched too greatly and missed the camper shell altogether. He hurled himself forward and came down quietly on the aluminum roof—toes, knees, palms—as if in bending prayer. The limb whipped back up over his head, sounding like a group of startled birds, wings aflutter.

His good eye, which he had shut unknowingly, lighted on the open skylight, only a scant few feet away. He crawled carefully as the roof curved beneath him, spreading himself flat to keep from caving it in. He attempted to keep most of his weight over the ribs where the rivets showed and where he could feel support; the area to either side seemed fragile and weak. Inch by precious inch he wormed toward the open skylight, like a puppy stretching itself out on a rug. The frame of the skylight was wood, with heavily caulked edges; it looked as if it had been added, not part of the original shell. Ben slipped his head into the gap and peered down inside. It *was* a gun, lying on the padded bench. And next to it, on the floor, on top of an open sleeping bag, was a green army duffel bag. On the floor were several empty beer cans and an open copy of *Playboy* magazine. Ben pushed on the skylight, and it resisted. Then he spotted the hook and three different eyelets, allowing the skylight to be hooked open at different heights or locked shut. He pulled on the hook and it came undone and the skylight opened.

Ben heard voices to his right. "You're sure today is okay?" the deep voice asked. "It's sudden, is all."

"It's fine," Emily answered.

At first, it didn't register. But then Ben formed an image of what was going on: The guy who owned the truck and the *gun*—Nick—was at the door. He was *leaving*.

Ben glanced up. The man was standing at the door, just pulling it shut. In a matter of a second or two he would turn and face his truck; he would see Ben spread out on the roof, his head halfway inside the plastic skylight. Ben would be caught.

He couldn't breathe; his heart felt as if it had stopped, but then it swelled to a painful size and tried to explode in his chest. Ben never thought about choices or about excuses he might use; his reactions were entirely instinctual. He pointed his head down, reached up to grab the lip of the skylight, and slithered inside. He swung down into the camper space, his toes nearly touching a folding table, and let go. He dropped to the floor, rolled partially under the homemade couch, and held his breath. The blood in his ears sounded like thunder; he couldn't hear anything else. His racing heart felt as if someone were gargling in the center of his chest. On the other side of the truck's cab the driver's door came open with a loud complaint. The two spaces, cab and camper, communicated by a small sliding window hidden on the other side of a curtain that was—thankfully—closed.

The man's words echoed inside Ben's head: "I'll be back." Perhaps he was simply retrieving something left in the cab; perhaps he needed a cigarette break. Perhaps, like Ben's stepfather, he had a bottle of booze hidden under the seat or a joint in the ashtray. He wouldn't be the first; Emily's readings could get to people.

The truck's engine came to life with a roar. Ben glanced up at the skylight. It seemed so small, so far away. So out of reach. The truck rumbled and backed up.

Ben scrambled on hands and knees for the half-sized back door. He reached up and turned the handle, preparing for the moment when the driver paused to shift into forward. He would use that instant to leap from the truck.

He twisted the doorknob, and to his joy it moved. It wasn't locked.

The truck slowed and then braked, and the gears made a sound as the driver shifted. Ben pushed on the door. It stopped abruptly, only open an inch—padlocked from the outside.

The truck roared off. Ben tried the door again, but it would not open. The pavement blurred through the open crack in the door.

He was trapped inside.

14

PANIC seized every muscle in Ben's body. For the first few minutes of the drive, he couldn't help but focus on how much trouble he was going to be in. He had violated Emily's one rule—once and only once—and yet here he was locked in the back of a pickup truck, heading who-knows-where, with a suspected criminal behind the wheel. Surprisingly slowly, his fear of getting into trouble migrated into a realization of his predicament and focused on the importance of figuring a way out of the camper. Fast. The truck was moving quickly and not stopping at lights anymore. It seemed increasingly apparent to him that they were on a highway, and the only logical candidate was I-5, either north or south. North was Canada; south, Oregon and California. What if the truck never stopped? What if Nick had been checking out a date with Emily because he intended to commit a crime? Fear ran his blood hot and his skin cold.

The side windows were tiny things with locking screens; there was no way he could go out through one. He kept looking up to the skylight—to the heavens—his only way out. It might be possible to jump from the folding table, catch his hand on the lip of the skylight, and pull himself up and out, but only if the skylight were open, and it had fallen shut behind his less-than-graceful entrance. He realized in a calculating and determined way that escape was a multi-step process: force the skylight open and keep it open in a way he had yet to figure out; climb up onto the table and jump; pull himself up and out; wait for the truck to slow; and either climb down or jump off. All this, without being seen or heard by the driver. He felt on the edge of tears—it seemed an impossible task. He felt afraid for his life.

The gun in the holster and the duffel bag both kept staring at him, as if alive and with eyes of their own. He crawled around the soiled carpet searching out a broom handle or some other device to help him push the skylight open. As the truck changed lanes, he was thrown off balance and onto his stomach, and he struggled back to his hands and knees. It was a tiny space, and he quickly realized there was nothing in plain sight to help him, and he felt convinced that if he opened the tiny closet or any of the drawers, Nick would catch on to his presence, kill him, and leave him dumped along the highway, which was where all bodies were found anyway.

He lost his balance again and was tossed up against the duffel bag, and he couldn't resist looking inside. One end was clipped shut, using a webbed strap that ran from the fabric handle. He unclipped this, opened the canvas folds, and stuck his head inside, hoping something might prove itself useful to his cause. What he found instead scared him half to death: large, clear plastic containers filled with milky fluid. A chemical formula was handwritten on the nearest container in black marker.

He didn't have to know chemistry to know what it was. Drugs! He had seen a police raid of a meth lab on TV. The thought that he was trapped in the back of a pickup truck being driven by an armed drug dealer sent his head dizzy, and he swooned, nearly losing consciousness, only brought back to reality by the swerving of the truck and its sudden slowing—the whine of the engine lowering and softening in pitch. He looked up in time to see the green flash of a highway sign outside the window:

SEA-TAC AIR TERMINAL
EXIT ONLY

He glanced at the duffel bag. Nick was taking a trip. He would be coming after his bag in a matter of minutes! Ben had not considered the possibility that the truck might stop and the driver come into the back. He had pictured himself heading off forever. Suddenly, he found himself a victim of the clock; they were only a matter of minutes from the airport. Time was running out. He needed a place to hide.

Panic-stricken, he glanced around as if seeing this place for the first time: a tiny, claustrophobic space with the only obvious hiding place a broom closet that seemed too risky to open, given the small break in the curtains that hid the back from the cab. It was this gap in the curtains that kept Ben low, on hands and knees. Where else to hide?

The truck slowed more and took a strong right turn at a light. It was the entrance to the airport.

The few drawers were far too small to consider as possibilities. Ben thought about taking out the drugs, placing them in the drawers, and hiding himself in the duffel bag, but that would backfire badly if Nick took the bag with him, which was likely. Hiding inside the sleeping bag was a possibility, but seemed far too risky. Then he saw it.

The bench that supported the cushions where the gun was resting was a big wooden box, shaped like a coffin. A storage area with a lifting lid! Ben pushed and the cushion lifted up and the gun slid against the back. Cluttered with tools, extension cords, cigarette cartons, rags, and boxes of ammunition, there was still plenty of room inside for a boy his size. He crawled inside and lowered the lid, hoping the change in the position of the gun wouldn't raise the driver's suspicions. The truck came to a complete stop, and Ben heard faintly the sound of a mechanical voice say, "Take ticket, please."

The truck began spiraling up the airport's corkscrew ramps to the elevated parking. Ironically, Ben had never been to the airport.

The only time he had been out of the city had been to take a bus with his mother down to see his dying aunt in Kent, at the age of six—but he had seen this very parking ramp in a cop movie and could actually picture the pickup truck, held in a tight corkscrew turn, accelerating up the steep ramp. He felt both apprehension—at the idea of the driver coming into the back of the truck— and relief that the truck was certain to park and the driver to leave, offering him the chance to escape. The truck slowed and took another hard right, and Ben had to move an electric drill that was stabbing him in the back. The truck made two more sharp turns and stopped abruptly. The engine died and Ben heard the driver's door slam shut. He caught himself holding his breath in order to hear better. His heart beat painfully in his chest, his eyes stung. His mouth was dry and his tongue was sticky. He tried to think what he would do if Nick suddenly opened up the bench and caught him. His right hand searched blindly in the dark. He found a bag of small nails and quietly gripped a fistful of them.

The truck jostled, rocking Ben side to side. He heard the padlock snap open, followed by the sound of the clasp coming undone.

Nick was coming inside. The driver. The drug dealer. The man with the gun. It felt about a thousand degrees in the box. Ben was suddenly overcome by claustrophobia, the tightness and darkness of the uncomfortable space getting the better of him. He wanted out. He *had* to get out. Now!

A loud noise caused his whole body to stiffen. The driver had sat down on the bench. Ben thought it sounded like he was strapping on the gun, getting ready for whatever it was he had planned. And this discovery sent another electric bolt shooting through him. If the man was taking a gun with him, he wasn't getting on any plane. So how long would he be gone? Or worse, maybe he was not going anywhere but had come to the airport parking garage to do a deal.

Ben did not want to be a witness to any drug deal. All he wanted, more than anything in the world, was to be back in his own room, the door closed and locked; he didn't care if he had to listen to his drunken stepfather screw his girlfriends; he didn't care if the guy lifted a hand to him every now and then. He just wanted to be *home*. He hated himself for everything he had done. He wanted nothing more than to set the clock back and start all over, get a second chance.

The bench creaked as the man stood up. Ben heard the duffel bag dragging heavily on the floor; the guy let out a grunt as he struggled with it. The back door slammed shut.

He didn't think about getting to the police and stopping the deal from going down; he thought only of freedom, of his flight to safety.

There was no sound of the clasp or the padlock. Nick had left the back unlocked. Ben didn't stop to think why. For him, this was the green light. He pushed the bench top up a crack and ventured a look. His eyes stung with the light, and he blinked furiously. The camper was empty.

Now was his chance.

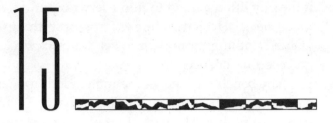

TERRIFIED, exhilarated, Ben climbed out of the storage bench, his one good eye trained on the camper's back door, no plan in his head on how to deal with what the next few minutes might bring. He behaved more like a caged bird discovering the cage left open. He carefully approached the camper's only door, distrustful and cautious, bravely venturing a look out the window into the parking garage. He ducked just as quickly, glad he had not charged out the back of the camper as he had been tempted to do: Nick stood waiting for the elevator with the large green duffel bag at his side. It was stenciled in bold capital letters USAF. Ben impatiently waited him out.

It was strange how with just the one eye Ben could see so much, or perhaps it was his lack of peripheral vision that sharpened the importance of those objects he *could* see. So many times he had been struck by a football or a stick or even another kid's fist, because it moved too fast into his range of vision and caught him by surprise. Little by little his brain had adjusted, sending early warning signals far ahead of the warning signals received by people with stereoscopic vision. Ben lacked depth of field—the world played out on a two-dimensional television screen. He was a terrible judge of distance, and his hand-eye motor coordination suffered measurably from his impairment. But if something entered his visual field it registered fully, taking on an immediate importance.

It was just a shape. Dark. About as tall as his stepfather. Standing between two parked cars. Watching. Perhaps he—she?—was standing there waiting for someone with the car keys to arrive from baggage claim, but it felt far more sinister than that, as if Ben himself were being watched, or even the man over at the elevator. Worse, the presence of this man caused Ben to fear leaving the back of the truck; he would be seen, and something warned him to avoid this at all costs. (Although he didn't see it as such, this was his first real glimpse of Emily's true powers. He experienced the ability to tune in to the subtle signals inside him that, if trusted, offered a vision of the future: If he stepped outside this camper, there was trouble waiting.)

The figure in the dark possessed him; he couldn't take his eye off him. When the man—he suddenly saw clearly that it was a man—turned his attention away from the elevator and toward the truck, Ben *knew* that he was headed for him.

The elevator arrived.

He twisted the handle, tempted to flee, regardless of that dark shape. He wanted out so badly he could taste it. At that same instant, however, the figure moved, walking out from between the parked cars, and headed straight for the truck. A voice inside Ben's head warned, "Don't!" and he found himself releasing the doorknob.

Nick stepped into the elevator, hauling the duffel bag with him. The doors slid shut.

The other man suddenly approached quickly, taking long strides, nearly at an all-out run. Patches of light flashed across his face, but even so, Ben had trouble actually seeing that face. It was as if the man were wearing a mask.

Ben lifted the bench and dove inside, driven back into hiding amid the tools and oily rags, feeling ever more involved with something he wanted no part of. How many times had Emily warned him not to so much as touch a customer's car? It felt as if his situation was designed as some kind of lesson; he half expected the approaching figure would turn out to be Emily, having created and acted all this out with Ben in mind. He promised himself that if he got out of this, he would never, ever in a million years, lay a finger on another person's property. He hoped this promise might in some way protect him from the man who now approached, for his stomach churned with fear and trepidation.

The camper door made a noise as it opened. Ben felt his insides go watery. He could barely breathe, his throat was so dry. Where the driver had seemed a threat, this dark figure was the one to fear.

As quickly as the door opened, it shut. Ben never felt any movement of the truck's springs, any indication that the man had come inside. He waited and listened, blood pounding in his ears and chest. The tips of his fingers felt cold, and all at once a shiver passed through him. He felt on the verge of crying. He swallowed his fear and ventured to lift the bench a crack and peer out.

Empty. He wanted to shout a thanks to God. Instead, he hoisted the bench, climbed out, and hurried to the smudged glass of the back door.

The parking garage appeared empty. He didn't trust this and looked back and forth, intent on spotting the other man lingering in the shadows or wedged between two parked cars, but he was nowhere to be seen. Ben twisted the doorknob and pushed, thinking that with his luck the door would prove to be . . .

. . . locked!

The second man had re-padlocked the door. A wave of nausea coursed through him. He banged the door against the clasp several times, paying no attention to the possibility of being heard or noticed. Where was good luck when he needed it?

He dropped to his knees in an effort to study the clasp and lock, in order to see if there was any chance it had been hooked but not locked. As his knee touched the filthy carpeting, he felt an unexpected bulge below his kneecap and glanced down to see the corner of a plain white envelope protruding. He slipped the envelope out. It was thick and bulging, but lightweight. He couldn't resist looking inside. He lifted the flap to see the squiggled edges of money. Dozens of bills. Fifties and twenties and some tens. Old bills. Worn money. Lots of it.

To him, it seemed like a million dollars. Cash, right there in his hand. He would need money to get home. He had none on him. He reached in and fished out a twenty. And then another. With each bill the temptation grew. Who would know if he took the whole thing? So many times, as Emily slipped her ten-dollar payment into the cigar box she kept in the freezer, she had spoken the words to Ben: "Money is freedom." They lived in him as a kind of mantra. Money meant independence. Money offered people the chance to be themselves. And here was this envelope of cash in his hand and no one around to see him. He could give the money to Emily; he could pay for his food; he could live with her.

The presence of the money was overwhelming. There was no drug deal. He was not trapped in the back of a truck. He was free. He didn't return the envelope to where he had found it. Never even considered it. He folded the envelope and shoved it into his front pants pocket. He had a chance at a new life. He felt giddy. Then, all at once, the confines of the camper shell got to him. The envelope seemed to be burning his leg. It suddenly felt heavy to him, as if anyone looking at him would see it. But not for a second did he think about putting it back. He moved quickly, as if he had done all this before. He checked the tiny closet. He didn't find a broom or a mop, but instead an aluminum baseball bat. Hurriedly, he climbed atop the camper's tabletop and probed skyward with the bat, pushing open the skylight. It took three tries to get the hook to catch, and even then it was not *through* an eyelet but only resting on top of one. Nonetheless, the skylight remained open, and Ben returned the bat to the closet. Once again he felt the pressure of time bearing down on him. He sensed that the trouble was not over but only in a lull. Despite this pressure he moved fluidly, accustomed to the anxiety of searching a car while the customer remained with Emily inside the purple house. His senses remained on full alert. His hands were sweaty, his skin hot.

He climbed back on the table, trained his eye on the edge of the skylight, and knew he had to make it in one jump. There were no second tries. To miss would be to fall backward on the table; he would break something or knock himself out. He had one try in him.

A voice inside reminded him that this required hand-eye coordination, this was something everyone agreed he had no talent for; the voice grew louder, warning him not to even try. But the drive for survival spoke louder, and he overcame this nagging voice and blatantly disregarded it. There was no choice. He simply had to make the jump. And he had to be successful.

He squatted down, feeling the strength in his tree-climbing legs, aimed his single eye above him, having little judgment of the exact distance he had to travel, and jumped, fingers outstretched.

The wood edge slapped his palms and he gripped down and hooked the lip and held himself dangling, suspended in midair. But he had rocked the truck, causing the hook to slip off the eyelet, and the skylight came down like a Chinese poultry knife onto his knuckles. Ben cried out, but he did not let go. Could not let go.

He pulled, as he had so many times in a bad situation in a tree, as if lifting himself to the next branch. He did this twice but sank back down to his dangling position, his fingers aching under his weight. The third time he coordinated all his efforts simultaneously: He pulled himself up, banged the skylight partially open with his head, hooked one elbow, then the other, and pulled even higher, worming his torso up and through the skylight. Kicking his legs, as if swimming for the side of the pool, he wiggled up and out of the hole in the camper's roof. He clambered over a rusted rack, where a tire and wheel was chained and locked, and slipped over the back to a narrow ladder fixed to the side of the shell. His feet touching pavement, he was off at a run, as if hearing footsteps immediately behind him.

He wasn't going on that elevator, no matter what. Instead, he entered the stairs and descended two at a time, his fingers skating down the banister, his legs feeling rubbery from the excitement. He leaped onto the landing, grabbed hold of the railing, and pulled himself up short, stopping like a car caught by a red light.

Nick, the buzz-cut driver of the truck, the drug dealer, was standing on the stairs, wearing an expressionless face, his full attention riveted on Ben.

Ben stood there, chest heaving, recalling that the slight bulge on the man's right side was a handgun, and that he was in the military, which meant he was a crack shot, and that Ben had been inside his truck, and that he no doubt knew this and had been thinking, planning, what to do about it, and now his hand was forced and the time had come, and Ben had served himself up on a silver platter.

He thought about the fold of money in his pocket, suddenly so heavy that he couldn't move that leg. Surely the man saw the outline of the envelope there. Surely he knew. Caught!

The man Ben feared so much smiled and said, "Slow down there, buddy. Good way to knock some teeth out."

Ben heard very little except something about getting his teeth knocked out. Nick climbed the stairs. Ben was directly in his path and so terrified that the man looked blurry, and his already untrustworthy legs felt on the verge of total failure. Their eyes met, and Ben felt a sick, hollow spot where his stomach should have been, and he felt a trickle of warm urine run down his left leg.

"Excuse me," the smiling man said, and Ben stepped aside for him. Nick walked past, turned on the landing, and headed on up the stairs.

Ben sneaked onto a downtown hotel courtesy van, pretending to be with a pair of parents who didn't notice what he was up to. The driver, who didn't even count heads, seemed to care little about anything but getting the luggage in the back and moving on to the next curbside pickup. Any other day of his life, Ben might have considered this a major accomplishment. But not on that day. Instead, he spent the twenty-minute drive into the city debating exactly what he had seen take place: Nick had left with a duffel bag; he had returned without it. The dark, short, faceless man who had come out of the shadows had left an envelope of money and then locked the camper. An exchange. A drop. A drug deal.

From downtown he rode a city bus over First Hill toward home, walking the last mile and a half. Exhausted, he headed directly to his room and locked the door, well ahead of his stepfather, but not taking any chances. A few minutes later he went downstairs to the kitchen phone. He felt more like a robot than himself. It was something that had to be done; that was all there was to it. He knew this in his heart, even if his mind was engaged in a continuous dialogue to the contrary. He dialed 911. A woman's voice answered.

Ben said calmly, "I want to report a drug deal. I saw a drug deal—" He caught a glimpse of himself in the glass of the cabinet on the wall. He could just picture himself explaining this to his stepfather. His butt hurt enough already. He slammed down the phone and sprinted back upstairs to his room.

Down a drab and unremarkable hallway in the Public Safety Building, the Seattle Communications Center, equipped with Enhanced 911 communications software, identified and recorded not only Ben's telephone number but the physical address of that phone number as well, all before the operator ever answered. Every moment of the call was recorded, every nuance of his slightly hysterical voice. The call would be logged both by computer and by hand, Ben's voice reduced to a data stream, compressed, and stored temporarily on a hard disk that was backed up on magnetic tape every twelve hours, the tapes stored in a former cannery repossessed by the city for back taxes a decade earlier. The operator mistakenly classified Ben's call as a juvenile prank, which meant that if another two offenses were attributed to the same phone number, an officer of the juvenile court would pay that home a visit.

However, all so-called "dead" calls—calls not acted upon by dispatchers—were reviewed for free by a volunteer hot-line association whose main goal was to locate possible sexual and physical abuse victims where the caller lost his or her nerve to report.

As Ben drifted off to a much-needed sleep that night, downtown the Seattle Communications Center was processing his call along with several dozen others received in the 6 P.M. to midnight shift. The billing name on the phone number—his stepfather's—the physical address, and the phone number were all part of the system. The gears of a slow-moving but determined bureaucracy continued to grind.

Ben hung up the phone and headed straight upstairs to his room, his heart still pounding as hard as if he had only then stopped running. He felt a little dizzy, a little sick to his stomach. It was at moments such as this that he missed his mother most of all. She would have helped him; he believed this with all his heart. He wasn't sure what, if anything, to tell Emily; she was all he had. He shut his door and sat down heavily on the bed. At first he didn't believe the empty feeling under his butt. An even deeper fear than what he'd been living with for the past few minutes wormed into his stomach. It didn't seem possible. He reached back to the seat of his pants tentatively, afraid of the implication of what this emptiness meant to him.

His wallet was gone.

16

ARSON investigator Neil Bahan noti-
fied Boldt by cellular phone that the ATF chemist had arrived at
the fire site. Boldt hung a U-turn at an intersection on Aurora and
cut across Wallingford on 45th, passing a movie theater marquee
that advertised a Richard Dreyfuss film.

He hadn't been to a movie in over two years. Before the birth
of Miles, he and Liz had seen three movies a week. He called his
wife on her cellular phone, because the cabin didn't have a phone,
but got the message service recording of her voice. He told her he
missed her and the kids, how he couldn't wait for them to come
home. He left out any mention of a second body, of the anxiety
compressing his chest and restricting his breathing, of the nagging
sensation that yet a third victim was being targeted at that very
moment, and that he, the investigator, had only a couple of ladder
impressions and some fibers to go on. Any mention of that and Liz
might decide to call the bank and take a week's vacation. He ached
to see his kids.

Dr. Howard Casterstein looked like one of the profs over at
the U where Boldt occasionally guest-lectured for a criminology

series. He wore a white shirt and tie with an undershirt showing beneath. He had a military cut, making it difficult to judge his hair color, and the square shoulders of a man in shape. Boldt didn't like him on first glance. He resented the federal involvement before he heard a word of explanation. He introduced himself on the edge of the property where the fire-gutted house remained under police watch. It was no longer smoldering, and only two patrolmen were to be seen.

Casterstein had penetrating eyes and a firm handshake. He introduced himself as Howie and said immediately, "If the body you found was Melissa Heifitz—the owner, as we believe will prove to be the case—then the match violated an act of interstate commerce by torching the place. Heifitz made huckleberry jam and did catalog mailings out of her house; that qualifies as interstate commerce. It allows us in, *no problemo*. I'm here strictly as a chemist. I mean no invasion of your investigation whatsoever, Sergeant. Just so we're clear on that. Let the desk jockeys fight it out over who's running the show—not for this boy to hassle with." He added, "One of your arson dicks, a guy named Bahan, contacted us concerning the Enwright evidence. Your lab up here wasn't picking up hydrocarbons in the samples. We didn't pick them up either, so when we got a whiff of this one on the wire last night my boss sends me up as a solo NRT man—National Response Team." Boldt couldn't get a word in edgewise. "The NRT is for Podunk towns that don't have fire investigation units, or for massive hits like Oklahoma City. We can be on any fire, anywhere in the country, in twenty-four hours or less. That's me. That's my story. What can you tell me?"

Boldt wasn't sure where to start. "I'm Homicide," he said.

"I know who you are," Casterstein said, perfecting the art of compliments. "Me and a couple of the boys attended that talk in Portland a few years ago. The thing about the victim. It was good work."

"Oh, yeah, 'the thing about the victim,' " Boldt muttered, offended. Off to a bad start. He attempted to clarify. "You're here as a chemist or a spy? At what point do you boys move in and take over?"

Howard—call me Howie—Casterstein grinned artificially. "It's not like that. Bahan wants our lab involved. We've got the neat toys," he said. "That's all it is, Sergeant, nothing more."

For now, Boldt was thinking. Trying for a new start, he said, "Well, we need all the help we can get. If Melissa Heifitz was in that fire, we've got two homicides and precious little evidence. Anything you can supply is greatly appreciated." How did the Feds know the victim's name before he, the investigating officer, did? He felt humiliated. "And if she's single, we have a city of terrified women on our hands. The press is making this front-page."

"So we get to work," he said, holding up a pair of shiny metal paint cans used to collect fire evidence. "This match of yours has us puzzled. And by God, Sergeant, that's something we just won't tolerate." He turned toward the burned-out structure. "If you'd care to join me, I'd appreciate the company. These road trips suck."

Lou Boldt followed in step, ready to learn something. Howie Casterstein had that look about him.

Boldt spoke loudly enough to be heard over the whine of a passing motorcycle. "If you value your shoes," he warned, "I wouldn't go in there."

17

DAPHNE Matthews danced with the
devil. It was the same devil, nothing new. And though all her training, all her experience in the field of psychology, told her that to
share it with another living person might exorcise it, might help
purge it from her memory bank, she had never allowed it to come
to that. To speak of it was to risk the fear of bringing it to life; being
haunted by it was altogether different—controllable, in a strange
uncontrollable way. Subconscious versus conscious. Dream versus
reality. At all costs, she would never allow it to come back to life.
She could not afford it. And so it went unmentioned. And so it ate
into her at times like this, wormed into her like a bug trapped
inside her ear and turning toward darkness instead of light. She
lived with this darkness. She had even come to believe she had
tamed it, which wasn't true and was probably the most dangerous
lie that she told herself. Her conviction remained in living with it
rather than confronting it. The hypocrisy of her position was not
lost on her; she was not that far gone. But there were times like this
when she realized she was close.

When the devil possessed her, all else was lost. Gaps in time.

Sometimes minutes, sometimes half an hour or more: a form of short-term amnesia, where she sat in a trancelike state. One day of her life, eleven years earlier, and still it managed to overcome her at times, force her to relive each dreadful, terrifying minute.

The images came to her in black-and-white, which she had never figured out. Snapshots, but with blurred motion to them: the gloved hand—the smell of him!—the pain as she was shoved into the car's trunk. . . . At times vividly clear, at times disjointed and hard for her to see. Like flipping through the pages of a photo album too quickly.

Perhaps it was the privacy of her knowledge that prevented her from sharing it. Perhaps it was that no one, not even Owen Adler, was that close to her. Or perhaps she didn't want to give it up. This thought concerned her most of all. Why hold on to such a thing? Why protect the horror? What sickness accounted for such behavior?

She caught him out of the corner of her eye. She protected her feelings for him as well. No one knew. It was their secret. Theirs to share, but never with others. And who had such answers? Who could possibly understand? Her heart still beat furiously when he passed in the hall, when she heard a Scott Hamilton cut and was reminded of him. He wasn't particularly good-looking—although to her he was; he didn't hush a crowd when he entered a room. He was an observer. He blended in. He was a student: of people, of behavior, of music, science, the arts. He was better at math than anyone else, and yet no one knew this of him. He could name the key of a song within seconds. He could remember the page number of a particular line he had read, a caption, a photograph. His eyes saw things before the techies ever uncovered them. He noticed things that no one else noticed and wasn't afraid to mention them, but never in a bragging way. "You're wearing a new scent." "You cut your hair." "You look tired today. Anything wrong?" He could tell a story and hold her captivated, regardless of its importance. And yet, around the building, he moved fairly unnoticed. No one seemed to know much about him, despite his twenty-odd years there. They talked of him, religiously sometimes—absurdly so. But no one noticed.

People had noticed her all her life. It was just something she lived with.

"Interrupting?" he asked.

Considerate. Humble. Cautious. Apprehensive. All that knowledge chiseled into him, like a figure cut of granite, and yet none of it showing. He couldn't dress himself no matter how hard he tried. Missed buttons. Stains. Five-o'clock shadow for two days at a time. *Disheveled* didn't do him service. Marriage didn't help. Scuffed shoes. Knotted shoelaces. Hair uncombed. No one could change him. They could share time with him, be a part of him, but not change him. She envied Liz her chance and felt angry at times at how she had passed up the opportunity because of her own ambitions. Lou Boldt needed someone to nourish him, to draw out the genius, to stimulate. Liz missed so much of this in him. If only things had been different. . . .

"No," she answered. "Never."

"New flowers," he said.

"Yes."

"And what is that, a Wonder Bra?"

She blushed. It was, in fact.

"You're the talk of the bull pen."

"And what do you think?"

He sat without invitation. "You don't need it. Throw it away."

"Okay."

"Just like that?" he asked, surprised.

"Yes."

"What does Owen say?"

Owen hadn't noticed, but this wasn't something she would share—even with him. "It's under consideration."

"Lucky Owen," he said.

"Lucky Liz," she fired back.

"Oh, yeah, lucky Liz," he replied in his best self-deprecating tone. The trouble was, he believed it.

"How long since you washed those khakis?" she asked,

knowing she was perhaps the only person from whom he would tolerate such things.

"Too long?"

She nodded.

"Yes, dear," he mocked. He glanced down at himself, like a child looking for the problem. He said, "What's up?" She had asked for his time.

"You're aware that Shoswitz is hanging you out to dry for this?" she inquired.

"So what's new?"

"He uses your name in every press conference, spouts fire and brimstone about how this killer will be caught and brought to justice. How you're the one to do it, to bring him in. God, he makes it sound like something from a spaghetti Western. Truthfully, I don't like it one bit. It makes you a potential target."

"Now, Daffy—"

"It *does*, I'm telling you. This is *my* field, not yours, not Shoswitz's. You don't taunt a person like that; you don't offer up targets. Listen, if the Scholar's attacking a particular kind of building, or if he offered to sell these women aluminum siding and they declined, that's one thing. But if he's focused on Garman, if this is about revenge, if that's his mind-set, Shoswitz is wrong to build you into a gunslinging bounty hunter. These guys operate on hair triggers, Lou. He could switch targets like *that*." She snapped her fingers.

"What's done is done," Boldt replied. "Shoswitz only takes credit, never blame. It's what preserves his job, his position. It's what turns me off of ever wanting to take a desk here. You have to know how to play the game, and frankly it doesn't interest me."

"Thank goodness," she replied. "I'm going to speak with him," she declared. "Tell him to stop it. Just so you know." She knew he wouldn't argue with her; he chose his battles carefully.

"Melissa Heifitz," Boldt said. "Dixie confirmed it this morning. Dental records. They found five teeth in the ashes. Two of them are confirmed as Melissa's. Twenty-nine years old. Widowed mother of one. Husband was a construction worker, cement. She was a bookkeeper for a professional building up on Eighty-fifth. Doctors and dentists. No connection that we can see to Dorothy Enwright. A nice looking woman," he said, passing her the driver's license photo. "Parents live in Lynnwood. A sister in Portland. One very normal life abruptly brought to an end." She could hear the knot in his throat. He took every victim on as a member of his own family. It made him unique. Perhaps it explained his brilliance, but it made him vulnerable as well. He said, "You know they used to burn people at the stake." He left it hanging there for her.

"Do you see it?" she asked him, the driver's license photograph still in hand. "The coloring? Even the shape of her head?"

"What are we talking about?" Boldt inquired, sitting forward.

Daphne craned herself over her desk and fingered through a stack of manila file folders. She extricated one and opened it. She passed Boldt a bad photocopy of a snapshot of Dorothy Enwright. "How about now?" she asked.

"Oh, shit," said the man who rarely cursed.

"I think we can rule out the structure as the target. I think we can let Garman off the hook. There's a specific look to his victims: dark hair cut short, thin face. He's chosen death by fire—"

"Which is ridiculous," Boldt interjected. "There are a dozen easier ways to kill someone."

"Not ridiculous," she corrected, "symbolic. The fire holds some kind of symbolism for him, or he wouldn't go to all that trouble. Right? It's important to him that they burn. Why? Because of the image of Hell? Because his mother intentionally burned him as a child? Because she's unclean and he's attempting to purify her?"

"You're giving me the creeps here," Boldt said, crossing his arms as if cold.

"I'm giving you motives, the psychological side of what fire may mean to him: religion, revenge, purification. They're all relevant here."

"Some guy tapping brunettes because he's screwed up about his mother?"

"Or a girlfriend, or a teacher, or a baby-sitter, or a neighbor.

He tries to have sex with a woman and he can't perform; she laughs at him, teases him. I'm telling you, Lou—and I know you don't want to hear this—sex and rejection probably play a part in this. His mother catches him playing with himself and takes an iron to him—"

"Enough."

"We see that kind of thing," she pressed.

"I don't need this."

"You do if you're going to catch him," she cautioned. "You have a premeditated killer burning down structures in a way that is confounding the specialists. He's confident enough to send poems and drawings in advance of the kills. He has a specific look to his victims. He's getting into their homes somehow and rigging their houses to blow so that they don't have time to get out. You better know what makes him tick, or you're operating on blind luck. The only way you'll catch him is to run him down in a super-market parking lot."

"We isolate his fuel and we trace it back to a supplier. That's how it's done with arson," he informed her.

"That's fine for some guy torching warehouses for the insur-ance, but that's not what we've got."

"In part it is."

"In part, yes. But the other part is your turf; he has victims. Listen to the victims, Lou. It's what you're so good at."

"There's nothing left here," he gasped. "As sick as this sounds, I deal in bodies, in crime scenes. These fires steal both. It takes me out of my game plan."

"Forget the fire," she advised.

"What?"

"Leave the fire to Bahan and Fidler, to the Marshal Fives. You take the victims and whatever evidence you can dig up. Divide and conquer."

"Is this what you called me for?" he asked angrily. "You want to tell me how to conduct the investigation? Doesn't that strike you as just a little bit arrogant?"

She felt herself blush. They fought like this, but only on rare occasions. She said, clinically and pointedly, "I wanted to forewarn you that I intend to speak with Shoswitz. I wanted to tell you that I made an appointment with Emily Richland, and to check if you had any direct question you wanted asked of her."

"Emily Richland," Boldt muttered.

"I spoke to her by phone. She mentioned a man with a burned hand." That caught his attention. "Possible military service with a badly deformed hand. A blue pickup truck." She could feel his resistance. She snapped sarcastically, "Why don't you like it? Because she actually helped us solve a case once?"

Emily Richland, who ran a ten-dollar-a-throw tarot card operation on the other side of Pill Hill, had helped lead police to the location of a kidnap suspect. At her request, the police had withheld her involvement from the press, which impressed Daphne because she figured such a stunt—if it could be called that—was done in part for the notoriety, publicity, and legitimacy it afforded her. At the time, Daphne had been recovering from injuries sustained in another case involving an illicit organ donor ring and had missed the kidnapping. She had never had personal contact with Emily Richland.

"You're saying that because it's Richland we should listen?" he asked.

"Is that so wrong? Test the source? What if she's a part of it? I'm not saying she's psychic, I'm saying we listen. A burned hand? Come on!"

"What of the other calls, the other self-proclaimed psychics? You going to interview them as well?"

"I might. Emily Richland proved valuable once before; that's all I'm saying." She caught herself huffing from anger. "Your call, Sergeant."

Boldt conceded. "We investigate every lead." He sat back. "You're absolutely right. Maybe she has something."

"Try to think of her as a snitch, not a psychic," she suggested.

"She has visions?"

"Don't look at it that way. Define it in terms that are acceptable to you."

"A snitch," he said, testing it.

"Leave it to me," she recommended.

Lou Boldt nodded. "Good idea," he said.

Emily Richland did not answer her phone, but the recorded message said she was open for readings. Daphne tried again the following day, at ten in the morning. Again the machine answered. That second time, she wrote down the address given in the recording. She rode the elevator down to Homicide and marched up to Boldt's cubicle, aware of the mountain she was attempting to climb.

She said, "How much did we pay Richland last time?"

Boldt's khakis were clean, she noted. His shirt was fresh and his shoes polished.

"Two, two-fifty I think it was."

"I need authorization to offer her that same amount."

Boldt appeared paralyzed. "You're going out there," he stated.

"Yes, I am. And if I have to pay her, I will."

"Shoswitz will blow a gasket."

"I'm not asking Shoswitz, I'm asking you."

"You know what they say around the bull pen?" he inquired rhetorically, not allowing her to answer, even had she had a comeback, which she did not. "That I can't refuse you anything."

"Oh, but you *do*. They don't know the details."

"List her as a snitch in the requisition," he instructed. It was a small compromise, easy for her to live with. It was as good as an approval. She had the finances necessary to pay Emily Richland. She felt ecstatic.

"And don't look so smug," he added.

"Is that an order?" she asked, directly reminding Boldt that she outranked him.

"I hope you're enjoying yourself," Boldt quipped.

"Oh, I am. I definitely am."

18

DAPHNE knocked loudly on the door to the purple house. Hearing just how loudly and impatiently she knocked, she questioned whether or not she had the open mind necessary for the ruse she intended. A majority of psychics were nothing more than clever con artists. Dial a 900 number, and through the miracle of caller ID and on-line computerized credit information, the so-called psychic on the other end knew more about you—income, marital status, spending habits, the car you drove, the house you owned, the catalogs you shopped—than could possibly be used in a single session. Though she was loath to admit it to Boldt, she didn't trust any of them, not even Emily Richland. There was no telling what connection Emily might have to the arsons. She lived in a low-rent neighborhood and made her living telling lies. She would have to prove herself one hell of a mind reader to convince Daphne otherwise.

Daphne's mission was multilayered: to reverse roles, tell lies of her own, and subtly interview Emily Richland in an effort to test the woman's authenticity; to attempt to trap the woman into admitting some connection—professional or personal—with the arsons or the arsonist; to offer to pay the woman for information, but only as a last resort.

The door opened.

The woman's long dark hair was pulled back, stretching the skin of a freckled face that took ten or more years off her forty. Her eyes were a haunting blue under too much mascara. She wore a thrift-store black velvet gown that emphasized her breasts even though the rest of the dress appeared a size too large, and was cinched tightly around her narrow waist by a blue-and-white beaded Indian belt. A string of dime store pearls hung around her neck, and a pair of earrings featured black-and-white photographs of Elvis. Her smile was radiant and yet mysterious—surprisingly natural; her eyes, probing and curious.

"Welcome."

"Do you have time?" Daphne feigned embarrassment, awkwardness.

"Please," Emily said, gesturing inside. She wore peach nail polish with silver-blue glitter. She was wearing ballerina slippers with black ribbon bows and worn toes, as if she had been on point. "I'm Emily." She made no more small talk. She led Daphne to an upholstered chair with a green chenille slipcover that faced a small unadorned table with a pack of thumb-worn tarot cards waiting in one corner and a giant stump of a candle that might take years to burn itself out. There were nudes painted on the wall.

Daphne saw the woman's hand gently brush the edge of the table as she took her seat. It was a clever, practiced move. The lights dimmed and established themselves at the level of the candle that the woman lit next, using a yellow Bic lighter. The room then smelled faintly of incense, reminding Daphne of her radical years at college.

"You have a question that needs answering," the woman stated. She studied her. "You're having trouble with a man."

Daphne felt her heart in her throat all of a sudden. How on earth could she know about the problems with Owen? Then she realized that on entering the neighborhood she had spun her engagement ring around so that Owen's absurdly sized engagement diamond was hidden under her finger, not showing on top. The good ones can read a subtle change in skin tone, voice inflection, body language, she reminded herself. Daphne had studied paranormal phenomena in her undergraduate years. For any psychologist with an open mind, it was a fascinating area.

She felt her face flush, at which point there was no sense dodging the question. "Yes, a little bit of trouble," she admitted, "but that's not why I've come."

"Something to do with work," Emily said, eyes searching Daphne's left to right, left to right. Slightly hypnotic. "You're a doctor," the woman speculated, then shook her head no. "Something close, but that's not it. A paramedic maybe . . . no . . . not a nurse. Something medical. Am I close?"

Daphne shifted uncomfortably in the chair, then chastised herself for giving herself away so easily. Concentrate! she demanded of herself. The woman was good. Better than expected. She worked fast. Calm voice. Penetrating eyes. She missed nothing. She was staring at Daphne's neck, probably counting my pulse, the policewoman thought. Or curious about the long scar there. *Focus!*

"My fiancé's a doctor"—Daphne lied convincingly—"of economics, not medicine. Can't put a Band-Aid on his own finger," she said, amused. "But he's rich as Croesus," she included, completing the picture. "But no, it's not about work, not about him." She prepared her fiction carefully. "I came to you because of a dream I had. Have you ever dealt with a person's dreams?" She knew the weight psychics put in such things.

"Dreams can be windows, my dear. Into the past, the future. Do you want to tell me about the dream, or should I tell you a little about you first? You're not a believer, are you. It's all right, you know. I mean, not trusting in the powers. They aren't my powers, you understand. Not mine at all. It's important to me that you understand. I'm not channeling, I don't mean that. I'm not a channeler, not a conduit. But I do *see:* the past, the future. I see wonderful things; I see terrifying things. I can't help what I see, so I may not please you with what I tell you, but I'll tell you what I see." She spoke quickly but without a sense of urgency, so it came off as a smooth monologue that one wouldn't want to interrupt. Her voice was musical and lilting, her eyes calming and warm. "You're someone who's well prepared. You think out potential problems in advance. You're neat. You keep a clean house and you pride yourself on the little details. You're angry at your fiancé, but it's not about another woman—a young girl, perhaps."

Daphne felt a chill all the way to her toes. As quickly as Emily talked, Daphne attempted to reconstruct how she might arrive at such things. Some of it might be explained by Daphne's appearance, her choice of dress, her use of makeup, but how could she know about Owen's daughter Corky? How could that be explained? She couldn't allow herself to be led; she needed to take control. "It's my dream I'm concerned with," Daphne said definitely, in a dry, flat tone.

"No, my dear. I don't think we can deal with the dream until I've convinced you, and I haven't convinced you, have I? Not yet. Not entirely. I'm sorry. It's a two-way street, and I feel you tensing, and I'm afraid I haven't got much else to offer. If you like—no charge. You can go. We can try again another time or not, as you like."

One hell of an effective sales tool, Daphne thought. Offer the door for free, or more to stay. Amazingly, Daphne found herself more convinced of this woman's authenticity than she was willing to admit. "No," she said, "I'd like to stay."

A quiet descended over them as the psychic appraised her, only the light New Age music playing. The other woman's brow knitted and she whispered, "There's another man, isn't there?"

Daphne felt her eyes pool with tears, her gut wrench. This was too much! "This is not about me," she blurted out, feeling violated and invaded, taken advantage of. The only image before her was the face of Lou Boldt. She felt saddened to her bones. She felt exhausted. Finished. She wanted no more of any of this—no psychic, no Owen, no police department.

"Of course it's about you," Emily said. "It's in the past now, isn't it? In the past, but always in the present."

"I will not talk about this!"

"No," Emily said. "There's no reason to talk about it, is there? What's in the past is better left there."

"You're staring at me."

"I'm looking at you, yes." She hesitated and then said, "I think we can talk about that dream now. What do you think?"

A guess, Daphne decided. The woman had made a lucky guess, had scored a bull's-eye, and had pursued it until to try for anything more risked the guess revealing itself as such. She knew nothing of it. She was no mind reader. Daphne had not been thinking about Lou. Or maybe she had been; she wasn't sure. She felt confused and angry. Confusion was a foreign country to her; she didn't speak the language or know the customs. She returned to her years of reading, of study, of conducting interviews, of forming psychological profiles. She stepped toward its safety as a person lost in the dark will head for even a faint glimmer of light.

Daphne inhaled a long slow breath, collecting herself. She closed her eyes slowly and said dramatically, "In the dream it is always the same: a man . . . I can't see his face. He never looks at me, never directly at me. He's a strong man. Imposing. And I see people burning," she said, in a hoarse, dry, frightened whisper, knowing without opening her eyes that she had gained control of the other woman. "Houses burning. White-hot flames. Dancing flames. Women burning." She saved the best for last. "Never his face. Just his . . ." She squinted tightly and shook her head no. She waited for the other woman.

"What, dear?" Emily asked.

"His hand. A burned hand. Disgusting. Fingers burned . . ."

Emily gasped audibly.

Daphne opened her eyes, containing her delight. *Touché!* The psychic paled considerably. Daphne asked, "What is it?" And then, reversing roles completely, she sat up straight and said, "Do you know this man?"

The psychic shook her head no.

"You've had the same dream?"

No again. Emily's eyes remained enlarged. She was preparing some comment to make, preparing to take back control.

Daphne had to speak, to maintain her position. "You've *met* him," Daphne stated plainly. "He came here." She looked around the room and put onto her face her best mask of terror. She crossed her arms tightly, as if fending off the cold. "He's been in this room," she stated, noting with great satisfaction that Emily remained pinned by her comments. "Who is he?" Daphne asked. "Why have I seen him in my dreams?"

She waited, uncrossing her arms and placing her hands on the table before her. She leaned forward. "Who *is* he that he enters my dreams this way? Is he going to kill me? Is that it? Is it the man burning these houses? Is it the news? Is that all?"

"Who are you?" Emily choked out.

"You've seen that hand. I *know* you've seen that hand."

The other woman's face took on a look of terror. "You're a friend of his. His girlfriend? You're checking up on me?" She allowed it to slip.

"You *have* seen him!"

"You're lying to me," Richland said, her eyes lowered dangerously. "Do not lie to me."

"The hand," Daphne repeated. "You've seen that hand. I know you have. I saw how you reacted. I can tell you've seen that hand. Why? Why have I come here to you?" She tried to sound as emotionally unstable and fearful as possible. "I could have gone to any psychic. Why you?" *Feed the ego*, she reminded herself, having used this same principle on dozens of suspected felons.

"Because I can help you," Emily answered, the suspicion in her eyes lessened. "Tell me about the dream."

Daphne asked, "Am I psychic? Is there a way to stop it, control it? I don't like these dreams. I don't want any more of them. Is that how it starts? A dream? Dreaming?"

"We all have the ability to glimpse the future," the woman answered clearly. "We've all done it: thought of an age-old friend whom we haven't seen in years just moments before the phone rings and it is that friend on the line. Worried for a friend or relative, only to discover something terrible—or even something wonderful—has happened. Although I'll tell you this," she said, as an aside. "The dark, the evil, is somehow more powerfully transmitted than the good. It has been said that people close to those who have died have experienced a pain or even fallen to the floor, which, when traced later, can be connected to the exact moment of this other person's death. Skeptics call this coincidence. I call it the Power. The difference between those people and me—between you and me, my dear—is that I can summon the Power. I can harness it. Connect with it, at my choosing. But at its core, it is no different from your dreams. Yes, I can tell that you've connected during those dreams. Something in this man has stirred a place in you. There may be others with this same dream; there may be none. None of that matters. What matters is that you've connected. And yes," she said—answering honestly? Daphne wondered—"so have I. I know the man. I've seen him. He has sat in that chair."

Daphne leapt from the chair and bumped the table in the process, and although the psychic reached out a steadying hand, the tarot deck separated and spilled across the surface, and a single card fell to the floor. The psychic stared at the card—which was face down—and a growing menace filled the room. "I'm sorry," Daphne apologized. But Emily Richland waved off her apology and, stooping, reached for the card and turned it face up.

"Death," she announced, her eyes finding Daphne's. "It can be a good card," she said, "but not always."

Death had occupied a place in Daphne's life since she was a child. Through her years of study and soul-searching, and some time on the therapist's couch, she had come to understand that death is an integral part of life, but as a child she was far from that knowledge, that understanding. For years she had identified with the character of Scout in the movie version of *To Kill a Mockingbird* (she had not read the book until a young adult): the young tomboy, raised in Kentucky bluegrass country, surrounded by wealth, privilege, and death. Her father, like Atticus, a defense attorney, had won and lost cases where men's lives were at stake. Her first close look at death was when her pony, Dell, got colic and died on a Saturday night in August. Daphne had spent that night in Dell's stall; despite everything done for her, the old girl cried out in pain and died, Daphne's arms clenched around her sweet-smelling neck, tears pouring out.

Death had followed her closely from that day forward. Her dearest friend on earth, her neighbor Jon Crispell, had been hit head on, killed on his twelfth birthday, coming home from a fishing trip with his sixth-grade teacher, a close friend of the family. In college, a sorority sister, made drunk by an oversexed football player, fell backward out of an open window and broke her neck in the front lawn of the Phi Gam house. Janie Whimfiemer, Daphne's roommate during graduate school, had traveled to Africa and died there in her sleep, the cause of her death never discussed, as if the reasons for death did not matter, only the event itself. Janie was flown home to Indiana in a metal casket. Daphne had met the plane along with the family, and this had been her first sight of an actual coffin. She could remember the horror of that day still. When she drew close to people, they died. So for years she had avoided that opportunity.

She looked down at the card and shuddered. "Death and I are old friends," she said, the room noticeably colder.

Emily picked the card off the floor and restored the deck on the table. "Tell me about the dream," she repeated.

"I never see his face, just that hand. There's fire, a woman screaming."

Emily nodded gravely. She'd witnessed that hand.

"I thought about going to the police," Daphne said, "after reading about the fires. But what's to tell?"

"They won't believe you," Emily said. Her voice sounded far off, and there was weariness in her tone.

Daphne hesitated and said, "You can see the connection, can't you? The possible connection? A man with a badly burned hand, the newspaper articles. I'm sorry. I've never believed in this kind of thing—psychic phenomena—but now it has happened to me, now I've experienced it. . . . What I was thinking: Maybe *you* could make the call to the police for me."

Emily swallowed dryly, her throat bobbing, eyes glassy. "I can't help you. I wish I could, but—"

"But you can," Daphne emphasized. "Of course you can. You've seen him, met him; he's been here. You could call the police and tell them that."

"I think we're all done here. If that's why you've come, there's really nothing I can do."

Daphne allowed a long silence to settle over them. Still maintaining eye contact, she said, "Maybe they would pay you for such information."

Her lips trembling, Emily gasped hoarsely, "What?"

"It's the car, isn't it? My car? You see, I remembered that I had left mail in the front seat. That's how you knew I belonged to the Northwest Medical Society, which is why you were guessing doctor." The words hit Emily as small bombs. "You know I'm neat, that I keep things clean, because that's the way I keep my car. That's what gave you away. I thought it might be my appearance at first, orderly and all. But the comments about my fiancé—the ring, of course—and mention of Corky—the young girl—threw me off. Kept me off balance for a moment. But Corky's notebook is in the back of the car, and her name is on it. Whoever you're working with told you the name, didn't she—he?—but you elected not to use it." Daphne stood from the chair.

"Sit down!"

She took two quick steps toward the door behind Emily and pushed it open in time to see the kitchen screen door thump shut. She heard Emily right behind her. Daphne reached the back door and pulled it open, but whoever had been there was long gone. Fast, she thought.

"Stop it!" Emily cried out.

Spinning on her heels, Daphne said loudly to the woman, "You have nothing to say about this!" She took a step forward, driving Emily back. "I make one phone call, and we bring you in on a handful of fraud charges. You're out of business."

"You're a *cop?*" It was a question, but also a statement—a realization—at the same time.

They stood only inches apart, Daphne a full head taller. She searched the other woman's eyes and asked pointedly, "Are you part of the arsons? Straight answer: yes or no?" Their eyes locked, darted back and forth in unison.

"No," Emily gasped, eyes averted for the first time, head lowered in submission. Exactly where Daphne wanted her.

Daphne believed her, but she waited just the same, for the woman's next movements and words would be the final test of her guilt or innocence, whether to take her downtown or leave her here and work with her.

"It was some kind of business deal. Drugs, maybe." Emily glanced away, then directly back into Daphne's eyes. She drummed her thigh absentmindedly with her peach-glitter nails. "A decent amount of scratch involved—he was willing to pay the sixty for the chart. It was the date he was worried about, why he came to see me. People consult you for dates, you know: weddings mostly. One woman, I think it was because she was having an affair . . . or wanted to." Emily appeared nervous and scared. Daphne fought off a grin of satisfaction. She lived for these moments. "Because of the astrology," she said, pointing toward the neon window. "I do charts, you know. And I do have the Power."

"The sixty bucks. Cash or check?"

"Honey, do I look like I'd take a check? Gimme a little credit here."

Daphne's hope for a quick and easy solution slipped away. So did her hope that this woman would soften for very long. Then a second thought occurred to her. "The car. His car."

"A truck."

"His truck," Daphne corrected. "Description?"

"Light blue. Old model. Maybe ten years old. White camper shell, not in good condition."

"The dates?"

"October second the first time. I checked the papers on the third. Nothing much had happened. No *fire*," she emphasized.

The Enwright fire had occurred September tenth; Heifitz, October fourth. "The second? You're sure?" He might have set the accelerant for a future fire, she thought.

"Positive. And then again just—" She caught herself.

"*When?*" Daphne shouted.

"This last weekend," Emily answered. "Saturday."

Daphne's pounding heart occupied her chest painfully. The timing seemed off—too rushed—unless October second had accounted for Heifitz. In which case, what was the significance of the weekend just past, another victim yet to come?

Daphne said, "We need to talk to this man with the burned hand. We need your help."

"You could have just offered me the scratch. We'd been jake. I'd have told you what I knew. But now . . . this. I don't like this. I don't like the way you do business."

"You helped us before," Daphne reminded. "Was that the Power, or was that smoke and mirrors?"

"You remember that?"

"We credit you on the case report."

"People talk when they're in that chair. What can I tell you? They open up. And you know why?" she asked, shoving Daphne back and away to create some space between them. "Because they want to believe. They don't believe in much anymore, but they'll believe in me because they want to. They open up to me."

Daphne understood. The detectives she saw as clients were no different. Solid at first, tight, unwilling to share. And then little by little she convinced them to believe in her, and suddenly the dam unleashed and they were spewing intimacies about impotency, suicide wishes, abusing their children, stealing from their day job. An endless laundry list of failures, both personal and private, and all because they discovered a sanctuary, a person willing to listen without judgment—they believed. Daphne realized that she and this woman before her were not so very different. The thought troubled her. "I need everything you have on the man with the burned hand."

"Why should I?"

"Two hundred dollars in your pocket, and I walk away."

"You—people like you—never just walk away. You'll be back. That's the thing about you."

"Will *he?*" Daphne asked hurriedly, hopeful. "The man with

the hand? Be back, that is?" Her heart pounded strongly in her chest—the possibility had not occurred to her—but people who believed in such things returned for more.

Emily met her eyes and nodded slowly. "Probably," she said reluctantly. She nodded more strongly. "Yes, I'd say he will be back." And then she added caustically, "But, honey, that one's going to cost you people. That one's gonna cost big."

19

LIVING in Seattle had taught Ben about rain, the way living in Alaska teaches one about snow. There was mist and spray and teardrops and pearls, curtains, sheets, and waterfalls. On that day it began as a mist, light and delicate like the soft spritz at the end of a spray bottle. It changed the way the air smelled, from metallic and oily to fresh and clean. Exciting. It evolved quickly through wind-driven spray to teardrops, a pelting and unforgiving rain that drummed loudly on fall's colorful leaves. The sidewalk before him became peppered with black teardrops, then consumed by them, transformed into a dark mirror reflecting Ben's footfalls.

He suddenly felt as if someone were watching him, and he wondered if it was guilt or reality. But then the sensation sharpened into the same invasive feeling as when Jack stared at him from the chair in front of the television, stared as if looking right through him.

Ben didn't want to look, didn't want to know the truth. His ears remained alert, his heart pounding, his palms suddenly damp, a lump growing in his throat. His scalp itched. He was afraid.

The urge to look back, to assess his situation, pulled at him like a kind of gravity. He wanted out of this feeling.

He ran. He couldn't simply walk. He looked forward, not back—never look back is what Emily had told him. He tore through the veil of pouring rain like a bat through the darkness of night.

Guilt soaked through him like the rain on his shoulders. Payment for his crime. He picked up his speed. Seen by others, he would be thought to be attempting to outrun the rain, though it was impossible, just as it was impossible to outrun that guilt from which he wished so desperately to distance himself. He crossed at a red pedestrian light, unaware; unable to face the reality of his theft. His legs grew leaden, his heart heavy. He could not live with himself. He wanted to be good; he wanted Emily to like him, to want him. He didn't want to tell her, and yet he felt driven to do so.

When Ben arrived at the purple house, Emily saw the worry in his eyes, or perhaps she read his mind, he thought, and she immediately led him around back to the small porch overlooking the equally small back garden, so carefully cared for. Ben needed that same kind of care and attention.

Rain splashed only inches from them, and the wind swirled, filled with its fragrance. Emily's skirt danced against her calves, and she absentmindedly swatted at it, like a horse's tail after flies.

"So, young man, you have something to tell me."

He would never understand her completely, though he longed to be given the chance. "The world is such a huge place," he began, avoiding any mention of what was really on his mind. "So many people going so many places, doing so many things. I don't see how I'm supposed to fit in. Where I belong."

She wrapped a warm arm around him. It was all he lived for. How would she react if he told her what he had done? "You know, you have an advantage in life, Ben," she said, confusing him. "You've grown up quicker than most people. No, I mean it," she said, answering his expression. "You think things that even some adults never get around to. But the point is, the world is a good place, despite the way it looks sometimes. Life is good, despite the way it feels sometimes. Where you are right now, your age, the best thing to do is enjoy it as much as you can. I know that's not always easy. Don't think about it too much. Just kinda let life happen around you, you know? Basically, I think what you'll find is that things pretty much work out if you let them, if you don't get in their way. If you think good thoughts. If you do good things."

His throat tightened, his eyes stung, and he felt himself begin to shudder and then cry. She consoled him with another squeeze of her arm, but it made him feel even worse, and he struggled to be free of her, leaning away.

"Ben?"

"I'm not good."

"Sure you are. Of course you are."

"I'm not."

"You mustn't let Jack do this to you, Ben."

He shook his head, the tears falling all the harder, tears like the rain falling only a few yards away. How easy it would have been to allow her to believe it all Jack Santori's fault. How simple and convenient. "It's not that," he squeaked out.

"Your mother," she whispered.

He shook his head again. His memory of his mother was only a face, a smell, a smooth hand rubbing his back or tousling his hair. His mother was something, someone, too long ago to remember. "If I lost my wallet in his truck, he'll know where to find me. My address is in the wallet." It just kind of tumbled out of him.

"Who, Ben? What truck?" He heard concern in her voice.

He looked up at her, his vision blurred by his tears. She looked back with sympathy and love, and he knew he was about to tell her everything. He was about to offer her the money—the whole $500—and ask if he could stay with her. He knew her answer long before he uttered his first stuttered sentence of explanation, but that didn't stop him. Nothing stopped him. The truth fell hard, like the rain. It poured out of him.

Emily Richland, reaching out to comfort him, never stopped holding him. She drank up the truth like the garden with the rain.

She listened to every word, nodding as he spoke; her own eyes filled with tears; and the two spent over an hour there on the back porch, right through the squall and into a patch of blue sky, welcoming the sun's penetrating warmth that followed behind, flowed through it, like the intense love that Ben felt for this woman.

20

WHEN his pager sounded, Lou Boldt cringed. The effort to pull its tiny LCD screen into view was as automatic as turning the ignition key of his car or pulling on a pair of socks. At that very moment he had been wondering what to do about his suspicions about Liz, because if he was right about her it started a series of unthinkable, problematic choices that questioned the survival of their family.

Liz was taking a bath. Taken in and of itself, this was no big deal, except that in this family it was Boldt who usually took the baths and Liz, ever in a hurry, who always took a shower. But three times this week she had come home from work and immediately drawn herself a bath. And it was only a few minutes earlier that Boldt realized she had taken baths on the same days the week before: Monday, Tuesday, and Thursday. All three days she had come home an hour and a half late. His imagination raced. As a detective he was trained to see patterns. He regretted this ability, this talent; most of all he resented that his work should intrude into his private life to this degree. He was engaged in maintaining a thoughtful surveillance on his own wife, based on distrust and fear and driven by palpable memories of the past. He hated himself. Coincidence was not in Lou Boldt's vocabulary. He heard Sarah crying and felt on the verge himself.

He scooped up his infant daughter from the crib, nuzzled her, and inhaled the sweet-milk fragrance of her skin that he treasured. She reached out, her tiny fingers locking onto his hair.

"Knock, knock," he said, toeing open the bathroom door, trying to release the vise of her grip on his hair.

Liz's face was bright red, her chest flushed, her body stretched in the tub and magnified by the water. She looked so incredibly appealing, the florid skin tones of a Rubens. He felt a pang of protective jealousy. There was no such thing as ownership; he knew this consciously, and yet . . .

"I think it's dinnertime," he said, his voice cracking, emotions and memories welling up from within him. She had betrayed his faith once before; was it so impossible again? Many of the same elements were in place: both of them working too hard, ignoring the other's needs. The two kids placed impossible burdens on their attentions. There was little time left for their marriage. It was all about the family now. It was different.

He didn't want to cry in front of her, to set her off, to start something he felt so unclear about, so incapable of articulating. He wanted to treasure her, to trust her, to believe. He feared the truth; he didn't want to know—and the realization swept through him that this was the first time he had purposely and intentionally not wanted the truth. As an investigator, curiosity drove him, fed him. It was the fuel of his professional existence, and yet now he stifled it, like throwing a wet blanket over a fire. To him this was a profound and significant difference, and one he interpreted as a weakness. A crack in the armor.

The mother beckoned with outstretched arms, and the child, seeing this, stopped crying and wiggled to be free. Boldt envied Liz this biological connection and for a moment felt himself a visitor in his own home. Liz sat up high in the tub and, cradling the child, offered her ripened breast. The hungry lips drew her mother into her and Liz smiled slightly, closed her eyes, and leaned her head back against the tub. Boldt studied his wife's nakedness from head to toe, her youthful breasts, trim waist, the grassy swatch of black hair between her long legs. He didn't want anyone else having this. He felt possessive. He wondered why he had allowed his own body to train-wreck the way it had. He blamed himself.

"Didn't I hear your pager?" she questioned, her eyes still closed.

Did she want him out of the house? He felt a flood of anger surge through him. He stood taller and drew his stomach a little tighter. He suddenly wished he looked different, less disheveled, more hair, better tone to his muscles. Had her eye wandered? Was he aging too quickly for her?

"Yeah," he answered. Was she going to blame the pager for awakening Sarah? It wouldn't be the first time. She had fallen into the habit recently of blaming him for all sorts of things, many out of his control. He had let most of these complaints pass unchallenged, but they had eaten into him like dry rot, damage unseen to the naked eye.

"You going to call it in?" she asked. The lines of her naked form were a work of art. He wished the tub were big enough for both of them. He wanted to feel her skin against his, warm and wet.

"Yeah." When had he not called it in? he wondered. He was a slave to his work. He lived for it.

She opened her eyes slightly, like a person drugged—dreamy and quiet. The baby suckled her. Again he was struck by how he envied that connection. He wondered what it must feel like to her, the aching swelling of the breast relieved, her fluids giving life to another. "You okay?" she asked, her brow knitted sharply, her eyes suddenly pained.

"Sure," he replied.

"I don't think so."

"Fine," he lied to her, wondering when and how that had become such an easy thing to do.

"You know what it is?" she asked. He looked back at her curiously, wondering if this was to be her moment of confession.

Strangely, he didn't want that just now. "The pager," she explained. "Do you know what it's about?"

"No, it's not that," he informed her.

"Then what?"

"Regrets. Concerns." He heard his voice betray him. Betrayal fed on itself, he thought, like those insects that eat their mates.

Her eyes came open wider. Her hips rolled in the water as she leaned toward him. She floated there, motionless. She cradled the baby tighter to her. "Honey?"

He had an urge to make love to her. Possess her. He knew it was for all the wrong reasons. "Maybe we should talk at some point," he said, though he sounded defeated and he knew she picked up on it.

"I'm all yours," she said.

I wonder, Lou Boldt thought. He nodded, though insincerely. She took the baths to clean herself up, to keep him from knowing. A cleansing. Purify her from whoever else had been with her. He ached, wondering what drove such thoughts.

"Go to work, Sergeant," she ordered. "I'm not going to get mad about it."

"I'll call in," he said. "Check it out."

"I'll wait up," she told him, acknowledging with more certainty than he wished that the page was going to take him from their home. She was right, of course, it nearly always did. The pager was the giant stage hook, designed, it seemed, to steal him from his home life. To disrupt. He had come to hate it. "Or I'll try to, depending how late you are." She chuckled. The baby lost her mother's nipple, and Liz helped her to find it again.

"You two are beautiful," he said, still living with the urge to have her sexually. He felt his throat choke and turned toward the phone to prevent her from seeing the betrayal of tears that filled his eyes.

Out of the frying pan and into the fire, Boldt thought, the wind blowing through his close-cropped hair—what was left of it; her silhouette caught by a streetlamp that lit the running path that surrounded Green Lake. Daphne Matthews was a little too fit, a little too pretty; she never quite looked the part.

The lake was several acres of black water surrounded by the running path, a perimeter road lined on the east with cafés and a quality restaurant or two. Lush wooded hills, densely populated with neighborhoods of two- and three-story clapboard houses built in the city's first big boom—the timber era—seventy years earlier, rose on three sides, containing the lake in a jeweled bowl of window lights. Green Lake was picturesque and charming, like something from a New England village postcard. South of the lake were recreation fields for softball and soccer, lit at night by steel towers projecting a harsh, stark light visible at a great distance. At 8 P.M. the lake's running path still saw a great deal of use, men and women running or walking alone for the most part, as contrasted with the pairs of couples and friends and associates that exercised in the early morning and at lunchtime.

Daphne wore jeans and a stone-washed blue silk jacket over a crisp white shirt buttoned to her neck. He joined her and they started walking, holding to the right side of the path, allowing the breathless joggers to pass. The lake was convenient to both their houses. She had recommended they meet there, as they had so many times before.

"Emily Richland uses a shill who checks the cars of her clients. Information about the cars is passed to her, and she can make some damn good educated guesses as to who is sitting in front of her."

"Am I supposed to be surprised?" he asked, his mind elsewhere.

"The guy with the burned hand came to her place looking to check a couple of dates: October second, two days before Heifitz; and then again on Saturday. Lou, I think it's the arsonist." Before he could speak, she said, "His right hand—the last three fingers are fused in a kind of paddle. Badly burned. He's military. Air Force, maybe. I think she's holding out on me. I think she has more."

Boldt's mind raced away from him, removing his concern

about Liz's affair and focusing solely on the suspect. He realized that he buried himself in work for a reason. "His car?"

"A truck." She gave Boldt the description that Emily had given her.

"Air Force," Boldt mumbled.

"She thinks this guy is involved in drug deals, not arson. And maybe that's right, maybe he's dealing in drug lab chemicals, maybe that's how he got the burned hand, maybe it has nothing whatsoever to do with arson, but I think it's one hell of a lead."

"A psychic," Boldt said. "Do you know how Shoswitz is going to react to this?"

"A fraud," she reminded him. "If we get her accomplice, the one who actually saw this guy's truck, Jesus, I think we've got a hell of a witness. The two of them? Are you kidding me? One of them studied the truck, the other spoke to the man. He was nervous, real concerned about October second."

"Or maybe he's just a middleman," Boldt was thinking aloud. "Maybe he's selling some chemicals to our boy. Maybe he even thinks they're for a drug lab. We won't know until we get there."

"I paid her two hundred. I think another two and we'll get more. I think if we sat on the place we'd ID her accomplice. She needs the spy. The scam doesn't work without the spy. Furthermore," she added, pulling on his elbow to keep him from interfering with an approaching runner, "she thinks he'll return."

Boldt stopped walking. Daphne went on a step or two. He said, "Return?"

"He's already been there twice," she said proudly.

"Military? Maybe Garman was military, maybe Air Force. Maybe they served together. Maybe that's the connection."

"A woman was involved," she said, reminding him of the connection between the two victims. "A *divorced* woman."

Boldt walked to catch up to her. The two started walking again. "Heifitz was *widowed*," he reminded.

"She was *separated*," Daphne corrected. "As good as divorced, I'm told, when her former husband up and died on her. Went down on the records as widowed." She walked a few more steps and then said emphatically, "Divorced single moms, Lou. That's what we're looking at. Count on it."

He was a cop who based his investigations on the information a victim could reveal. He caught himself walking faster, out of excitement. Thoughts sparked in his head; he could barely contain them. "We can link the victims!" he nearly shouted.

"Why do you think I paged you? Link? I don't know. But we've got some obvious common denominators."

"Divorced single mothers," Boldt repeated. "Both of them," he stated. He could barely contain his excitement. He felt like screaming. The victim! he thought. The victim can tell more about a homicide than a pile of crime-scene evidence.

"That's it," she confirmed. "Age of the kids?"

"Didn't check."

"We need to." Searching for a way the two women might have been targeted by the killer, Boldt listed, "Group therapy—you know, coping-with-divorce classes—church groups, what else?"

"Book clubs," she suggested.

"Cooking classes, gyms."

"Plumbers, electricians—"

"Ladders!" he barked, stopping again. His excitement bubbled out of him. He could see it become contagious in her. "We're close! Plumbers, electricians . . ."

"Roofers, masons, chimney sweeps . . ."

"A house painter!" he exclaimed. "The cotton fibers at the base of the ladder."

"What?"

He spoke so rapidly that his words blurred. "We found cotton fibers alongside the ladder . . . at the base of the ladder. Bernie's working on them. What do you want to bet they come up positive for petroleum products?"

"Slow down," she said. "I mean, slow your walking. You're practically running."

"Both of them divorced," Boldt repeated for the third time.

"Dating services," she offered. "It's hell out there as a single mom."

"Both divorced," Boldt said gleefully. He stopped her, grabbing her by the shoulders, overwhelmed with a feeling of accomplishment. "You're a genius!"

They stood face-to-face, both breathing hard, the path light
catching half their faces, their eyes locked, his large hands firmly
gripping her narrow shoulders. Electricity sparked between them,
a familiar energy, and Boldt sensed how precariously close he was
to kissing her.

He released her and backed off.

"Oh, God," she gasped, maintaining eye contact, confirming
her own desires.

Lou Boldt nodded imperceptibly, his heart pounding in his
chest and then breaking into pieces.

21

WALKING to the school bus stop on a wet Friday morning in mid-October, cars everywhere, their drivers anxious and agitated, everyone in such a hurry, Ben sensed he was being followed. Spilling the beans to Emily had not quieted the sensation, as Ben had hoped. He dreamt about it. He felt it at all times. He had absolutely no doubt that someone was back there. It was not something that needed proof. He *knew!* If Emily could know things, why couldn't he? Perhaps he possessed the Power as well.

For Ben, all fear, all terror, all misgiving had previously existed in the form, the shape, the image of his stepfather. He had compartmentalized it, defined it, so that he recognized it. For years it had been the only fear he knew. All else was tame by comparison.

Tame, until that moment when Ben realized a second, more palpable fear: fear of the unknown, the unexpected. He had an idea about the identity of the person following him. And of this he had no doubt: He was being watched. It had to do with the money from the truck. Emily had said that things would work out. Ben was not so sure.

To Ben, the sidewalk suddenly felt soft, spongy, like walking across a mattress, and it took him a few strides to realize it was his knees, not the sidewalk. His vision darkened on the edges, as if he were suddenly walking down a poorly lit hallway. As he hurried, nearly running, he gained the courage to glance over his shoulder and sneak a look.

The blue truck! He staggered, nearly collapsing. It moved so slowly that traffic rolled around it as it held to the curb. Ben could not see Nick's face, but he knew the identity of the driver. He knew what the driver wanted.

At the next intersection, he turned right, cut through traffic, and joined fifteen other kids at the bus stop, hoping for cover. He watched for the blue truck.

"Hey, Ben"—he jumped at the sound of his name—"you want to come over after school?"

Finn Hershey was a school friend with blond hair and a thin face. Like Ben and the others, he was soaking wet from the rain.

"I don't know," Ben said, shifting his glance from left to right, bus to truck. He couldn't think about such things; he had the truck to worry about. The yellow school bus appeared, its big nose topping the hill and dropping toward the waiting kids. At the same instant the blue truck appeared in the intersection, creeping along incredibly slowly as it passed. Thank God it didn't turn, though for Ben it felt as if he locked eyes with the driver, who was bent low and clearly searching the bus stop. The bus chugged forward, seemingly more slowly than ever. Ben mentally encouraged it.

"If it keeps raining we could hit my Sega. I got a new *MK* magazine. Some cool stuff in it."

Mortal Kombat. Ben was something of a pro. Finn was always trying to beat him at the video game, but he wasn't very good. "Sure," Ben said.

"It would be cool."

"Sure."

"We could call your mom from sch—" Finn caught himself.

"I don't have a mom," Ben reminded him.

"I didn't mean to say that."

"I know."

"We could leave a message. You know."

"Sure."

"What is it with you?"

The bus arrived, its door swinging open, and the kids fought toward the door. The pickup truck rounded the far corner, heading for the bus stop. Ben shoved his way into the bottleneck, followed by Finn.

"What is it with you?" Finn repeated.

"Nothing."

Ben was never anxious to get on the bus. Today he was acting different. Fear had changed him, he realized. He clawed his way to a seat near the back of the bus and was forced to relinquish it when told to by a junior Ben had no desire to mess with. He found a seat farther forward.

He looked back in time to see the pickup truck through the rain-blurred back window. Forced to wait behind the bus, the driver sat idle, craning close to the fogged windshield and rubbing it in an effort to see. A line of vehicles had formed behind it, waiting for the school bus to decommission its warning lights and move on.

By the third bus stop, when Ben looked back, the truck was no longer in sight. He decided that it had either moved on or gone ahead. Whichever, it hardly mattered; by that point the driver knew the name and location of his school. He thought back to the airport, to that stupid moment of taking the money. For the hundredth time since that day he touched his back pocket, praying his wallet had reappeared.

The bus stopped in front of the school. In the chaos of the rain and the rush for the front steps, Ben crouched and ducked into the foundation planting alongside the stairs. His head swooned as he caught sight of the blue pickup truck. Out there waiting. For him. Like a wild dog at a rabbit hole: patient and hungry. Ben knew the way it worked. The rabbit never stood a chance.

22

THE pressure had built up behind Boldt's eyes like water in a pipe. Based on the timing established by Emily Richland's client, another woman was likely targeted to burn. She would be close to thirty years old, a divorced woman, mother of a boy younger than ten. Daphne had followed up as requested. He bore the responsibility to prevent this death from happening, and he had frightfully little evidence to pursue.

Boldt gave a regular morning briefing to LaMoia, Gaynes, Bahan, Fidler, and two other homicide detectives loaned to Boldt from the other squad. ATF had offered agents but Boldt had politely refused, fearing that once he allowed the federal agents inside he might never get them back out the door.

The ATF lab chemist, Casterstein, was an exception to that rule. When he requested a video conference with Boldt, the sergeant accepted, though not without trepidation. SPD lacked video-conferencing capability, requiring Boldt to pay a visit to the ATF offices in the Federal Building, which he feared might be little more than a ploy by ATF to hold him hostage while they convinced him of the importance of their joining the investigation. As an insurance package, he brought along the police lab's Bernie Lofgrin and all four of his detectives, LaMoia, Gaynes, Fidler, and Bahan. If Casterstein wanted a conference, Boldt would give him one.

The federal offices were newer, cleaner, and quieter than SPD's, a source of irritation for any cop. ATF and the FBI had access to, or owned outright, state-of-the-art surveillance equipment, computer technology, weapons, and communications systems. Although they were always generous with the equipment, it nonetheless irked Boldt and the others to have to ask, which they did often. Using the video conference room was partly embarrassing for that reason, even though an ATF agent was involved. Boldt and his five ducklings moved through the ATF halls like kids on the way to the principal's office. The room itself was nearly identical to their own fifth-floor conference room, except for the projection television screen at one end and the video camera mounted on the wall alongside and aimed back at those sitting at the table.

Boldt and the others took seats, several with notepads open in front of them. The lights in the room seemed brighter to Boldt. Two gray devices in the middle of the large oval table, which looked like large square ashtrays, were actually conferencing microphones. At ten o'clock sharp the screen sparkled, and the face of Howard Casterstein appeared, greatly oversized.

Boldt wished that Daphne had joined them, though she wasn't to be found. Her ninth-floor office was locked, her voice mail on, and no one seemed to know where she was, although rumor had it that she was off working with local forensic psychiatrists on a profile of the arsonist.

Casterstein's face was slightly washed out by the light. To Boldt's surprise and delight, the ATF agent who had showed them to the room had not tried to sit in on the conference. That impressed Boldt a great deal.

Boldt introduced the face on the wall to his squad, at which point Casterstein, polite to a fault, began the discussion. "We've been looking at the fire debris, hoping to support a cause and origin. I thought you might want to see some of this, which is why I suggested the video room. I suppose my first comments are directed to"—he looked down at a piece of paper where he had scrawled the names of those in attendance—"Sid Fidler and Neil Bahan. In reading your reports of interviews with the neighbors, and from the pilot reports you cited, the first item of significance to those of us in the lab is the purple flame associated with these fires. That, along with the spalling and bluish color of the concrete, suggests a flammable liquid accelerant or propellant. The lack of hydrocarbons in your testing has been confirmed here in Sacramento. This boy was not burning dinosaurs, which is highly unusual for a residential structural arson. Of special interest to us were the Vibram soles of Sergeant Boldt's hiking boots, which most of you probably know dissolved after walking the site. We looked at ions, at pH. We expected to come up with chlorine, but we weren't able to support that. In fact, the more common tests turned up little of interest. We thought we might be looking at thermite mixtures, but they should leave a slag, and we have no evidence to support such a by-product."

At this point Bernie Lofgrin nodded and took down some notes. He asked, "Metals?"

Casterstein answered. "Mr. Lofgrin is asking about residual metals found on-site because magnesium and a number of other metals burn exceptionally hot and are often associated with high-temperature fires such as the two that killed Enwright and Heifitz. Unfortunately the answer is no. We have found no trace of such metals in the debris or in our samples." To Lofgrin he said, "We used the EDAX—x-ray fluorescence analysis—along with chemical spot tests and are showing some inorganics that were probably used in building this device, though the actual accelerant initially proved elusive."

"Initially?" Boldt asked, sensing a breakthrough that Casterstein wasn't revealing. He might have complained about Casterstein's college professor approach, but he knew Lofgrin to be much the same and had come to accept that labbies gave elaborate explanations but only once. It was up to the investigating officer to inform others, from the ranking superior to the jury. The detailed explanations were a way for these forensic scientists to move on to other analyses without a dozen follow-up inquiries. For this reason, Boldt took meticulous notes.

"We have some interesting clues in these burns," Casterstein suggested. "Of primary concern is that at least Enwright was viewed walking around inside before the fire. Sergeant Boldt raised the appropriate question: Why did Enwright not get out of the house?"

Bobbie Gaynes answered. "We're assuming she fell through the floor, into the hole created by the fire, and, injured in the fall, was consumed in the basement."

"A justifiable theory," Casterstein said diplomatically, "but not supported by evidence. To explain such a fall, I'm afraid we would be looking at an explosion, something that instantly took the floor out from beneath her."

Boldt couldn't take this kind of talk without his imagination running wild. He could picture Dorothy Enwright breaking through the flaming floor and falling to her eventual death in the fiery confines of the basement. The helplessness of such a moment overwhelmed him, and briefly he neither heard nor saw Casterstein but, instead, felt himself inside Dorothy Enwright, weightless and falling, the flames licking up from below. Casterstein's voice brought him back.

"We have no reports of any such explosion, only fire. A devastatingly fast, enormously hot fire—a spike of purple flame jettisoning into the air. This is not timber burning. This is not the explosion of a gas barbecue stored in the basement for winter. This is an unknown accelerant, somehow ignited, most likely by timer, or less likely, radio-controlled from a distance, that spread so quickly through the house that the resident never had time to react. What I find of particular interest, and what I wanted to show you today, is this." Casterstein put on a pair of latex gloves. He held up a black blob, and whoever was operating the camera zoomed in on it. "Found by you, Mr. Bahan, according to our documentation."

Those at the conference table looked over at Neil Bahan. His thin brown hair and big build reminded Boldt of the kids in school who never joined in, always standing on the edges and watching.

Boldt was reminded then of Daphne's warning that a fire inspector is dangerously close in mind-set to an arsonist—two sides of the same fence. He paid particular attention to both Bahan and Fidler for this reason: If they were investigating fires they themselves had set, Boldt might never find the truth.

Bahan said, "I found it up the street from the Heifitz place, by where my car was parked, actually. It was still warm to the touch, so I included it as evidence. But I put a note on it, because it seemed awfully far away—a hundred yards or more."

"We think it significant," Casterstein said, spinning it in his fingers. It was a hard piece of plastic the size of a large golf ball. "We've x-rayed it, and there is apparently a piece of a wire melted into it, leading us to believe it to be—"

"The detonation device," Bernie Lofgrin said quickly.

"Precisely. Or part thereof. Yes," Casterstein agreed. "Further tests are needed, of course, and may take a month or two—"

"A month?" Boldt shouted. "We haven't got a month! We have a—an informer," he explained, stopping himself from using *psychic*, "who may have information indicating another fire is planned within the week."

Neither Casterstein, Lofgrin, nor Gaynes were aware of that development, and they all sat stunned. Casterstein finally muttered, "I see. Well, something like this takes time." He held up the melted plastic. "Our principal concern is the identification of the accelerant. If we can give you the accelerant and you can trace its components to their sources, you just may be able to end-run this guy. Detonators are a dime a dozen, and though sometimes, when in better shape, they offer latent prints, we're not going to see that in this case."

Lofgrin said, "Why don't we handle the possible detonator up here? Spread out the manpower and consult you guys on what we find?"

"That works for me," Casterstein agreed. "We'll send this and some other evidence back up to you."

Bobbie Gaynes said, "I'm still confused as to why both women were unable to get out of their houses in time. These fires were late afternoon, early evening. It's not as if they were asleep."

All eyes turned to the wall.

"We can't answer that at this time. It might be explained by the fire going off so fast, so hot, that it sucked the oxygen out of the structure and suffocated the resident instantly—kind of like being kicked in the chest."

"But if that were the case," Fidler suggested, "we would have seen some of the windows imploded—glass *inside* the structure. We have nothing to support that."

"Agreed," Casterstein said, glowing on the wall, still spinning the black plastic ball between his fingers. "If there had been accelerant in every room," he suggested, "if the device was of multiple origin with simultaneous detonation, the choices for egress would be limited."

"Trapped like a rat. That's what you're saying," LaMoia said, speaking for the first time. "He rigged the whole fucking place to blow at the same time." He glanced at the others and then said to the wall, "In which case there should be more than enough evidence for you guys to tell us that." LaMoia had never been fond of the Feds, and Boldt nearly kicked him under the table. The detective went on. "Lemme ask you this, Doc. What is it you boys aren't telling us? What is it you're leaving out? I'm feeling a gaping hole here, and the wind blowing through it stinks kinda bad."

A silence hung over the conference room. The speaker spit static. When Casterstein moved, the image blurred slightly. It did so as he looked off-camera and then back at those in the room. He said softly, "We're seeing what we term a *mixed profile*. We need to see through that, to separate out the elements. It takes time. They aren't the common hydrocarbons that we would expect. So we start over and try again. We fail, and we try again."

"Like us," Boldt said. Casterstein was describing an investigation perfectly.

"We're both detectives in our own way," Casterstein said.

"Bottom line?" LaMoia demanded harshly. "What's the bottom line here, Doc? We got people this guy's planning to barbecue here shortly. I, for one, would like to see something we can take away from this powwow, lovely as it's been to visit the Federal Building. A black golf ball? That's not exactly the treasure I had in mind."

Casterstein remained unruffled. He allowed a slight smile, as if he had expected a LaMoia in the group. "I appreciate your honesty, Detective. I asked Sergeant Boldt here," he emphasized, "because I wanted to show him this piece of evidence. I also wanted to show him this." Casterstein nodded to someone off-camera at his end. The screen went blue. Casterstein's voice said, "Stand by. What you're about to see is a test conducted by the Fort Worth Fire Department."

The image was of a large deserted supermarket in an open sea of empty blacktop. Where the windows should have been were sheets of plywood. Grass grew up through gaping cracks in the pavement. Surrounding the structure were twenty or more fire vehicles, all parked at a good distance. Crews stood on the ground with hoses, but there was little water on the ground, no evidence of a fire having been fought. A digital clock counted down in the lower right-hand corner.

Casterstein said, "Pay particular attention to the speed of the burn and the color. I think you'll find it interesting."

The clock counted down to zero, at which point Gaynes and LaMoia, closest to the screen, actually jumped, leaning back in their chairs and away from the bright purple flash that rose into the sky like the flame from a wick. The roof of the building melted away, creating a hole in the doughnut. Everything seemed to burn at once. It lasted for three minutes and forty-two seconds, at which point the crews moved in and began to hose water onto the structure. The only water able to reach the center, shot from ladder trucks, exploded into flames as it arrived at the burning core. Those firefighters shut off their hoses, and the ladder engines were pulled back some distance from the inferno. Boldt had never seen a fire so ferocious.

The video stopped; Casterstein's image reappeared, fuzzy at first and then clear. "They fought the fire for another twenty minutes, but it's that initial burn that is of interest. I don't know if you noticed, but this burn went off at temperatures that caused water to separate into its elements, hydrogen and oxygen, literally exploding the attempts to suppress it. Never seen anything like it. The fire was an attempt to discover the accelerant used in a series of arsons that swept the country from '89 to '94. Our Washington office had a hand in it, which is how I have a copy of the tape.''

Boldt could picture a person inside such a structure. He shuddered from head to toe and wondered if Bahan, next to him, saw him shake. All of a sudden the lack of human remains discovered on-site made sense to him; it explained the inability of Enwright and Heifitz to flee their homes. The pressing urgency of preventing another fire welled up from within him, and he immediately felt filled with self-doubt. Perhaps he should have moved on to lieutenant, he thought. Perhaps the work required younger minds, more agile thinking. Had he grown staid and incapable? Could he do his job effectively while worrying that his wife was having another affair? He had too much on his plate, too little time. *Time.* The word haunted him. Not another fire, not for anything.

"The recommendation coming out of Washington—and I have to agree with it—is that, should there be a third fire, we let it burn. No fire suppression, certainly no overhaul." An uncharacteristically long silence hung over the room.

"What the hell did we just look at?" Boldt inquired, uncharacteristically brash. He glanced over at LaMoia, feeling respect for the detective; only LaMoia had dared to push Casterstein. Only LaMoia had sensed something lingering under the surface. Boldt couldn't help but wonder if he'd lost his touch.

Casterstein pursed his lips and leaned into the camera, going slightly out of focus again. "I don't know yet what we're looking at in these fires of yours," he said flatly, his voice suddenly dry. "But I can tell you what they set off in that test fire. I can tell you what they're thinking back East. I can tell you what they're looking for, now that they've culled the test site and run the necessary analysis." He allowed it to hang there for a moment, suspended on a telephone line somewhere between Sacramento and Seattle, a ball of spoken information surrounded on both sides by static. He brushed his hair back like a pitcher debating a signal sent by the catcher. Then he took a deep breath and spoke two words that flooded Boldt with heat and caused his eyes to sting. "Rocket fuel," he said. "The accelerant in the Fort Worth test was liquid rocket fuel."

23

THE grounds of Owen Adler's residence intimidated Boldt despite the fact that he had been there three years earlier. One measured Owen Adler's kind of wealth by the size and range of his private jet. It was a Gulfstream 3 with the wings of a 4 for extra fuel. He was on the Seattle A-list. His marriage to Daphne Matthews was to be performed by Robert Fulghum in a private ceremony on the grounds of the estate, overlooking Shilshole Marina and Puget Sound. The marriage had been postponed twice, although only their closest friends knew this—no invitations had ever been sent. Daphne claimed it was because, in putting his food empire back together, Adler had encountered repeated scheduling problems, but for Boldt there were other signs. Daphne had allowed the tenant of her houseboat to leave without penalty; she had made no attempt to rent it again. She was back to volunteering at the Shelter, a church basement for teenage runaways, a commitment she had dropped during the infatuation days with Owen Adler. For his part, Adler had twice been photographed in the company of other women for the society pages. Boldt had not asked any questions. Any man who could lift a multimillion dollar company out of ashes the way Adler had deserved some kind of medal. There was no doubting the man's power to overcome financial obstacles. On the other hand, Boldt thought, Daphne Matthews might be a kind of challenge he had never faced.

The picturesque marina, so pretty at night with its white lights, black reflecting water, and regimented lines of white boats, their masts as delicate as frost on a window, was nestled inside a stone seawall, far below the hillside compound.

Using the front door's intercom, Daphne asked him to go around the house and wait for her out on the patio. When he circled the sprawling mansion, he saw that both pool and patio lights were on. It felt more like Italy than Seattle. He and Liz had not been back to Italy since Miles was born, another of those lifestyle changes that at moments like this registered in him as regret.

Daphne had it all. This would be hers soon. He wondered what that felt like.

The French doors opened and she ducked through chintz drapes wearing a pink robe and a towel wrapped around her head. "Sorry," she apologized. "I was . . . I wanted a swim. A shower first. I was just getting out—"

"Then it's me who's sorry for interrupting."

"Corky's asleep," she said, referring to Adler's adopted teenage daughter. "I didn't want to wake her."

"No."

"Does this make you uncomfortable?" she asked, clearly referring to the robe and the fact that there probably wasn't much in the way of clothing underneath it.

"Are you living here?" Boldt asked. He wasn't sure why this came out of his mouth, wasn't sure why it was suddenly so important to him.

"I could change, if you want. The clothes," she clarified. She looked away, back in the direction of downtown and the Space Needle and the city skyline. "He's in South America this week. Peru, I think, tonight. Another deal. I didn't want Corky to be with a nanny. Not as long as I'm around. It doesn't seem fair to her."

"He travels a lot."

"Yes, he does." Regret. Maybe some resentment that Boldt would voice such a thing. The way two people relate changes with each different situation, he realized, wishing it didn't have to. He wanted to always share an intimate closeness with this woman, that liberating closeness where anything goes. But it was not the same any longer, and he resisted the change. He blamed Owen Adler. Her secret life was now shared with this other man; Boldt was the outsider.

She sat down in a Brown and Jordan chair and crossed her legs, and a knee and then a thigh popped out of the robe. Boldt looked off into the cleanness of the pool. Interwoven lines of serpentine light ribbed the pool walls. A plane flew over the bay, its wing lights flashing.

"Rocket fuel."

Her head snapped up. A line of shower water ran from her wet hair down her neck, chased the line of her collarbone, and leaked down into the robe between her breasts.

"That was my reaction as well," he said.

"Emily Richland mentioned the Air Force." Her eyes were wide, her cheeks flushed.

Boldt said, "There's more. Bernie says the ladder impressions put his—or her—weight at one-forty tops. That's light."

"A juvenile?" she asked. "The second poem was Plato: *Suddenly a flash of understanding, a spark that leaps across to the soul*. Big stuff for a juvenile."

"Messed-up kid, ugly divorce. It's possible, I suppose." He added, "You're the judge of that."

"I'm thinking mid to late twenties, college educated. He could be thin, even gaunt; I could buy that." She leaned forward. The bathrobe fell away from her chest. He looked away, back toward the pool and its dancing waves of light. He didn't want to stare. Daphne had always been dangerous for him. It was inescapable.

"LaMoia is trying to track down the Werner ladder sales. Something about computerized cash register receipts. He's optimistic we'll get something."

"John? Since when doesn't he think highly of his own abilities?" She said sternly, "I know you're thankful to have LaMoia. Believe me, I love him dearly. But we all should be grateful that there's only one of him. He stretches the envelope enough, thank you very much."

"Bernie can't swear by those impressions. It's a best-guess situation. If he's wrong, he's wrong; there's no backup guesstimate. The ground was soaked by the fire fighting, which made conducting any kind of field test impossible." He mused aloud, "Funny, isn't it, how the act of suppressing the fire goes a long way to destroying the evidence that might be found."

"*Ironic* would be my word of choice."

"Twenty-five and a college grad?" He attempted to keep the disappointment out of his voice.

"That bothers you?" she inquired. "All I'm saying is that's the collective wisdom based on national averages. In talking with others, that's the best I can do: twenty-five to thirty, college educated, sexually inadequate. He hates his mother, girlfriend, whatever. Maybe all of the above. He is judge and executioner. He's intelligent, quiet and lives alone. He's working at a job under his abilities."

"You've been busy!" Boldt said. He was never comfortable with these profiles, but he did his best to trust them—they had proven accurate too many times.

"He probably carries a library card and rides city transportation. If we put this information from the ladder into the mix, then he's slight of build."

"Library card? City transport?" he asked.

"Comes out of his income, which is limited if any. These guys like their labs. They like to tinker with their stuff. He works a job that requires no thought. He thinks about his kills, about his bombs, all day long. He may not sleep much, or eat much for that matter, and that fits with what you're saying about his being slight. He leaves work and goes to his lab."

"His apartment?"

"Unlikely. No. Someplace away from it all. Someplace he won't be bothered. A garage. An abandoned building."

"None of those in this city," Boldt snapped sarcastically.

"I know it's not what you want to hear."

"Fidler gave me a report on Garman. Steven Garman, the Marshal Five, the fire inspector—"

"I know who Garman is," she reminded him, a little hot under the collar. "The one receiving the threats is always the first one to look at."

"Have you looked?" he pressed.

"We talked about Garman, that's all. What is it with you?"

He met and held her eyes. He found her beauty intoxicating. He had often wished she could make it go away. "I don't know that I'm up to this," he confessed.

"Don't be ridiculous."

"I teeter on the edge. My self confidence goes out the window, and there I am, teetering."

"It's called anxiety. It's healthy." She studied him thoughtfully and asked rhetorically, "You didn't come here because of Bernie Lofgrin or rocket fuel or Steven Garman, did you?"

"Sure I did."

"Talk to me, Lou."

"Another woman is going to burn."

"Not necessarily."

"Sure she is. And I'm at the helm, and I don't particularly want the wheel."

"Understandable. But you've got it."

"Thanks loads."

"You want to turn it over to Bobbie?" she asked, eyes penetrating. "John? Whom would you pick to run something this size? Pfoutz? Lublanski? Tell me."

"Garman lives alone. He went through what he characterized to Fidler as an ugly marriage. He's been with SFD for twelve years. Highly regarded but keeps to himself. No beers with the boys. At constant war with his superiors."

"Don't do this, Lou. Let's talk about you," she encouraged.

"He's a stickler for details. Meticulous. Demanding. No one can remember his having even dated a woman—or a man either, for that matter." He knew he had her then, for the color of her eyes changed and her brow tightened.

She said, "We can talk about Garman later," but in a tone that suggested she didn't mean it.

"I wouldn't mind if you could find a way to chat him up," he informed her. "Open him up."

"You can pass the case to someone else," she told him. "Shoswitz will grumble and piss all over you, but in the end he'll relent if he thinks you aren't up to it. You want me to tell him I think you need a breather? I can do that."

"He's a big son-of-a-bitch, Garman is. Certainly no one-forty. But by his own admission, Bernie could be wrong about that, and he is, after all, at the center of the case: a Marshal Five inspector, the guy receiving the threats."

"You know there are any number of cases from any number of wars where a soldier fights with heart and soul, wins medals, fights to the death, invincible. Then he gets married on leave, and sometime later has a kid, and that's the end of that phase of his military career. There's a line he won't cross any longer. It's dangerous for him *and others* for him to be out there."

Her comment hit Boldt in the center of his chest. He didn't want to hinder the investigation—this went to the core of his concern. He wanted to keep pushing back at her with comments about Garman, but he heard himself say, "If we lose another, I don't know what I'll do."

"You'll go to work in the morning," she said calmly. "Same as you always do, as you've always done. It's what we do." Again, she studied him carefully. "It was the mother and sister, wasn't it? You humanize the victims, where others intentionally do the opposite. Why? Because it motivates you," she stated. "Because it reminds you what these victims were *before* the incident— whatever the incident. It's the not knowing," she said definitely. "If you had more, you'd be a dog after a bone, but there isn't more, there isn't enough, and for the time being you feel aimless. How does he meet them? How does he rig their houses? How does he ensure they're alone? I can't say I know what it's like in your shoes, because I don't. No one does, or damn few, at any rate. But there's no one better, Lou. You never see this, but the rest of us do. No one. And if another woman dies, she dies. And another? Maybe so. You have to live with that. I can't even imagine the strength that requires. The rest of us—we have you as a buffer. Even Shoswitz uses you this way. But don't think for a moment that John or Bobbie or any of the others could do any better. They would do it differently, I can't argue that. Better? No. You work your squad for their strengths. You run it like a team. You're admired for that behind your back. There are other ways to do it, God knows, but none better. You get up in the morning and you go to work. Some days it sucks; some days it's almost tolerable. Those are the ones we come to cherish. You want me to raise a flag, I will. I'd do *anything* for you."

He felt light-headed. He didn't like her saying that, not wearing a pink robe with a lot of leg showing. He didn't need a pep talk or want one. He needed freedom from the pressure inside his head; nothing anyone said was going to cure it. What would cure it was the foreman of a jury standing and reading off a litany of guilty charges. And that was at the end of a road so long that at times he needed to look for off-ramps. He begged for air.

"Thanks," he said, because it seemed only fair.

"I'll figure a way to get to see Garman so he won't think anything of it. I'll chat him up," she promised. "Try for some sleep," she suggested.

He nodded. He was sorry he had come.

"And I won't say anything. Not to anyone."

He wanted inside that robe. Comfort. Escape. He lusted after this woman who was not his wife but was also no stranger. He wanted to stay, to get close to her.

Boldt thought about Liz, and his suspicions of her having an affair, and wondered about his intentions of wanting to find her in the wrong. Was he looking for an easy way out of a complicated situation? Were the kids more than he could take? Did he dare have such thoughts, even in the privacy and secrecy of his own conscience? Was he worried about Daphne actually loving Adler for real, of losing her for good? Or was he, as he wanted to believe, so in love with his children, his wife, his life that it seemed too good to be true—and, if too good to be true, then certainly something had to come along to challenge it, even destroy it if left unchecked. An affair. A serial arsonist. Something.

Nothing surprised him any longer.

24

BEN kept watch for the pickup truck. He had not seen it today but he sensed it was out there. He feared it. He had little doubt that his wallet had fallen out while hiding in the camper, and his wallet contained not only four dollars but his school picture and an ID card that had come with the wallet, carefully filled out with address and phone number. The guilt over having taken the money occupied his every thought. He figured he had two choices: give it back or run away. Emily wouldn't take it; she called it dirty. And the thought of giving up that much money was repulsive. Running away remained at the top of the list.

His current plan was to go home with Jimmy for the afternoon. Avoiding his own house—the address in the wallet—was of utmost importance. Jimmy was big for his age, with narrow-set eyes and big pudgy hands. He wasn't the coolest of Ben's friends, but he never teased Ben about his glass eye the way some of the kids did. Jimmy was okay. Ben realized they would probably play video games or watch a movie—what would normally have been a great way to avoid homework and going home to his empty house—but as the school day came to a close, Ben wished he had never agreed to go. He was terrified to leave the building.

He had an urge to visit Emily, as he so often did on his way home from school, but the possibility remained that the driver of the pickup truck, Nick, had connected Ben to Emily, which meant he might be watching her place just as he might be watching Ben's place. With few options, going home with Jimmy seemed the smart thing to do: He would ride a different school bus to a different part of town. Meanwhile, he debated how he might go about running away, how far the money might take him, where he might go. He also debated buying his very own Nintendo.

Ben wore a sweatshirt with the hood up on the way to the school bus. Jimmy was big enough to use as a screen, and Ben followed him to the bus, head down, trying to force himself not to look up and give anybody a chance to see his face. His stepfather would be home about seven or eight, sometimes later. By then it would be dark, easier to move around without being seen. Ben was slowly formulating a plan. Survival was everything. He was no stranger to the game.

25

To confront a possible murderer face-to-face was the moment Daphne Matthews lived for. As departmental psychologist, she tolerated that aspect of her job which required her to listen to grown-up men with badges whine like little boys; she put up with the sexist environment of a cop shop that would never change. The boys could paint over their discrimination with regulations and the occasional slap on the wrist, but they would never be rid of it: Men who wore uniforms and oiled their guns on a regular basis saw women as a reservoir of soft flesh and a means to a hot meal and children. She helped out the alcoholic patrolman, the suicidal detective, the wife abuser, all as a means to an end: to interview killers, to see herself through herself, to explore the darker realm.

She walked a little lighter, stood a little taller, grinning non-stop as she hurried down the 1500 block in Ballard, home to SFD's Battalion 4 and its Marshal Five, Steven Garman. The firehouse was a beautiful brick structure built fifty years earlier, outclassing everything in the block. Ballard was Seattle's neighborhood of Norwegian ancestry, its southern boundary Salmon Bay and the Ship

Canal, whose piers and marinas housed much of the city's smaller commercial fishing fleet, the mom-and-pop vessels owned and operated by generations of Ballardites. For some, Ballard was the target of ethnic jokes, about smelling like fish and talking with accents; to others, an object of respect, one of the only neighborhoods in the city to have maintained its heritage and identity through the Californication of the mid and late eighties.

As Daphne climbed the stone staircase to the firehouse's second floor, she focused on establishing her own identity while preparing herself for whatever, whoever, Steven Garman turned out to be. She would begin with no preconceived notions of innocence or guilt, no judgment. She accepted that he was the recipient of the poetic threats, both of which had been accompanied by an as yet unidentified piece of melted green plastic. She intended to establish a rapport, whatever this required of her: professional psychologist, sexual flirt, disinterested bureaucrat, attentive listener. Such interviews required her to be an actress, and she loved the challenge. She could use her beauty to lull a man into an unwitting cooperation; women were a far tougher sell.

The firehouse had undergone little if any renovation. Daphne was struck by the depressing atmosphere, well aware of the role environment plays in psychology. There were photographs on the walls, black-and-whites of blazing out-of-control fires and a color copy of the mayor's official photograph. The requisite gunmetal-gray file cabinets, ubiquitous in all government offices, were full to overflowing, and the hallway smelled of a combination of chewing gum, hot dust, and industrial cleaner, as if something electric were burning somewhere out of sight—an odor appropriate for the office of a fire inspector.

Daphne knocked lightly on Garman's door and entered.

Garman was ensconced in a large leather chair in an immaculately kept office. He was a big, handsome man with soft brown eyes and a bushy mustache, younger than she had expected. There was a picture of Einstein on the wall, and another of Picasso. These seemed out of place to Daphne; a blue-collar fireman up on his Impressionism? What were his tastes in poetry? she wondered.

There was a color shot of the space shuttle *Challenger* at the moment of its explosion, the entrails of white fumes caught in a tight corkscrew spiral, shuttle debris frozen forever in a sky of blue. Daphne remembered exactly where she had been on that day. Garman caught Daphne staring.

"I worked on that one," Garman explained. "The debris reconstruction." Maintaining strict eye contact, he said, "Like working on a jigsaw puzzle with cranes."

"You were Air Force?"

"Does it show?" he asked, coming out of his chair and introducing himself with a handshake.

Maybe it did show, she thought, as she looked more closely. Maybe it helped explain the hard handshake and the riveting grip of those eyes. She wanted to like him right away, which only fueled her suspicion of him.

"Aircraft carriers, land-based, or what?" she asked.

"Bases," Garman answered, motioning Daphne into a chair.

The desktop held a couple of faded snapshots of Garman with a very young boy. Wheat fields. Blue sky and lots of it. Kansas? she wondered.

At the forefront of her thoughts were Emily Richland's mention of a military man and Boldt's information that the accelerant might be rocket fuel. Steven Garman, ex-Air Force, had to be considered carefully.

She said, "Sergeant Boldt wanted to thank you for not opening the most recent note."

"Listen, I wish I could tell you why he's sending this stuff to me. I really don't want any part of it."

"He?" Daphne asked. "What makes you think so?"

"A girl? No way, no how. I've been around fire most of my life, arson investigation for the past seven years, and I gotta tell you that in all that time I've never had a female suspect. Not once. Some women trying to be firefighters, sure, we've gone through that. Maybe a few teenage girls as accomplices to their boyfriends. But primary suspect? No, ma'am. This is a man lighting these fires. I'd bet my badge on it." He added, "Are you on Boldt's squad?"

"I'm part of the in-house task force," she answered. She felt compelled to skirt the truth. Garman might freeze up if he discovered she was a psychologist.

He had bright red cheeks and either dark skin or a 200-watt tan.

"The last note read, *Suddenly a flash of understanding, a spark that leaps across to the soul.* Mean anything to you?"

"He's one sick mother, you ask me. Sparks leaping? I don't know. You can overanalyze this stuff, you know? It's some shit-bird's way of playing heavy. It's a power trip—send this stuff ahead of time. He's a tease is what he is, but he's a killer too."

"It's Plato."

"Is that right? Plato? Probably got it off a box of cornflakes."

"Can I ask you a couple of personal questions?" she said, feeling for the cassette tape recorder that ran in the pocket of her coat, counting on it for transcripts later.

"Shoot."

"Did you know either Dorothy Enwright or Melissa Heifitz, personally or otherwise?"

"Certainly not," he said defensively, his voice strained with tension. He looked at her quizzically, suddenly more curious.

"The reason I ask is because it might help explain the threats coming to you—someone who knows you're connected with the women."

Garman said brusquely, "Not connected. I never knew either of them, never had so much as heard their names. Listen, I don't *want* these things. Have you guys checked with the other Marshal Fives, other firemen? Do we know for sure that I'm the only one getting them?"

"I haven't heard otherwise."

"Well, neither have I, but that doesn't mean anything."

"One of the things Sergeant Boldt has asked me to do is act as liaison. There's the Arson Task Force investigation, and there's the Homicide investigation," she said, indicating one of her hands for each department. Weaving her fingers together, she said, "My job is to help marry the two, now that Bahan and Fidler are so actively involved. We don't think the weekly meetings are enough, and Boldt is no fan of meetings to start with. He says everything gets talked about and nothing gets done."

Garman allowed a grin. "I'd go along with that."

"You've worked over two hundred arson investigations," she informed him, without consulting any notes. She wanted him to know she had been researching his record, wanted to have her eyes on him to judge any reaction. She was disappointed by the slight blush to his neck. He averted his eyes in what to her was an act of modesty. She realized she had lumped all firemen into cocky macho types despite her efforts to avoid prejudging.

"Suspicious fires," he corrected. "Some we call as arsons. Some not."

"Twenty-two arrests, nine convictions," she added.

"Listen, I don't keep notches on my gun or anything. It's a job. You quote those numbers, and it depresses me. We only clear fifteen percent of our cases. You guys, it's what? Seventy or eighty, I think? Vehicle fires are the worst. Last year we lost forty-five thousand vehicles in this country to suspicious fires. Forty-five thousand! Can you believe that? And we wonder why our insurance costs so much! Maybe half my stuff is vehicles. Most of the rest, abandoned structures. Every now and then revenge or a vanity fire.

"First thing I did," he continued, "when I connected the Enwright fire to that note, was go back through my files. That's what Boldt asked about; that's what you're going to ask too, so I'll save you the time. I can't place a single one of those shitbirds in something like this. A couple are still locked up, a couple more moved on. And every one of them was an obvious pour. Gasoline. You don't convict them on anything less. Every drop of gasoline has its own fingerprint, did you know that? Every batch that comes out of a refinery is a little bit different, chemically speaking. A guy does a pour; we pursue him as a suspect; we find a can of gas in his garage and, bingo! the lab gives us a match. At that point we convict. Anything short of that, they walk. And I'll be damned if I can make any one of my convictions stick for this thing."

"Your arrests?"

"Same thing."

"But why are you receiving these notes?" she asked. Again, Garman's neck went florid, but this time his soft eyes went cold and hard; he nervously rolled a pen between his fingers. It was not what she expected; she registered that look, not wanting to forget it.

"Marshal Five, I suppose. There are only a few of us. Could have mailed it to any one of us. I got lucky, I guess."

"Enemies?" she asked. "Anything in your past that might—"

"No," he interrupted. The pen began to spin again. She used it as a barometer.

"How about your Air Force serv—?"

"Listen!" he interrupted again. "What is it with all the questions about *me*? It's this torch we're after, okay?"

"He's chosen you for some reason, Mr. Garman."

"Steven," he corrected.

"Do we chalk it up to coincidence? To chance? Let me tell you something about Lou Boldt, if you haven't already heard it. The word *coincidence* isn't in his lexicon. It doesn't exist. He's a fatalist: Everything happens for a reason; there's an explanation for everything. These victims?" she asked rhetorically. "Chosen at random? Don't suggest that to Lou Boldt. There's a reason, no matter how obscure. And Boldt will find it, mark my words." The pen stopped moving. "These notes coming to you?" she asked in the same tone. "To Boldt there's a reason for that. No roll of the dice is going to explain it. And my job is to provide him with a believable explanation. There isn't a hell of a lot to go on in this one. *You* are about all he has. Why Steven Garman? he keeps asking. He wants an answer—and let me tell you something else about Boldt: He gets to the truth." The pen started spinning. "He gets the answers. You want to talk clearance rates? Boldt's is in the nineties—and we're talking over a fourteen-year career on Homicide. You want to talk amazing?" The red flush crept back into Garman's neck, and Daphne knew she had a live one. Like every other living human being, the man had secrets.

"So that's the question he wants answered: Why Steven Garman?" A thin film of perspiration glistened under his hairline. "I'm asking myself if it doesn't go back to your Air Force days. Something out of your past."

Garman swallowed heavily. His eyes were soft again, but they were scared. His pupils were dilated; he was mouth breathing.

Talk to me, she encouraged silently.

"Nothing I can think of," he said. His voice cracked and belied his words.

Got you!

She wanted to stay there the rest of the day, to keep working on him until he asked if she were hot or loosened his tie or opened a window. She had no idea what was hidden inside him, or if it bore any real significance to the investigation. People inflated their own self-worth. But she wanted to get at it. She wanted to sweat him. There were a dozen ways to trip him up, but she would go gently. Consult Boldt, play it his way. She said, "You mentioned that you were stationed on a base."

"It isn't relevant. Seriously. It was—what?—nine, ten years ago. The world changes a lot in ten years."

"You were married then," she said, adding a little tug to the hook.

Garman's eyes went to glass. If the pen had been a pencil it might have snapped between his powerful fingers. He glanced away, then back at her, then away again, unable to decide where his eyes should light. There was anger concealed within him. Rage. Its bubbles broke the surface, indicating the roiling boil below. "Exactly what is the purpose of this meeting?" he inquired tightly.

Instinctively, she switched off the role of interrogator. She had more than enough to present to Boldt. To push further without backup, without surveillance in place, would be a mistake. Garman was a suspect. She felt a flood of hot, almost sexual energy pass through her chest and through her pubis and down to her toes. "The purpose of this meeting was to get to know each other, that's all. I have the jump on you in that regard. Sorry if it came off as the third degree. Product of the profession, I'm afraid." She had saved one last gem, held it in her bag of tricks from the moment he had

confirmed his service in the Air Force. Kept it ready, compartmentalized in her mind, one hand on the door. She opened that door
by telling him, "The ATF lab believes the accelerant was some kind
of rocket fuel."

For a split second Steven Garman appeared chiseled in stone.
Daphne wished she had a camera.

She continued, "You see the possible connection to the Air
Force, I'm sure."

Garman seemed incapable of speaking. She knew that look.
She had seen it a dozen times: He was devastated. She had touched
his most sensitive nerve. Rocket fuel, she thought.

She looked over at the photograph of the *Challenger* explosion.
Framed beneath it, she recognized salvaged pieces of the craft
spread out on a hangar floor. He must be something of an expert.
That was how Garman looked too: blown apart, his world a mass
of smoke and flames.

26

"LOOKING good, Detective," a
female voice cooed from behind Boldt.

The sergeant turned in time to see the target of the comment,
John LaMoia, strutting his stuff—creased blue jeans and all—
heading in the general direction of his sergeant. LaMoia was style:
those pressed jeans, a crisp Polo shirt, ostrich cowboy boots, and a
rodeo belt for taking second in bronco riding when he'd been seventeen and stupid enough to enter. He had a bony, thin face, wiry
hair, and a prominent nose. Exactly what women saw in LaMoia
was a mystery to his senior in rank, a man whose job it was to
solve mysteries, but women flocked to him, even if one discounted
his reported conquests by half, which was only sensible given La-
Moia's tendency toward exaggeration.

Maybe, Boldt thought, it was that walk—confident and tall,
with a certain swagger to the hips. Maybe it was the large brown
eyes, or the way he used them so unflinchingly on his targets. Or
maybe it was simply his self-centered, cocky attitude, a quality that
clearly endeared him to the uniforms as well as the brass. Whatever the case, LaMoia led, he didn't follow. He'd have his own

squad someday if he wanted it. He'd have a wife and five kids, or a woman in every part of town, or both. One liked the man from a distance, trusted him up close, and could rely on him, unequivocally, in any situation. Boldt tried to disguise his admiration but not his fondness. He didn't need a loose cannon—and LaMoia trod dangerously close most of the time.

LaMoia began as he so often did, without any greeting. He simply rolled an office chair into Boldt's cubicle and straddled it backward, leaning his frame on the chair's hinged back. "Needless to say, you have no idea where any of this came from." The detective had enviable connections to the private sector: credit unions, insurance companies, banks. Some believed it was past or current women who supplied him with such broad access. Shoswitz said it had to do with LaMoia's military service, though Boldt thought it was nothing more than the man's undeniable charm and his incredible ability to network. If you met him, you liked him; if he asked a favor, one was offered. If he received a favor, valuable or not, he reciprocated. He knew people: how they thought, what they wanted. He knew the streets. He could probably supply anything to anyone, though Boldt turned a blind eye to this possibility. He had the knack. He was envied by most, hated by few, and always at the heart of controversy.

LaMoia placed a folder in front of Boldt. He explained the contents. "Enwright and Heifitz—their financials: credit cards, banking. Nothing there to connect one to the other—in terms of buying patterns, restaurants, health clubs. Nothing that I could see. But there it is for you."

"Too much cologne," Boldt said.

"It wears off. It'll be all right in another hour."

"We could suffocate by then."

"You like the shirt? It was a gift."

Boldt said, "You're saying there's nothing at all to connect them to each other? It doesn't have to jump out at you; I'd take something peeking around the corner. A department store they both shopped? A gas station?"

"The wheels."

"What?" Boldt asked.

"Has anyone worked the wheels?"

"Cars?"

"The houses were torched, right? Toast. So what was left behind?" LaMoia asked rhetorically.

"Their cars!" Boldt said, his voice rising. Investigations took several sets of eyes—that's all there was to it. Boldt had not given the victims' cars a second thought.

LaMoia shrugged. "Not that it means shit, mind you. How would I know? But I'm not seeing a hell of lot of physical evidence to chase. The wheels kinda jumped out at me—or maybe they just peeked around the corner," he teased.

"Check them out," Boldt offered.

"*Moi?* And here I was thinking you'd be more interested in the ladders." LaMoia studied his sergeant's expression.

Caught by surprise, Boldt asked, "The ladders?"

The grin was contrived, full of arrogance. "Are you feeling lucky?"

"I could use some luck."

"Werner ladders are sold through a single distributor here, which is good for us, but they do one hell of a lot of business, and the chances of our tracing sales back to a particular buyer would typically be zilch. But we got lucky for once. The model with this particular tread pattern had a manufacturing problem with the shoes—the little things bolted to the bottom of the ladder—and the production run lasted a total of six weeks. They issued a recall, which meant this particular model only stayed in stores for a little over two weeks. The distributor can account for all but a hundred of his initial inventory."

Boldt understood the significance of such a number. There were several hundred thousand people living in King County. LaMoia had just narrowed the field to one hundred.

The detective continued proudly. "With the one distributor it's a piece of cake to track down his retail customers: hardware stores, building supply, a couple rental shops. Count 'em! Seventeen in western Washington, but only *four* in King County. It's a high-end ladder—pun intended—the BMW of ladders, which is nice for us because they restrict the number of retailers allowed to carry them. Another thing: They're spendy things, meaning that when some Joe buys one he pays by check or credit card. Check it out: Not one of these ladders went out the door for cash. We've gotten that far already."

"You've already talked to the retailers?" Boldt felt a surge of optimism; LaMoia had a way of making even the smallest crack of light seem blinding.

"You bet. And this no-cash thing plays well for us," LaMoia continued. "Because all these places use computerized cash-register inventory systems, we've asked for itemized sales records. Some have been able to supply those directly to us. Others provided their cash register tapes for the couple of weeks in question."

Boldt felt all the air go out of him. "We're supposed to go through a bunch of cash-register tapes item by item, pulling ladder sales?" he complained. He considered this a moment. "I'd say forget it, John. Too big a long shot. Abort. Too time-consuming."

"Wait a second!" the detective objected, still wearing his trademark cocky expression. "Do you want to know who bought those ladders or not?"

"Not if it requires that kind of manpower. In the past, I might have handed off a job like that to one of the college criminology courses, let them do our dirty work, but—"

"Wait!" LaMoia repeated, interrupting. "You're not listening."

There were few if any other detectives who could talk to Boldt that way. He crossed his arms tightly and withheld comment. La-Moia was careful about how he played his cards; he would not have been so abrasive without something to back it up.

"We've got scanners," LaMoia said. "Hand-held jobs you run over a newsprint article, or an ad, or a map you want on your desktop machine. We've got OCR—optical character recognition—software that converts printed text from a scanned graphic image to data that word processors and database programs can manipulate. We're in the fucking computer age here, Sarge. Leaves Neanderthals like you in the dust."

"I understand scanning technology," Boldt countered. "Not real well," he conceded, "but the fundamentals."

"So what we're in the process of doing is *scanning* those cash register tapes. Doesn't take long at all. When that's done, we run OCR on them, and then we can search for anything we like: Werner, the word *ladder*, the product code, the price point. Guaranfuckin'-teed to give us a hit for every ladder sold. Every sale is accompanied by method of payment, check or credit card. The account number is right there on the tape. By this afternoon . . . tomorrow . . . day after, we'll have every sale of every ladder accounted for. We'll have a checking account or credit card number we can trace—right back to the individual buyer." He said proudly, "I'm telling you, Sarge, we've got this guy."

It was good work, and Boldt told him so. What he didn't bring up was that a hundred names might not get them any closer to the arsonist. They still needed the method of selection, the method of entry into the victims' homes. There were too many unanswered questions, too many loose ends. He didn't want to deflate LaMoia. They needed a decent break—perhaps the ladder was one of them, as LaMoia believed. The job of lead detective was to cast a dozen nets into the water and hope for fish in a few.

"Mind you," LaMoia interjected, "the ladder was probably ripped off. Ten to one, that's what we find out. But from what neighborhood, when? We might get something out of it yet, Sarge. You want me to chase down the wheels, I got no problem with that. But don't drop this ladder thing. I'm telling you: I can smell it. The ladder is a good thing. It's worth going after."

"It's good work," Boldt repeated, though with discouragement sneaking through. "Honestly."

"This computer stuff helps." For the first time, LaMoia sounded tentative. "Something's gonna break, Sarge. We've got six dicks on this thing working damn near around the clock. That ups our odds significantly."

"Get someone to look at the cars. Maybe they shopped the same convenience store, ate a burger at the same place; maybe that's how he spotted them. Maybe there's a wrapper on the floor or a receipt or something. A bag. I like the cars. I want to work the cars. But if you want the ladders this badly, John, go ahead and stay with them. We need a quick education about rocket fuel, as well. We need Bahan and Fidler to step up to the plate. An arson is another world, at least to this cop it is."

At that moment, Daphne burst through homicide's security door, her face flushed, her chest heaving. It was a Wonder Bra again, as far as Boldt could tell. She marched over to Boldt and LaMoia with a defiant stride that at once alerted the sergeant to some kind of breakthrough. He knew that fire; he had tasted it. There wasn't a male eye in the bull pen that missed her.

She stopped in front of them, attempted to collect herself, and, filling her chest with a lungful of air, said, "Steven Garman is hiding something. He knows a hell of a lot more than he's letting on. I want to hit him, and hit him hard. I'm going to crack the son-of-a-bitch wide open."

27

HE was late, and terrified of the consequences.

Ben had turned and locked the door from the inside before he ever smelled the guy.

He wasn't exactly thinking about it, but his mind was registering that a house, a home, is a sacred place, with sacred sounds and sacred smells; a place of familiar sounds and familiar smells; each with its own identity. These markers represent safety and sanctuary.

That smell did not belong: sharp, salty. Not at all the sour smell of booze he had come to live with, not the smell of a girl. It was . . .

The smell inside the back of the camper.

At that moment of realization, a hand clutched at his shoulder and Ben screamed and took off for the stairs. The low, angry voice said something from behind him, but Ben missed all but the sensation of it, the strange tingling inside him, coupled with the palpable echo of that hand locking onto his shoulder. His reaction was born of instinct: make it to his room, lock the door, get out the window, run like hell for Emily's, never come back.

A plan. Something upon which to focus. A few years earlier he might have thought about it. But he had learned that thought slowed you down. He glanced over his shoulder. The face belonged to Nick, the driver of the pickup truck, the guy with the burned hand and the leather belt. He was faster than Ben's stepfather, sober, in better shape. "My money, you little shit!" A flood of fear ran like a hot liquid over him. He slipped on the stairs. Nick grunted, precariously close behind. For Ben, the hallway seemed to shrink, the seconds shortened. The world was a painful place, a voice inside him reminded. Panic seized his chest. No more plan, only the certainty that bad things happened to bad people and that by taking the money he had made himself a bad person, had crossed over to where little separated him from the man scrambling quickly up the stairs.

The strength in the man's one good hand was not like anything human. It strangled his left ankle, tripping him, and his chin banged on the stairs as he was dragged downward. He bit his lip, and the metallic taste of his own blood filled his mouth. He understood vividly that it would not be the last blood spilled. The man dragged him closer, the rug burning against his face. Ben reared back with his right leg and drove the sole of his sneaker into the center of his attacker's forehead. The man let go.

Ben recaptured the stairs and once again began his ascent. The suffocating fear dissipated somewhat; Ben was in his element, he knew all about escape. This was a game he understood.

As he cleared the top of the stairs, Ben heard the man right behind him. He didn't look back. He didn't scream. He hurried.

His bedroom door loomed at the end of the hall—a safe passage, freedom.

The entire house shook as the back door slammed shut. "Kid?" the familiar drunken voice called out.

Ben couldn't remember a time when that voice had sounded so good.

The footsteps behind him paused.

"*Help!*" Ben shouted. "Look out!" A few steps from sanctuary,

Ben skidded to a stop. Nick was suddenly more concerned with
Jack. Ben's drunken stepfather wouldn't stand a chance.

"Who the fuck are you?" Jack had reached the bottom of the
stairs. "Get out of my fucking house!"

"He took my money!" the intruder shouted. "Your fucking
kid's a thief."

Ben hurried back to the top of the stairs. If his stepfather believed what he heard, Ben was dead. Nick was standing on the
stairs, looking down at Ben's stepfather. A gun was tucked into the
small of his back. "Dad!" Ben shouted, wondering where that
word had come from. Overcome by an unexpected protective instinct, he began to slide feet first down the stairs like a runner
going for home plate, undercutting the intruder, knocking him off
his feet, and propelling him toward Jack, who stood there unflinchingly, numb, gazing drunkenly at the spectacle.

A fight erupted between the two men, but it was nothing like
television. They rolled around on the floor in a tangle of limbs and
a blur of swearing. Ben clawed for purchase as he continued to
slide down the stairs, his chin banging against each step, his brain
rattled. He scratched and clawed, attempting to brake, finally grabbing for the handrail.

He stopped just short of the fray. The one called Nick was
pummeling his stepfather. Ben was strangely torn by the pleasure
he took in such a sight.

"I . . . want . . . my . . . fucking . . . money," the intruder said
with each hit. "My fucking money!" He slapped the man with that
grotesque paddle and hit hard with the opposing fist. There was
blood coming from his stepfather's swollen eye.

Nick glanced hotly over his shoulder and met the boy's eyes.
Ben felt his stomach go to jelly. Nick grabbed hold of Ben's shirt,
which tore off in his hand as Ben jerked away. Ben screamed, stumbled back, and fell.

The intruder sprang like a cat, blocking Ben's chance at the
front door. Boxing him in, he stepped closer, arms spread wide.
Ben threw a lamp at the man, turned over a chair, and reached for
the door of the downstairs closet, the only escape available to him.

From the corner of his one good eye, Ben picked up movement to his right; his stepfather was conscious and coming to his feet, unseen by the intruder, whose full attention was fixed on the boy. The man said clearly, "I want my fucking money."

Ben realized that by standing there he could buy his stepfather time to come up from behind. But instinct won out—he grabbed the closet doorknob and turned.

The intruder lunged for him. Ben kicked out, blindly connecting with something that cracked. The man let out a ferocious cry. Ben slipped into the darkness, yanked the door shut behind him, and held the doorknob tight. It rotated despite Ben's efforts. The door opened a crack. That burned hand, with its shiny pink skin, slipped through the crack in the door.

At that moment there was a huge crash. The flipper was smashed in the door and the intruder screamed again and withdrew it. Ben, retching, was sent reeling backward onto his butt, onto the trap door that led to the basement crawl space.

How many times had his stepfather cautioned him not to go down there? He had put the fear of God into him, which of course had done nothing to convince Ben to stay out. Even nailing the trap door shut had not prevented Ben from prying it open, but his subsequent expedition, his encounter with thick spider webs and a terrible smell, had finished off his curiosity once and for all. That had been over a year ago, and yet he still remembered that disgusting smell.

The enormous crash was followed by total silence. Someone's dead, Ben thought. He pulled hard on the trap door, shaking it left and right to wiggle free the nails he had loosened a year earlier. It opened. He slipped down inside, the trap door closing above him.

The crawl space was perhaps three feet high. He had to crouch in order to move. At the far end, light seeped through the cheap construction, casting a dusty gray light throughout. It smelled damp and foul, though better than a year before. Ben crab-walked toward the darkest corner, immediately caught in a sticky tangle of spiderweb. He smacked his head on a cold, sweating water pipe.

He froze in place as he heard slow footsteps overhead. Fear

pumped through him. The next sound was the closet door coming open. "Kid," the muffled voice cautioned, "you're pissing me off here."

The trap door squeaked as the man stepped on it. He was in the closet!

Ben inched toward the darkness, heart pounding, chest heaving, throat dry, skin prickly. A heavy foot thumped loudly on the trap door, testing. It thumped again.

Ben dragged himself deeper into the darkness, consumed by spiderwebs, convinced that his stepfather was dead and his own death imminent.

Light flashed sharply behind him as the trap door came open. "Don't fuck with me, kid. You're pissing me off something bad." He tested. "Kid?"

Ben stopped, suddenly wanting to answer. He didn't care about the money; he would gladly give it up. He opened his mouth to reply, but nothing would come out. Slowly, carefully, as if someone had let the air out of him, Ben laid himself down prone on the dusty gravel. He would hide. It was all that was left.

The ground was disturbed there, humped, the gravel mixed with dried mud. He tried to make himself as thin, as low, as invisible as possible. The intruder's leg entered through the hatch. The man was coming down after him.

Ben had run out of options. He couldn't think what to do. Face pressed low to the gravel, he peered toward the open hatch and the flood of light there.

Ben's one good eye shifted focus, the resulting perspective out of proportion. It was not gravel or stone or mud that he saw. It was not the wooden supports rising at equal intervals from poured concrete pads to support the floor overhead. Nor was it the pair of legs groping for where to land. All this remained within his field of vision, yet all that Ben could see, the entire focal point of his attention, was an arc of dull yellow metal a few inches in front of his face.

He reached out and pinched the yellow metal between his fingers. A ring. A gold ring.

At once he knew. It spoke to him in the familiar soft, tender, feminine voice that he had longed to hear. Hearing that voice brought a tightness to his throat and blurred his eyes.

His mother's wedding ring. He knew this absolutely and without doubt. His mother's grave.

Impelled by anger, rage, and grief, without a second thought, he sprang to his feet, crouched low, and flew through the crawl space, fingers clutching the ring. He charged wildly, knocking over the man named Nick without any outward effort other than the sheer determination to be gone from this place as fast as his feet would carry him. The intruder fell back. Ben leaped through the trap door access and hurried out of the closet.

His stepfather was just coming to, dazed and badly beaten. Ben stopped abruptly and stared down at him. Disappointment drained him: The man was *alive*. Their eyes met. Ben held up the ring for him to see. He reared back and kicked with more force than he knew he possessed. Jack's head snapped back sharply and thudded onto the floor.

Ben had never dared raise a hand to the guy. The realization of what he had just done, coupled with the knowledge of his mother's grave and the presence of the intruder behind him, sent him out the door at a full sprint. The call to 911 would come, but not until he reached a pay phone several blocks later. "I want to report a murder," the terrified young voice was recorded as saying. "He killed my mother! She's under the house!"

For the second time that youthful voice was recorded by the Seattle Communications Center. This time, the address given by the boy matched the address of an earlier recorded call, though that connection was missed. The center's computer-aided dispatch system assigned the call to a patrol car near Seattle University. The driver of that car, officer Patrick Shannon, would find an unconscious man on the living room floor, the victim of an assault.

As directed, he would hold this man for questioning and pursue evidence of a possible body in the crawl space.

A second car was dispatched to the pay phone from which the

911 call had been made. The phone was back on the hook, the receiver warm to the touch.

Far away from this phone, a small boy sped through the night. Running, running, running. Running until his legs would carry him no more.

28

BOLDT was thinking that there are many shades of gray, many moods to accompany these shades, and not all dark, as many people believed. There was the gray of morning, leaning more toward the color of lint in a laundry dryer; there was the gray of noon, a dripping gray that bleeds from the sky and enhances the lush greens of the ivy and the grass; there was the gray of evening, dark and foreboding, warning of a pitch-black nighttime that turns all men blind and all children scared. One learned to live with gray in Seattle. The gray of moods. The gray area between right and wrong.

Sergeant Lou Boldt was one of many who saw the paperwork on the decomposed female corpse discovered in a crawl space. Boldt felt convinced all they needed was a few hours in the Box with the suspect. They would win the confession. A grounder, as the saying went. If this failed, Dixie would need to ID the remains, and they would work up a connection between the victim and the suspect. Time-consuming, but feasible. It was just the kind of case that attracted Boldt, though, due to the arsons, all he could do was manage it from a distance. Based on neighbors' statements, city services was looking for a young boy believed to be the suspect's stepson and more than likely the source of the anonymous 911 call that had led to the discovery of the corpse. To Boldt, it added up to another runaway somewhere on the streets of Seattle—a possible witness, a scared and terrified young boy, whose picture had been found at the house and was already part of the case file.

He had no choice. Without telling anyone, Boldt left the office and drove the streets looking for that face. KPLU announced a Clifford Brown cut. Boldt pumped the brakes. The pool cars weren't serviced well anymore.

Traffic was light for a change. He tried the streets of downtown, drove aimlessly over to Capitol Hill, and then to the address listed in the file. No face, no little boy. He stopped at a supermarket and shopped. He drove home and left off the groceries and tried to speak Spanish to Marina, who looked after his kids. He hugged Miles and kissed Sarah and wondered what the streets were like for a twelve-year-old.

Back in the car, jazz found its way into his bones, like the lingering warmth that follows a bath. It lived inside him. He let it out as often as possible, not often enough. He thought that people who lived without music lived tragic lives, but realized that others would say the same about modern art, or poetry, or even dog racing. Each to his own. For him it was jazz, sad and dreary at the moment, like the noon sky. He felt gray all over.

Bear Berenson owned and operated Joke's On You, a comedy club and music bar with a fish-sandwich menu, a mirrored porthole behind the bar, and, during the evenings, several coeds in their late teens working the tables. On any given night, Bear could be found, slightly stoned, moving between his customers' tables, one eye on the backsides of the coeds and the other on the bartender, to make sure he wasn't failing to use the register. After a protracted legal battle with the federal government, Bear, although the victor, had failed to save The Big Joke, his first club and a longtime haunt of Lou Boldt and other cops. Joke's On You was in Wallingford, up on 45th, a long way from downtown and his former clientele. This time Bear was aiming jointly at the imports to the U, the young kids with their parents' credit cards and loose change, and the yuppies turned parents who had abandoned the Beamers for the Caravans. Wallingford had changed a lot in the last ten years, and Bear was there to take advantage. The five-to-seven jazz and cocktail hour was for what Bear called the Headin' Homes, the young professionals too tired to think, too tired to play mom or dad, but strong enough to stop for thirty minutes of courage. At nine the place rolled into stand-up, the drink prices dropped by a dollar, and the waitresses shed short skirts for black jeans and white tops with a logo of a laughing bear on the breast pocket. In jokes.

At three in the afternoon there were two barflies at the bar, a haze of smoke in the air, and a man behind the bar playing solitaire on a laptop computer. He was a barrel-chested guy but with droopy shoulders, black hair—lots of it—and thick lips. His eyes looked perpetually sad; his lips held back a cynical grin. Bear always looked like he knew something he shouldn't.

"Rip Van fucking Winkle," Bear said, the partial grin giving way to a full smile. "How goes, Monk?"

Thelonious Monk was Boldt's favorite jazz pianist—he played the entire Monk book. Bear had called him this forever. "Just like the Energizer bunny," Boldt said.

"Lots of dead people keeping you busy?"

That caused one of the two barflies to take note of Boldt. This man nodded at Boldt and Boldt said hello. "Enough to keep me busy," Boldt answered.

"Obviously too busy to play," Bear complained. Boldt, who had virtually owned the Headin' Home happy hour piano slot, had passed it off to Lynette Westendorff, a friend who knew more about jazz than Boldt did police work.

"You don't like her playing?"

"She's fine. Better than fine. And she's better-looking too."

"And still you're complaining," Boldt said, reaching the bar then but not taking a seat on one of the vinyl stools.

Bear shrugged. "Gotta stay in shape," he said.

Bear's eyes were bloodshot. He'd been smoking pot already. He used to wait until eight or nine at night, but since the move he started midafternoon and smoked right through until closing. Boldt had tried several times to put him off the habit, but when the friendship seemed threatened he had backed off—he rarely even joked about it anymore. Bear was probably his most consistently loyal friend.

"How long?" Bear asked, meaning the investigation.

It was Boldt's turn to shrug.

Bear poured his two patrons a drink on the house, locked the cash register, and led Boldt to a far corner table under a large black speaker cabinet from where the owner could keep one eye on the bar. "Afternoon business is really cooking," he said, gesturing toward his two drunks.

"Lunch?"

"A little better. I don't know: You like those curlycue fries or good old plank fries?"

"Curlycues."

"Yeah, me too. You can get an extra quarter for them, but they come frozen, or else you gotta do 'em yourself and they're time-intensive. The plank fries we can do fresh—simple, easy. I don't know."

"Fresh curlycues," Boldt advised. "They add a touch of class."

"Probably right. We could use a touch of something around here."

"New location. It takes time."

"It takes luck. And advertising. Good talent on stage, and a couple of babes working the floor. I don't know; I miss downtown."

"It's going to work," Boldt encouraged.

"Not so far it isn't. People don't want to part with their money, that's the thing. It's not like the eighties. And the stand-up humor has gone into the toilet—it's all fuck this and fuck that. These kids don't know anything about structure."

"There's always *Monday Night Football*," Boldt teased. Bear hated football, refused to show any of the games.

"Yeah, and opera," he followed quickly. "The subtitles certainly changed the experience for me."

Boldt warmed and smiled, realizing that it had been a while since he'd done so, and this was followed by the thought that life is choices, not fated paths, and perhaps his choices had been misguided lately. This was exactly why he stopped to visit with Berenson occasionally: perspective.

"I've resorted to backgammon and Monopoly," the bar owner admitted reluctantly. "Had a Monopoly tournament last Saturday and packed the place with college kids. Sold a lot of beer. The winner gets a free meal."

"The loser gets two free meals," Boldt quipped.

They exchanged grins and were silent a moment.

"Is it Liz?" Bear asked.

"You a mind reader?"

"A psychic."

It reminded Boldt of the case. Of Daphne. The wrong reminders just at that moment.

"I say something," Bear asked.

"Liz is okay."

"That means things are fucked."

"No, they're okay."

"Oh, yeah. I know you. Is that why you gave Lynette the gig? Listen, here's the thing. My take on the problem with adulthood," began the barroom philosopher who sought to remain as perpetually stoned as possible, as childlike as possible with his bawdy jokes and quick one-liners, "is that you grow up as a kid saying exactly what you're thinking. You know the way kids do: 'Hey, look, Uncle Peter's not bald anymore, but his hair's a different color in the middle!' That sort of shit. And as a kid you do basically what you feel like—torture little sisters, take clocks apart. Only over time do you find out what's acceptable and what's not. Which is the entire problem; this way, we teach kids to get it wrong. Because as adults it's just the opposite: We rarely say what we're honestly feeling or thinking, and we end up doing a lotta stuff we'd just as soon not do. Someone at a dinner party asks how you're doing, and you answer that everything's fine, when in fact it might suck big-time but you're not about to say it; you get up at six every morning, take the trash out, and drag yourself off to a job you hate, all for those three weeks of vacation a year. What's that all about? How is it we end up getting it all so screwed up?" He added, "As a parent, Monk, you owe it to yourself to think about this." Wide-eyed, he trained his attention on Boldt. After a moment he asked, "So?"

"Things with Liz are okay."

"You or her?" Bear asked.

"Her," Boldt answered.

"Serious?"

"Don't know."

Bear said, "It's work. Your work, not hers. Right? That's why Lynette; that's why the long face and the heavy heart. This is the way you get when it starts to eat at you. I know you, Monk. You need to lighten up. You should come by and play a couple of sets. You should have never stopped drinking."

Boldt laughed, amused that Bear always simplified unhappiness to a lack of appropriate drugs. "My stomach stopped me drinking, not me." He had never been a serious drinker anyway, and Bear knew this, but the two carried on a constant dialogue centered on Boldt's taking up a few beers every now and again. Bear couldn't stand the thought of anyone approaching life entirely sober. It frightened him, like a kid afraid of the dark.

"I'm hunting a guy who's burning women to death," Boldt said, using a verb he seldom voiced aloud. It cast him in the light of a predator instead of a protector. He preferred the latter. But the truth was that in an open-ended homicide case the detective often became a hunter, like a rancher trying to identify and trap whatever animal was decimating the herd. Bear looked shocked. He furrowed his brow and squinted across the table. Boldt answered the expression. "What went wrong, Bear? Where did we cross that line, and what drove us there? You know? It's not the same as it once was. People will tell you it is, but it isn't."

"I agree," Bear said in a soft voice; the comedian had left the room. "The rest of us read the headlines, Monk. You guys live with this shit."

"I think it's God," Boldt said immediately, because he'd been thinking about this for a long time and Bear was the kind of friend he could say this to. "Or, more to the point, a lack thereof. I was raised with church. Sunday school, that sort of thing. You?"

Bear nodded. "Temple."

Boldt continued. "Yeah, and in all those stories, all those lessons, you had good and evil, God and the Devil—no matter what significance you put in either—but they were there, and you had faith, some sense of faith, some belief in something larger than yourself, no matter how small or on what level. Maybe you look at the night sky a little differently or maybe you go to church twice a week, but it's there, it's *in* you. And without it, without that sense of God, there's no flip side, there's nothing to fear, and as much as I hate to say it, maybe fear is a good thing in this case. A sense of God—whatever you choose to call it—gives you a soul; without a soul you're left with unfocused eyes and a sense that you're at the top of the food chain and anything goes. And that's what you see in a killer's eyes: no humanity, no consciousness, no thought or concern for their fellowman. Some kid blows away his best friend over a pair of sneakers—so what? I'm telling you, it's no act. They have no soul. I interrogate these guys, I look them right in the eye, and I'm telling you they're beyond recognition. They aren't human. I don't know what they are."

"I've seen it," the bar owner said, nodding in agreement and pulling the skin on his cheeks so that his eye sockets stretched open and he looked slightly monstrous. "I think it's television. The movies. It desensitizes us. All that killing, the blood, even the sex—and I gotta admit, I *like* seeing the sex; it's about as close as I've gotten lately! But that's what I'm saying about the fuck jokes, you know? We've bottomed out. The only thing that draws a laugh is bathroom humor about your mother and father's sex life. You should hear some of the stuff."

"I'm hunting this guy and part of me doesn't want to catch him; I don't want to know. Daffy, she's all eager to interview this guy, see what makes him tick—take his clock apart. But what if you open up that clock and there's nothing inside? Come to find out it's only a face and hands disguising an empty shell? What then? What if there's nothing to learn? Nothing to change? Nothing to gain? Nothing to do?"

"You need to lose this one, Monk. Pass it off to someone else. Spend more time with Miles. Come back and play happy hour for me."

"He sends pieces of melted green plastic and notes that look like the work of an eight-year-old."

"What's with the melted plastic?" Berenson asked.

"No one knows."

The melted plastic remained important to Boldt. He had given it to Lofgrin for analysis but had yet to hear back.

"Green plastic," Berenson said thoughtfully. "You got a weird job, you know that?"

Boldt nodded.

"How big?"

Boldt indicated the size: smaller than a quarter, bigger than a nickel. Berenson loved puzzles.

Berenson speculated. "Not poker chips . . . whistles—they must make green whistles—jewelry?" he asked. "Some kind of jewelry? A trinket, a key chain, something like that?"

"Jewelry, maybe." Boldt liked this idea.

They didn't talk for a while. One of the barflies signaled Bear, and the bar owner served him another drink. Boldt went over to the stage, climbed up and opened the piano, and played a long, rambling mood piece in E minor. It released him.

In the corner, he saw a stack of six backgammon boards and a matching number of Monopoly games. And there was Bear, in a chair, arm resting on the stack of board games, eyes closed, listening.

Bear said, "You could have done it for real, you know? The music. You're that good, Monk."

"I'm not that good—you're just that stoned—and I can't feed a family on what you pay." It was a sensitive issue; perhaps Bear had forgotten; perhaps not, Boldt thought. Boldt had taken a two-year leave of absence following the Cross Killer investigation; only Daphne had possessed the persuasive techniques to lure him back to the department. For those two years he had been a good father and a better husband. He had been a happy hour jazz pianist, and Liz had brought home the paycheck. Those times seemed like a decade ago, instead of the five years it had been.

Bear was a little too stoned. He leaned his weight on the stack of board games, and the pile went over and onto the floor, spilling with a racket. "Hey," Bear said, his lap piled with play money, "I'm rich." He held up the money. "I'll give you a raise."

Boldt knocked off the trumpet fanfare that starts a horse race.

"Then again," Bear said, down on his hands and knees to clean up the mess, "maybe you won, not me." He threw something toward the piano player, and Boldt caught sight of it out of the corner of his eye in time to lean back, swipe the air with his large right hand, and snag whatever it was.

He glanced down into his open palm and saw there a small green plastic cube in the shape of a building, complete with a peaked roof, used to mark the purchase of a house on the Monopoly board: green . . . plastic. . . .

Boldt said, somewhat breathlessly, understanding the significance of the find, "A house!"

"A game," said Berenson.

Boldt pocketed the small green house, gave his friend an appreciative hug on the way out, and headed directly to the police lab, where he met up with Bernie Lofgrin, who, anxious to leave for the day, nonetheless understood the possible importance of the rush job that Boldt requested.

With the sergeant looking on, Lofgrin ran a comparison analysis of the melted green plastic sent by mail and that of the game piece delivered by the sergeant. He did so on the lab's Fourier

Transform Infrared Spectrophotometer, a device Boldt could name only with a struggle and which Lofgrin referred to by its initials, FTIR. The results offered the first real sense of progress: The two green pieces of plastic were identical in chemical composition; he had a match. The torch was sending melted Monopoly houses as part of his threats. Boldt tried to reach Daphne, hoping to connect some kind of psychological significance to the find—he had a lead and he wanted to run with it; he felt an urgency, a need to follow this to completion—but she didn't answer, either at her houseboat or at the Adler mansion.

As Boldt headed home, he barely focused on Aurora Avenue, slowing when the red taillights brightened, speeding up as they grew distant, following the other cars but not entirely conscious of them. His focus was on Steven Garman and Daphne's suspicions that he knew more than he was letting on. He pulled into the drive and sat quietly behind the wheel for several long minutes.

Liz's car was there—and suddenly he was flooded with an entirely different set of suspicions and concerns.

29

DAPHNE knocked on the door of the purple house with the neon sign in the window and then hurried off the front porch to get a look down the driveway. She was uncomfortable to be a white woman, alone, in that neighborhood. Seattle was not a racially tense city like some other American cities, but gangs were of increasing concern: Asian against Asian, black against black. Women were occasionally gang-banged, sometimes to death. Car jackings were on the rise. And there was Daphne, white, attractive, driving a red Honda Prelude with aluminum mags, suddenly well aware of the ghetto surroundings.

He was small, and he was fast. A white boy, ten or twelve years old. He dodged around the corner of the house, froze as he saw Daphne, and then took off like a shot.

The front door came open and Emily Richland stood there in a black pants dress with an embroidered yellow robe over her shoulders. It took her a second to locate Daphne in the driveway.

"Is he your son?" Daphne asked.

"Leave him out of this," Emily protested.

"Is he?"

"No."

Daphne approached the woman, who stepped back inside and made an attempt to shut the door. "I wouldn't," Daphne warned.

Emily considered this and hesitated, the door still partially open.

"I haven't heard from you," Daphne told her.

"I haven't heard from *him*."

"How do I know that?" Daphne asked.

"I would call you."

"Would you? I don't think so." Daphne forced her way inside and closed the door. "Who's the boy?" she asked, pushing past the psychic into the lavishly painted room. "And don't play with me, or you and the boy will end up downtown, having your pictures taken and rolling your thumbs and forefingers in little boxes. The press loves to destroy people like you."

"You do whatever it is you have to do. You're pathetic. You know that? He hasn't been back. I would have called."

"You con people for a living. How am I supposed to trust you? The boy is part of it," Daphne said, keeping the boy's role in the foreground. The boy was clearly the wild card, the way to get at the woman. "Maybe you lied about this man with the burned hand."

"No, he was here."

"Maybe I can help the two of you," Daphne offered. She caught a flicker of what looked like hope in the woman's eyes. "Is he from a bad home? A runaway?"

Emily looked hateful. "You leave him out of this."

"I'll do that. I'll leave him out of it, but you're going to have to help." She wandered around the bizarre room, dragging her finger along the naked women painted there. "City Services would be interested in talking to the boy."

"Don't do this."

"Help me!"

"How can I? You don't believe me. He *has not* been here. Do you ever listen, or do you just like to threaten?"

The question stung Daphne, though she hid it by looking at the murals. She removed a photograph of Steven Garman from her pocket, crossed the room, and handed it to the psychic. "Is that the man?" she asked. "Look closely," she said as Emily began to shake her head. "Forget the face hair. Look at the eyes, the shape of the head."

"Absolutely not. Not even close."

"You're sure?"

"Positive."

"You would swear to that in a court of law?" With each question, Daphne studied the woman's face, putting little value in her words. But what she saw there was discouraging. Emily Richland had never seen the man before. Daphne felt crushed. She had convinced herself that Garman could have created the burned hand for himself as a disguise for the sessions with the psychic.

"It's not him. Not even close."

From sour to sweet: Daphne produced a hundred-dollar bill. "I need an *exact* description. You withheld some details last time, didn't you?" Every snitch did so, in order to collect more money a second time. Emily regarded the money carefully but seemed reluctant to accept it. Daphne said, "Or maybe the boy can fill in some of the blanks."

Emily bristled, took the money, and began a thoughtful and exacting description of her client, covering some of what she had told Daphne the first time around but embellishing upon it greatly. She mentioned Sea-Tac airport, a possible drug deal. She described the man in more detail. An image formed in Daphne's mind—the close-cut hair, the strong build, the farm or rodeo background. The more she heard, the less she liked it. The man known to Emily as Nick—this, from the back of his belt—did not make the most likely suspect for a person quoting Plato. *Two* suspects? she wondered, knowing that even the suggestion of such a thing would send Boldt ballistic. A conspiracy? What would that do to the investigation?

"Perhaps I'm wrong about this," she said, hearing the words tumble out of her mouth and wondering from where they came. There were times she seemed possessed of two minds: one eager to solve the case, interview the suspect ahead of everyone else, even the arresting officer if possible; the other, to help keep things less complicated for Boldt and his squad, to ease the tension, improve the working environment. Most of the time, these two objectives existed in direct opposition to one another and forced her to make a choice. She heard her words and wondered if she had subconsciously already made it.

"Perhaps you are," Emily said spitefully, no longer holding the one hundred dollars: part psychic, part magician. The money had disappeared.

"I want to talk to the boy."

"No."

"This isn't up for negotiation," Daphne warned. "The more trouble you create for me, the more you bring upon yourself. At the moment, we're staying clear of warrants and statements and trips downtown. At the moment, as far as you're concerned, it's still business as usual. You're open; you're seeing clients, I presume. As far as I know, the kid is still working the cars for you the way he worked mine. That can all change, and quite quickly. No work, no little boy. The prudent thing to do at a time like this, Ms. Richland, is carefully weigh one's options. Obstinacy for its own sake is such a terrible waste."

"The boy stays out of it," the other said defiantly.

"By attempting to protect others, we often endanger them further." Daphne took a few steps closer. "Are you sure you want this for him?" She asked, "Tell me how you know what you know. A drug deal at Sea-Tac. Are you sure? Did *you* see it, or did *he?* What if it isn't drugs? What if it puts both of you at risk? What if you or the boy were seen at the airport?"

Emily's throat bobbed and an eyebrow cast a lower slant, despite her admirable attempts to prevent any such reaction. Her eyes darted nervously, searching Daphne's.

"It's my duty to tell you this, although quite honestly I would prefer not to, because I don't want to frighten you any more than you already may be. Two women about your age, with about your looks, are dead. You will have heard about the arsons, they've been all over the news. This man Nick, or perhaps someone close to him, may be responsible. The military connection works for us . . . the burned hand. You saw the possible connection, or you wouldn't have offered your services to us."

"You're trying to scare me," Emily said. "Take a look around at this neighborhood and ask yourself if I scare easily. My age, my looks? Come on! You think he's targeting me? You think I'm next?" She grinned and laughed. "Where do you get your material, Detective?"

"I'm not a detective," Daphne clarified, for the sake of the tape recorder running in her pocket.

"But you said—"

"I told you that I'm working on the investigation. That's true."

"You told me you were a cop."

"Also true. Just not a detective. Listen, my role is unimportant here. It's *your* role that's of concern to me. And yes, for all I know, he's targeting you. We have no idea how he targets his victims, how he rigs the structures, how he gains access." She hesitated. "Did you ever leave him alone in this room?"

All color drained from Emily's face. She collected herself well enough not to allow her panic to filter into her voice, but Daphne saw it all over her: the rapid blinking, another attempt at a dry swallow, the twitch in her left eye. She had left the man alone.

Glancing around nervously, Daphne said, "I think it might be to our mutual advantages to work together."

"You're messing with me to get at—to get at the boy." She had almost slipped and spoken his name aloud. Daphne wondered: If she had pushed a little harder would the name have come out? Everything was measured in degrees. She didn't always guess right.

"Messing with you?" she questioned. "What I'm telling you is that we can't protect you. That protection stuff works fine in the movies, but not in real life. You think we can afford the manpower to watch your place?" Daphne was hoping to confuse the woman. The truth was mixed: They could afford the surveillance, but witness protection on a local level was nonexistent. Daphne's role was not to deliver the truth, nor did any regulation explicitly state she was obliged to. Suspects were routinely told falsehoods in order to win confessions; it was one of the techniques of interrogating, tricky at best, and a matter of pride for police entering the Box: The best liar wins. "At best you could hope for the bomb squad to do the two-step through here and try to sniff out any devices. We'd bring someone in like he was a client of yours, in case your place is being watched."

"Shut up!" Emily threw her head back and forth, her hair whipping the air. "Stop it!"

"But I need the boy for that," Daphne continued, knowing she had finally gotten through to the woman. "I have to show my sergeant that there's some currency here, some give-and-take. You must understand that. On some level I know you do. Trust me. Let me work with you and the boy together—no warrants, no arrests. Just a little collaborative effort to put this guy Nick where he belongs."

Emily's face showed rage and resentment. Daphne wondered if the woman might strike out at her.

At the same time, Daphne hoped she had cracked the shell, hoped Emily might give her the benefit of the doubt, prayed for a shot at the boy. Child witnesses were among the best. Little kids and old ladies—Daphne knew the statistics. Juries and judges loved them. If the boy had seen something, if Daphne could get it on tape or in a statement, Boldt would be beside himself.

Suddenly, Daphne questioned her own motivations. Was this effort for the betterment of the investigation or to please Boldt? Was she trying to solve a crime or win points? Her belly knotted in pain, and she felt light-headed and weak in the knees.

"You're lying to me," said the woman in front of her, a woman as familiar as she was with reading body language. "We can have all the currency you want, but the boy is not in the equation."

Daphne recovered nicely. "They have electronic sniffers. Have you seen one? A guy comes in here with a briefcase and he leaves, telling you if the place is rigged or not. Five, ten minutes. Peace of mind. Are you a target? I don't know. I wish I could tell you that you weren't." The sniffers were for hydrocarbon accelerants and certain drugs. She'd never heard of one for rocket fuel. She didn't share this. "Let us help you. Do this my way and it's completely low-profile. Stonewall and you lose control. You strike me as a woman who wants to maintain control."

The woman looked confused. Daphne didn't like that. She anticipated Emily's reaction before it ever came.

"Get out of here." Emily stepped to within inches of Daphne's face, strong and defiant. "You're here uninvited, and you're not welcome. I'll file a complaint against you. Don't think I wouldn't."

"You're overreacting," Daphne cautioned. "Take a minute to think about this." She absolutely *hated* losing. There was nothing worse. Her job was about wins, about steering people away from some thoughts and toward others.

"Out!" Emily reduced the space farther, closing to where Daphne could feel the warmth of her breath across her face.

"I'm going," Daphne conceded. She stormed out, more upset with herself than with the psychic.

The outside air was not cold, but it stung her face. She stood on the front steps for a moment, admiring the quirky six-foot metal sculpture of the world that sat on Emily's front lawn. And then a frightening feeling overcame her: She was being watched. She glanced around—but casually, carefully—and saw no one.

She walked a little more quickly to her car, feeling unsafe and exposed. And as she drove away, a little faster than polite for a quiet neighborhood, she wondered who had been watching. The boy? Or was it the arsonist?

How much to tell Boldt and how much to keep to herself? How much was paranoia, how much real?

And how was she going to feel if and when Emily became the next victim?

30

ANOTHER poem. Garman had delivered it downtown while Boldt had been visiting Bear. Both his pager and cellular phone had sounded nearly simultaneously. He drove home to tell Liz in person that it was going to be a long night. He didn't want to tell her by phone. The claw-foot tub was the first place he checked, placing his large hands against the side wall, searching for evidence of lingering warmth. Stone cold, like his heart. He felt an immediate pang of regret. Trust had been the cornerstone of their renewed attempt at marriage, and here he was, creeping around and feeling up bathtubs.

Together they put the kids to bed, Boldt looking for a chance to tell her he was going to leave her alone. Getting the kids down took longer than he expected. Things rarely went the way he expected. He finally sat down to a reheated dinner at a kitchen table cluttered with several days of mail—bills, mostly.

"You know," she said, absentmindedly opening a piece of mail, "I was thinking that I might leave Miles with you and take another weekend up at the cabin." The announcement—for that was what it was, an announcement, not a request—stunned him.

She had never been a big fan of the cabin. What had changed? "Maybe this weekend."

"By yourself?" he blurted out.

"No, with my lover," she snapped sarcastically. Or was she using sarcasm to hide the truth? Would she, when he finally found out, remind him of this evening when she had mentioned a lover over the dinner table? "I'm whipped, Lou. Burned out. I could use a weekend by myself. I'll take Sarah, of course. A good book." She added, "Not away from you, just this." She motioned around the room. He knew she meant him. She meant Miles, who at three and a half was a handful. Although a good mother—especially, he thought, for a working mother—she reached these tolerance points with Miles; it wasn't the first time. More important, he thought, trying to see the positive, she trusted him to take good care of their son.

"It's not the best time," he answered honestly, aware that he had worked three seven-day weeks in a row. Aware he needed to get back downtown. "This case—"

"Oh, come on," she complained. "Marina can help you. Besides, you can't work *every* weekend. Phil won't allow that. If he knew the schedule you were pulling he'd throw a fit." Then she caught on and he winced before she voiced it. "You haven't filed for the overtime, have you," she stated incredulously. Liz ran the household budget—being the banker in the family—and Boldt knew he had serious trouble with this discovery: unpaid time at work was time he could be with the kids, or working on the house, or spending time with her. This could provoke a firestorm.

"It isn't as simple as that. I'm sort of on loan to the fire department. I'm essentially pulling double duty as it is; managing the squad and working these arsons."

Her expression remained hard. "If you're expecting violins, forget it. I need this time, Lou. That's what I'm trying to tell you. If I could do it without Sarah—if I could express enough milk—I'd leave her with you too, but I can't right now."

Boldt went over to the sink to pour himself a glass of filtered water and noticed immediately that the view out the window was

remarkably cleaner. He noticed this because cleaning the windows
was his responsibility and he had let this duty slip, and it seemed
inconceivable that Liz had washed them, which meant she had
paid to have them washed, and this in turn helped him to understand her independent and somewhat foul mood: If he slacked off
on his jobs around the house, she came in behind him and hired
them done, and it annoyed her to no end. He asked, "Is it the
windows? Is that it? You got them washed, didn't you? Listen, I
meant to."

"No, it's not the windows," she countered.

"You got them washed," he objected. He could see that they
had been washed—and a good job at that. Professional. He even
felt a little envious at how good a job it was.

"It was a mistake," she said, clearly frustrated at his attempt
to steer her away from the issue of the overtime pay. "The point is,
if you're not filing for over—"

"Getting the windows washed was a mistake? I don't think
so. They look great to me." He hoped he might be able to press
this toward humor and deflect her anger, because taken together
the two added up to real trouble: He wasn't charging the department for his overtime, and he wasn't home enough to do his
chores, so the overtime pay wasn't there to cover the added expense of hiring people to pull his weight.

Speaking in a patronizing, condescending way in which she
accented every syllable, she told him, "A mis-take. The . . . wrong
. . . house. I did not hire any window washer. *You* are the window
washer. The guy was off by one street. It was a mis-take . . . on . . .
his . . . part."

Boldt smelled a scam. "Did he try and charge you for—"

"No. We cleared it up. He packed up, and he took off. He was
perfectly nice about it." She lightened up a little. "In fact," she
said, "he did a pretty good job."

"Better than that other guy you've got," he said, meaning
himself.

She came out of the chair then and, suppressing a slight grin,
approached her husband and threw her arms around his neck and

drew them close together. He felt like stealing a glance at his watch, but he didn't. "Why is it I can't stay mad at you?"

He felt better than he had in ages. He didn't want to let go. He clasped his arms around her waist and squeezed tightly, and she got the message and squeezed back, and he could feel her breath beneath his ear, and he put his lips to her ear and said, "I miss you."

"I *need* this weekend, Lou. I wouldn't ask if I didn't." She added, "Please."

He felt himself nod, although it wasn't automatic; it was born of great reluctance and trepidation. He felt some fear along with his love, some suspicion, even some anger. He wanted to keep squeezing until the truth came out of her, but Liz took her time. She needed time to think; he understood this. Her return from the cabin would bring with it a request to talk with him alone. He knew this woman well enough to understand that a change was coming—a decision. The baths were part of it: isolation, a time to think; perhaps that was all they were about. He leaned back and looked at her; he thought her darkly handsome and intelligent-looking. She looked a little tired. Troubled. "You okay?" he asked.

She squinted. That meant don't ask, so he didn't push it. A pit of concern burned inside him.

"I'll take Miles," he conceded.

She hugged him thanks.

"And I'll get the rest of the windows."

She kissed him on the lips. "We'll talk," she said.

"I know we will."

"It's going to be okay." She attempted to reassure him, but his years with her contradicted this; her tone of voice belied her message. It was *not* going to be okay, and this realization terrified him. He forced a smile, but he thought she probably saw it was forced. Their moment of peace was passing. They released their hug.

Boldt headed to the refrigerator and poured himself a glass of milk.

He heard Miles calling from the nearby room. "Da-a-ddy." It was not a cry of alarm but of longing—the father could easily discern the difference—and it caused a warm stirring in Boldt's heart. He stopped at the kitchen doorway and turned toward his wife, the first nibble of concern beginning chew on the inside of his chest. "How old?" he asked.

Liz, who had poured the teakettle full of water and headed for the stove, replied, "What are you talking about?"

"How old?" he repeated, this time more strongly.

"What? Who?"

"The window washer," Boldt answered, and by then his body had seized on the idea, and it infected him, from the center of his chest outward through his shoulders, groin, and into his limbs. He felt this flood of heat like a sudden fever. "A *ladder?*" he barked at his wife, passing along his alarm to her, for her head snapped up disapprovingly, and even to his son, whose nearby cry suddenly raised in pitch and severity.

Her hand trembling, she placed the kettle onto the stovetop, attempting to carry on as usual. She knew that tone of his. She detailed for him: "Mid-twenties. Early thirties? Thin."

"His face?"

"He was up the ladder. His face? I don't know. I was over by the garage. He wore a sweatshirt up over his head. We said about five words. I went inside, and he was gone. Lou?" She reached down to turn the knob on the front of the gas stove. That knob was suddenly all that Boldt could see—it loomed huge in front of him, occupying his vision: a trigger.

"Don't touch it!" Boldt shouted loudly.

Liz jumped back. Terror filled her face.

Miles cried out, the fright contagious. "Daddy!"

"Don't touch anything!" he cautioned. "Don't *move*, for that matter."

"Lou?" she pleaded, anxiety dissolving her.

His mind racing, Boldt hurried outside, into a dark and gripping terror. *A window washer. A ladder.*

It was dark out, and as he ran down the back steps he headed directly to his car and retrieved the police-issue flashlight from the trunk. He hurried around the side of the house, the glaring white light fanning out across the grass and throwing moving shadows in its wake. Boldt glanced up at the kitchen window and saw Liz, wide-eyed with concern, looking directly out at him. Her expression told him not to bring this sort of thing into her home, her life, onto her children. In all his years of service, no physical threat or trouble had found its way across the threshold of his home. There had been phone calls once—even with the number unlisted—but these had been quickly handled. Never this close.

He inspected the grass bib alongside the narrow apron of foundation planting that surrounded the house. He could picture Liz in summer shorts and a scoop-necked T-shirt, toiling over the flower beds. Flooded by such memories, he felt a stopwatch running inside his head. He imagined flames, concave walls sucking the life out of everything within . . .

The light illuminated two parallel rectangles pressed down into the grass. The evidence-sensitive cop in Boldt prevented him from stepping forward and contaminating the area. He looked carefully for any boot or shoe impressions, cigarette butts, matches, any possible evidence, while his heart was tugging at him to step closer and check those ladder impressions for the telltale chevron pattern left at the two arsons. The two homicides, he reminded himself grimly.

Any grass lawn collected and concealed evidence. As empty as it appeared under the glare of this light, the area of grass surrounding the ladder impressions was a potential gold mine to evidence technicians. Technically, he should have waited, but instead he stepped forward and trained the light down into the first of the impressions. Recognizing the chevron pattern, he cursed and ran toward the back of the house, Liz staring coldly at him through the freshly cleaned glass of the kitchen window.

"Get the kids!" Boldt ordered frantically, once inside. His imagination created an inescapable inferno at the center of the house, oxygen starved and impatient. He hurried toward their bedroom, where Sarah would be in her crib. "You get Miles," he shouted. He reached inside the bedroom door for the light switch, but his mind's eye suddenly enlarged the action to where he saw

only a fingertip and the toggle of the switch, and as the two connected and Boldt was about to throw the switch, he caught himself.
A trigger!

"Don't touch *anything!*" he shouted as a panicked Liz sprinted
past him. "Just get him and wait for me."

He suddenly saw everything as a potential detonation device.
Sarah, startled by her father's voice, began to cry.

Liz stopped at the doorway to their room, held by the sound
of her daughter's crying. "Be gentle," she said. Boldt turned
around in time to see Liz reaching for the light switch.

"No!" he hollered, stopping her. "Touch *nothing*. Watch for
wires. Anything that doesn't look right."

"A bomb?" she gasped, suddenly catching on.

"Get Miles, Liz. Quickly. We'll go out the back door, not the
front. We've both used the back door, right? So it's okay. Just
hurry."

When residents panicked, they fled out their front doors regardless of their clothing or appearance—any cop, any ambulance
driver, any fireman had experienced the half-naked family standing out on the front lawn, toward the psychological safety net of
the neighborhood. But to Boldt, the front door could be the trigger.

Liz scooped up Miles. Boldt snagged his daughter, drawing
her into his arms and pressing her warmth and her sweetly per-
fumed baby skin close to him. He was drenched in a nervous sweat.
"Good girl," he said, as she calmed in his embrace.

The parents met at the door leading into the kitchen, each
bearing a child. Liz was fraught with raw nerves—eyes wide, jaw
dropped, breathing heavily, panting from fear. "Let's get out," she
said hoarsely.

"We're going," Boldt answered, his voice cracking, his eyes
scanning the kitchen floor for anything unusual. His paranoia ran
rampant. He pictured everything a potential trigger. He suddenly
froze, fearing the trigger immediately before them. Miles struggled
restlessly in his mother's arms. Sarah wiggled to be free of Boldt,
reaching for Liz, who pleaded, "If we're going, then we're going.
Please."

"We're going," Boldt announced dryly. He cut a straight line across the kitchen, out the door, down the steps. "No," he called out, stopping Liz as she headed for her car. He stepped closer to her and kissed her on her damp cheek. "We're out for a walk with the kids. Leisurely. Easy does it. Okay?"

Tears ran down her cheeks. She nodded, glancing around.

"No," he cautioned. "It's just us. The two of us with our kids, out for a walk. Nothing to it."

She nodded again.

They walked west on 55th up to Greenwood and a corner convenience store run by a pair of Koreans whom Boldt knew by name from so many trips for eggs or milk.

He dialed 911 into the pay phone mounted outside the store, with Liz and Miles at his side and Sarah in his arms. Graffiti was scrawled around the phone, foul jokes, and a message: *Zippy was here.*

"You can go in," Boldt told his wife.

"No," was all she said. She stayed close, to where her elbow pressed against him, and he felt her warmth with the contact. That simple touch was enough to tighten his throat as he spoke into the phone. In his twenty-plus years on the force, he had never dialed the emergency number. He asked to be put through to Homicide and was informed that it couldn't be done. He asked, sternly, for the on-call identification technician and received the same curt reply. He hung up and, lacking a quarter, borrowed the use of the phone behind the counter.

He called his lieutenant, Phil Shoswitz, at home rather than the department. He explained his suspicions, requesting the bomb squad, a backup fire truck, and evidence technicians. He suggested the adjacent homes be evacuated, but Shoswitz refused this last request, wanting more proof before attracting "that kind of attention."

The comment reminded Boldt of a conversation with Daphne that the majority of convicted arsonists admitted to watching the burn. Witnessing the burn was itself a major if not primary motive for committing the crime. Boldt debated returning to the house to get Liz's car, but decided instead to ask a friend to come pick them up at the convenience store. A plan was forming in his head. He was a cop again, the father's panic subsiding.

The ladder, and whoever had scaled it, had been in their side yard that same afternoon. The arsonist, if the house had been rigged, could be watching the house at that very moment. Depending on what vantage point he took, what distance he chose, he might or might not have seen the family leave. It seemed possible he was still in the neighborhood. Boldt suggested this to Shoswitz. Listening in, Liz went noticeably pale.

After a short argument, in which Boldt found himself on the side of sacrificing his home if necessary, it was agreed that the various squads—lab, fire, bomb—would be placed on call but would not arrive at the residence until a police net had been put in place in an area extending from Woodland Park to 5th Avenue, Northwest. The net would be tightened, in hopes of squeezing the arsonist into its center. Shoswitz, typically tight with the budget, responded admirably. Faced with a possible crime against a police officer acting in the line of duty, he made not one comment about money. No crimes drew more internal support.

If and when the bomb or accelerants were found, their existence proved, then whoever had perpetrated this act had, in the process, crossed a sacred boundary, a boundary Boldt and his colleagues took seriously, one that was intolerable and unforgivable, the reaction to which would be the unvoiced but unwavering goal of revenge and punishment.

Twenty minutes later, Liz and the kids were headed to Willie and Susan Affholder's house for the night. If possible, Boldt would join them later. He and Liz kissed through the open window of Susan's Explorer, a heartfelt, loving kiss that meant the world to him. As they drove away, as the red taillights receded, Boldt knew in his heart that even if there had been an affair, it was over now. His wife and his family were whole again. They were reunited by this incident.

By 9:15 P.M., eight unmarked police cars had taken up positions along the corners and side points of an area roughly a half mile square, with Boldt's house at its center. Two decommissioned school buses, painted blue, typically used for the transportation of convicted felons, awaited the drop-off of thirty-four uniformed officers, nine of whom were on walkie-talkies with earpieces, the rest on hand signals. The buses were placed to the north, at Greenwood and 59th, and to the south, at Greenwood and 50th, seventeen uniforms each.

Before this, a black Emergency Response Team step van deposited nine of SPD's most highly trained field operatives onto the southwest corner of the zoo. Woodland Park was believed by the ERT to be the suspect's most likely route of escape. Each of the nine ERT officers was armed and wore a hands-free radio headset and night vision equipment.

Boldt climbed into the back of a maroon step van marked in bold gold letters, TWO HOUR MARTINIZING. The van had been confiscated as part of a greyhound gaming bust several years earlier and was presently in service to the police as a field communications command center. It was parked on a hill on Palatine Place, a block and a half from Boldt's house.

Shoswitz occupied an office chair bolted to the floor, as did the two techies—a communications dispatcher and a field operations officer. Shoswitz owned a long, pale, pointed face, overly large eyeballs that registered perpetual shock, and busy fingers that reflected his nervous disposition.

Boldt checked his watch. Even secured radio frequencies could be, and occasionally were, monitored by the more creative members of the press assigned to the police beat. The best technologies could be compromised, given time and determination. He knew at least two reporters capable of such tricks. He estimated the operation had about fifteen minutes in the clear. Boldt made specific note of the time: 9:23. They needed to be well along by 9:45, or the press might spoil the operation. Impatience tested him.

"All set?" the field operations officer asked Shoswitz. Phil glanced over at Boldt through the dim red light of the step van's interior. There was no other chair, so Boldt squatted on an inverted green plastic milk crate. The sergeant nodded at the lieutenant; it was an uncomfortable moment for Boldt, this prerequisite use of chain of command necessary to all multitask, multidepartmental operations. With one hot glance in the sergeant's direction, Shoswitz let Boldt know that responsibility for the hurried operation was all his. Phil Shoswitz was already distancing himself.

The dispatcher flipped some toggles and said, "Attention, all units."

Boldt closed his eyes and, listening to the continuous stream of radio traffic, envisioned the events unfolding in the dark outside.

As residents in the neighborhood watched TV, ERT and uniformed police stole through their lawns, down the alleys behind their homes, and around their garages and carports, with almost no one the wiser. One child of nine announced from his bedroom that outside his window he had just seen a Ninja in the backyard. The father hollered up the stairs for the kid to go to sleep and stop bothering them.

A human net constricted toward its geographical center: Lou Boldt's home.

Boldt, eyes closed, pictured a cool and hardened killer, lurking somewhere out there in the dark, anxiously awaiting the spectacular light show he had planned, awaiting an event that Boldt prayed would never come to pass.

ERT officer Cole Robbie was one of the voices Boldt heard speaking across the nearly constant radio traffic. He was a tall man, a little over six foot one, and on that night he wore all black, including a flak jacket and leather jump boots. He wore his black ERT baseball hat backward, the brim covering the back of his neck, the adjustable plastic strap biting into his forehead. Robbie had a young daughter, nine months old, named Rosie, and a wife of four years called Jo, for Josephine. Rosie was, without a doubt, the most amazing thing that had ever happened to him. Jo was probably the finest woman on the face of the earth, given that she pulled two jobs and still managed to keep Rosie happy and the house happening. Only a few days earlier, in the middle of prayer at church, Cole Robbie had realized he had everything he had ever hoped for, everything and more than a person dared ask for. On that night, sneaking through people's backyards, aware that many if not all people in these neighborhoods armed themselves, aware that his job was to apprehend some unknown, unidentified assailant, quite possibly dangerous, quite possibly a murderer, his heartbeat was clocking a hundred and ten, and he was thinking, *Let it be someone else*. He had no intention of being a hero. He was, in fact, seriously considering applying for an interdepartmental transfer. After all his years of training and angling for a place in ERT, a desk job suddenly looked real appealing.

Cole Robbie crept over a low fence and into a fire alley, which was considered city property and therefore public land. Sneaking through backyards was not exactly legal, it was just easier at times.

He remained in shadow as often as possible, moving slightly hunched, shoulders low. In his right ear a constant stream of radio traffic became a din, and though he listened for key words that might have relevance to his own situation, for the most part he tuned it out. In any field operation that involved uniforms there was too much radio traffic. Left to ERT—as it should have been, in Robbie's opinion—an operation like this one would have been substantially simpler.

His wrist vibrated silently under his watch face. He stopped, stepped out of shadow, and looked once left and then right. He waited. A moment later he looked again and this time saw both of his fellow squad members, one on each side, perhaps twenty to thirty yards away. There was no attempt made at hand signals. Conserve movement.

In four more minutes his wrist would vibrate again, and he would wait for visual contact with his team members. If, within a minute of this, either should go missing, Robbie would attempt radio contact through Command Center Dispatch. If this failed, he and his fellow ERT teammates would search for the missing officer until the reason for his absence was explained. Sometimes it proved to be nothing more than a neighborhood dog preventing egress. Sometimes it was a matter of the officer getting lost or forgetting his route; even the best trained made mistakes. Once—only once, Robbie reminded himself—a missing ERT operative had been found with his spinal cord broken in two places and his skull cracked open. He lived through it, but David Jefferson, who had changed his name to Abdul Something-or-other, now worked the phone bank for a telemarketing firm from the confines of a wheelchair. Robbie had had a pizza with him a couple months earlier. The man's life was a wreck: He had lost his wife in a bloody divorce and was twenty grand in debt. Cole Robbie wanted nothing to do with that. He stepped quietly forward. The section of park on the far side of the zoo that the suits believed was this perp's most likely escape route lay just ahead and was Robbie's destination. It was pitch dark beneath those trees. Visual contact was out of the question once they were inside there. His heart rate climbed above one-ten. He loved this work.

Boldt opened his eyes and craned forward in the odd red light, attempting to see whatever it was that the field operations officer, Tito Lee, was attempting to show him.

Pointing to a map, Lee said, "We got ERT in a line right through here. They're moving good and should be in position within five, maybe ten minutes. At that point, we got a human wall between Phinney Way and the zoo. Our perimeter patrol cars are all in place. The two buses are in position as we speak, but no one's going anywhere until we give the high sign. You want to start to close this gnat's ass, you let me know."

"What—who?—was that woman I heard a couple of minutes ago?" Boldt asked.

"What we got there is an undercover officer working the streets in an Animal Control vehicle up to the west side. She's driving around real slow, like she's after something, which of course she is, technically speaking." He seemed proud of this concept. He grinned. "It gives us an operative on the specific street; she's headed for your place. She'll get out of the vehicle there and go door to door, heading toward Woodland, asking about a Doberman reported wandering loose."

"She's alone?" Boldt asked apprehensively. "I thought everyone was going to be partnered in this—"

"Who's alone?" Shoswitz interjected, suddenly interested.

Lee answered the lieutenant, turning from Boldt. "The dogcatcher. One of the Vice dicks, Branslonovich. She's undercover as a dogcatcher," he repeated, for the sake of the bewildered and concerned Shoswitz.

"No one goes unpartnered on an operation like this," Shoswitz echoed, suddenly concerned. "Who authorized?"

Lee said defensively, "We put this together in forty-five minutes, Lieutenant. It's not like—"

"I want her out of there."

"Yes, sir."

"Now."

"Yes, sir."

"Team her up with someone. I don't care if her partner ends up in a dog cage in the back, I want everyone paired. I thought I made that clear!" Shoswitz delivered this invective and then glared over toward Boldt; the lieutenant hated the unexpected. He dreaded these operations—he was too close to retirement to risk his career on hunches. He disliked Boldt at that moment; the sergeant could feel it.

Cole Robbie moved evenly and fluidly, avoiding jerky motions. If one were to have caught a glimpse of his dark form, it might have been mistaken for a tree trunk or a waving shadow from the occasional car headlight that sneaked into the copse of trees through which he navigated. He was, at that moment, no longer a corporal entity, no longer a body of heartbeats and sensations, for as he negotiated through the trees, so did he negotiate a transformation of spirit, divesting himself of the material and turning himself over to God. That was something he never discussed with anyone other than Jo, who fully understood such transformations and, even had she not understood, would have supported anything that might keep her husband alive through another tour of duty. Through this surrender of spirit, Cole Robbie believed himself an instrument of God, all knowing, all encompassing. If he were meant to engage with a psychotic arsonist, so be it; he would do his best and hope for divine guidance. He trusted that same divine guidance to carry him on the proper route through the forest, to deliver him to a point, the significance of which he might not understand but would willingly accept. Understanding, even knowledge itself, was beyond his capacity at that moment. His training occupied a spot within him far inferior to his trust and confidence in the correctness of the moment. He accepted his role, his route, his destination without question, and whereas others often mistook this for an admirable sense of loyalty to his team, the truth was far different. His misperceived loyalty was nothing more than an adherence to the doctrines of faith and the acceptance of Divine Principle.

"Come and get it," was Cole Robbie's last conscious thought before he surrendered completely and turned himself over to his Keeper. From the corner of his right eye, he registered the quick white wink of a flashlight signal, and he returned and then relayed this signal to his left without thought. Through the trees it sparked, linking the various members of ERT, connecting the chain. All was well. His confidence was second to none. He knew and he accepted, though he did not dwell on the fact, that at that moment he was the best cop out there. He was part of an entirely different team. Only time would tell, but something told him this was his night.

"Where then?" Shoswitz barked from the back of the step van. The pale red light cast from above created hollow black eye sockets and doubled the size and distorted the shape of his already prominent nose. He looked to Boldt like something satanic. His teeth shined wet and red in that light. His index finger pointed straight and shook authoritatively at Tito Lee. The lieutenant's question was in response to Lee's having said that the Vice officer Branslonovich, who was posing as a dogcatcher, was clearly not in her vehicle.

The operations officer answered by asking a question of the dispatcher. "Can we raise her in the field?"

Shoswitz, rarely content to speculate, shouted into the cramped confines, "I want her back in that truck and the doors locked, and her rolling, this instant. How we deal with this can be discussed later. Copy?"

Lee shot Shoswitz a hot glance.

The radio dispatcher looked distressed as well, and that troubled Boldt because the dispatcher's role was critical to such a complex and quickly conceived operation.

"All we can do," Boldt offered, weighing in on the side of Tito Lee, "is try to raise her. Is she carrying a hand-held?" he asked the dispatcher, in part to get him back on track.

"She's carrying a unicom," he replied, explaining that she should have been hearing all directives from the step van. "I put it out on the unicom," he offered. "But even if she heard it, it would take her a minute to get back to the truck and respond. She's not authorized," he explained, and Boldt understood that she, along with others in the operation, was not in possession of a walkie-talkie capable of transmitting on secured frequencies—only a few of the hand-helds could do that. This technical restriction isolated her.

Boldt said, "Am I mistaken, or will an animal control van have a radio capable of—"

"Oh, shit, you're right," interrupted Lee. "She's restricted to line-of-sight reporting over the unicom. Emergency reporting of contact with the suspect." To minimize radio traffic and to reduce the chance of the press catching on, most of the radios in use were under the same restrictions.

Shoswitz chimed in. "So we put it out over the unicom that we want Branslonovich to make a land line call to headquarters. That will force her back into the truck, to a pay phone, and we can deal with it from there. Settled?" he asked rhetorically, his mind already made up. "Do it," he instructed the dispatcher. He glanced over and caught Boldt staring at him. "What?" he asked, still at a shouting volume.

"I didn't say anything," Boldt objected. But inside he was thinking that Branslonovich was Vice and was more than familiar with field operations, and such a summons would mean only one thing to her: She was being called in. So, he reasoned, the first time she received the message over the unicom she would ignore it and say later that bad reception had interfered with the signal. The second time she might be forced to respond, but at her own speed; she would take her sweet time about coming in. With each successive attempt by dispatch, she would increasingly suspect that the only explanation for these attempts was that she was in a hot zone and because she was a woman officer the male pigs that controlled such operations were recalling her. This, in turn, would keep her in the field all the longer. And the truth was, as far as Boldt could tell, she probably *was* in the operation's hot zone, somewhere within a city block of Boldt's house.

"You're pissing me off," Shoswitz declared, glaring at his sergeant.

"Then give me your keys," he said, standing up from the milk crate and hunching into an uncomfortable stooped crouch. He sensed that at first Shoswitz was reluctant, but the change in expression on the lieutenant's face revealed his decision to pick his fights carefully. This fight would be lost on his part, no matter how adamant his attempt. He handed Boldt the keys. They both understood that Boldt intended to go after Branslonovich himself. He rarely felt prescient about a situation, but Branslonovich was in danger. Lou Boldt felt certain of it.

Shoswitz directed his anger to the dispatcher. As Boldt slipped out the back of the step van he heard the lieutenant bark, "Try sending it out over the unicom again."

It was a moonless night, inside-the-stomach dark. An ocean smell permeated the chilly air and brought back images of Alki

Point, where Boldt had once stood staring down into the crab-eaten eyes of a decomposing corpse.

A dead body, he thought, hurrying toward Phil's car. All at once it felt as if he might be too late.

Cole Robbie found the darkness of the trees comforting. A moment earlier he had been ordered to adopt his night-vision goggles, which meant discontinued use of the flashlights. It was a good call on the part of the ERT commander, because it allowed a return to hand signals and silenced the winking flashlights that seemed to shout every time a signal had been sent.

The world was now a green and black place, with few shades of gray. The tree trunks rose like black cornstalks from the forest floor, looking to Robbie like irregularly placed bars to a jail cell. Three dimensions were reduced to two—he felt as if he were walking inside a green and black television set. Inside these goggles, motion blurred; fast motion sometimes vanished completely. It was rumored that the FBI had seriously superior night-vision headgear presently "in testing," which was a euphemism for proprietary ownership. What the FBI got, others waited for— sometimes for years.

A hand signal from his right. Robbie caught it, returned it, and then passed it along to the officer twenty-five yards to his left. All this occurred with Robbie feeling as if he were on autopilot. He noticed that the line was stretching apart, stretching thin. Pretty soon they would be too far apart for hand signals. He wondered if anyone else had noticed. It was just such sophomoric mistakes that hurt operations. Just the kind of thing that got someone killed.

Up ahead to the north, the park fed into a hillside neighborhood falling toward Green Lake. The occasionally glimpsed light from those houses momentarily blinded the night-vision goggles, burning a bright white hole in the dense green and black. For that reason, no sooner had Robbie donned the night-vision goggles than he shifted them to his forehead and avoided their use. Previous experience with "golf balls"—the ERT name for the blinding flashes and burnouts in the light-sensitive goggles—had educated him to avoid the goggles in the presence of *any* artificial light. Whether or not any of his other teammates also elected to skip the goggles, he couldn't be sure. He would still need to use them every four minutes for hand signals, but in the meantime he preferred the uniformity of the darkness.

Immediately a slight glint of yellow light high up in a distant tree caught his attention and provoked him to stop. An airplane light seen through the towering limbs? he wondered. Something wet in the tree, reflecting light from the ground? A person? He quickly tried the goggles but preferred it without them, his peripheral vision expanded. He hadn't seen exactly where . . . the sound of an airplane briefly convinced him that it was nothing. . . . There! Another glint of light, thirty or forty feet up in a tree perhaps fifty yards directly ahead.

He depressed a small button on the device clipped to his belt that allowed him radio transmission within the ERT team. "Operative Three." He announced himself at a whisper. "Eye contact with possible suspicious object. Five-zero yards. Eleven o'clock. Elevation: four-zero feet. Advise."

"All stop," came the commander's voice through Cole's earpiece. The line hissed static as the commander checked in with the command van, but Cole knew what was in store for them. A minimum of four operatives would converge on that tree.

With God's guidance, Cole Robbie thought, this one was over before it had barely begun. They had their man. He stayed where he was, eyes fixed on that elusive spot, hoping beyond hope that what he had just witnessed had nothing whatsoever to do with aviation traffic and everything to do with the suspect they pursued.

As it turned out, because of his disdain for the night-vision device, when the first and only firestorm occurred Cole Robbie was the sole ERT officer not wearing goggles and so not blinded, the only operative able to function, the only operative to see a spinning body burning as clearly as if it were a Christmas tree afire. He was immediately struck by the irony of an arsonist setting himself aflame.

But then, as he began to run toward the animated orange puppet that spun like an unpracticed dancer, he heard it screaming like a woman—worse, in a voice familiar to him. It was, in fact, a woman, a woman consumed by pain and fear. By fire. Worse yet, the voice of a friend. The closer he drew, the more convinced he was that *it*—however indistinguishable, for it was no longer human—was the voice of Vice officer Connie Branslonovich.

Boldt found the animal control truck parked well up the hill from his house, half a block from Greenwood, two blocks from Woodland Park and the well-discussed anticipated escape route of the arsonist.

He glanced down driveways, around corners of houses, up and down the road, hoping for a glimpse of Branslonovich. He carried a unicom walkie-talkie concealed inside his sport coat, a single wire leading to an earpiece. He hoped like hell to hear Branslonovich or the dispatcher announce that she had reported in. Instead, he heard the order for the thirty-four uniforms to leave the buses and begin closing the net. The operation was in full swing.

The radio channel came ablaze with communication traffic as a small army of uniformed patrol officers was unleashed onto a four-block area.

ERT was somewhere inside the park setting up a back line to net the escaping arsonist. Suddenly the entire effort seemed so futile to Boldt, so absurd. It was based on the assumption that Boldt's house had been rigged with accelerant, as yet an unproven fact. He reviewed the logic, aware he might need it later to defend the decision to the brass. But the more he examined the thinking, the more he liked it. If the uniforms were presently being deployed, the sirens and the lab truck were only minutes from screeching to a stop in front of Boldt's house—an act certain to dislodge the waiting arsonist, accepting the theory that the arsonist was indeed watching. Although he could make sense of it in his head, he wasn't too confident how it would sound to a review board. He had convinced Shoswitz easily enough, but he and Shoswitz had a long history together, a working relationship, and the lieutenant had grudgingly come to trust his sergeant's decision-making process. It didn't mean that others would understand it. Not at all.

His current thought process was more clear to him: Thinking like a cop, attempting to retrace Branslonovich's steps. He stopped and looked around, realizing what a dark night it was. He glanced back at his own house, seeing it differently for the first time—as a target. The arsonist would want a good view, and that seemed most clearly offered from up the hill, which explained the location of the parked animal control truck. Branslonovich had quickly discerned the importance of the elevation of the hill. If the arsonist didn't care about seeing anything more than the flames, a position in the park would suffice. Boldt chugged up the hill, winded immediately, shoulders hunched, wondering how he had allowed himself to fall into such bad shape and vowing to do something about it. Sometime.

The arsonist would need a lookout, someplace either secretive—inside an empty house, perhaps—or right out in the open but with a convincing excuse to be there: electric lineman, telephone or cable repairman. Boldt quickly glanced up and scanned the area; he didn't want to spend too much time with his head up, for fear of being seen and giving away his intentions. A pang of dread swept through him. If Branslonovich had gone around scanning the poles and roofs and windows, she might have given herself away. Perhaps, he thought, she was clever enough to have done so while calling out, "Here, kitty. Here, kitty." Branslonovich had her share of smarts. Or had she, too, been drawn toward the park?

He climbed the hill a little faster. He had a bad feeling about this. He felt like calling out, Here, Branslonovich. Here, Branslonovich. The higher up the hill he climbed, the more houses he passed, the more inviting the park seemed. Just across Greenwood, dark, full of places to hide. Branslonovich might have felt this same thing: Why bother with the houses, or any exposure, when the park offered such sanctuary? Furthermore, went his reasoning, an animal control officer had every excuse to roam a wooded area. Boldt walked faster. Branslonovich was in the park. He knew this as a fact, however unexplainable, just as he knew his house was rigged to burn.

He dodged traffic, cutting across Greenwood, suddenly more hurried. He pushed himself faster and faster.

He entered the park at a run.

He heard her before he saw the sweep of her flashlight breaking through the stand of tree trunks. She was moving through the park, perhaps thirty or more yards ahead of him. Her flashlight was aimed high into the overhead limbs. He couldn't actually identify her as Branslonovich, not at that distance, but he knew. She was on the arsonist like a bloodhound; Boldt could feel this as well.

"Hey! Are you the dogcatcher?" Boldt shouted, attempting to maintain a modicum of professionalism by maintaining her undercover status. "You looking for a Doberman?" She didn't seem to hear him, his voice absorbed by the woods. He took a deep breath to shout loudly, but before that same breath escaped his lips, the ground immediately to her right erupted in a billowing column of purple flame. She had tripped a wire, perhaps, or stepped directly on a detonator.

The figure ahead of him ignited instantaneously in a bluish yellow flame, as did a nearby tree trunk. She spun once, arms held out, crying for help, a searing, painful cry. And then she seemed to explode. Yellow-blue pieces disembodied from the spinning creature, arching through the black night air like fireworks. As what was left of the body slumped forward and collapsed, the bark on the tree trunk exploded—sap combusting like fuel—punctuating the quiet night with what sounded like cannon fire. The concussion of the erupting flames lifted Boldt off his feet and deposited him onto his back, ten feet behind where he had been standing. He felt deaf, blinded, and as if his back had been broken in several places. Branslonovich issued one last bone-chilling cry; how this was physically possible escaped Lou Boldt as he lay on a damp bed of decomposing leaves, immobilized by the fall, his ears filled with the haunting wail of the detective's final moment on earth.

In the distance, sirens.

Lou Boldt managed to get his hand on his weapon, thinking

to himself that in all his career he had only fired it on three other occasions. He aimed straight up toward where the stars should have been and let off three consecutive rounds. With any luck at all, someone would hear it and find him, before the whole forest burned, and he along with it.

Cole Robbie saw her spin in a complete circle, an all-consuming plume of blinding light, as pieces of her shot out like sparks from the fireplace, streaming through the air like shooting stars. The cacophony in his earpiece distracted him, for the commander had clearly been wearing his night-vision goggles at the time, and the string of cursing that ensued poured over the airwaves. Robbie heard three live rounds, yanked the earphone from his ear, and broke into a run, thinking, *Someone else is out there.*

At that same moment he caught a flicker of a shadow to the left of the inferno and tentatively identified it as an object—a human form—moving away from the fire and indirectly toward him, off to his left. The image was there and then gone, the light of the fire so intense, so bright, that one glance induced temporary blindness—like a camera's flash—and the resulting collage of shifting, slanting shadows turned the landscape into an unrecognizable, eerie tangle of sharp black forms, as if he were suddenly at the bottom of a pile of brush trying to look out.

He had played team sports in high school and junior college, and his resulting instincts moved him to his left in a line calculated to intercept the path of the human form he had spotted. A few strides into it he dropped all conscious thought, electing instead to turn himself over once again to the power and force that guided his life. He ran like the wind, free of his own misgivings, thoughts and calculations. As if to confirm the correctness of this attitude, he picked up sight of the moving form once again, heading right at him. He felt his hand reach down and locate his weapon without any such thought in his head. Then his hand released the stock and found the TASER stun gun instead—a weapon similar in appearance to a large handgun but one that delivered twenty thousand volts of electricity instead of bullets. The TASER had to be fired within fifty feet of the target—twenty to thirty was preferable for accuracy—as two small wires carried the charge to the inductor needles on the projected electrode. Once hit, a subject was knocked unconscious for a period of four to fifteen minutes by the jolt of electricity. He would take him alive; he would bring home a prisoner, not a dead trophy.

There was no sense of time, except that measured by the change in tone and color of the shadows thrown by the fire. The same hand that held the TASER found the small button on his radio transmitter. Robbie said breathlessly, "Position Three. Suspect sighted. Foot pursuit. Identify before weapons fire." Whatever the real time, it all happened fast. In a mix of moving shadow, shifting light, and the running human form dodging through it toward an imaginary point directly ahead, Cole felt a part of the forest, comfortable and unafraid.

The suspect was closing fast from his right.

Cole planted his feet, skidding to a stop in the sloppy ground, dropped to one knee, leveled the TASER, aimed into the blackness of space directly ahead, and squeezed the firing trigger. He saw the twin shiny wires glimmer in the brightness of the fire as the electrode raced into space. The suspect, at a full run, having not seen Robbie, bumped into and grabbed hold of a low branch, knocking it out of his way and, as luck would have it, absorbing the electrode into the branch which otherwise would have struck him. The suspect appeared completely unaware of Robbie's presence, never breaking stride. The ERT man dropped the TASER and reached for his weapon as he came to his feet and continued the chase from behind. The sudden appearance of round white holes in the darkness—flashlight beams—alerted him to his change of angle and the reality that he could not fire the handgun, except in warning, since his teammates were now directly ahead. Robbie, a fast runner, initially gained on the suspect as with his right hand he found the dangling earpiece and returned it to his ear. Then, all at once, the suspect was gone. He had ducked behind a tree in hiding, somewhere up ahead. Robbie instinctively dove to the forest floor, anticipating weapons fire. He tripped the radio transmitter and said quietly, "Operative Three. Kill the flashlights. Go to infrared but do not fire. Repeat, do not fire. Copy?"

"Copy, Three," said the commander. Robbie heard the instructions repeated.

The ERT weapons were equipped with heat-responsive sighting devices that alerted the shooter to a warm body fix. The infrared devices allowed for nighttime "blind" precision targeting, their only drawback being that they could not distinguish between wildlife and human forms, and occasionally a deer or large dog was shot in lieu of a suspect. What Robbie intended, and what the commander had just ordered, was that the sighting devices be swept through the forest in an attempt to locate a warm-blooded body in the hope of identifying the suspect. If Cole Robbie saw any red pinpoints of light strike his person, he would alert the ERT to a "bad hit." The lights in the forest went dark; the flashlights were turned off in succession. Between Robbie and the dispersed line of operatives some fifty yards away—and closing—the suspect was hiding.

All senses alert, Cole Robbie rose to his knees and then to his feet and began to creep ahead, one quiet footfall at a time. He realized in that instant that he was dominated by his senses, that he had lost his magical connection with the power of being, of guidance, upon which his confidence relied, the source of all good in his life. He didn't want to be thinking, listening, watching; he felt trapped in himself.

The suspect came from above, completely unexpectedly, falling out of the darkness and onto Robbie painfully and with determination. A pair of hands found Robbie's head. One firmly gripped his chin; the other pressed tightly against the back of the cop's neck. Cole Robbie lay on the ground, face first, still reeling from the impact, unable to gather his senses. He knew this grip and what was coming. The intention was to break his neck with a single jerk, a spine-twisting snap, and leave him lying here. Robbie could defeat the move with a simple anticipation of which direction the suspect would choose. But there was no time for such thought. God help me, he thought, and forced his chin left, just as the suspect made an identical move with his hands.

People would say that Robbie instinctively felt the guy's fingers against his face and his brain registered that the fingers were on the right side of the face, and therefore the guy was left-handed and would attempt a twist to the left; when combined with Robbie's choice, the attempt was in part defeated. They would say that all his training and all his experience had combined to save a cop's life. For the devastating crack the suspect heard, before abandoning the cop for paralyzed or dead, was not Cole Robbie's neck but his jaw. Robbie would drink from a straw for the next eight weeks, but he would live; he would walk; he would run with his daughter and make love with his wife. And he would know for the rest of his days that his moment of decision had nothing to do with training or experience but was born of those final words he voiced internally before the deed was done.

The suspect cut through the woods, heading back toward the very fire he had himself set, perhaps aware that heat-seeking devices were useless when aimed in the direction of such an inferno, perhaps only lucky to have made such a choice. Cole Robbie watched him run. On that night, it was the last anyone saw of the man.

Boldt was of good stock. After firing those shots, he immediately regretted doing so, because he didn't want to be in the position of needing anyone's help. It was the spreading fire that had put the fear in his heart; he wasn't outwardly afraid of many things, but fire was one of them. He rolled and came to his knees. All he needed for motivation was the sound of those approaching sirens, fire and police. He struggled to his feet, tested out various limbs, and pronounced himself sound. He would be badly bruised, and he would need a hot bath, but he wasn't going to be admitted to any emergency room. He would accept responsibility for the warning shots, explaining that at the time he was down and unable to move. The truth nearly always worked best.

The fire crews contained what remained of the fire. Strangely, what had begun as a white hot inferno had quickly petered out into one burning tree and some smoldering underbrush. When no detonator and no can or jar that might have contained the accelerant was found at the scene, speculation ran rampant among those in the know. Many theories surfaced; but with no physical proof, excepting some broken glass fragments found much later, the fire that consumed and killed detective Constance Branslonovich was listed as "arson assault by mysterious causes."

The Seattle press had for some years worked in concert with law enforcement. It was a relationship for which the city government was grateful. The press could kill you if they so chose. The Night of the Burning Tree, as it came to be called among law enforcement officers, proved an exception to the rule. The purple cone of fire had been seen from five miles away and was said to have stretched nearly three hundred feet in the air. An eyewitness put the top of the flames above the Space Needle, but this was gross exaggeration and journalists elected to ignore it. Whereas the fire in the park and the death of an animal control officer (Branslonovich's identity was temporarily withheld by mutual agreement) were reported at the top of the eleven o'clock news and on the morning edition's front page, the subsequent detailed search of Boldt's residence went unreported, based almost entirely on the fact that the press agreed to keep secret the residential addresses of law enforcement officers for reasons of security. The bomb squad, the scientific identification unit, and the Marshal Five arson task force, including Steven Garman, gathered at the Boldt home at 11:45 P.M., thirty minutes after the last of the fire trucks had departed Woodland Park. The bomb squad and their dogs led the first wave, searching doors, windows, switches, and flooring for triggers. The Marshall Fives followed next. Nothing indicating attempted arson was discovered.

At 1:00 A.M., Bernie Lofgrin's identification unit went to work, beginning with the lawn and perimeter grounds. Plaster casts were

made of the ladder impressions, although Lofgrin agreed with
Boldt's assessment that the impressions "appeared consistent"
with impressions at the two prior burn sites, an analysis later confirmed by the lab comparison tests.

By the time Boldt entered his own house there were nine other
people inside, including an electrical engineer who was using a
sophisticated voltage tester to, as he put it, "measure line resistance," and a carpenter who was drilling holes into various walls
so that a fiberoptic camera could be inserted and the inside of the
walls examined. This study revealed that the house had adequate
insulation, as well as a piece of newspaper dated 1922, and a Stan-
ley screwdriver that was probably equally as old. At the end of
three hours of intense scrutiny, the head of the bomb squad and
Lofgrin pulled Boldt aside and pronounced his home "clean,"
which after that invasion it was anything but. A more thorough
examination of the outside wall where the ladder had been placed
was scheduled for daylight, and Boldt was ordered to sleep elsewhere, though nothing suspicious had been found.

Garman, who joined the huddle, said, "Your wife's arrival at
the house probably put the guy off his mission." Boldt was not
comfortable with Garman's presence in the first place. The sergeant grunted a response that no one understood.

Lofgrin said, typically technical, "That would explain the discovery of the impressions and help to explain the absence of any
accelerant."

"It doesn't explain what happened in the woods," Boldt
pointed out.

Arson detective Neil Bahan said, "Ah, but it might! We don't
know that whoever that was, let's call him the arsonist, was there
to watch or wait. He may have, for instance, been awaiting a chance
at a return visit. To finish the job." Boldt wanted everyone out of
there, even if he couldn't stay. He wanted some peace and quiet.
Branslonovich was dead; Robbie was in an emergency room getting his jaw wired. There was no proof that Boldt's house had been
rigged. He was being asked to believe that the arsonist had been

hanging around the forest waiting for a good time to return. He didn't like any of it.

Shoswitz asked to see him in his office first thing in the morning. Boldt feared he might lose the case—a case he had not wanted from the beginning but was, by that time, too personally involved to want to surrender it to someone else. Thirty minutes later the last of them was out the front door. Boldt locked up tight and called Liz at Willie and Susan's and woke them all. He spoke to his wife for nearly half an hour, explaining everything as best he could. He felt both embarrassed and ashamed that he had brought this onto his family. She told him that, with the kids asleep, she was there for the night.

Boldt said, "I think the cabin is a good idea for you."

"For all three of us, you mean."

"Yes."

"You're scaring me."

"Sorry." He had all sorts of pat answers ready. Stuff like this happened to cops. They had been lucky all these years to have seen so little of it. He felt tempted to share with her the sight of Branslonovich exploding—for that was the only way to describe what had happened—not so much to frighten her but because he needed to tell someone, needed to vent some of the anger and fear that the violent death had instilled in him. He still saw her spinning around like a dancer—yellow, blue, then white. He still heard that cry.

"You there?" she asked.

"Yeah. Here."

"You want to come over? Sleep with me? They gave me the guest room."

His wife asking him to sleep with her, to hold her, to comfort her. He wanted nothing more. He said so.

"But you're staying," she said.

"I couldn't sleep if I tried. I'll go downtown, try to sort some of this out." He wanted a look at the most recent poem sent to Garman.

"I'd rather just lose the house, you know. I wish—and I mean this!—I wish he'd gotten the house, that he'd taken the house and left us alone."

Boldt was silent for a long time.

"I know that silence. You're saying he doesn't want the house, he wants *you*." She gasped. "Oh, God."

"I didn't say anything."

"He wants you. Is that it?"

"We don't know what he wants. We don't know who he is. We don't know much."

"Someone you put away before?"

"Doubtful."

"I hate this. Jesus God. What do we do?" she cried into the phone.

"Can you get a leave?"

"I'm owed *weeks*."

"Do you mind?"

"Being driven out of my own home? Of course I mind," she snapped. He waited her out. "No, love, I don't mind. No, of course not. But I wish you'd join us."

"The Sheriff's Department will watch the road. The cabin too, probably."

"Oh, God. I can't believe this is happening."

"Could Susan go with you?"

"I can ask. She might. I love you," she blurted out. "God, how I love you!"

"No music so sweet," he whispered into the phone.

"Always and forever," she added.

"We'll get through this," Boldt said, "and we'll reevaluate and we'll make sense of the last few months."

"We need to talk," she said, and to him it rang as something of a confession, and his heart wanted to tear from his chest.

"Yeah," he agreed. If tears made noise, she would have heard them.

"You amaze me." Her voice trailed off. "Have I told you lately how much you amaze me? What an incredible man you are?"

"A little overweight," he said, and she laughed, barking into the phone.

"Not to me," she said.

"I love you, Elizabeth."

"Sleep if you can."

They hung up.

Boldt ignored orders and took a long hot bath in the old claw foot that had come with the place, running the faucet twice to reheat the water. When he got out, he pulled the drain plug. Ten minutes later, the tub was only half empty. He searched the house for a plunger but couldn't find one. Not one damn plunger in the entire house!

The kitchen sink still filled with dishes hadn't drained either, but Boldt didn't notice it. He was already out the door and on his way downtown, off to prepare for that dreaded meeting with Shoswitz.

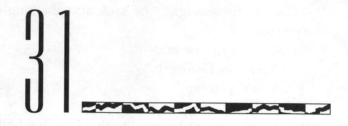

31

THE death of a fellow police officer was
like a death in the family. For the Seattle Police Department, death
incurred while on duty happened so rarely that in his twenty-four
years on the force, Boldt had only attended three such funerals.
Staged as pageants more than funerals, they gripped the city's collective consciousness. Flags were lowered, streets were closed, and,
on a marbled hillside high above the rat race, weapons were aimed
into the gray sky and fired in bone-chilling unison.

By sunrise the morning after the botched attempt to net the
arsonist, all the crews had left both the park and Boldt's home.
Only a ribbon of yellow and black police tape remained at both
sites. A single cruiser with two patrolmen cruised between the two
crime scenes. Identification technicians were scheduled to return
to both at first light.

Boldt beat them to it. Perhaps it was the look that Shoswitz
had given him in the operations van just before the exercise began.
Perhaps it was Branslonovich's spectral dance among the towering
trees. Perhaps it was his arrival at Bronslonovich's torching, only
seconds too late. Whatever the reason, Boldt felt directly responsi-

ble for her death. The image of her twisting body, arms outstretched in a crucifix, remained seared into his consciousness,
plaguing him. Eyes open or shut, it didn't matter, the image remained. His to live with. Or try to.

Chief among his frustrations was that the only apparent witness, an ERT officer by the name of Robbie, had a jaw so badly
broken he could not speak. His one scribbled message was that he
had not gotten a clean look at the suspect.

Boldt's fascination remained with the crime scene in the park.
He ducked under the police tape, unseen. Overhead, the stark
limbs of the deciduous trees captured the orange-ruby glow of a
spectacular sunrise, bleeding a rosy daylight onto the forest floor.
The conifers and cedars towered overhead majestically. Boldt
walked among the fallen limbs and the wintering weeds and
shrubs, avoiding the downtrodden path created hours earlier by a
dozen anxious firemen and patrol officers responding to the scene.
He cut his own path, the symbolism not lost on him. Although
there would be a pulling together of SPD because of Bronslonovich's death, Boldt was certain to find himself isolated, cut free by
Shoswitz, and the subject of several briefings and reviews. If he
were determined "solely responsible" for "recklessness" in the
hasty fielding of the operation, it was conceivable he would be
suspended without pay or even asked to retire. More than anything
else, those last few hours planted firmly into Boldt's mind the reality of his advancing years of service. He was at that time the most
senior homicide cop, considered old guard and, in a department
looking to reinvent itself in the wake of national disgrace in other
inner-city police departments, an endangered species.

The burned section of trees stuck out like a charred cancer.
Boldt steered his way toward it, eyes alert in the shimmering light
for any stray piece of evidence particular to a human presence. The
arsonist had been in that area, and despite the trampling caused
by the emergency crews, Boldt held to the possibility, the probability, that evidence had unintentionally been left behind, as was
nearly always the case.

Circling the area several times, he found nothing of significance on the outskirts of the burn, but his imagination began to place the killer hiding there. He worked his way in toward the center, like growth rings on a cut stump. He chose two trees at the relative center of the burned area, a circle of roughly twelve feet of cleared ground blanketed in a white ash, only two tall trees remaining intact, their bark badly burned, rising a distance of ten to twenty feet. Searching the area, Boldt realized the brilliance of the deed: The arsonist had burned any and all evidence of his being there along with Branslonovich, a complete and thorough job. Another example, the detective thought, of the kind of forethinking mind responsible. He didn't appreciate having a worthy adversary; he would have preferred an ignorant, emotional, mistake-ridden sociopath who inadvertently left evidence at every crime scene.

Keeping the arsonist's intentions and motivations in mind—a point of view critical to an investigation—Boldt shifted left and right, side to side, in an attempt to provide himself with any kind of a view of his own home. But all he saw was Phinney Way, all he heard was the traffic on Greenwood. He glanced up.

That one simple movement set off a flood of thought and emotion. With it, Boldt confirmed to his own satisfaction that the arsonist had been up in the tree. Branslonovich had appeared on the ground below him, and he had bombed her. The bottom limbs of both tall trees were black with soot. Boldt studied both trees carefully. The branches of the one nearer him began lower to the ground and were clustered in a way that seemed the easier climb of the two. Boldt chose that tree and began to climb. The limbs offered a natural ladder. He struggled with his balance and his big frame, realizing that even climbing a tree was a physical effort for him. With each branch, as he pulled himself higher, the view improved. His hands and clothes were black with the soot of the fire. Ten feet . . . twelve feet . . . fifteen feet. . . . He could not yet see the second story of his house. He pulled himself up yet another notch, and another—flirting with acrophobia, light-headed, slightly nauseated. Higher and higher he climbed, his attention on the view, not the ground. There. Nearly a quarter mile away, he spotted the roof of his own house. The sighting charged him with energy. He shifted focus, looking for the next limb to climb, and came face-to-face with letters and numbers freshly carved into the bark.

d A n 3 : 27

He held tight, staring at it for several minutes, his heart racing in his chest. From that higher perspective Boldt's house was entirely in view. A surge of adrenaline coursed through him. The arsonist had sat right here, in this very spot.

By the time he reached the bottom of the tree, Boldt already had his cellular phone in hand. He called LaMoia and said without introduction, ''Meet me at Enwright's and bring some running shoes.''

''Running shoes?'' the vain detective protested.

''Yeah,'' Boldt answered dryly. ''You can't climb trees in ostrich cowboy boots.''

32

"THREE different biblical quotations," Daphne said from the end of the fifth-floor conference table. Reading from a copy of the Bible, she said, "Daniel three, twenty-seven, carved in a tree with a good view of the Boldt home:

> And the princes, governors, and captains, and the
> King's counsellors, being gathered together, saw
> these men, upon whose bodies the fire had no
> power, nor was a hair of their head singed,
> neither were their coats changed, nor the smell of
> fire had passed on them."

She continued, "This is clearly aimed at us—police, firemen, *governors and captains*—and is much different from the others, both of which are aimed at retribution. At Dorothy Enwright's it was Ezekiel twenty-four, twelve:

> She hath wearied herself with lies, and her great
> scum went not forth out of her; her scum shall be
> in the fire."

"This guy has fried his circuits," LaMoia said, annoying her. "The anger is directed at a woman. That helps us."

"You, maybe," LaMoia said. "Doesn't help me any."

Boldt and LaMoia both had pine sap smeared on their clothing, their hands, and their faces. Locating the carved quotations had been time consuming, but easier than Boldt had expected; they had isolated the highest ground near the two victims' homes and had looked for the tallest trees and, of those, the easiest to climb. Between them, they had climbed a total of eight trees, two with a view of Enwright's and six with a view of Heifitz's. LaMoia had found both quotes.

"What's of interest to me—to us—is not only the quotes but the confirmation that this individual watched his fires or, at the very least, had a view of them. He's a fire lover. That's consistent with what we'd expect."

"Or he triggered them from up there," LaMoia suggested. "Quarter of a mile with some altitude," he reminded. "Even a bunch of the shitty hobby-type radio control devices would work at that distance."

"And he was carrying some kind of explosive accelerant on his person," Boldt contributed. "To be used just the way he used it on Branslonovich, I assume."

"Or as a distraction," LaMoia suggested. "A diversion, if necessary."

"So he's a planner," Daphne said, "which we already knew. He's voyeuristic, which works with what we know of arsonists. But what comes as a surprise are these biblical references. The earlier use of poetry suggested an intellectual, college educated, well read; the use of biblical references is typical of a different psychology, a more pathologically disturbed individual."

"The God squad," LaMoia said, well aware of Daphne's aversion to such terms. "A fruitcake. A nuthatch. I knew it all along. I said so all along, didn't I, Sarge?" He smiled thinly at the psychologist, mocking her. Despite their friendship, LaMoia and Daphne continually butted heads on matters of the criminal's psychology.

"Where's it leave us?" Boldt asked, ignoring LaMoia's outburst and hoping the pair of them would leave it alone. The discovery of the quotations, the physical carving of the bark, had humanized the killer for Boldt. Along with the ladder impressions, he had Liz's image of a thin man dressed in jeans and a dark sweatshirt. With the killer increasingly defined, so was the urgency within Boldt.

"The third poem, the one received yesterday," Daphne said, "was Nietzsche. This one was accompanied not by melted plastic but melted metal." To Boldt, she said, carefully and tactfully, "If you hadn't made your discovery last night, perhaps we wouldn't know the significance of the substitution of metal for plastic. And if Bernie Lofgrin's identification crew wasn't so consumed with working up evidence, they might have time to check the metal for us, but I know what they'll find anyway, so it really doesn't matter. Remember as a kid," she asked them both, "the pieces you moved on a Monopoly board? The hat—"

"The car!" LaMoia exclaimed.

"Metal," Daphne answered. "Aluminum? Pewter? Doesn't matter. The message is simple: The metal pieces were the players." To Boldt she said, "You're a *player* in the investigation. The arsonist sought a means to differentiate between one of his victims in a *house* and a *player*—namely, you," she said, meeting his eyes. "Shoswitz spread your name all over every press conference."

"Damn!" LaMoia gasped.

She had warned Boldt that he might be targeted, but neither of them brought it up.

She said, "What's of significance here is not only that he had the wherewithal to target the man running the investigation but the determination to see it through to fruition. Your family was in your house," she reminded him. "Would he have gone through with it if he'd had the chance?" She loved such theory. "He torched the two women only after they were alone, without their children, which is also why we assume he watches the houses prior to detonation. He doesn't want to kill any kids. That's significant. That's something I can run with. He has a conscience, Lou, which, quite frankly, makes him all the more dangerous. No nuthatch." She said this derisively to LaMoia. "Worse, the decision to take out the lead investigator indicates to me a man with a bigger plan, someone who needs more time, is willing to take a chance to buy him-self more time. Why?'' she asked rhetorically. ''To complete some larger goal? Kill more women? Burn more houses? Who knows? But more. Something more.''

Boldt felt restless. He got up and paced the room. A monster, he thought, no matter what she called him.

''You get like this,'' LaMoia said to her, ''and you give me the weebees. You freak me right-the-fuck out. You're guessing, right? Because it doesn't come off like that. It's weird, the way you get.''

''Educated guessing,'' Boldt clarified for her. He didn't want to tell her that he too felt an added urgency. Was it that the cor-nered animal strikes out? He wasn't sure. But it bubbled down inside him like something bad he'd eaten.

''My advice,'' she said, ''is that we get cranking on every damn aspect of this case we can. We pull manpower, whatever it takes.''

''I've been putting in sixteen-hour days,'' LaMoia complained. ''I've got a shitload of stuff to go over. I've got sap in my hair and pine needles down my pants. Don't tell me to get cranking. I thought you were going to produce some witness, this kid of yours. What about it?''

''Easy,'' Boldt chided. ''For two people with such mutual re-spect, you sure have a weird way of showing it.''

Daphne bristled at the detective. ''I'll get the witness,'' she declared harshly. ''There were other considerations at stake.''

''I'm sure there were,'' LaMoia snapped.

''Children, children,'' Boldt soothed.

Daphne slid back her chair and grabbed her paperwork. ''I'll get the witness,'' she repeated to LaMoia. She stormed out of the conference and shut the door.

''Proud of yourself?'' Boldt asked his detective, who looked smug.

''Damn right,'' LaMoia answered. ''When she gets pissed off her nipples get hard. You ever noticed that?''

''Cool it, John. That's enough.'' Boldt hated playing school-teacher. He decided to call LaMoia on his claims. ''What's all this 'stuff' you say you have for me? Anything useful?''

"Sarge, it's *me!* Useful? What do you think?"

"I think you're full of shit half the time," Boldt said angrily.

"Yeah. True enough. But what about the other half?" He held up his detective's notebook.

Boldt broke down and grinned. LaMoia had a way with him. "Go on," the sergeant encouraged, "I'm waiting."

"First thing is these ladder receipts. We're actually getting somewhere with this scanner stuff. It's taken a little time to get the bugs out, but yesterday—before all the shit hit the fan—we finished the scanning and dumped the data into an indexing engine, and we culled over eighty hits: eighty actual transactions of a Werner ladder being bought, complete with credit card or checking account number."

It felt like old news to Boldt, though he didn't say so. He had sat in that tree in the very spot the killer had sat, his wife had talked briefly to the man; he didn't want to hear about tracing back receipts for ladders, and yet he understood the importance of such evidence. They needed names, addresses. If LaMoia produced them, as he claimed he could, Boldt was interested. Until then, he felt like telling his detective to keep it to himself. But he understood well the need to voice one's accomplishments, no matter how small. Any detective was left defeated more often than not. Any win was worth a little applause. "That's great," Boldt said, attempting to sound enthusiastic.

"Tomorrow or the next day I should have the names that belong to those account numbers. We run the list by our military friends, we use the computer to compare it against the fire department's employee roster, present and past, and maybe we get a break. Stranger things have happened." He waited for Boldt to say something and, when he didn't, asked, "You okay, Sarge?"

"Fine."

"This thing shook you up. I can see it. *No problemo.* It would anybody. You want to blow this off for the time being?"

Boldt told him to go ahead.

"Yeah, okay. Fine. Cars is next," he said, changing papers. "I don't have shit. Nothing worth your time. Some hassles getting access to the vehicles. The Mazda belonging to Heifitz was impounded—based on what, I have no idea. Enwright's Ford, on the other hand, found its way over to her ex-husband's place. You ask me, that borders on grand theft auto, but what the fuck. He's going to let me take a look at the wheels, so what do we care? Stay tuned."

"That's it?"

"Best for last," LaMoia explained. "This possible Air Force connection—Matthews and her snitch saying this guy was Air Force. I greased an ATF guy with a pair of Sonics tickets. Preseason. No great loss. Decent guy at that. Says this isn't the first time they've investigated rocket fuel."

"Texas," Boldt said.

"Yeah, right, that video. Sure. But an arson in St. Louis as well. Another in the Raleigh–Durham area. One in Miami. Turns out a person can cook up some rocket fuel with a little bit of knowledge and a lot of balls. But the thing is, the homemade shit leaves crap behind—metals, shit like that. They can see it's homemade. What's bugging Casterstein, my friend says, is that if it's rocket fuel, it's clean stuff, and if it's clean then it's military quality. Well, you can be fucking sure that if it's military, it's Air Force, so I started kinda nibbling around at the edges, you understand, trying to get a fix on how a person scores Air Force quality rocket fuel. And the ATF guy is as baffled as I am. And I believe him, Sarge. I mention Mc-Chord," he said, referring to a base south of Tacoma, "and I don't get much of a rise out of him. But he says to me that if it's rocket fuel it's ICBM stuff, because the space shuttle fuel is produced privately in Utah, and their lab has the book on that shit. They can recognize it post facto." He lowered his voice intentionally. "But McChord is a major airlift center, Sarge. Shit coming and going constantly. And I get to thinking, What if some of what they're shipping is rocket fuel? I don't know to whom, I don't know why, but it's possible, isn't it? The Japs have a space program; maybe they're buying our shit to lift their rockets. Maybe it's bound for Korea for defense. Something hush-hush. But shit, it's worth looking into, don't you think? You know those military ordnance guys.

They'll freak out if they think someone has lifted some of their hooch. All we gotta do is tickle them a little bit."

"Do it," Boldt said, thinking back to Daphne's comment and the need to pursue absolutely every speck of evidence, every lead.

LaMoia had a devilish look. He said, "Or I can cut to the chase without involving the fruit salad boys. I kiss a few butts and see what I can get for us. Press some flesh. You'd be surprised what a bottle of Stoli and a night of lap-dancing can get you. Most of these MPs guarding the bases are just kids in uniforms. I flash my badge, they think I'm straight off the tube. You get these kids lip-walking drunk with some topless nineteen-year-old coed doing the Watusi in nothing but a thong, about an inch over their woodies, and they don't remember nothing about confidential." He said sarcastically, "I hate this work, Sergeant, you know that. But as long as I'm helping out, I'm there for the betterment of this investigation."

"Just exploratory," Boldt suggested. "A fact-finding mission."

"If the facts play out," LaMoia said, "then we obtain the necessary paperwork and we go through the front gate, nice and proper." Similar techniques were used in every investigation. It saved the investigator from the paperwork of pursuing any dead leads.

LaMoia sat uncharacteristically quiet for a moment.

"What?" Boldt asked.

The detective said, "Sarge, if you need it, you can hang in my crib for a while. I can make myself scarce over to a friend's."

"Who said anything about that?"

"Just if you need it," LaMoia offered.

Boldt saw that LaMoia meant it. A rare moment of outward compassion from the king of one-liners. Boldt thanked him and asked what they had on the movements of Enwright and Heifitz on the days of their murders.

LaMoia informed him they had credit card records and bank statements. He would check them out as well.

Boldt studied the detective. He looked exhausted and haggard. Boldt returned the concern: "What about you, John. Are you holding up?"

LaMoia didn't answer directly. His voice cracking with emotion, he said, "Just so you know, Sarge. If anything should happen to you, I will personally whack this guy. This is a promise that I swear on. So help me God, I'll kill him dead."

Boldt had no words. He reached out and briefly took the other's hand in his own. LaMoia had tears in his eyes. It was the first time Boldt had seen him cry.

33

BOLDT

had not stopped thinking about the runaway boy who had called in the homicide. He had been distracted, first by Bear's discovery of the Monopoly piece, then by the arsonist's targeting of his home, but each time he climbed into his car and drove the streets, he thought of the boy.

He was reminded of him again when Dixie's preliminary report on the crime scene arrived on Boldt's desk. A body discovered in a crawl space was not an everyday occurrence. The papers had run the story; a radio show had somehow gotten hold of the boy's 911 call and played it. There was an outcry from a domestic abuse group that too many women disappeared and too few of the disappearances were investigated thoroughly. The group, jumping to conclusions ahead of the medical examiner's report, pointed to the fact that the woman victim had been found in the crawl space of her own home.

The lead detective was typically present at an autopsy, but Dixie requested that Boldt attend as well since the investigation was being conducted by his squad. A press conference was anticipated; Dixie wanted a senior cop present.

When Tina Zyslanski showed up at the door to Homicide requesting Boldt, he agreed to an impromptu meeting despite his schedule, not because Zyslanski was a Community Service Officer but because the woman she was with, Susan Prescott, worked for Human Services and wanted to discuss the "crawl space murder," as Zyslanski put it. The boy! Boldt thought.

He walked them down to the conference room, Zyslanski making small talk along the way. She was an anorexic-looking woman with thin, lifeless hair and a nervous disposition. She hadn't seen the sun in too long; her skin was jaundiced and onion-skin thin. Susan Prescott was a cream-color black, broad-shouldered and slight-chested, hourglass waist and legs to the ceiling. She wore large gold hoop earrings that nearly touched her shoulders and walked like a woman who had worked the fashion ramps. She held her chin high, her neck stretched. She carried an air of indifference and alarming self-confidence. Boldt kept his eye on her. He held a chair for her as she sat.

She thanked him and said, "It's my job to do everything I can to find this boy, the one who called in the nine-eleven. It's your job to sort out the evidence. My hope is that maybe that evidence will point to where we might find the boy. I understand that he's a possible homicide witness and that's fine. I want him because he's likely to be traumatized, alone and scared. Every day he is outside of adult supervision is another chance he'll be swallowed by this city. The homeless. The child pornography rings. Drugs." She leaned on the word. "We would like to avoid that at all costs."

"I have a son, Ms. Prescott. I'm as anxious about this as you are."

"Then perhaps you will allow me into the home," she said, in a tone that sounded like a complaint.

Zyslanski explained. "The home is sealed with police tape and warnings. Human Services is requesting access to your crime scene."

"You are aware, are you not," asked Prescott, "that your primary suspect required outpatient hospital attention prior to his detention?"

Boldt had not studied the case carefully. He had left the case to the lead detective, focusing his own concerns on the kid's whereabouts. He didn't dare explain that. It wouldn't come out right.

When he failed to answer quickly, Prescott said, "From what I've been told of the injuries, from what I was able to see through the windows of that house, your suspect was certainly not beat up by a child. That implies the presence of a third party, and we at HS are concerned about the child's safety."

"The possibility of an abduction," Zyslanski explained.

"I have no problem with you entering that house. The lead detective on the case will want to join you, I would think, just to—"

"Keep an eye on me," Prescott answered, interrupting. "That's fine." She sounded dissatisfied.

"To protect the chain of custody," Boldt clarified. "It's a technicality, is all."

"It's the drug connection that has us most concerned. They use everything from five- and six-year-olds up to seventeen-year-olds to run their drugs. I don't need to tell you that."

"Drug running is certainly pervasive, yes. But I would hope—"

Prescott cut him off sharply. "It's not a word I can live with. One loses hope quite quickly in my job. One substitutes hard work, believing that in the occasional case it will make a difference. It doesn't very often, just for your information. But maybe this time, right? That's how you start every case."

"Maybe this time," Boldt agreed. He didn't need this woman soapboxing to him.

She inquired, "You are aware of the earlier nine-eleven call, Sergeant, aren't you?"

"I don't believe I am," Boldt admitted.

"I thought something was wrong here," Prescott said to her escort, Zyslanski. To an even more angry Boldt she said, "There was an earlier nine-eleven call, placed October fifth of this year. The Communications Center identified the number making the call and the address from which it was made. The report was made by a young boy who remained anonymous. It was believed a hoax but was passed on to us, as is required. The address of that first call is the same address where the body was found. The boy is the same boy," she explained. "But that earlier call is especially troubling to us, given the horrible condition your suspect was found in. Pretty tough stuff going on in that house. We assume it was a drug deal gone bad."

"A drug deal?"

"That first call?" she asked rhetorically. "It wasn't a hoax, as the dispatcher thought. The boy was trying to report a drug deal he had witnessed at the airport."

"Airport?" Alarms sounded inside Boldt's head. In a rare inability to control his emotions, he came out of his chair and he shouted, driving Prescott back from the table, "The airport? *A drug deal at the airport?*" Daphne's write-up of her second interview with the psychic had reported a drug deal at Sea-Tac involving the man with the burned hand. There were no coincidences in Boldt's world; everything could be explained.

"Ms. Prescott," Boldt said more calmly, regaining control, "I think you may have just found your runaway."

34

THERE were many times in the course
of a day that Daphne wondered what she was doing with her life.
Engaged to a man she was finding hard to love; loving an unavailable man; pressed between uniforms and suits, one of a handful of
women above the rank of patrol; volunteering a few nights a week
at a homeless shelter for kids who had seen too much and lived
too little; a scientist longing for the spiritual; a loner longing for a
partner.

Her car was parked in front of and across from the purple
house with the neon sign and the giant globe in the front lawn. At
exactly 3:07 P.M. a small boy came walking down the sidewalk and
turned into the driveway. He walked around to the back of the
house and was not seen again, presumably having gone inside.

Daphne glanced over at Susan Prescott sitting alongside her
and said, "Are you ready?"

"As ready as I'll ever be," answered the woman.

Daphne climbed out of the car. It was colder than earlier. She
shoved her hands into her pockets, still searching for alternatives.
She hated the idea of separating the boy from Emily, only to put

him in the custody of a public agency. She had paid plenty of visits to the King County Youth Detention Facility on Spruce. What if he somehow ended up there? Who was to blame then? It was all about pressure. It was about bringing Boldt a witness. It was about forcing Emily Richland to deliver.

She stayed as far to the edge of the property as possible, not wanting to be seen. Susan would wait to knock on the front door.

Daphne felt heavy and sad. The gray and the drizzle weighed her down that day. She wanted out. She wanted to be somebody else—a woman with a different past, a different job, a different life. Mrs. Owen Adler? She wasn't sure anymore, and one had to be sure. She was sick of herself, of the predictability of things.

Take a boy from someone willing to love and protect him and turn him over to the custody of the state? Life sucked. Susan knocked loudly. The sound bounced off the trees like gunshot reports. Daphne tensed, pulled her hands from her pockets, and climbed the back porch, placing herself immediately before the door. Pressure. It could be used to drill tunnels through mountains of solid rock; it could push people out backdoors.

She heard the muted sounds of a heated conversation between Susan and Emily. It started low but quickly grew to shouting. It was strange how, without hearing the actual words spoken, Daphne nonetheless could predict the conversation down to the punctuation. Susan represented herself as the authority that she was: City of Seattle Human Services, Child Custody. Emily mounted a quick but useless defense, objecting, interrupting, raising her anguish and decibel level to the point that Daphne clearly distinguished the words, "You cannot take him!"

Daphne spread her feet apart a little wider, like a boxer in a stance, braced for the collision that seemed imminent. She had mild cramps. She hadn't eaten anything all day. The two cups of morning tea sat in her stomach like a pool of acid. She had her period. A little nausea. It was a day to be in bed with the covers pulled up, or in a hot bath with some music playing. She decided she had been spending too much time at Owen's, not enough time on the houseboat; her priorities were all screwed up. Flat out hated herself. Bad time to be doing business.

"So there I was," Daphne said. "He came through the backdoor like a train running down hill, head down and hell bent."

Stretched out on the bed in Boldt's hotel room, Daphne was into her second beer. The room wasn't much—paid for by the city until Boldt was allowed to return to his house. He wanted back badly. He didn't feel right about Daphne stretched out like that. She wore tight black jeans and a white button-down shirt. She toyed with her watchband, spinning it around and around.

"I caught him in my arms, and he squirmed like . . . I don't know, a fish or something. Fought like hell. Poor kid. And of course she couldn't prove he was hers—because he isn't—which was all Susan required in order to take him. And now it has back-fired. We know exactly who he is, but he won't say one word to us. So . . . you know. . . ." Her voice trailed off.

"Don't beat yourself up over it," he advised. He was staying pretty much in the room's pullman kitchen, keeping his distance.

"Listen, if you'd been there," she said. "He was crying for her. She was crying too—begging us. It was awful."

"You're killing yourself over this," he said.

"It backfired," she repeated. She was beginning to sound a little drunk, to slur her words. "You want to stay out of trouble, don't mess with kids."

Boldt leaned forward.

"Don't lecture me," she cautioned, anticipating him. "I'm a big girl, and I want another beer."

"You drink it, and I'm driving you home."

"Promises, promises," she said. "Maybe I'll just sleep right here." She asked too loudly, "What are those?"

Boldt felt caught. He'd been about to attempt to talk her out of a third beer. She patted the edge of the bed, for him to sit closer, but he declined.

"Dorothy Enwright bought this from a hardware store the day

of the fire. John pieced it together." It was a can of compressed air, a roll of silver tape, a can of Drano and a pair of rubber gloves.

"Susan's letting let him stay with me—the boy," she stated.

"A hardware store," Boldt said, not wanting to look at her. "Might be a connection."

"It's that or some halfway house till things are sorted out, and I just can't do that to him. They have this thing called a Big Sister sponsorship. Susan has to bend the rules a little, but by tomorrow afternoon he's mine. And he won't run away, because we've told him that if he does, Emily Richland goes out of business, maybe to jail. He won't do that to her. See how good I am at my job? I thought you'd be proud. It's down to threatening twelve-year-olds."

"It's never easy," he answered. "Especially where kids are involved. Remember Justin Levitt?"

"They *look* so innocent. That's the thing. It's hard to get around the way they look at you." She added, "You miss them, don't you? Your kids?"

"Sure I do."

"She's got you forever. That's the thing. The day Miles was born I knew I'd lost you forever."

This was exactly where he didn't want the conversation straying. "What will Owen think about the boy?"

"I'll stay at the houseboat," she answered. "Owen and I . . ." she didn't finish, electing to drink the beer instead. "Really quite good," she said.

"You haven't lost me," he said.

"Of course I have." She wouldn't look at him. "We had our chance," she reminded him. "I'm not sour grapes." She said thoughtfully, "Maybe it wouldn't have worked with us. Who knows?"

They both knew better, he thought; it would have worked. It had always worked between them. He was thinking that, but he said, "I was separated at the time. Married."

"Don't remind me. Believe me, I remember that night well. Funny, what sticks with you and what doesn't. I'm the one who's supposed to be able to explain all that, right? All this training. But when it's my life? Forget it. That's the thing: objective, subjective. 'Tangled up in blue.' Was that Dylan or Joni Mitchell? Probably both. Hey,'' she added playfully, "did you grow up liking jazz, or was there a transition period? Folk rock? Rock? Or were you jazz right from the crib?''

"There may come a day when we're old, and our spouses have died off. For us, I mean.'' He wasn't sure why he was saying any of this.

"Like *Love in the Time of Cholera*, you mean?''

"Never read it.''

"Your loss.'' She said dreamily, "That's us, I suppose. Maybe you're right.'' She added, "It's a little morbid, though.''

"The thing of it is,'' he said, changing the subject, "the boy may break this open.''

The way she positioned herself on the bed—rolled up on one hip, her legs split, up on an elbow with her hand supporting her head—was too much. That lush hair, eyes a little drunk and dreamy. She said, "I wonder why I'm so hung up on you.''

"You're not.''

"Oh, but I am. We both know it.''

"We'll place Richland under surveillance,'' Boldt said. "Garman also, I think.''

She added, "I see the way you look at me sometimes. You don't think I feel that same stuff? Right down to my . . . bones,'' she said.

"She'll call us if he shows up?'' he stated.

Without missing a beat, Daphne answered, "As long as we have the boy, she will. If I'm her, my big worry is that the state gets him in their system and never lets him out.''

"Will Human Services ever let him go back to her?'' Boldt inquired dubiously. "There's no blood relation, is there?''

"He loves her,'' Daphne said painfully. "And she him. Does it really matter?''

A cellular phone rang. Boldt stood and reached for his, but it was hers, coming from her purse. She answered and listened. She mumbled, "Yes, I heard you." She flipped the phone shut. To Boldt she said, "We used the last name of the crawl space suspect. Susan cross-checked school enrollment. We know the boy's name: It's Benjamin Santori." She misted. "Nice name, isn't it?"

"It's a start," he said, trying to be upbeat.

"Just the point," she fired back. "A start for us, an end for him. Twelve years old, Lou. Murder. Some kind of exchange at the airport. She was protecting him from us: the courts, the truth. Can you blame her?" She sucked down a good deal of beer.

"I'll drive you and take a cab back. I insist."

"Then I'll take another," she said, holding up the empty can.

The beers were on ice in the ice bucket.

"First class service," Boldt said nervously, delivering the beer.

"I won't bite," she said, popping the top.

But Boldt wasn't so sure. He wasn't sure of anything anymore. The cellular phone rang for a second time. Boldt didn't even bother going for his, but when Daphne answered hers and shook her head, the sergeant thought better and lunged across the small room.

"Boldt!" he answered curtly. Cupping the phone, he told her, "LaMoia." He grunted into the receiver several times, impatient for his detective to get to the point. He was talking excitedly about scanners and hits and making a big point about his personal contacts in the banking industry.

Boldt listened intently as LaMoia finally got to the point. Boldt disconnected the call with a heart in his chest that couldn't find the beat.

"Good God!" she said, seeing his reaction. "What was that?"

Boldt took a deep breath, exhaled, and closed his eyes. When he opened them he said, "He got back the information on the ladders, the credit card accounts, and the bank accounts—the names, the mailing addresses . . ." She knew better than to interrupt. Boldt met her eyes and said, "Steven Garman bought one of the Werner ladders two years ago at a hardware store up on Eighty-fifth." He took a breath. "The thing to do now is see if he still has it."

• • •

Boldt did not drive Daphne home. Having interviewed Garman in the first place, she insisted on tagging along. During the hurried drive to a neighborhood twenty blocks north of Boldt's house, she spared no opportunity of reminding Boldt of that initial assessment of hers.

"One doesn't make arrests based on opinion," he replied, following her third reminder.

"It's the beer talking, not me," she apologized.

"Well, please ask the beer to be quiet when we get there," he snapped testily. "This is an inquiry, nothing more."

But the beer spoke again. "Bullshit, and you know it. If that ladder's there, its pads match. But it won't be. He knows all about that evidence."

"Which leads one to ask," Boldt countered, "why, if he knew about the impressions found at Enwright, did he use the same ladder at my house?"

The words flew around the inside of the car like trapped birds. Boldt ducked from them, shrinking from the logic of his own statement. Why indeed?

"You're not going there just to chat him up, and we both know it. Why did you ask for a patrol backup? I'll tell you why: Because you intend to cuff him and bring him downtown for the Box. That's why you need me along." She grabbed for the dash as Boldt pulled sharply off the road. "What are you doing?"

"I never thought I'd be glad about an espresso shop on every corner." She looked blank. He told her, "You're right. We had better get you a cup of strong coffee."

Despite her protests, at Garman's Daphne remained in the car. Boldt and LaMoia, who arrived only two minutes behind, approached the front door. The patrol car and its solo uniformed officer idled at the curb.

Garman wore reading glasses, a cotton sweater, and blue

jeans. His pager was clipped to his belt. "Gentlemen," he said, not a trace of concern or anguish in his voice.

There were times when Boldt liked to skirt the issue, make small talk, or bring up a subject completely away from his central point, establish a rapport, and ease his way into it, but he had a working relationship with Garman, and that evening he went straight for the jugular. "You bought a twenty-four-foot extension ladder manufactured by Werner Ladders from Delliser Brothers up on Eighty-fifth."

"Summer before last," Garman informed him, nodding. "You boys are thorough. I'll say that. You might have asked. I could have saved you the trouble."

Boldt and LaMoia engaged in a quick eye check, both surprised by Garman's forthcoming nature.

"We'd like to see that ladder," LaMoia told the fire inspector. The detective had called in a telephone search warrant that had been authorized by Judge Fitz. He informed Garman of this, hoping he might ruffle the man.

"You're welcome to come inside," Garman offered, opening his door wide. "You don't need a flipping warrant." The two detectives stepped in. Boldt heard a car door shut. He didn't need to look to know it was Daphne. "But you won't find a Werner ladder," Garman added, without a hint of remorse. "I replaced it with a different brand, one of those aluminum numbers that hinges in a couple of places. You know the kind?"

"Replaced it?" Boldt asked.

"It was stolen," Garman informed them. "Six, maybe seven months ago." He nodded, his lips pursed. "Swear to God." Daphne knocked. Garman admitted her. They shook hands. "Listen," Garman said, "you want to do this downtown, or can we do it here?"

Boldt felt out of sync, the fireman anticipating his every move, his every question. He wanted to take him downtown, use the Box, intimidate the man. Work a team interrogation, LaMoia the bad guy, Boldt the friend, Daphne the outsider. Loosen him up at the edges. Trip him up. But he wondered all of a sudden if it would work with a man accustomed to conducting his own investigations, his own interrogations. It felt a little bit like looking at himself in the mirror.

"Here will do," Boldt said, wanting to give the man nothing, wanting an explanation for the two dead women and the threat on his own family, but torn by the necessity of an assumption of innocence. Cops didn't work from such an assumption, they left it to the judges and juries. Boldt saw the man as a killer—clever, perhaps, professional, but a killer nonetheless. He owed him nothing.

"I'll look around," LaMoia said, directing one of his patented expressions of loathing toward the suspect. LaMoia was a cop who cut to the chase, rarely, if ever, electing subtleties. His method was more head-butting, beating a suspect down into submission. He produced a flattened Dunkin Donuts bag with a bunch of writing on it. He said, "Just to make it official. This is the warrant the judge signed off on."

The bag was oil stained, the writing illegible. Garman accepted it, looked it over, nodded, and handed it back. "Very official," he said, trying for a joke.

LaMoia recited the Miranda. Garman just smiled, miming the words along with him.

Boldt wanted to pop the guy. Garman was too smug, too prepared—or innocent as the day he was born. Boldt knew before they started that they weren't going anywhere with this one. Daphne asked for a cup of coffee. Garman made her a cup of instant; made one for himself as well. Boldt and Daphne sat on a couch that had seen better days. Garman took the La-Z-Boy recliner upholstered in a maroon Naugahyde.

Fifteen minutes into the questioning, Boldt taking furious notes and double-checking Garman's exact language, LaMoia joined them. He shook his head at Boldt from behind Garman and held both hands into a large zero. Boldt was hardly surprised.

They talked in circles for the better part of the next hour, returning to some of Garman's statements and attempting to catch him in a misspeak, but the Marshal Five's performance—if that's what it was—seemed utterly convincing. Here, Boldt realized, was a man who had achieved an honored position among firemen. He had served his city well, earning several merits of distinction for both his professional life and his volunteer work with teens. Put him in front of a jury with all the damning evidence in the world, and you might not win a conviction.

One hour and twenty-two minutes into the interrogation, Daphne scored the first big points. "Tell us again about your service in the Air Force."

He nodded. "I was stationed two years at Grand Forks AFB and six at Minot. I was married then. Young. Good times, for the most part."

"Not much up there," Daphne said.

"Even less than that," Garman replied, winning a smile from her.

"Must get to know the other guys real well," she said.

"You know everybody real well: guys, wives, families. Grand Forks is a big base. It's a town, a small city really."

LaMoia said, "Those are missile bases, aren't they?"

Garman smirked at the question. "Look it up, Detective. It'll give you something to do."

LaMoia bristled and shifted uncomfortably where he stood. He sought out a kitchen chair, brought it around to face Garman, and straddled it backward.

The lines were drawn—and by Garman himself, Boldt noted. He would work with Daphne, respect Boldt at a distance, and spar with LaMoia. What bothered Boldt the most was that he had sussed out the exact way Boldt would have done it.

"Your marriage?" Daphne asked.

"Out of bounds, counselor," Garman replied.

"I'm not a lawyer."

Garman stared at her. "We never did establish your exact role in this, did we? As I recall, you kind of skirted the question."

LaMoia said, "Look it up. It'll give you something to do."

That caused a brief crack in Garman's armor.

Boldt felt a little more optimistic. He said, "So you didn't lose the ladder or loan it to a friend—it was stolen."

"I'll answer for a fourth time if you want," Garman replied. He pursed his lips, looked each of them directly in the eye and said, "You'll find this out anyway. The ladder was the least of my concerns. It was my truck that was stolen. A white pickup. Damn nice one, too. Ford. Bucket seats. Electric windows. The ladder, some turnout gear, my clipboard. Cars . . . trucks . . . stolen every day in this city, right? I figured it was probably chopped and on its way by ship to Singapore or wherever they end up. Until the poems, the notes. Then I wondered if maybe I was some kind of target all along." He looked directly at LaMoia. "Of course, maybe I stole it myself and stashed it somewhere to use later in these arsons. Great excuse, a stolen truck."

LaMoia had his hands full. Boldt was used to rapid-fire comebacks, but the detective was slow off the blocks. All he managed to say was, "Yeah, great excuse."

They did the dance for the next forty minutes, but nothing worthwhile surfaced. Only LaMoia's questions were answered sarcastically. If Daphne repeated the question, Garman answered it. Boldt saw through the ruse. It meant that Garman feared LaMoia most of all—and he was correct in doing so. LaMoia didn't do the dance, he just stepped on toes and crashed his way through. When he got on a roll, when he got hot, he could pin a suspect in a matter of a couple of questions. Garman had sensed this quickly and did his best to prevent LaMoia from getting a rhythm going. That particular session was won by Garman, but there would be others.

He was the closest thing they had to a suspect, and Boldt was not about to let him go. He would cut him distance, give him some rope—hopefully enough to let him hang himself.

The interrogation was, in fact, little more than a stall for time.

Twenty-four-hour surveillance began thirty minutes before their departure.

Steven Garman was suspect number one.

35

BEN'S world had gone down in
flames. First the guy trying to kill him, then the discovery of
the body . . . he couldn't even think about it. Calling 911 and returning to watch his stepfather being arrested. It had a dreamlike
quality, distant and yet present at the same time.

And whereas he had forgotten so much of his mother, her
reality clouded by his stepfather's unyielding demands and pun-
ishments, she was suddenly a much greater part of him. He found
her present in his thoughts, before him as a vision, a soothing,
calming force at once transparent and yet palpably real, like an
ocean current. Taking him somewhere new and different.

The days immediately after the incident had been among the
best in his life. Emily had given him his own room, his own towels;
she had cooked his meals and even made him a sandwich for
school lunch. He didn't tell her that he didn't go to school for those
days—he was too terrified the blue truck might return, that the
nightmare might start all over again. So he skipped school, climbed
trees, and watched boats and Windsurfers out on Lake Washington, looking like moths on a window. He didn't even have the five

hundred bucks. It was at the house, hidden in his room, and he sure wasn't going back there.

They were good days, even though Emily wouldn't let him help her with her clients, something Ben didn't understand but didn't protest too loudly. He wasn't going to push things. At night she turned off her neon sign and locked her door, and together they either played cards or worked on a jigsaw puzzle. Emily didn't own a television, something that stunned Ben when he had first learned of it, but he hadn't missed it at all. Before bed she would read to him, which was a first. Aside from teachers at school, no one had ever read to Ben in his twelve years.

Being caught by the police had scared him to death. Convinced that they knew about the five hundred dollars, he had refused to speak at first. But when Daphne Matthews had given him the choice of a juvenile detention center or going home with her to her houseboat, Ben had spoken up loud and clear. He had never seen a houseboat; he could just imagine the detention center. Speaking had broken the ice. It had been hard not to talk, given all that had happened. Daphne proved to be both a nice woman and someone easy to talk to—almost as if she knew what he was thinking before he said anything. She amazed him that way.

Even so, he missed Emily with an ache in his heart unmatched since he discovered his mother's ring in the crawl space.

At that moment he sat on a couch in Daphne's houseboat, the television tuned to a black-and-white rerun on Nickelodeon.

For the past two days he had never been alone, except in the bathroom. When Daphne wasn't there, Susan was. He considered running away, though the only place he could think to go was Emily's, and it would be the first place they would look for him. Besides, Daphne had warned him that if he "misbehaved in any way whatsoever" it would hurt Emily. She hadn't spelled it out, but it was pretty clear to him that Emily would be out of business and he would lose any chance of ever living with her again. That was unthinkable. Emily was all he had. No running away. He missed her something awful.

Daphne picked him up every afternoon from "school," a place

surrounded by wire fence, for juveniles in detention. They went for snacks. They drove around. She had taken him to the Science Center, a place he'd never been. After dinner she took him to her houseboat and he watched television or read a book. The houseboat was small, but he liked it okay. The walls were thin. When she thought he was reading, he was actually listening to her on the phone. She spoke to someone named Owen, and he knew enough to know that things weren't going great between them. Twice she had hung up and started crying. It had never occurred to him that police ever cried.

Twice, he had stolen a look at Daphne's papers, because she wrote at the little desk downstairs where Ben slept, and he had to know if it was about him or not. So he read everything he could find, including the thick file she carried back and forth between home and the office. To Ben it wasn't much different from peering in car windows.

He wasn't sure exactly why, but she made him write one page in a diary every day. If he wrote in the diary, he didn't have to sit down and talk to her at night—only to the other woman, Susan, during the day. To avoid the extra talking, he did the writing. She had told him he could write about anything—school, home, Emily's, his dreams—or he could make up a story.

The night before, he had dreamed about being part of an Egyptian archaeological dig, like on the National Geographic specials. He had to crawl on his belly inside the pyramid, crawl over rocks and dirt and mud. It reminded him of Indiana Jones. And when he got to the tomb, there was all this gold—gold rings of every size—and a mummy of the queen, all wrapped up in gauze. And when he unwrapped the mummy, it was his mother's face. Frightened, he had run from the place, leaving all the gold behind. Losing his way. He had awakened right there on that fold-out couch.

He put his pencil on the third page of the diary and began to slowly scrawl out his dream.

Last nite I dreamed I was in Egipt. . . .

36

BOLDT likened an investigation to an enormous rock or boulder on the summit of a mountain. Initially, the investigator's job was to climb that mountain, gathering up whatever tools made themselves available—whatever evidence could be found. Reaching the rock, tools in hand, the investigator went about trying to leverage the rock, summoning whatever size team was necessary. Together, the team went about the job of displacing the rock, prying, pushing, shoving. The better organized the team, the better directed, the quicker the boulder gave way. Once displaced, the investigation was rolled toward the edge, given one final push, and gravity took over, at which point the task was to stay with it—all teammates pursuing it simultaneously—a mad, frantic race down hill in the midst of a landslide created by the beast itself. The job at hand by now: to keep the rock from exploding into bits at the bottom.

Boldt was caught in that landslide.

He didn't recognize it at first, and this typically proved the most difficult task of all—understanding what phase of the investigation one was in—for inevitably some of the team were still uphill with the pry bars while the rock itself was hurling toward the bottom. The possible involvement of the psychic's military man with the burned hand, the ATF lab's suggestion of rocket fuel as the accelerant, and finally Garman's purchase of a Werner ladder had sent the rock tumbling downhill. At that point it became Boldt's job to stay with it, to shape the investigation into something manageable. That task was made more difficult by two subsequent occurrences.

The first was Garman's receipt of a fourth poem and piece of green plastic—this *following* his interrogation. Was he brazenly taunting the police, Boldt wondered—or was he, as he claimed, an innocent go-between?

The second was a phone call received by Daphne from Emily Richland on that same day. She hurried into the bull pen, out of breath from having run downstairs from the ninth floor. Her voice was frantic, her words rushed as she shouted, "That was *her*! Emily! Nick, the guy with the burned hand, just made an appointment with her for five o'clock today. That's only two hours from now. Can we handle it?"

Boldt felt an immediate knot of tension, from his stomach to his pounding head. Two hours, he wondered. Surveillance, ERT, bomb squad—a repeat of the team assembled just over a week earlier. Branslonovich was barely in her grave. His memory of that spectral vision haunted him. "We'll try," he said.

37

AT 4:49 P.M., a bald-headed man wearing khakis and ankle-high deck shoes came out through the front the door of the purple house on 21st Avenue East. The detectives had nicknamed him the General. The General wore wire-rimmed glasses and a blue beret. He carried a small brown leather briefcase as he walked briskly to a nondescript station wagon and drove off. The briefcase had contained a lavaliere condenser microphone and a battery-powered wireless radio transmitter, presently taped to the bottom of Emily's "reading" table. A wide-angle black-and-white fiber-optic camera was installed into the kitchen peephole, giving those in the operations van a look at Emily's back and shoulders and a slightly distorted fish-eye view of the face of her client. The video's transmitter was connected to a Direct TV dish mounted on the outside of the purple house.

The operations van, the same steam-cleaning van used less than a week before, was parked a block down 21st.

A FOR SALE sign had been placed on the lawn of the adjacent house. Above the sign was a small plaque announcing OPEN HOUSE, complete with six colorful balloons, and a floodlight lighting the sign. The lights to this house were all ablaze. The mustached man in the green sport jacket boasting the real estate logo wore pressed blue jeans and ostrich cowboy boots. LaMoia came and went from that house, greeting other undercover cops who arrived on schedule to view the house, all of whom kept one eye on the purple house next door and a flesh-colored earpiece embedded in their right ears. In the back room of this house, two members of the bomb squad and two ERT officers awaited orders.

Two other members of the bomb squad ran the tow truck that was busy—albeit slowly—hoisting an illegally parked car up onto the flatbed. Their location, immediately outside of the driveway to the purple house, allowed them quick access to the light blue truck and white camper shell that was expected any minute.

Boldt, Bobbie Gaynes, and Daphne occupied fuzzy padded seats that faced a large Mylar-covered picture window in a cream brown customized recreational van parked across the street from the open house. Gaynes had the body of a gymnast and the bright blue eyes of a child on Christmas morning. She wore a quilted white thermal undershirt and blue jeans and leather Redwing work boots with waffle soles. Boldt had his cellular phone in hand, the line open to a phone set that connected directly to the headset of the operations van dispatcher. At his feet were two portable radio systems, one that allowed them to communicate with, and to hear, the secured channel of radio traffic; the second, a live feed from the transmitter inside the purple house. A cellular phone in the seat next to Gaynes was wired to a battery-operated portable fax machine. On the floor lay two shotguns, a nightstick, a TASER, and two boxes of shotgun shells. Next to these were two flak vests marked POLICE in bright yellow letters. Boldt looked around, realizing they seemed equipped for a small war.

On the second floor of the open house, in a storage room left dark, a police photographer operated a pair of 35-mm Nikons, each with a different speed film. Every movement would be recorded, every word.

A bicyclist, a motorcycle rider, and two unmarked cars were spread between the surrounding streets, ready to follow the truck when it left the area. The drivers of these vehicles also were keeping an eye out for the camper's arrival.

At 4:57 P.M. the motorcycle rider's voice came clearly over the radio.

RIDER: *Suspect's vehicle, Washington tag 124 B76, just passed checkpoint Bravo, headed in a westerly direction. Copy?*

DISPATCH: *Westbound. Copy.*

"Right on time," Boldt said, checking his watch.

Daphne, wearing her game face, was prepared to deliver a real-time psychological evaluation of the suspect.

DISPATCH: *124 B76 is registered to one Nicholas Trenton Hall, a male Caucasian, twenty-six years of age. Residence listed as 134 232nd Street South, Parkland.*

"Here he comes," said Gaynes, from where she had her eye to a crack left between a pair of brown curtains that kept the van's two forward seats separate from the passenger area. Seeing the truck approaching, Boldt felt a stirring of vengeful anger. He recalled Bronslonovich twirling in flames in the circle of trees, like an effigy burning. One man responsible for the death of so many.

Daphne said, "Is he Air Force? Can we confirm that?"

Boldt repeated this question into his phone. Dispatch replied that a "full query" was under way. He reported this to Daphne. She nodded, her sober face revealing no emotion.

Not thirty seconds had passed before Boldt, holding the phone loosely to his ear, pressed it closer and relayed to Daphne, "He was Air Force for eight of the last eleven years, a civilian employee at Chief Joseph for the last three."

"The discharge—his employment change—coincides with the hand injury. Bet on it."

"Is he our guy?" Gaynes asked from the front where, she watched the slow approach of the truck.

Boldt shrugged. He glanced out the window. LaMoia was on the porch of the open house, shaking hands and saying goodbye to Brimsley and Meyers, a pair of Narcotics detectives. Brimsley and Meyers were among the best shots on the force with handguns. Boldt had wanted them outside, on the playing field, at the time of the suspect's arrival. If the surveillance went bad, he reasoned, case histories showed it would happen in the first two minutes. He wanted his best people out there. He knew Brimsley and Meyers well enough to judge them oversized; they were wearing police vests, he beneath his sport coat, she beneath a blue rain slicker. The two cops stopped on the path, turned, and waved goodbye, Brimsley shouting his thanks to the real estate agent, both officers facing the purple house slightly, ready for weapons fire.

Nicholas Hall left his truck and followed the path past the huge globe, his face reflecting the colors in the neon sign. He pushed the button. The doorbell was heard over the surveillance radio.

Boldt, tight as a knot, muttered, "Get him inside."

The suspect took notice of Brimsley and Meyers next door. He then glanced around cautiously, suspiciously. He looked right at the police van. "Freeze," Boldt said. "No one breathes." Hall's attention on his surroundings continued even after Emily answered the door. His attention focused on the two men struggling to hoist the car up onto the tow truck. The bomb squad crew was not particularly adept at car towing.

The fax machine began to whine. Boldt glanced hotly toward it as a poor copy of a black-and-white photograph of the suspect slowly wound out, an enlargement of a driver's license photo. Nicholas Hall looked average in every way.

Into his phone, Boldt whispered, "Find out about that right hand."

The hand. Even from a distance it was noticeable. Boldt snagged a pair of binoculars, glad to have the porch light. The hand. A single piece of red flesh with three fingernails growing out of the end. It looked as though the man had put his real hand into a pink ballerina slipper or a costume glove. But this glove would not come off. A moment of panic surged through Boldt at first sight of that hand: Could such a person climb and descend trees?

Could he carve biblical references into a tree trunk? Boldt snatched up his phone and told the dispatcher to reach him on the radio if necessary. He ended the call on the cellular and dialed Lofgrin's office, hoping the man had stayed late, as he often did.

Gaynes handed Boldt the fax of Hall's face. Boldt accepted the fax but put it quickly aside.

At the front door, Hall continued to watch the two at the tow truck.

"Welcome," the three in the van faintly heard Emily say as she greeted Hall. The microphone was some fifteen feet and a room behind her, yet it still grabbed some sound. "Come in," she encouraged.

"You seen 'em tow cars around here before?" he asked her. "That something they do here up in the city?"

"All the time," she lied.

"Ticket them, sure. But tow them?"

"They make more money towing them. What do you think it's about, parking spaces?" she asked cynically. "Besides, what do you care?" she asked. "You're okay in my drive."

"One cool woman," Daphne said under her breath.

"I'll say," Gaynes agreed.

One of Lofgrin's assistants answered Boldt's call. The boss had gone home. Boldt asked for his home phone. The assistant gave him the number for a car phone, adding, "He just left a few minutes ago."

Boldt reached Lofgrin, who was in slow traffic on the floating bridge. The sergeant asked him, "Those tree carvings?"

"Yeah?"

"The guy was right-handed or left-handed?"

"I don't believe we checked for that."

Surveillance operations were conducted on a need-to-know basis. Lofgrin had no idea that Boldt was in a department-owned repossessed luxury van with his eyes on a possible suspect.

"We shot some macros, with the digital. My people can enlarge them. You want me to look at it, I can have them faxed right here to the car. Otherwise, they should be able to handle it for you." Boldt had seen the inside of Lofgrin's department-issued vehicle. Equipped with a Motorola Communication terminal, printer, cellular phone, and fax machine, it served as the Identification Division's field office at crime scenes.

"I need it ASAP. I'm on a surveillance, Bernie."

"Give me a number."

Knowing his might be tied up, Boldt checked if Daphne was carrying her phone. She was. Boldt gave Lofgrin that number.

Lofgrin said, "Traffic sucks. That's in our favor. I can get some work done. Right back to you."

Boldt thanked him and disconnected the line. He redialed and was once again connected with the steam-clean van.

Nicholas Hall stepped through the front door, which closed behind him. Emily's voice grew louder as she led him into the room and toward the microphone.

Daphne sat with her eyes shut, concentrating. She sensed Boldt looking and said softly, "He didn't like the tow truck." She added, "I suggest we lose it."

Without hesitation, Boldt passed this along to dispatch. Less than a minute later the towed vehicle was secure on the flatbed, and the truck pulled away and down the street.

For the next minute, the only radio traffic was between operations dispatch and a pair of ERT officers concealed behind a hedgerow immediately to the north of Emily's purple house.

One of these ERT officers, identified only by the number seven, checked several times to determine beyond a doubt that the suspect was known to be inside the structure. Then, in what appeared to be nothing more than a shadow moving across the grass, Boldt witnessed this same agent roll out of the bushes and under Hall's truck. Less than five seconds later, he rolled back out from under the truck and vanished into the darkness beneath a large cedar tree.

"GPS is in place," this man announced over the radio. Dispatch acknowledged, repeating the statement. A sophisticated location device had been attached to Hall's truck, enabling police to track its movement and identify its whereabouts. This accom-

plished, mobile surveillance could then follow blocks behind the
suspect's vehicle, well out of sight. It was a major accomplishment,
and one that helped Boldt feel at ease and in control.

"Good move," Daphne said, eyes still closed. She added, "I'd
tell LaMoia to keep the frat party atmosphere to a minimum. Might
be wise, in fact, if he packed it up, made the house dark, and left
behind whoever needs to be there. Mr. Hall is a control freak," she
announced in a cold, authoritative voice.

Boldt felt a chill down his spine.

She continued, "He's used to the military way: everything in
its place. Everything explainable. He doesn't like variations on a
theme. He listens to country music. He's macho. He'll take her as a
hostage if he's pushed." This came out as a warning. Allowing
Emily to conduct her fortune-telling had been a huge risk for Boldt
to take. He had trusted Daphne's assessment of the woman—that
they could work with her. Putting a civilian at risk was absolutely
forbidden within the department; nonetheless, it was done on rare
occasions—with all sorts of legal waivers in place—and this evening was just such an exception.

Daphne explained her reasoning without Boldt asking. "The
belt Emily described is a Western thing. Rodeo. That's country
music—that's a macho attitude: little woman in her place, and all
that goes with it. He's angry about that right hand, angry every day
of his life. He believes he's owed something for that hand. That
could be at the heart of all of this—retribution. I don't trust him
with her. We want to make him comfortable in there."

A phone rang in the heart of her purse. For the first time Boldt
noticed a walkie-talkie sitting in her lap and wondered where it
had come from. She took the phone from her purse and passed it
to Boldt.

The sergeant answered. Lofgrin's voice said, "Ninety-percent
chance whoever carved that tree was right-handed." Static.

Dismayed, Boldt said, "I owe you."

Lofgrin answered, "True story."

Boldt passed the phone back to Matthews.

"It wasn't him in that tree, was it?" Daphne said.

"What makes you say that?" Boldt asked.

"Well, I'll be damned," she replied, not answering. She jumped ahead of him. "Garman's back in the picture."

Astounded, Gaynes said, "Are you saying Hall is *not* the arsonist?"

"Where Nicholas Hall fits in is anybody's guess." Daphne held up her index finger, halting conversation. She pointed to the radios. "Here we go," she said.

EMILY: *Welcome back.*
HALL: *I want to check a date with you.*

Daphne hoisted the walkie-talkie and said softly, "Like before."

EMILY: *Like before.*

Boldt glanced over at Daphne. She answered the look in a calm voice, saying, "Nicholas Hall isn't the only control freak." Bobbie Gaynes grinned.

HALL: *Yeah, that's right. Like before.*

Daphne said, "Ask him if the dates worked out."
Boldt asked her, "When did you arrange this?" She chastised him with a look that told him to hold his questions for later.

EMILY: *So, did our other sessions work out for you? They did, didn't they? The stars are a powerful tool, aren't they?*
HALL: *It's next week. Next Thursday. You can check that, right?*

Daphne spoke into the walkie-talkie. "Check the charts and tell him it's a bad day. Something sooner would work better."

Over the radio Boldt heard Emily stand and open a drawer. There was a rustling of paper; she returned to the table with the microphone and sat down.

EMILY: *You have a descending moon next week.*

The psychic's voice sounded ominous and foreboding.

Gaynes quipped, "My moon's been descending since I passed thirty. My planets too!" She of the perfect body.

Daphne shot her a hot, annoyed look, but Boldt grinned.

HALL: *What's that mean?*
EMILY: *It's not a particularly fortuitous time for you to be making a business deal. You said this was business, not pleasure, isn't that right?*
HALL: *Does it make a difference?*
EMILY: *Very much so.*

Daphne announced to her colleagues, "This is interesting. How can someone quoting Plato believe this stuff? I think he takes it quite seriously."

Boldt had no comment. For him the interview with the psychic was only the beginning. They needed hard evidence against Hall. Probable cause to raid the truck and his residence. Bust it open, a voice inside him urged. The discovery that Hall was unlikely to have carved those trees left Boldt with a pit in his stomach. The wrong guy? He felt impatient and edgy. He didn't want any hostages, any shooting; he wanted this clean; they had to follow Hall, make something happen. Justify a raid.

HALL: *Business, yeah.*

"Bingo," said Daphne. Into the walkie-talkie she said, "Try to draw it out of him."

EMILY: *The kind of business can influence the way the charts are read. Sales for instance. Sales are particularly bad in a descending moon. Negotiations, however, don't suffer so much. You could negotiate next week, if you're careful. But if it's sales, I would suggest you advance the date. (Paper rustling) The next two to three days would be far superior. (Pause) Is there a date in that range you'd like me to check?*
HALL: *(Pause) How come you didn't mention this before? Last time? This moon thing.*
EMILY: *There was no descending moon involved. Your chart was good*

last time. Not as good this time. (Pause) Is it sales then? It influences the way I read the charts.

HALL: *Sales. Yeah. You could say that.*

Daphne said into the walkie-talkie, "Well done. Number of people involved. Location."

EMILY: *(Clears voice) You have a good Mars and Venus. But Pluto is way off. . . . That says something about numbers. There are not a lot of people involved in this sale, are there? (Pause) One other. Am I right about that?*

HALL: *This shit amazes me.*

EMILY: *Cars. Darkness. Lots of cars. Parked cars. Am I seeing that clearly? Loud noises. What's that noise? Roaring, like animals.*

HALL: *Jets.*

EMILY: *Of course, the airport. (Pause) You work at the airport.*

HALL: *Something like that. You fuckin' amaze me.*

EMILY: *There's a man, isn't there? There's another man involved in this sale. One other man.*

HALL: *Whatever.*

EMILY: *But not a group of people. That's important.*

HALL: *Not a group.*

Boldt sat forward. "The airport drug deal the boy called in."

Bobbie Gaynes said, "Well, at least it's not a militia or something like that. At least it's not another Oklahoma City."

"He trusts her," Daphne stated. "He's displaying a great deal of trust in her."

EMILY: *The next day or two. Three at the outside. I wish I had better news.*

HALL: *You missed something last time. (Pause.) I nearly didn't come back to you because of that.*

EMILY: *(Long pause) I'm seeing something outside of your business arrangement. Something unexpected. Something missing, perhaps. You lost something?*

HALL: *It was stolen.*

Daphne said anxiously, "I don't know what this is about."
Boldt answered, "I bet our friend Ben does."
Daphne shot him a surprised look.

EMILY: *Money.*
HALL: *Damn right.*
EMILY: *A lot of money.*
HALL: *Fuck yes, a lot of money. It was a boy. A boy stole it. Right out of my truck. (Pause) I want that money.*

Daphne met Boldt's eyes. "Ben," she said agreeing with him.
Boldt nodded. "No wonder he's scared of us. He's worried we're after *him*."
"She knows the whole story. Ben told her," Daphne said, sounding a little wounded.
Boldt worried about her relationship with the boy. "Or she got Ben to steal the money for her. Maybe it's not the first time," Boldt suggested.
"No," Daphne countered, "I don't believe that."
Boldt, thinking aloud, said, "He's Air Force. It wasn't drugs. It was rocket fuel." The silence in the van was shattered by the speaker.

HALL: *I thought you could see this shit! Why didn't you warn me?*
EMILY: *You asked me about a particular date. That was all.*
HALL: *Well, now I'm asking about complications. The unforeseen shit. I don't need any of that.*
EMILY: *And I'm warning you that the longer you allow the descending moon—*
HALL: *Fuck the descending moon! What about complications?*

Daphne said, "I don't like the hostility. He's in a mood swing here. Something triggered that swing." Into the walkie-talkie she said, "Placate him. Go easy. Be vague. I'm not liking what I'm hearing." To Boldt—the walkie-talkie back in her lap—she said, "Can we kick it if we have to?"
Boldt felt his scalp prickle with sweat. He didn't want it heading in that direction.

HALL: *What about if I pull it off in the next few days?* (Pause) *What if I can't get it together in the next few days?*

EMILY: *You* can *get it together. The stars support success.* (Pause.) *The moon isn't good for some time.*

HALL: *How long?*

EMILY: *How long?*

Daphne depressed the talk button. "Make it a long time. Force this on him."

EMILY: *The moon won't ascend for another month.*

HALL: *What?*

EMILY: *This isn't a good month for you where business is concerned. Love, on the other hand, is on the rise.*

Gaynes said, "This woman is a piece of work!"

EMILY: *No more complications if you act quickly. This boy, whoever he is, won't bother you again. You frightened him.*

HALL: *He's got my money.* (Pause) *Listen . . . Can you help me find him?* (Pause) *There would be a bonus.* (Pause) *He's kinda disappeared.*

Boldt said excitedly, "We can use this."

"No!" snapped Daphne.

Boldt held his eyes on her, his determination. "It takes Ben out of the loop and just might give us our probable cause."

Daphne, eyes still on Boldt said into the walkie-talkie, "If you know where that money is, sweetheart, it's time for a vision. You tell him. We all want Ben out of this."

Collectively, they held their breath as they awaited Emily's decision.

EMILY: *I see a brown house. Small.*

Relief flooding him, Boldt said, "There we go!"

HALL: *That's the boy's place!*

EMILY: *The money is there.* (Pause) *A second story?*

HALL: (Sounding anxious) *Yes!*

EMILY: *The boy's room. A box. A plastic box. Wait a second . . . (Pause)*
    Rectangular.
HALL: *A cigar box.*
EMILY: No.
HALL: *A toy safe? A lockbox? Something like that?*
EMILY: *A lunch box? (Pause) Ah! There it is clearly. It's a video. A box*
    for a video tape.
HALL: (Excited; the sound of a chair moving*) How much?*
EMILY: *What?*
HALL: *How much do I owe you?*

Daphne said into the device, "Let him go."

EMILY: *Ten for the reading.*
HALL: *I'm giving you twenty. (Pause) I'll try for sometime in the next*
    three days.
EMILY: *Yes. Better than next week.*
HALL: *I'll be back to check with you.*

Bobbie Gaynes asked, "Do we follow?"

Boldt answered, "No, we lead. We know exactly where he's going. Sooner or later he's going after that money."

Daphne said, "That personality? He'll go for the money right away. Bet on it."

38

BOLD T planned to take Hall into custody at Ben's house.

He confirmed that Hall's residence—identified as a mobile home in Parkland—was already under surveillance. A backup team was put on standby.

Hall left Emily's, the object of a dozen pair of eyes, climbed into his truck, and drove away while Homicide, ERT, and bomb squad officers looked on. Many of these people experienced disappointment, the accumulated adrenaline of the past hour finding no outlet.

The blue-and-white truck drove down 21st and turned left on Yesler.

With Gaynes driving, the brown recreational van negotiated a U-turn and headed north on 21st, right on Spruce, and right again on 23rd. The police radio identified the truck as paused for a light at Yesler and 23rd.

The police van drove through the intersection heading south. Boldt spotted the truck to his right, four cars back, waiting for the light.

"There he is," Boldt told the others. They drove past. Boldt held him in sight as long as possible. He scrambled for a map.

As expected, a moment later the blue-and-white truck turned south on 23rd.

Boldt cautioned Gaynes, "He could be heading south to Parkland—"

"He's not," Daphne interrupted.

"We want to continue south until he commits," Boldt finished, annoyed by Daphne's confidence.

Boldt found himself willing Hall to turn left on Jackson in the direction of the Santori house. His muscles ached from holding himself so tight. He caught himself grinding his teeth.

Dispatch announced, "Suspect vehicle turning east on Jackson Street East."

"Told ya," Daphne said proudly.

Gaynes checked the outside mirror. "He's too far back. I've lost him."

Checking a street sign, Boldt instructed her, "Left on Norman."

The surveillance car following Hall at a distance reported in. Boldt directed them to remain on 23rd and pass Jackson. "It's too small a street," he told Daphne and Gaynes. "He might spot them."

Jackson was a dead end, up a steep hill; the Santori home backed up to Frink Park.

Boldt ordered the surveillance car left on Dearborn, two blocks behind where the van turned. The van and the surveillance car then ran parallel to each other on two adjacent avenues, the van turning right one block south of Jackson and the surveillance car, one block north. A third unmarked vehicle was told to park with a view of the intersection of Jackson and 23rd.

ERT was deployed into Frink Park, in case Hall fled on foot.

Dispatch confirmed that the vehicle came to a stop a half block from the Santori home.

With the suspect effectively boxed in, Boldt checked his weapon and sat forward to leave the van.

"I'm coming with you," Daphne said, removing her weapon from her purse. Before Boldt could contradict this, she added, "I outrank Bobbie. No offense," she said to the woman, a veteran homicide detective. "Lou," she said, in a gentler voice, "I need to be reading this guy from the word go. If I'm there at the bust, it gives us a leg up."

Daphne had always allowed her ambition to get in the way. She carried a large scar on her neck because of this. Boldt had witnessed that wound as it happened. He couldn't put either of them through that again. She could be something of a loose cannon, in her determination to be the first inside a suspect's psyche. But even so, Boldt did not argue. The more they understood about Hall the better. "We partner on this, Daffy. And I'm the lead." He said it in a way that humbled her briefly.

"You're the lead," she agreed.

Boldt nodded. To Gaynes he said, "You're our backup. I'll be on radio." He indicated for her to pass him a walkie-talkie from the front. She handed him a large flashlight as well, that could double as a near deadly nightstick. He stuck the earpiece in his ear and secured the radio in his coat pocket. The dispatcher's voice announced that ERT was in place and the truck had been spotted and was empty.

Boldt told Gaynes, "We call for help, you send in the cavalry."

"Understood," replied the driver, her disappointment apparent.

Daphne was a faster walker. Boldt grabbed her arm and tugged. The two hurried up the hill and cut in behind the house on the far corner of the property. They made for a decrepit gardening shack.

Its doors were held closed by a board that spun on a nail. Boldt got the door open quietly and pulled Daphne inside with him, leaving the door unfastened.

Daphne whispered softly, "Did I mention that I absolutely hate places like this?"

It was dusty and dank, spiderwebs and mildew. There was a '57 Chevy on blocks, too much dust across its skin to discern a color. It was ensconced in a cocoon of sports equipment, storage boxes, and milk crates. There was barely enough room for the two of them to stand. There was a boy's bike to her left, shiny and well-kept.

Daphne threw one arm around him, like a child seeking comfort. Her body was warm and it moved behind her heavy breathing.

With the shed door open an inch, they had a good view of the house. Light from a flashlight flickered in a window, but only briefly. Boldt heard an exchange between ERT and dispatch. His heart raced in anticipation.

"He's in there," Daphne said, sounding excited.

A shadow moved in the same window.

Nicholas Hall stood less than twenty yards away, his attention fixed on the back yard. Boldt whispered, "He senses us. This guy has good instincts."

He felt her nod.

Hall's shadow crossed the window. Boldt felt it as a cold breeze.

Daphne remained pressed close. Boldt wanted to push her away, but he didn't. Instead he drank in her warmth, the feel of her breath against his neck, the gentle touch of her fingers on his waist. "Come on out," she whispered, encouraging the suspect.

Boldt willed the man to find the money, knowing he wouldn't have taken that much time if he had found it right away.

"If he comes out without the money?" Daphne asked quietly.

"We'll have a mess," Boldt answered. He didn't need to elaborate further.

Daphne whispered, "Five hundred dollars is a fortune to him. He'll find it."

Boldt elbowed some distance between them. He couldn't take her talking into his ear, even at a whisper. He couldn't take her hands on him. His skin was hot and his pulse racing. She felt the elbow and held him all the harder.

Hall could be heard hurrying down the steps inside the house. Boldt worried that the man had given up. Disappointment surged through the sergeant. To bust him *without* the money on him was a simple B and E. The prosecuting attorney would laugh at Boldt. He had to make the call to arrest or return to surveillance.

The back door cracked open. Hall hesitated, unseen.

Reading Boldt's thoughts as she so often did, Daphne said, "What about the bones? What about a suspicion of murder charge? Wouldn't that hold him?"

Bingo! Boldt thought. "You're worth your weight in gold," he whispered. He handed her the flashlight and withdrew his handgun. "Ready?" he asked.

The suspect stepped out of the dark house and shut the door behind himself.

"On your count," Daphne hissed.

Boldt clicked the walkie-talkie button three times.

He spun to face her and their lips brushed. He leaned back and held up his fingers. *One . . . two . . . three . . .*

He kicked open the shed door. Daphne snapped on the light.

"Police!" Boldt shouted. "On the ground *now!*"

Hall dove to the earth, hands outstretched. The move surprised them.

"One thing about those military boys," Daphne quipped. "They know how to follow orders!"

Daphne realized that she loved him but would never have him. Her mind was not on the suspect or the house or the attempted theft but on Boldt, the man, the sergeant, the lover, the friend. The unattainable. Her thoughts had been on the suspect, and they returned quickly to him, but for that brief instant of time between leaning against him and being asked if she was ready, her thoughts had strayed to encompass the idea of a life with him and the realization that any chance for such a thing had passed. It was a thought she had entertained and refuted an equal number of times, as she did once again, though she eased incredibly close to acceptance. Her move to Owen had felt like love but in truth had been little more than a late rebound, an attempt to shed the burden of Lou Boldt.

The attempt had failed, something she had acknowledged within herself only over the past few weeks, something Owen had sensed immediately. She faced the reality that her personal life was once again a train wreck. Did she think too much and feel too little, or was it the other way around? If she listened to her friends, she was opinionated and stubborn, inflexible and bossy. These were the same friends who told her how much they loved her. If she listened to Owen, she was beautiful and brainy, ballsy and supportive. If she listened to her own heart, it said that what had once been respect for Lou Boldt had matured into unconditional love. She admired him for his musicianship, his leadership by example, his intelligence, and his humanism. He was flawed: full of self-doubt, misplaced compassion, and a tendency to hide inside his moods. He was an amazing father, a loyal husband, and she wanted him for her own. Liz be damned.

He stepped toward the suspect. There was enough ambient light to see shapes but not details.

She didn't want any surprises. "Let's wait for backup, shall we?"

Boldt never broke his concentration. He nodded. Then he called out to the man lying on the ground, "Nicholas Hall, you are under arrest. You have the right to remain silent. . . ."

He glanced over at her—only for an instant—and their eyes met. His were full of joy.

She cherished the moment. She tucked it away and saved it. Safe from harm. Hers always.

39

THEY took turns with him, as if working
a punching bag. Nicholas Hall had been processed like a side of
beef: his fingerprints inked, his possessions stored in lockup in a
brown paper bag bearing his name and record number, his clothes
replaced with the humiliating orange jumpsuit with CITY JAIL
stenciled in huge white letters across the back. Boldt had requested
"full jewelry"—handcuffs and ankle manacles. He wanted Hall to
think about it.

The prisoner had not yet requested a court-appointed attorney, a privilege that had been offered him during three separate
readings of the Miranda. They were taking no chances with Nicholas Hall. The lack of an attorney meant that Hall spent three consecutive two-hour shifts in Homicide's eight-by-eight interrogation
room A, the Box. He was given a twenty-minute break between
sessions, escorted to the toilet, and offered food and water. Boldt
took the first hour and the role of the heavy. Daphne took hour
number two and played the friend. Boldt took hour three. By the
fourth hour, Daphne had begun to loosen him up by pitting Boldt
against her and telling him how the old guard, the hard-liners like

Boldt, didn't like a woman doing their job, didn't like the suspects forming any kind of relationship with her.

"I put up with a lot of shit around here," she informed him. Hall had rough hair and soft brown eyes. The left side of his lower neck was discolored—beet purple—a birthmark, not a burn. That hand hid in his lap, shackled to its partner. "They think of me in terms of my sex," she said. "I'm all tits and ass to most of them, that's all. I'm different," she said, attempting to appeal to that hand of his, "so they don't trust me."

"I know all about that."

In the three hours and twenty minutes they had worked on him, this was the fourth full sentence that Hall had spoken. Daphne felt a tingle of excitement in her belly. "The hand," she said.

He nodded.

"People think you're a freak."

"You got that right."

"Me," she said, "I'm a freak around here because I don't pee standing up." She wanted to place as many images in his head about her as possible, hoping to mislead him into seeing her strictly as a woman, not as a cop but as opposing the cops, the same way Nicholas Hall felt at that moment.

He smiled.

She could tell a lot about him from that smile: considerate, kind, thoughtful. Not that she trusted it. "Do you have brothers or sisters?" she asked, knowing the answer.

"Yeah. Kid sister."

"Parents?"

"Dead. My dad on the highway. My mom . . . she kind of drank herself to death, you know? After my dad and all."

"My parents too," she lied. "It trashed me at the time. Tough stuff."

"My dad was driving pigs, Des Moines to Lincoln. Can you imagine? They say he caught a wheel on the shoulder. The pigs all swung at the same time and carried the trailer over. Trailer took the cab. Rolled down into that middle part. I was fourteen."

She nodded sympathetically. She reached up and scratched the back of her neck, giving Boldt the signal.

The sergeant came charging into the interrogation room, red faced and angry. "It's my turn," he announced. "You're out of here."

"No way," Daphne complained. "He doesn't want to talk to you."

"What the hell do I care what he wants?" Boldt asked. "He killed a woman and left her in a crawl space—"

Sitting forward, his handcuffs dragging on the table, Hall said, "That's bullshit."

"You're interrupting me, Sergeant." She glanced at her watch. "Nick and I aren't through," she said, using his abbreviated name. Until that moment she had only called him Nicholas. The idea was for her to develop a rapport and isolate Boldt as far as possible. "You mind if I call you Nick?" she added, checking with the suspect, who looked confused and afraid. To Boldt she said, "If Nick wants to speak with you instead—" She left it hanging there.

"No!" objected the suspect.

"There you have it," she informed Boldt. "You'll have to wait your turn."

"You're not going to get anything out of him," Boldt complained. "Let me have him. I sense *Nick* and I are on the verge of some real progress here."

"I don't think so," she countered. "The door is that way." She added, "If your head isn't too big to fit through it." She glanced at Hall. The suspect grinned. Just right, she thought. He's all mine. "Out!" she told Boldt.

The sergeant glared at them and left the tiny room.

"These charges are bullshit," Hall stated. "I didn't kill no woman."

"You know, it's better if you don't play dumb," she informed him. Quietly, she said, "If they think you're cooperating with me, we can keep you up here. Otherwise it's down to lockup. And once they arraign you, you can spend weeks there—months in County. The backlog in the courts is awful right now."

"I am not playing dumb," he protested. "I don't know nothing about no dead woman."

"Listen, the thing is, they can place you in the house. What were you doing there, if not trying to cover up your knowing her?"

"I don't know her."

"Didn't," she corrected. "I'm telling you, these guys are not real long on brains." Raising her voice, she said, "They're just about as dumb as they look."

"Are they watching us?" he asked.

She nodded.

"Listening?"

She nodded again.

"Can we talk—I mean, just you and me? None of that?"

"I can check."

"Check it out," he said. "I'll talk to you, but in private. You know? Off the record."

"Right," she said. None of what was said in that room was ever off the record. It was written down in a notebook, or tape-recorded, or videoed. But the rule of the Box was to please the customer. "Let me check," she said.

"I didn't kill no woman!" he repeated, shouting at her. "Never been in that house before! You gotta believe me."

She left the room, immediately greeted in the office area by Boldt and Lieutenant Shoswitz. "You're a genius," Boldt said.

"He's coming around, I think."

"You think? You've got him by the stones," Boldt encouraged.

"I think he'll give us that airport meet," she said, "if we use the homicide charge to deal."

"We're holding Santori on that charge," Shoswitz reminded her.

"He doesn't know that," Daphne countered, then asked Boldt, "What about the truck, the mobile home?"

"The lab has been through the truck. The dogs didn't turn up anything."

"Is that possible?"

"No hydrocarbons," Boldt answered bluntly. "That's all

they're trained for. That's all it means." Boldt left them a moment and stepped over to his desk, returning with photocopies of several lab reports. He handed them to Daphne and said, "Here's your ammunition. You can hang him with these."

She looked them over, switching back and forth between the top report and the memo, which was indicated to have been written only twenty minutes before. "Are we wrong about this?" she asked Boldt, bewildered.

"Some answers wouldn't hurt any."

"You mind if I work this?" she asked. "Or do you want it?"

Shoswitz advised, "Be careful about the way you two do this. We want all the ducks—"

"In a row. Message received," she said.

Boldt told her, "They're yours if you want them."

She beamed. The lieutenant shook his head in disgust and walked away.

"He's not thrilled about you having the boy at your place. He's worried it'll come back to haunt us."

She felt her face heat up. "We've sequestered witnesses before. He's Shoswitz; he worries about everything." She indicated the interrogation room door. "Okay?"

Boldt answered encouragingly, "Go get him."

"They'll let us talk," she told the suspect. The small room was hot and she felt uncomfortable. "They won't eavesdrop without me knowing about it," she said. It wasn't a lie, though she used it to trick him. She *did* know about it, and they *were* listening in. Foremost in her mind was that she wanted Ben out of this as soon as possible. That required nothing short of a full signed confession. No matter how she worked and reworked it, she didn't see that happening. She felt discouraged but not defeated. In the right hands, an interrogation was something fluid and changeable.

Failure was at the base of most of the personal problems that as a professional she attempted to treat. Failure to beat a legal system that seemed stacked against law enforcement. Failure to take the slime off the street. Failure to make a promotion or convince a superior of the importance of a case. Failure at home: to communicate, in bed, as a parent, as a partner. It worked its decay slowly, at first, and unnoticed. By the time the pain struck it was virtually too late to stop the damage. The only recourse was to attempt to plug the hole, fill the void left behind. It took various forms: tobacco, alcohol, cocaine and amphetamines, sex addiction, physical abuse. Early warning signs were reckless behavior, vehement disagreements over trivial matters, absenteeism.

Over the years she had come to learn that suspects were no different: plugging the pain with crime. Nor was she any different. The idea of failure hurt.

"I didn't kill nobody," Hall mumbled. "Never. You gotta know that. Believe that. Nobody. Not ever."

"The hand," she said, knowing this was the source of the pain. "Tell me about that hand."

"No!"

"They stare at it, and they look away. They talk about it behind your back. They make you think about it at times when you'd forgotten all about it. But you can't get away from it. It follows you around, stuck to the end of your arm like another person—someone you don't understand."

"We're not talking about my hand."

"I am."

"We're talking about these murder charges. I ain't never—"

"I'm talking about your hand," she interrupted. "What, you think I'm working against you here? Maybe we find out she was strangled *with bare hands*. That's all you need, you know."

"Is that true?" he asked.

"I said maybe. Now tell me about that hand. How long ago?"

"Three years, seven months," he answered. His eyes grew glassy and distant.

"How?"

"An accident. I was in the service."

She replied, "Air Force."

"Yeah, so what?"

"How?"

"An explosive device. Phosphorus. It misfired. Detonator problem. Fired early."

She stared at his bad hand a moment, long enough to know that he too was engrossed in it. Then she asked, "Why were you in that house?"

He looked away.

"Why not tell me?" she encouraged. "If it had nothing to do with the victim—"

His nostrils flared and his eyes grew wide. He said softly, "A kid stole some money from me." Daphne felt ebullient. *More*, she pushed silently. "I got a tip it was in the house. I swear. You found it on me; that's *my* money."

She asked, "You know what they found when they found the body—the lab guys? Down in the crawl space, I'm talking about." She toyed with the papers Boldt had handed her, shifting them around on the table.

"I'm telling you, I have no idea about no body."

She toughened her demeanor and prepared herself for a more military attitude, one that Hall might understand. She took a deep breath of the room's sour air and said, "Listen, mister, when I ask you a question I expect more than an answer, I expect the *truth*. If the truth is too much for you, then we have no business here, you and I. Do you hear me, Mr. Hall?"

"Yes, ma'am."

"Good. Now I will tell you what they found down in that crawl space other than a pile of bones. And in return for this favor you will tell me the truth—for a change—and maybe, just maybe, I can save your sorry ass from Sergeant Boldt, who would just as soon send you down to lockup and never see you again. You think that Sergeant Boldt cares about your side of the story?"

"No, ma'am."

"That's correct. He does not. His desk is covered in open murder investigations, and as far as he's concerned this one is cleared. You're just a number to him. As far as he's concerned, the next stop for you is a court, a jury, and death row." She tapped the papers violently, summoning an anger that she expressed as an unrelenting and penetrating stare. "Do we understand each other?"

"Yes, ma'am."

"I'm getting a better feeling about this, Nick. I believe we're beginning to understand one another. Is that your assessment as well?"

"Yes, ma'am."

"Look me in the eye, Nick. That's better. Okay?"

"Okay."

"They found your fingerprints in that crawl space, Nick. Where they found the dead woman."

He wore a paralyzed expression, part shock, part realization.

She explained, "There is absolutely no question about this. Do you understand? That is what we call evidence. Proof. The stuff that puts you away for life." He couldn't get a word out. She watched as he relived some incident, his eyes suddenly blank.

He said hurriedly, "No, listen. You don't understand."

She told him, "No, I don't. But Boldt thinks he does."

"You got this wrong."

"What I *got*," she said, "is you, on tape, telling me that you had never been to that residence prior to tonight. *Never been in that house before. You gotta believe me*," she said, reading her interrogation notes. "So I believed you. Now I don't believe you, and neither does Sergeant Boldt."

"No, I *had* been there." He attempted to correct himself.

"I think we're pretty clear on that, Nick."

"Last week," he said.

"You're saying you just happened to be in the crawl space last week? Oh, well," she said sarcastically, "*that* explains it! Certainly fills in all the blanks for me." She straightened her posture and ran her fingers through her hair. She felt bone tired and yet almost high at the same time. This was the stuff she lived for. "There's no accurate way to date latent fingerprints. Did you know that? Last week, last year. . . . It's all the same to the lab guys. All the same to a jury." She fixed her eyes on to him and said, "Help me here.

What the hell were you doing there, Nick? How do we explain this to Boldt? *Did* you kill that woman?''

"No, no, no," the suspect said, shaking his head violently and gently slapping the table with that paw and its ungainly three fingernails.

"Talk to me."

"I was at the airport," he stated, breaking out of the dark and into the open ground of truth for the first time.

Confessions came piece by piece, by disassembling the fabricated truth and allowing the real truth to take its place. To her it felt like digging in wet sand as the waves came in—remove the sand, allow the water to fill the hole.

"You weren't alone there," she said.

He shook his head, the handcuff chains rattling on the tabletop.

"Help me out here, Nick."

She stood, leaned onto her outstretched arms. "A person can't dance alone. Boldt's way of doing this?" she asked. "He'll *misplace* you for a couple days. Place you 'accidentally' in the wrong lockup, in with the guys the screws call the soapies—the soap droppers. For you it's a few days of sitting on the toilet and screaming, a few months of wondering if you're carrying the disease or not.

"Who cares about capital punishment," she continued, "when there's the disease? It's free. No one pushes a button. That's Boldt's way for justice," she lied. "He's of the old school. He'll tell you he cares, but he doesn't. He wants a good, solid clearance rate. That's how his success is measured. You're a number to him. They made the arrest, now they want to clear the case. Take a good long look, Nick. This is your life walking out the door."

She stood and walked slowly toward the door, each step a lifetime: Dorothy Enwright, Melissa Heifitz, Connie Branslonovich. She reached for the doorknob deliberately, took her time in turning it. Pulled open the door. The air smelled better, felt cooler.

"It wasn't drugs," Hall admitted in a hushed voice.

Daphne turned, reentered the room, and pulled the door shut

behind herself. Suddenly that dreary, claustrophobic room smelled a lot sweeter.

"I was doing some business, you know? Some punk kid ripped me for five bills. Stupid asshole drops his wallet in my truck. First time I went there, he hid from me in the crawl space."

"You roughed up the stepfather."

"We tangled. I wanted my fucking money! Second time— tonight—I took the money. And that's the God's truth."

Daphne's pulse quickened, she felt warm in the small of her back. She focused on his body language and his facial expressions, searching for the signs. She measured his eye movement, waited for him to begin licking his lips—a dry mouth tipped off lying— watched keenly for how much eye contact he sought—eye avoidance often indicated insincerity.

After a long silence she asked, "What kind of business?"

"A phone call now and then. The guy knew more about my base than I did. I swear that's the truth." He checked her again. He was made nervous by her silence, which was exactly what she wanted, so she didn't change a thing. "I never met him."

Her skin crawled. A second person. No one would want to hear this, she realized. He looked over at her with the vacant eyes of a man on death row. "I don't know nothing about him."

She caught herself gnawing at the inside of her right cheek. She was full of questions but as yet unwilling to voice them, hoping instead to pressure him with silence, the most effective of all interrogation tools.

"I don't know his name," he declared solemnly. "I don't know what he looks like." He squinted and placed his pink paddle onto the table instead of hiding it below the lip as he had been. "A buck twenty a month. That's the disability pay our fine country sees fit to give me for this: a hundred and twenty a month. And what kind of job am I supposed to get? Tell me that. A typist?" He twisted his wet lips into a grin that caused her to shiver and made him feel dangerous. Was he looking to vent his rage? she wondered. She sat straight up and met his eyes, and silently told him not to try anything with her.

"It wasn't drugs," he repeated.

"Something available on the base," she replied.

He nodded. His mandible muscle locked up as big and firm as a chestnut. His eyes went wide. He was terrified. Of the military or the man with whom he had dealt? she wondered.

"What was it you sold, secrets?"

"Hell, no, I ain't no traitor!"

"What then?"

He answered, "I had access that he didn't have. Let's just leave it at that."

Her voice rose to a shout. "Leave it? I don't think so. Have you been listening, Nick? We're trying to build a credible story here. I don't know what you were selling, but it's not going to bring you death row. The murder charge will!"

His eyes hardened. His mandible muscle knotted again. "I want me a lawyer."

"We'll arrange one, of course, if you insist, but I should warn you that you'll regret it. You like me," she said. "We understand each other, you and I. But Boldt and the prosecutor? You think they care?"

"I'm not answering any more questions."

"Then I won't ask any more questions," she informed him. "Just tell me what was going on in that parking garage at Sea-Tac. Try the truth, in a way I can believe, and you may walk out that door with the charges dropped."

"Bullshit."

She stood. "You don't want the murder charges dropped? What am I doing trying to help you? You think I have time for this?" she complained. "You think I have nothing better to do than sit in this stinky little room listening to you bitch and whine? You want Boldt, you got him. You want the soapies, you got 'em. You want death row, it's all yours."

Her second false exit was less successful. She was mad at herself for trying it too soon. His chains rattled, but he did not speak up. No matter how many times she heard that sound, it gave her chills.

She could not be seen to give in. The temptation was to turn around and give him another chance, rather than let Boldt have him for a while, but there were no second chances to be given. The finality of his position was all-important. And besides, she thought, it was embarrassing to have the mark settle on a request for an attorney during her turn at bat. Hall had the look of terror. Better to give him a few minutes and let Boldt go at him for a while. But she gave him up reluctantly, like a pitcher coming off the mound in the early innings.

"Okay, here's the shit," John LaMoia said, approaching Boldt, who stood on the other side of the one-way glass watching Daphne debate her exit.

Boldt didn't like being interrupted, not even by LaMoia, to whom he granted an unfair amount of liberties. "I'm busy here, Detective," he said sternly.

"The . . . rocket . . . fuel," LaMoia said slowly, reminding Boldt of the way he talked to Miles when he wanted to get a point across. "The . . . suspect. *That* . . . suspect," the detective continued, pointing through the glass.

Boldt's mind wandered from fatigue. He spoke to Liz each night and some mornings. Though grateful at first for his efforts to protect his family, she was increasingly angry at him for her isolation at the cabin. She had spent nine days up there, and he had forbidden her to tell any friends or bank associates where she was, even though a close friend could guess immediately. The Sheriff's Department had two men assigned to her twenty-four hours a day, one guarding the road, one watching the cabin. She was feeling captive. He told her little of the investigation, just as she said nothing of the bank, with whom he knew she was in touch.

They ended up discussing social engagements, as if it were any other week in their lives. She sought the comfort of familiarity. He allowed it. There was a dinner party being thrown by one of her vice-presidents that she felt they were obligated to attend. Boldt hated these bank dinners, having little in common with the country club set. She then pressed him about the upcoming Fireman's Ball, a downtown gala fund-raiser they attended each year, again, Boldt reluctantly.

He softened and agreed to both, at which point she dropped the real bombshell. "I have to be back in the city on Tuesday. No questions asked, I *have* to be." Jealousy welled up within him and he nearly confronted her, but whereas confronting a suspect was easy for him, confronting his wife had never been simple. It was far easier for him to attempt a noncommittal statement such as, "We'll see," but he knew it wouldn't carry the day. He wanted to corner her into explaining the urgency, and yet he didn't want to know. He ended up procrastinating—putting off agreeing with her until another call.

LaMoia's voice brought him back. "What I've found out is this: The Air Force, in all its wisdom, decommissioned the Titan missile program in phases. The rocket fuel back then was either two liquids, or a liquid and a solid, that when combined self-ignited. No need for an igniter. Part A meets part B and *kablaam!*—fire, controlled burn. The chemical reaction produced its own oxygen, making it perfect for burns that continued up into space. The term is *hypergolic*: binary self-igniting rocket fuel. There's a whole family of them. But the point is, it takes the two parts to tango. They moved the two parts to separate locations, keeping them as far from each other as possible. The Minute Man program took its place. There was evidently talk of disposing of the two parts, but some fucking genius decided we might be able to sell the stuff abroad and make back some of the taxpayers' investment. It probably cost more money to ship it and store it than it did to make it," he snapped sarcastically. "So they didn't destroy it. They stored it. Part A went to Idaho, part B to California. Part A went to Texas; part B to Nevada. Keep brother and sister far apart. And then the base closures began. Base inventories were moved around like chesspieces. Some of that goes here, some of that goes there. Things get a little fuzzy at this point, but it would appear that either by just plain old government stupidity, or—if you accept the rumors—because a potential buyer came on the scene, parts A and

B were moved onto nearby bases here in Washington. But if that's true, the buyer must have fallen through, because parts A and B ended up here to stay, at which point, of course, we entered the second round of base closures, the second round of moving inventories like chesspieces, and—lo and behold!—parts A and B end up in separate storage facilities but both on the same base: Chief Joseph Air Force Base."

Boldt said, "Which was closed down in round three."

"But round three was not full closure for a lot of the bases. They reduced them to something called maintenance status. They maintained inventory but shut down barracks—it was a pork-barrel scheme to maintain the bases in an election year; no one had to say the bases were being closed, just scaled down. Fluff. The result was, a few administrators stayed on at each of these bases, a few MPs to watch the place, guard the gates. But for all purposes there was no one left. And the security details are less than twenty-five percent of what they were at full operation."

"Vulnerable."

"Exactly. Especially to an inside job."

Boldt speculated, "Nicholas Hall was an MP at Chief Joseph."

"That he was. Whether he figured it out himself or was paid off to do an inside job, who knows? But Mr. Paddle Paw in there skimmed off a little juice and cashed in his retirement plan." Looking through the one-way glass at the suspect, LaMoia said, "I wonder if he's considered a career in Ping-Pong."

Boldt exhaled loudly said, "Good work, John."

"Damn right. I'd say it earns me ten minutes with him, right, Sarge?"

Daphne stepped out of the Box at that moment and, overhearing the request, objected. "Let's give him a rest. Please. Then the sergeant will go back at him."

LaMoia had proved himself incredibly effective in past interrogations. Boldt thought of him as his wild card. He knew few boundaries. He could be a suspect's instant friend, or worst enemy. Boldt told his detective, "Don't touch him."

Daphne, knowing Boldt's mind was made up, advised La-
Moia, "Don't ask any questions. Just statements, John."

"Matthews," LaMoia said, "have I told you lately that I like
you?"

She repeated, "No questions. Push him with statements."

LaMoia moved to the Box, pulled up his pants at the waist,
and opened the door. Facing Boldt, he whispered, "You might
want to turn off the tape."

He walked in with a swagger—in his trademark pressed jeans.

Boldt and Daphne watched and listened. Through the speaker
mounted below the one-way glass they heard LaMoia say, "I bet
you're a killer at handball, Nicky." He kicked the empty chair away
from the desk and sat down in it, craned forward on the edge.
"You could always get a job as an inspector at a mitten factory. You
know: *Inspected by number thirteen*. That kinda shit."

LaMoia stared for a moment.

"What was life like out at Chief Joseph once everybody left?"

The suspect paled noticeably.

He asked this, breaking Daphne's request immediately. No
answer from the suspect.

"What else?" he asked. "You could play bass drum in a
marching band. Direct traffic! Hey, what about that? You could be
a traffic cop, Nicky. Pay sucks, and the company you keep isn't so
great, but you always have the fact that you're working for the
betterment of society, you know?" Then he said, "You could drive
a pickup truck, I bet. One-handed, but so what? You could sell out
your country. You could probably shove that thing up your cell
mate's ass, with a little help.

"You know who I am, Nicky? I'm the one you've been worried
about. I'm the one you've been thinking was going to come
through that door. You met me in boot camp. You see me in some
of your nightmares. I'm the one that those guys"—he said pointed
to the glass—"can't control. I'm the one who doesn't give a shit.
Boldt and Matthews, they're on a break. But not me. I'm the one
who does the dirty work around here. You know football at all?
I'm the safety, the last guy on the field between you and the end

zone. Safeties are always the crazy motherfuckers, you know? Stand in the way of a three-hundred-pound running back. You gotta be crazy, right? So what?'' LaMoia slapped the table so loudly that the speaker went fuzzy. ''You worked security at Chief Joseph. You decided to make a few bucks. Don't shake your fucking head, pal, because I know what I know. And I know all about you. You know I do. You want to nod, that's okay. But don't lie to me. Don't fuck with me. Matthews, she's the exception to the rule around here. And that makes me the rule. You're going to live with that, or you're going to die with that—I don't give a shit. But you're not going to lie to me. Under no circumstances are you to lie to me.

''Maybe I need a little introduction,'' LaMoia continued. ''I'm the guy who knows everybody. Ask anyone. I'm the guy who tells the screw to put you with the soapies and he does it; I'm the guy who says to put the roaches in the soup, and the cook does it. I have friends. I make friends easily. Like with you, right, Nicky? Buddies, right? Let's have a little nod, Nicky.''

If Boldt hadn't seen it a dozen other times, he might have been shocked to see the suspect nod.

Daphne, clearly amazed, said, ''I could study LaMoia for a decade and never write a comprehensible paper about how he does what he does. It's not simply intimidation, it's something beyond that.''

''It's LaMoia,'' Boldt said.

''That's what I mean,'' she agreed. ''He's despicable, and yet he's lovable.''

''I'm just glad he's on our side.''

''Sometimes I wonder,'' she said.

''He called me,'' Hall said, the first break in his silence.

Suddenly quiet and a fellow conspirator, LaMoia said, ''Give us what we need, Nicky, and you just might walk out of here. No promises. But the flip side is that we can make life hell for you. It's like a game show, Nicky. Choose the door. Go ahead and pick. But don't waste any more of my time, and don't make them send me on any more errands to clean up your shit for you. You got into this shit all by yourself. Now you need me to get out of it. The doors are right in front of you: Truth or Dare. Your choice. Pick one, Nicky, and pick fast, because I'm running out of time here. I'm going home at the end of the day, just remember that. You're not. Not yet. I'm going home to my own bed, my TV, and a warm little friend from Puerto Rico with a pair of cheeks that just sit in the palms of your hands, you know? Sweet stuff. Truth or Dare, Nicky? Time's up!" LaMoia was out of the chair, leaning across the table at the suspect. "Buzzer's ringing. Nicky Hall: Come on down!"

Even without seeing the detective's face, Boldt knew that the man looked insane and ready to crack. LaMoia lived on the edge, and at times like this it was impossible to tell how much was acting and how much was real.

Daphne said, "I can't believe this. It's going to work."

"Yeah," Boldt echoed. "I know."

LaMoia pounded the table again. "Truth or Dare, Mr. Paddle Paw! You start talking or I start walking. Matthews can't save you. Boldt can't save you. Only I can save you. What's it going to be?"

"He knew that both parts of the stuff were stored on the base," Hall explained. "He had to have either been stationed there or worked there at some point. I figured that out right away."

"Brilliant. Pray continue, my man." LaMoia kicked his feet up onto the table, stretched his hands behind his head, leaned into the cradle, and said, "I'm listening, Nicky. I'm listening." He glanced toward the glass and winked.

Boldt reached down and turned on the tape recorder.

As if cued to do so, LaMoia said, "My name is Detective La-Moia, Mr. Hall. Tell me what you know." He did this for the sake of the tape, which he knew was running by then.

Hall picked up where he had left off. "I was working MP duty. I'd driven by those buildings for *years* and never did know what was inside."

LaMoia glanced back at the window with a cocky, proud expression and grinned widely.

"Sometimes I hate LaMoia," Daphne said.

"Yeah," Boldt answered. "I know what you mean."

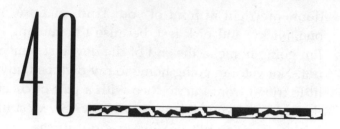

40

ON Saturday Daphne took Ben to the Seat-
tle Aquarium. He'd never been, and it was a place she enjoyed so
much that she often went there simply to relax, to stroll and think
in what to her was another world. She never took notice of the
tanks, rarely read the descriptive labels; it was the fish that captivated her attention, the unflinching eyes, the pulsing gills, the gen-
tle-paced wandering through the kelp and imitation coral. Despite
her frequent visits, she didn't know one fish from another, couldn't
tell a dolphin from a porpoise, a pilot fish from a pike.

Ben, on the other hand, was a product of TV documentaries
and knew the names of the various species, as well as their feeding
and mating habits. "I taped most of them late at night, once Jack
had passed out, because he only liked sports and sitcoms." He said
it as if this was to be expected, and it cut to Daphne's core. He
would toss such things her way, slowly opening the door to his
existence, and the wider that door opened, the more she glimpsed
of what Ben accepted as a normal life, the more she ached to
change his existence. It was this mutual desire to improve his envi-

ronment that connected Daphne, however indirectly, to Emily Richland.

"Have you ever felt that way?" Ben said, pointing at a red snapper kissing the transparent walls of the tank. They were in what to her was the most exciting section of the aquarium, a large open room exposed to several large fish tanks that housed entire communities of oceangoing species.

"Which way is that?" she asked. She wanted to see the world through his eyes, experience the world through his developing senses.

"Trapped like that," he answered pensively, stopping at the tank and studying the fish that appeared to be kissing the boy. "What's it like for him, banging up against that wall? He probably can't figure it out. And what's he think of us? This whole other place he can see but can't get to. Like that." He looked deeper into the tank at the lumbering fish. "They flush seawater in here at night. It has the nutrients and stuff. It feeds them. And then they filter it out to make the water clearer so we can see them."

"Do you feel like that, Ben? Trapped?"

"Not by you," he clarified. "Not you. But yeah." He pointed to the snapper, which continued to push on the clear barrier. "That's me at my window at night, you know? Looking out at other people's houses. Wondering what it's like. If their lives are any different." He led her a few feet forward but stayed with the same tank. "Emily says it doesn't have to be that way, but I'm not so sure. People are different than what they seem. That's just the way it is. Not Emily. Not you. But most people."

"I don't think you can group people together, lump them together like that." She wondered why she and Owen discussed the next party they were supposed to attend, and here she was with a twelve-year-old discussing the hard points of life. "I think it's possibly better to take people as individuals, weigh them on their own merits, and try not to be too judgmental."

"Yeah, but how do you do that?" Ben questioned. "First thing I do when I meet someone is size them up. You know? Like that guy," he said, pointing into the tank. "See him checking everyone out? Looking over there, over here. On the prowl. That's me. He's thinking someone's going to sneak up and try to eat him—that's what he's thinking. And that's right too, because one of those fish probably *is* thinking that. I'm telling you. That's how it goes out here, too, pal. You look the other way, someone's after your ass."

"Watch the language," she scolded, but Ben didn't respond. He walked on and Daphne followed. If Owen had been here, she would have tried to lead him around, she realized. Why was she willing to follow the boy, when she didn't like to follow anybody?

He glanced back at her. "Are you crying?"

"Allergies," she lied.

"I wonder if fish have allergies," he said innocently, turning back to the tank. "Check out that guy's fin. You see that? Someone womped on him, took a chunk. That's what I'm telling you, D. You turn your back, someone womps on you."

He had been using this nickname for her occasionally, and she had cautioned herself not to allow its use to draw them closer—to remain professional—but in this she had failed. Boldt called her Daffy. Everyone else, even Owen, called her either by her first or last name. Only this little bundle of energy called her by that nickname. It endeared him to her.

"Can you swim?" she asked.

"Nah. Not so you'd notice. Sink to the bottom if you put me in there. I'm a retard in water. Scares me, and I start flapping around, and that's pretty much it. Down she goes. You?"

"Yes. I swim."

"Teach me sometime?"

"Yes," she answered softly, wondering if this too were a lie. She thought him so special, and though it occurred to her that there were perhaps dozens, hundreds, just like him, she thought it wrong to lump people together. She refused to see it.

"If you could pick," he said, "which one would you be?"

Such a simple question, but for her it seemed profound. She studied the inhabitants of the tank. One was long and thin and exceptionally beautiful and she singled it out for him.

"But he's small," Ben complained.

"She," Daphne corrected, not knowing the fish's sex.

"Not me. I'd go for size. Speed. That guy, maybe. I'd pick the shark, but that kind doesn't eat other fish, only that stuff—what's its name?—in the water."

"Plankton."

"Yeah, that stuff. So what's the point of being a shark if you only eat that stuff? Maybe that guy over there," he said, pointing. It was a big, ugly fish that looked menacing.

"Do you love her?" she asked him, having no idea where the question had come from and wishing immediately that she could withdraw it.

"Emily? Yeah. She's the best. I know you don't like her, but she's really cool."

"I never said I didn't like her."

"No, you didn't say it, I guess," he offered in a voice that bordered on complaint. He attempted to quote her: "I think it's better to take people on their merits." He crossed over to the opposing tank then, carefully picking the moment so as not to have to look at her. She felt herself slip into his path, obediently following behind. Felt herself reach out and nearly take his shoulders in her hands. But she was tentative in this approach and she never did actually touch him. Instead, she lowered her arms in unison, a drawbridge going down but not quite connecting, and allowed him to slip away from her, like a prayer silently spoken, wondering if the words had found a home.

41

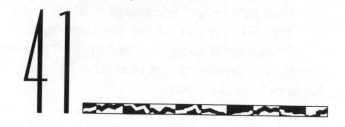

THE rock that Boldt and his investigators had started downhill began to run away from them, momentum and gravity prevailing.

The arrest of Nicholas Hall was broken by KOMO television and within minutes was the subject of talk radio. Both papers proclaimed Hall's arrest in splashy front-page headlines. For Boldt, the public euphoria was subdued by a memo received by him the Monday morning after the arrest.

TO: Sergeant Lou Boldt, Homicide
FROM: Dr. Bernard Lofgrin, SID
RE: Nicholas Hall, # 432–876–5

Lou: FYI, Hall's weight and height do not agree with our assessment of ladder impressions dated Oct. 4th this year. The suspect is twenty to thirty pounds heavy and, by our estimates, three to five inches tall (based on average weights) for whoever climbed that ladder. Furthermore, as so noted per our recent telephone conversation, the individual that climbed the tree at the Branslonovich killing was most definitely right-handed. Hall's disfigured right hand would suggest he was not a viable suspect for atten-

dance at that crime scene. I will write this all up for inclu-
sion in the file, but wanted to give you a first look. Any
questions, I'm around.—Bernie

They had the wrong man. An accomplice perhaps, a co-conspirator
possibly—but not the man the papers had dubbed the Scholar.
Boldt and Daphne had both sensed this from the start of the sting
operation and had felt more certain of it throughout LaMoia's interrogation, in which Hall detailed the theft, transportation, and
sale of the binary rocket fuel. Worse, Hall's story hung together
well. A search of his Parkland mobile home, on the north boundary
of the base, revealed no notepaper, no storage of hypergolic fuel,
no ladder. Hall had given up most, if not everything, of what he
knew about the hypergolic fuel. The man appeared to be a dead
end. One positive note of the follow-up investigation was lab man
Bernie Lofgrin's decision to run an analysis of the ballpoint pen
ink used in the threats, in hopes of discovering a like pen in Hall's
possession.

But Boldt knew the truth: The killer remained at large. The
one blessing was that the publicity of Hall's arrest had apparently
scared off the arsonist—no fire had followed the most recent poem.
Or had it merely delayed him?

He experienced an overwhelming bout of depression and frustration: so close, only to fail. He wanted an hour with a piano. He
wanted Liz home. The kids.

The investigation rolled on, regardless of his wants. He took a
walk downtown for forty-five minutes, up past the Four Seasons
and down 5th Avenue's fashion stores and office malls. He wanted
a shot at what the kid knew. Kids saw a lot more than adults.
Maybe a lead to the accomplice. Open him up with a lineup, something to jog his memory, work him into the smaller details. Pick
his brain. He bought tea to go at a coffee stand by Nordstrom's and
came back up 4th, stopping to window-shop at Brooks Brothers,
where a gray cashmere sweater costing most of a week's pay teased
him. He moved on, weary and worried. Pedestrians avoided him.

He used such walks to try to jog loose a fresh idea. He needed a fresh idea, if another life was to be saved. He mentally reviewed the most recent note:

You cannot look for the answer,
you must be the answer.

Daphne had traced it to Rita Mae Brown. The ATF's Casterstein had told them to let the next fire burn itself out—no water, no overhaul. Boldt understood that the fire could come any night, that another life could be lost. The responsibility he bore for that life was but one of the pressures he endured.

His present worries were twofold: the publicity generated by Hall's arrest might invite copycat arsons; or it could push the Scholar either into hiding or, worse, into a frenzy of activity—as Daphne predicted—fearing his own arrest imminent.

Boldt's best ideas came to him at strange times, so it was no real surprise to him that while coveting a gray cashmere sweater in a storefront window he hit upon a realization: With Hall's arrest, the arsonist's supply of accelerant would stop.

His cellular phone pressed to his ear, Boldt shouted people out of his way as he sprinted back toward quarters. Panting, he gasped through the phone to Shoswitz that they needed to conduct an immediate inventory of all fuel storage at Chief Joseph Air Force Base. Until that moment, under orders from the Captain of the Criminal Investigations Division, they had been intentionally leaving the Air Force in the dark, fearing a bureaucratic nightmare of jurisdictional infighting. "We blew it, Lieutenant. We had the trap all set, all perfectly baited, and no one was there to watch, to spring it."

"What trap?" Shoswitz demanded.

"If I'm right, there has been a break-in at the Chief Joseph base within the last forty-eight hours. *After* the news broke the story of Hall's arrest."

When Boldt walked into the office twelve minutes later, Shoswitz was waiting by the elevators. "How in the hell did you know about that break-in?"

Boldt answered, "I'm going to get LaMoia. Tell Bernie to rally some technicians. We treat it as a crime scene. We *share* it, no matter what kind of heat we take.''

"Yeah, but how the hell did you know?'' Shoswitz barked at his sergeant.

Boldt didn't stop to answer, but he turned and said, "Supply and demand.''

Chief Joseph Air Force Base was right out of a film studio back lot: parklike grounds interspersed with ugly shoe-box barracks and tightly grouped three-bedroom ranch-style brick houses for officers. With nine hundred family units and over one thousand dorm units, it had once employed or played home to 4,800 military personnel, 6,200 dependents, and 2,400 civilians, meaning its average population had once been over thirteen thousand people. It had its own movie theater, bowling alley, golf course, day-care center, beauty shop, bookstore, and PX. Base population was currently two hundred military, one hundred sixty dependents, and seventy-six civilians. A ghost town covering over two thousand acres, including what had once been the third largest airport in the state. The streets were straight and curbed and deserted. Grass grew out of cracks in the pavement. Boldt and LaMoia rode in the front seat, Shoswitz alone in the back. They followed a sheriff's vehicle that followed an FBI vehicle that followed an ATF vehicle that followed a Military Police jeep complete with camo green, black, and brown paint.

The base commander was a surprisingly soft-looking man in his fifties. The FBI team, led by a man named Sanders whom Boldt knew well, did most of the talking. The negotiations began to bog down, at which point LaMoia, uninvited to participate by anyone, said, "We've got several people dead, sir. We think we know exactly what was stolen—hypergolic fuel, but we need to know in what quantity. I for one would just love to listen to you guys jaw all day, but meantime we know for a fact that this wacko is preparing yet another fish fry. So what say we cut to the chase and you give us some keys to the appropriate buildings while you gentlemen rub the gums?''

Everyone in attendance stared at LaMoia dumbfounded. To which LaMoia, who could never keep his mouth shut, said, "Ah, come on, people! This is bullshit. We haven't got the time."

Boldt caught himself holding his breath. The base commander nodded to a uniformed aide standing at his side, and the young kid hurried inside and returned with a ring of keys, which he passed to his superior. The commander clasped his thick hand around the keys and said, "We will certainly cooperate to our fullest with an active homicide investigation, but at the same time it is imperative that we *share*, gentlemen. Our Ordnance Recovery Division is responsible for returning to base any stolen ordnance. Our Criminal Investigation Division will take the lead and report directly to Special Agent Sanders."

Shoswitz objected bitterly to military CID attempting to lead the investigation. Boldt grabbed his lieutenant firmly by the elbow and squeezed, expressing an attitude of cooperation—an act for which the hot-headed Shoswitz would later thank him.

The first of the buildings was called Arsenal D and was on the far western side of an enormous airstrip. Arsenal D was, in fact, a former jet aircraft hangar, in all appearances an oversized Quonset hut, ribbed galvanized sheet metal walls and roof, the latter with dull ivory skylights, the former with a minimum of windows. There were nine men involved in the fact-finding expedition, including Lofgrin's three-member forensic team and a pair of base MPs. In private, LaMoia whispered to Boldt that once CID arrived from McChord the trouble would begin. Special Agent Sanders led the way. A bright shiny padlock came off a bent and rusted door that swung open on complaining hinges.

One of the uniformed MPs explained that during morning rounds on Saturday between 8 and 9 A.M., the door had been discovered pried open. Lofgrin's team began work on the door itself immediately, photographing and dusting for prints. CID would later complain about this intrusion. Boldt and the others followed Sanders inside.

The sergeant was immediately struck by the effect of perspective. From outside, the hangar had seemed quite large; once inside, its size tripled. At the top of the arch of the curving roof there was perhaps sixty feet of clearance; the far wall felt as if it were a football field away. Between the two walls and perhaps forty feet high in twenty-two rows, each ten barrels wide, were stacked dark blue fifty-five gallon drums looking like spools of sewing thread. There had to be several thousand of them, Boldt realized, perhaps two hundred thousand gallons of fuel or more. Five gallons of that fuel, when mixed with its second element, could level a standard home. The firepower represented by this hangar was so staggering that at first, while the other men followed the MP down an endless aisle formed by the towering stacks of drums, Boldt stood transfixed, absorbing the absurdity of it all. Hall could have dipped into any one of these drums, siphoning off a few gallons here and there; in typical government fashion, the overkill, the embarrassment of riches, would provide the cover needed. An accurate inventory, especially given the small size of the crew on the base, seemed an impossibility—months, perhaps years away.

Boldt had not realized that LaMoia had remained with him, standing only a few feet behind his sergeant, respectfully awaiting orders. There were times, Boldt thought, when LaMoia actually resembled a cop.

Eyeing the thousands of drums, Boldt said, "He could have enough fuel to burn a dozen Dorothy Enwrights, a hundred! We'll never know."

Shaking his head, John LaMoia said, "God bless America."

42

BEN missed Emily. Daphne wouldn't answer any of his questions about her, pretending she didn't exist. He was shuttled back and forth, between talks with Susan, school classes with juveniles in detention, and evenings with Daphne. He used to think he had it bad living with Jack Santori, putting up with the parade of drunken women and the awful groaning downstairs late at night. But isolation was worse. The only thing keeping him from running away was Daphne's threat to put Emily out of business. Ben wouldn't do that for anything, not even his own happiness.

When Daphne showed up in the middle of classes, Ben knew it meant trouble. Anything out of the ordinary routine meant trouble. She briefly consulted with the teacher and Ben was excused, to the heckling of others. He met up with Daphne in the hallway, his heart beating fast with concern.

She was wearing black jeans, a sweater, and a leather jacket. She carried a large purse by a thick strap over her shoulder.

"We need to ask a favor of you, Ben."

"Who, you and Susan?"

"Boldt and I. The sergeant."

"I don't like him."

"You should," she said, a little stunned by his remark. "It's good to have him on your side."

He was loath to admit it, but he liked Daphne. He even felt sorry for her in a way, because all she seemed to do was work and talk on the phone. She said she liked to go on a run in the evenings, but she'd only managed one run since he'd been staying with her. "What kind of favor?"

"Sergeant Boldt wants to ask you some questions. Show you some pictures. You know what a lineup is?"

"Yeah."

"Maybe do a lineup."

He didn't want to show her how he felt about any of this. "What if I don't want to?" he asked sarcastically.

"Then I talk you into it," she answered honestly.

"And how are you going to do that?"

"Bribery, probably."

"Like what?"

She answered with a question. "How about seeing Emily?"

He felt like shouting a resounding "Yes!" but tried instead to hide his feelings, not give her too much leverage.

"It can't be at her place," Daphne said. "Maybe at the library, somewhere like that. I can work on it."

"Work on it," Ben said, but she glared at him and he added quickly, "please."

On their way to her car, Ben asked her, "Are you divorced?"

"No," she answered, clearly surprised.

"My mom was divorced before she met *him*." He had not told her much about himself, though she seemed to know a lot. Initially, he had feared the police were after him for the five hundred dollars, that they would arrest him and lock him up. But that was no longer the case; he knew it had to do with Nick. Putting Nick in jail would be a real pleasure.

"A lot of people get divorced these days," she explained. "It doesn't make your mother any less a person."

"I thought she went away," he said, his voice catching in his throat. Daphne started the car but glanced over at him before shifting gears. "She did, sort of. Go away. You know?" He felt tears coming and turned to look back at the building from which they had come. "He told me she left me. That she left us both. And I believed him." He felt a tear run down his cheek then, and he kept his face toward the glass of the window so she couldn't see. The car backed up.

"Ben, you're old enough to understand that people like Jack Santori do bad things. They hurt other people. Those of us who end up victims face some tough choices." She had started to drive, but she pulled the car over and put it in park and turned to face him. Her eyes moved as if she was thinking hard or remembering something. "If we dwell on being victims, we often never escape. The better choice is to move on. Talking about things can help." Too many memories for her. She felt herself break.

She had tears running down her cheeks; so did he. For an instant she reminded him of his mom, because his mom seemed always to be crying, especially in the months before she left. He thought of the lie—she had never left—and cried all the harder. She had been lying down there in the cold and the damp, down there with mice and spiders and ants and God knows what else. Nothing left but some bones and that gold ring.

He relived the experience of finding that ring for the first time since promising himself not to think about it. As Daphne reached over and hugged him he felt her warmth, and he smelled her sweetness, and he buried his face in her chest and fell apart, images surfacing, feelings surfacing that he had no idea were buried inside him. He saw himself as a child. He saw his mother naked in the bathtub, running her toes under the hot water and laughing. He saw her bruised face, her swollen eye, and her fat lip, and he remembered her warning in a frightened voice, "Don't you say a thing about this in front of him. When you look at me, you don't see it. When he looks at you, you act no different, Benjamin. You're my best boy, right? You gotta do this for me." She'd been protecting him; he realized that, though too late.

A tape played inside his head and he heard them arguing and he heard her being hit, and he heard her say, "I'll do it! I'll do anything. Just not my boy." After that the bed had pounded against the downstairs wall for a long time, and later he'd smelled smoke and, worried the guy had passed out while smoking, he went to look and found his mother sitting in a chair smoking a cigarette. He went down the stairs quietly and walked right up to her—she didn't smoke cigarettes, not as far as he knew, and it upset him to see her smoking and he told her so. She was staring at the drawn curtain; she didn't seem to hear him. The room was dark, and as his eyes adjusted, each time she drew on the cigarette a red light spilled over her body, and he realized she was sitting stark naked in that chair. Then, as the cigarette drew down, he saw that her body was covered in red, angry scratches, some of them deep enough to still be bleeding, black ugly bruises as big as potatoes. She exhaled and, without looking at him, said, "Go to bed." Tears ran down her cheeks. He hurried up the stairs, but he didn't go to bed; he sat in the shadows and watched her instead. She smoked four cigarettes in a row, found a coat in the coat closet, and put it on. She sat on the couch for a while, and when Ben awakened from an unplanned nap, she was in a different chair, looking out the window again, as if she wanted to be out there. She smoked two more cigarettes. Ben caught himself hugging his knees, crying into his pajamas. Jack called from the bedroom, "Get in here. We're gonna play a little more." Ben's mom glanced up toward where Ben was hiding, as if contemplating something. She snubbed out the cigarette—he would never forget that because she used her bare foot to grind it into the rug; he had looked at the burned spot often and thought of her. She unzipped the coat, shedding it and leaving it on the couch, and walked slowly toward the bedroom, almost like a zombie. He heard the guy say something, heard his mother's voice though not her words, and then caught the distinctive sounds of a hard slap and his mother's groan, and he had covered his ears with his palms and run to his room and buried his head under his pillow, as he had so many nights before.

"He killed her," Ben said to Daphne, between his sobs. She

squeezed him all the tighter. "He killed my mom and put her down there." Daphne didn't tell him to be quiet; she didn't tell him everything would be all right. That had been what he had feared the most, being told to shut up or that things would work out. Because they weren't going to work out, and Ben knew it.

Daphne said, "You can tell me anything that comes to mind. It doesn't have to make sense. I want to hear it, if you want to share it." These words seemed to come from the voice of an angel to him. He cried all the harder. She said, "You're safe here, Ben. Emily, me, Susan—we're not going anywhere. We're here for you. We're your friends. You can talk to us. You can share with us. It's safe." She squeezed him again.

"I'm afraid," he said, admitting aloud for the first time something he had lived with for what felt like forever.

"Me too," said Daphne. "And you know what? It's okay to be afraid."

He looked up at her then, and for a moment he forgot everything. There was only this woman and the feeling that whatever was wrong was suddenly okay. That he was safe.

He shut his eyes and tried to hold it there forever.

The big man was Boldt, he knew that much. He wasn't so much tall as big, and yet his hands belonged to a different person, with their long fingers. They looked like he kept them in his pockets all day or something. Hiding them. Protecting them. Ben had never seen hands quite like that.

The other guy to visit the houseboat was some sort of artist. He had a gentle face and kinky hair and went by the name of Andrew or Andrews; Ben couldn't tell if it was a last name or a first name. He set up his pad of white drawing paper under a lamp on the small countertop bar that separated Daphne's galley from the tiny sitting room that housed Ben's fold-out couch. There were three tall stools at the counter where Ben usually sat while Daphne cooked.

The one called Boldt brought a videocassette with him that

Daphne put into the machine and set up for Ben to view. Boldt explained, "You'll see five men, all standing alongside one another—"

"I know what a lineup is," Ben interrupted. He wanted these guys gone. He wanted Daphne to himself. He wanted that meeting with Emily she had promised. For the first time in a very long time he felt as if things weren't as bad, as scary, as they had seemed, and he didn't want to lose that feeling.

Boldt glanced over at Daphne, who asked Ben politely not to interrupt, saying that Boldt and this other guy had a job to do and it had to be done in a certain way, and even if all of them knew exactly what was supposed to happen, the sergeant still had to explain everything to Ben—which he then did, without interruption. Boldt thanked him at the end of the explanation, and it made Ben feel better about the whole thing. He wasn't used to a guy thanking him for anything, only ordering him around.

They played the video for him then, and it looked just as it did on TV, with a line of five guys shoulder to shoulder standing in front of a white board that had lines for different heights drawn onto it. They kept their arms and hands behind their backs. There was a short guy with a beard, and next to him a taller blond guy with a tattoo showing at his chest, and then Nick, and then another tall guy with a messed-up ear, withered and small, and then a guy who looked pretty much like Nick but not really. They all turned right, then left. They spoke the same line, one right after another, so Ben could hear their voices. But he didn't need to hear the guy's voice.

"The guy in the middle," Ben said. "The duffel bag had drugs in it."

"You're absolutely sure?" Boldt asked. "If this is the man at the airport, the one in the truck, that's important to us. We need to confirm that. We don't want to mix things up. But if not—"

"His name is Nick. He was a customer of Emily's. He has his name on the back of his belt. He drives a light blue pickup with a white camper shell. There's a Good Sam's Club sticker on the back bumper, and there was a gun inside the camper shell: a pistol like the cops use on TV."

"You saw the gun in the camper?" Boldt asked.

"I was *in* there," Ben said.

"Drugs?"

"Stuff to make them, I think. Milky stuff. I saw a TV show about a drug lab one time. Like that."

Boldt said, "And the duffel bag had this stuff in it."

"In plastic things. Like for leftovers. Must have been a dozen of them."

"Tupperware."

"Taped shut with silver tape. And they had chemistry stuff written on them. You know? Letters and numbers."

"What else did you find in the camper?" Boldt asked. Eye to eye with Ben, who remained on the stool, Boldt told him, "You know what immunity is, Ben? You have immunity. Nothing you tell us can get you in trouble. We didn't read you your rights, did we? Because you're not a suspect, you're a witness. Whatever you did is behind you. You can't get in trouble for any of it. And Emily's not going to get in trouble either. Okay? You don't have to worry about it."

"I didn't take any money," Ben stated.

Daphne said, "Ben, Sergeant Boldt didn't mention money. If you lie to us, even once, then we can't trust anything you tell us. Does that make sense to you? Do you see the importance of not lying?"

"Let's forget about the money," Boldt said, as much to Daphne as to Ben. "Let's talk about who was there at the airport. When you called nine-one-one you said it was a drug *deal*, didn't you, son?"

"I'm not your son."

"How many people were there, Ben," Daphne encouraged.

He didn't think he should tell. Emily had warned him to never so much as touch one of the cars. It was illegal. But Daphne's asking made it different.

"Two," Ben answered. "Nick and this other guy."

"The *other* guy," Daphne said.

Ben felt himself nod. The thing about Daphne was that she could get him to do things he didn't plan on doing. It was almost as if she played tricks on him. The guys scared him, but not Daphne. He wanted her to hold him again; he wanted the others to leave so he could be alone with her. "What?" he asked her, seeing a strange look on her face.

"Sergeant Boldt needs a description of the other guy."

"I didn't see his face. He was over by some cars. It was dark. I couldn't see him so good."

The artist, on a stool alongside Ben, started sketching. Ben watched in amazement as the inside of the parking garage came to life on the page. "You were looking toward the inside or the outside?" the man asked.

"Inside," Ben answered.

Boldt considered his words. "What's amazing about when you see something is that there is stuff you see that you don't even know you saw. You say you didn't see his face because it was dark. That's okay. Was he standing between some of the cars?"

Ben could recall the image clearly in his mind's eye: a dark shape looking toward the truck. He felt the fear he had experienced, not knowing what to do. He nodded at Boldt. "Yeah, between some cars."

"And was he taller or shorter than the cars?"

"Taller." Ben understood then. "Yeah, taller," he said proudly.

"My size? Danny's size?" Boldt asked, pointing to the artist, who was shading the cars and making the page look even more realistic.

"Not as tall as you," he told the sergeant. "Skinnier."

Daphne smiled, and Boldt looked at her disapprovingly.

Boldt said, "Smaller all around, then? Shoulders, waist—a smaller frame?"

"Yeah, I guess that's right."

The artist worked furiously. On the page the shape of a body formed between two of the cars. Ben instructed the man, "He was standing back farther . . . was a little taller than that." He couldn't believe how clear it was in his mind. Seeing the artist's sketch made it all so real for him—he knew exactly what was wrong with the picture. "There was a column there, you know? Yeah . . . like that. He was kinda leaning against it. . . . Yeah! There! That's cool. Real cool." He waited for the artist to get more of the guy on the page, then said, "His head was . . . I don't know . . . thinner, you know?"

"Narrower?" Boldt asked.

"Yeah. Narrow. He had glasses. Big glasses, I think." The artist corrected the head to where it was just right. He added the glasses three times until Ben said he had it. "A hat. One of those stretchy ones."

"A knit cap," Boldt said.

"Yeah. And a turtleneck up over his chin, I think. Or maybe a scarf or like the guys in the Westerns."

"A bandanna," Daphne said.

It amazed Ben how quickly the artist adjusted to every comment, how quickly it went down on the page. His hands moved in a flurry of activity, and when he pulled them away, it seemed like a Polaroid developing, the image growing out of nothing.

"Jeans?" Boldt asked.

"I couldn't see his legs much," Ben answered, more interested in the artist than Boldt. "No, not like that. Not a turtleneck, I guess." The man erased it and tried a bandanna. "No. I don't think so." A moment later the man's head changed completely. "Oh, wow! That's it. That's him." The artist had drawn a hooded sweatshirt onto the man, the strings pulled tightly under his chin so that, when combined with the glasses, almost nothing showed of his face. "That's it!" Ben repeated.

"The hood up like that?" Boldt asked.

"Just like that," Ben answered.

"Any markings on the clothes?" Boldt questioned. "A sports team? A company logo? The name of a city or town?"

"You can shut your eyes if it helps," Daphne said.

Ben tried shutting his eyes, and the image that was frozen while on the artist's page suddenly came to life. He could smell the car exhaust, hear the airplanes and car traffic; the guy moved his head back and forth, first looking toward the truck where Ben hid, then toward the elevator and Nick with that duffel bag. Light sparked off his mouth. Ben decided to mention this. "His teeth are shiny."

"Braces?" Boldt asked.

"I don't know," Ben said, his eyes still squinted shut. "Can't see. Not exactly."

"A gold tooth? A silver tooth?" Daphne asked.

"I don't know," Ben answered honestly. "Can't see much."

"What's the man doing?" Boldt asked.

Ben described the scene for them, the guy in the shadows checking out Nick and the truck. "He's careful, you know? He's waiting for Nick to get on the elevator. And then he does—Nick does—and the guy is coming for me, right at me!" He talked them through his panic as the guy headed toward the truck, the sense of panic, of diving back under the seat, of the truck never moving under the weight of the man, and then hearing that lock click into place. His terror at being locked up for a second time.

"As he walked toward the truck," Daphne said calmly, "he came closer to you, didn't he, Ben?" She added, "Maybe he stepped out of the shadows a little. Into the light a little. Go ahead and shut your eyes and try to picture that for me, would you? Can you remember? Can you see it?" Her voice was soothing, the same voice that had comforted him in the car, and so he closed his eyes, just as she said to do, and sure enough, the dark sinister form stepped out of the shadows, and for an instant Ben thought he could see part of the man's face. What made the experience especially strange for him was that he didn't remember this at all. Instead, it felt as if Daphne had made him see something he had never seen.

"I don't know. . . ." he mumbled.

"Go ahead," she encouraged.

"I'm not sure."

"It's all right, Ben. You're safe here. It didn't feel safe then, did it?"

"No way."

"You were scared. He was coming toward you."

"I can't get out," he told her. "The door is unlocked and I don't dare go out there."

"He's coming toward you."

"Yeah."

"But there's more light."

"Headlights. A car's headlights," he said, for he could see the image inside his head: it was in black-and-white, not color, and it happened quickly, and no matter how hard he tried, he couldn't slow it down. "He's wearing a mask, I think. Plastic. A white plastic mask. Shiny, you know? Like a hockey goalie, maybe."

"He wore a disguise," Boldt said in a voice of disappointment. "Damn."

The artist said, "A mask inside the pulled-up hood. Glasses over the mask. Hell of a disguise."

The artist held up the sketch for him. It was just the guy's head and shoulders, the parking garage a blur behind him. He had the sweatshirt up over most of his face, wore big dark glasses and had plastic-looking skin. The hat topped off the image. It was creepy to Ben how close that drawing came to real life.

"That's him," Ben whispered. He didn't want to talk too loudly. The picture seemed real enough that the guy might hear.

43

BOLDT thought of himself less as a public enforcer, more as a paid puzzle solver. Forensic evidence, testimony of witnesses, medical examiner reports, unforeseen events—all added up to a giant puzzle that the lead detective was supposed to solve. In the case of an ongoing serial homicide investigation, failure to solve the puzzle resulted in more deaths, the loss of innocent lives. It proved to be potent motivation. It robbed one of a private life, deprived one of sleep, gnawed at one's self-confidence. Boldt disliked himself and felt himself a failure—he couldn't even blame Liz for her affair, if it was real; he'd been consumed with work for months.

When he reached his hotel after questioning Ben and the clerk handed him a brown paper bag—and it wasn't his laundry coming back—the sergeant experienced a pang of dread. His first thought was that it was a bomb. He carried it to his room carefully and spent five long minutes inspecting it. Perspiration breaking out on his brow, he dared to uncurl the top of the bag slowly and open it equally slowly. Inside was a note from LaMoia and a half dozen items purchased from a hardware store—items purchased by Melissa Heifitz on the same day as her fire.

Boldt clicked the TV on to CNN and went about examining the contents of the bag: a compressed air canister called E-Z Flush, rubber gloves, a sponge head to a mop.

The items from Enwright were in the dresser's bottom drawer. He took these out and compared. Common to both groups were sponges and gloves. A bottle of Drano in the Enwright group, E-Z Flush in the other; a bottle of compressed gas to be used as a plunger to clear the stubborn drain. Boldt spun the device around in his hands. On the can's back panel was a simple illustration of a sink and another of a bathtub. In his mind's eye he recalled his own bathtub having trouble draining, and a moment later he placed it as on the night of his family's evacuation.

Clogged drains! he realized. A common link between Enwright, Heifitz, and even himself!

He called Bernie Lofgrin at home. The lab man answered cheerfully. Boldt did not introduce himself, for Lofgrin knew his voice. He said, "What are the chances that the hypergolics, that the ignition system, is somehow related to plumbing, to the house plumbing? To clogged drains?"

After a long silence, Lofgrin said, "I'm thinking." He mumbled, "Plumbing?" But Boldt did not interrupt. "Clogged drains?"

Boldt waited another few seconds and said, "One of the victims bought a New Age toilet plunger on the day she died. The other, some Drano."

"A plunger!" Lofgrin shouted excitedly. "A plunger?" he repeated. "Hang on. Hang on!" Then he said, "Just hang on a second," as if Boldt was prepared to interrupt. Boldt overheard Lofgrin calling out to his wife. Carol came on the line and asked about Liz and the kids, stalling while her husband busied himself. She sounded good. Carol was given to fits of depression but had been stabilized by some recently developed drug, and the word from Bernie was that she was "back to normal," though Boldt and others of his friends had come to distrust Bernie's assessment; in the last two years, Carol had been involved in two bad traffic accidents later deemed attempted suicides, these during periods when Lofgrin had been convincing others that she was stable. Bernie Lofgrin carried his own cross, same as anyone else—more than most, Boldt decided. Perhaps the man's work was his best escape. Perhaps it explained why he was so damn good at it, so dedicated.

Lofgrin's strained voice thanked his wife, interrupting her, and said, "Page two-fifty-seven. *Do-It-Yourself: The Visual Dictionary.* You got a copy?"

It was a rhetorical question. Lofgrin had given Boldt two copies: one for home, one for the office. He'd done the same for several of the other detectives in Robbery/Homicide. Boldt told him, "No. I'm in my second week at this damn hotel." His copy was in a small bookshelf that had been in his bedroom but had been moved to the front hall when the crib—currently occupied by Sarah—had entered their lives.

"Page two-fifty-seven shows a cutaway illustration of a house, revealing the plumbing. Everything from the water meter to a P trap. Left of the page is a stack vent. Right of the page, a waste stack. Drains from the toilet, a sink, a tub, another tub, are all connected by a common pipe labeled 'branch.' On either end of the branch is a vertical riser that passes through roof flashing to the outside air. The diagram shows two such risers.

"Draining water or waste creates a vacuum in the pipe," Lofgrin continued. "The waste pipes need to be vented in order to allow draining. Think of a drinking straw with your finger over the top end. As long as you keep your finger tight—no venting—the straw holds whatever fluid is in it. But if you vent the straw by lifting your finger, the fluid drains out. Same in a house. Only the drains have stinky stuff in them, so the vents go out the roof, so you don't smell them. Two of them, Lou. You get it?"

"You lost me," Boldt admitted.

"It's ingenious because it ensures the person living there is home at the time of the combustion. Two vent stacks: two parts to the hypergolics. Right?"

"What the hell, Bernie? The hypergolics are in the vent stacks?"

"I imagine so, yes. Seal the vent stacks with a thin membrane: wax paper? cling wrap? I don't know. Place the two parts of the hypergolics above those seals. It might not take much—maybe just draining a full bathtub or running the clothes washer—and those seals break and run down the vent stacks. The two elements of the hypergolics make contact in the branch pipe. You're looking for a way to burn the whole house, to destroy as much evidence as possible, and the plumbing gives it to you; it runs through the wall one floor to the next, one wall to the next. You open the bathtub drain or flush a toilet and suddenly every plumbing drain, every fixture in the house is a rocket nozzle. *The porcelain melts, Lou:* That was the clue I missed. Damn! That should have jumped out at me. Porcelain does not melt easily; it would have to be near the source of the burn. I let that confuse me. Every single piece of porcelain in the house was involved in the actual burn. You've got the answer, Lou. You figured it out!"

"A plunger?"

Lofgrin exclaimed, "He can set the explosives without ever entering the house. Do it all from the roof."

"He wasn't even in the house," Boldt mumbled. The method of planting the explosives had stumped him all along. He felt giddy. High.

"His cover. Sure. Wash a few windows, climb up on the roof, fill the vent stacks with the hypergolics. A matter of minutes is all. He takes off." It only took Lofgrin a second to make the connection that Boldt also made. "Jesus, Lou. Your house."

"I know."

"Your vents could be set. We could have *proof* here." He sounded thrilled. Boldt felt terrified.

"We need to evacuate the neighbors," Lofgrin said.

Boldt told the man, "Consider it done."

"Give me forty minutes," Lofgrin requested. "I'm gonna need a big crew."

Boldt wandered the sidewalk in front of his home in a daze, wanting to go inside and take everything with him in case Bernie Lofgrin's attempt to defuse his house failed. A home became a kind of kid's shoe box, a collection of odds and ends, books, music, furniture. Boldt owned over ten thousand LPs and about two thousand CDs. Every inch of wall space in the house not previously occupied contained music. Dozens, perhaps hundreds, of the LPs were priceless.

Each room through which he mentally wandered brought a tighter knot in his throat. His son had grown from an infant to a little boy in this house. Sarah had been conceived within these walls. His marriage had fully recovered here, resuscitated from the gagging spasm of its past.

If he could have gone inside, he would have taken the bronzed baby shoes belonging to his son. A photo album of their marriage pictures, another of Liz giving birth to Miles, and a video of Sarah's entrance into the world. A Charlie Parker first pressing, and a pair of ticket stubs to Dizzy Gillespie and Sarah Vaughan. An eagle feather found in the Olympics, and a lock of Liz's hair cut before the birth of their son. A blue bowling shirt that read, MONK over the breast pocket and THE BOWLING BEARS on the back; he had only bowled on Berenson's team once, but the shirt was a keeper.

It was more than a house, it was his family's history museum. The idea of losing it terrified him. It made him want to drive to the cabin and see Liz and the kids.

He prayed to God that the arsonist be caught.

The first man to reach the roof ridge of the house wore a fireman's turnouts complete with hat and mask and carried a hands-free walkie-talkie that communicated with Lofgrin on the ground. Lofgrin and Boldt and the others—Bahan and Fidler among them—stood behind a fire line established on the sidewalk. The six adjacent houses had been evacuated and two patrol cars blocked the street from vehicle traffic. Four ERT officers had sequestered

themselves in two of the evacuated houses, alert for signs of interest from the arsonist.

The roof man told Lofgrin, "Four stacks."

Lofgrin looked over at Boldt and said, "I gotta warn you:
we're gonna find hypergolics. Why else go up the tree and watch
the place, right? He was waiting for the show."

"I'm a nervous wreck," Boldt admitted.

"Think how Rick feels," he said, pointing to the roof man.
"That fuel goes and he's got about twenty seconds to get off that
roof before he's three thousand feet up. "If he doesn't jump, his
ass is ash. No time for the ladder. No time for the walkie-talkie. He
knows that," Lofgrin added, answering Boldt's curious expression.
"You ever seen a guy take a running jump from a two-story building?" He answered himself. "Me neither. And I don't intend to
tonight, just for the record." Into the walkie-talkie he said, "You go
easy up there, damn it. Use the scope."

The roof man was equipped with a fiber-optic camera about
the size of a pencil eraser on a flexible aluminum cable about the
diameter of a shoelace. His job was to lower the cable into each
stack and report what he saw. Boldt looked on as the man gingerly
crossed the roof between vent stacks. He knelt awkwardly and
fumbled with some equipment.

"He's nervous," Lofgrin observed. "Good. I'd rather that than
cocky."

The roofman's voice, made scratchy by the radio, reported,
"Going down."

"Nice and easy," Lofgrin ordered.

Boldt looked up as the man fed the cable with his right hand,
his left holding a Sony Watchman video monitor. "Two feet . . .
three feet . . ." he reported.

Lofgrin told Boldt, "The cable is marked in inches, feet, and
yards."

"Four feet . . . five feet . . ."

"You know what I think?" Lofgrin asked rhetorically. "That's
a front stack. Front of the house. Unlikely he would rig that one.

Too visible, right? If I'm him, I rig the back stacks and seal the front stacks. Less time on the front roof that way."

His radio squawked. "Seven feet . . . eight feet . . ."

Into the walkie-talkie Lofgrin said, "Let's try one of the back stacks, Rick. You copy that?"

"I copy," the roofman reported.

"Back of the house is where the action is," Lofgrin informed Boldt. "Count on it."

Overhead a news chopper aimed a blinding light down on the top of Boldt's roof, its cone sweeping back and forth, and isolated the man in the turnouts.

Lofgrin said, "Well, one thing's for sure: You'll never be invited to a neighborhood function again."

The spotlight left the roof, scanned the yard, and lighted on Boldt and Lofgrin. A considerable amount of wind was generated by the blades, and the noise was deafening. Lofgrin waved it off, but it continued to hover above them. The roofman lost his balance because of the generated downdraft; he slipped on the shake roof but managed to reach out a hand and catch himself. Boldt glanced over to the parked patrol cars. Shoswitz was shouting into his radio handset while looking up at the helicopter. Boldt didn't need to read lips to see how angry the man was. Thirty seconds later the helicopter gained altitude and the associated noise lessened, but the spotlight continued to jump between the roofman and Boldt and Lofgrin's position on the sidewalk.

"I'm at the northernmost stack on the back side," announced the roofman through Lofgrin's radio.

"The kitchen," Boldt explained.

Lofgrin said, "Go easy, Rick. This may be a live one."

"Copy that," answered the roofman.

Boldt could not see Rick working, and this bothered him. He heard him announce that he was feeding the camera into the stack, and Boldt could picture the tiny camera sliding down the black plastic vent; he could imagine the man keeping an eye on the Watchman while the fiber-optic camera with its tiny light disappeared down the tube.

"One foot . . ." the voice announced.

"Slowly," Lofgrin cautioned. Boldt sensed in him an added worry, a heightened concern.

"Howdy hey," the roofman said into the radio. "I'm showing a translucent membrane at the eighteen-inch mark."

"Hold it!" Lofgrin spat into the radio. He turned around and waved one of his assistants over. She had a handsome face, was somewhere in her early thirties, and was clad in turnouts too big for her. She carried a gray plastic toolbox in her right hand, heavy, by the look of it. Lofgrin told her, "The kitchen. Use the back door. Take it exceptionally slowly, as we talked about. It will be in the vertical somewhere. Give me a distance readout from the bottom of the vertical. Got it?"

"Yes, sir."

"Okay," Lofgrin said. "Go ahead."

"Young," Boldt said, as she hurried away from them, the toolbox dragging on her.

"They all look young anymore. She's got a four-year-old. Husband works for Boeing. Maybe the biggest overachiever I've got. She begged me for this assignment. Despite the risk, despite the obvious danger, despite the fact that the bomb boys were jockeying for this work, she wanted to run one of the cameras. She's the one who did the ventilation work over in the New Federal Building— you remember that camera work? Worked the thing up three stories and into the men's room. Remember that? It was a narcotics sting. Busted a seventy-thousand-dollar cash gift to a dealer from Vancouver. That was Goldilocks. You want fiber optics up somebody's butt hole without them the wiser, she's the one."

"Why send her inside?"

"We need to check the stack from below. Rick can't head down through that membrane, so now we go from the bottom up. That should give us some idea how to neutralize."

"Meaning what?" Boldt questioned.

"I see two options here. One is he trapped part A and part B in two different stacks. A thin membrane on the bottom, all the other stacks sealed off. Someone goes and uses a plunger, the membranes go simultaneously and the place goes up. The second option I see is both parts in the same stack. One atop the other, a membrane between. The advantage is you only have to break that bottom membrane. The point is, we don't know what he's done, so we sure as hell can't go popping membranes." He explained, "We're prepared to siphon off liquid, or vacuum up a powder, but there's a remote chance he's done this a third way. Casterstein found evidence of a possible detonator. We know the guy was up a tree watching the place. What if that detonator is a pressure switch?"

"What if it is?" Boldt asked.

"In the case of these single mothers—Enwright and Heifitz—he watches until he's certain the kids are gone. From his tree he activates the pressure switch—he could retrofit any remote-control toy to do the trick. Not a big deal. He can deactivate if necessary, should the kids return. And there's the kicker: Deactivated, the drains don't work well but the place doesn't blow. Activated, the first time she flushes a toilet—*boom*! Running a little sink water probably wouldn't do it. A toilet, five gallons all at once—*boom*! A plunger, same thing. If both parts of the hypergolic are in the same stack and we go messing around, we could make one hell of a Roman candle. Know what I mean?"

The next few minutes progressed painstakingly slowly. The woman technician maintained a running description of every wrench turn, every joint loosening. Finally, she announced, "Okay, I see an opening to a riser up ahead. I'm twenty inches to the right."

"Good. Let's follow it. But be careful, for God's sake. That membrane may be transparent."

"Copy."

Wincing, Lofgrin began nervously stroking the stubble on his chin, as if rubbing himself clean. The change in behavior made Boldt restless. The lab man pulled off his Coke-bottle glasses and cleaned them on his shirttail. Once the glasses were in place, he took to scratching the top of his head. "She's in the vent stack . . . heading up the vent stack. . . . If she breaks whatever barrier he has in place—" He didn't complete the sentence; there was no need. Their eyes met—Lofgrin's the size of golf balls behind the glasses—and Boldt understood that all the confidence in their techniques would not save this woman's life, did not guarantee this woman's life, and that Bernie Lofgrin was directly responsible. Lofgrin, dropping his eyes to the walkie-talkie, said in a coarse voice, "She's a good kid. A damn good kid. Hell of a worker. You hope for her kind. You don't often get them." Into the radio, he spoke in a voice suddenly stronger, for he would not allow her to hear any uncertainty. "What's the scenery like?"

The woman's voice sounded strained as she reported. "Thirty-one inches. Condensation on the pipe walls has increased noticeably."

Lofgrin said to Boldt, "We're close." Into the walkie-talkie, he said, "Let's use half-inch increments."

"Copy."

Boldt felt overly warm. He could picture the small camera creeping up the inside of the pipe.

Lofgrin said to him, "This is a little like aiming a pin at a balloon but not wanting it to pop."

"I understand," Boldt replied.

"Serious condensation," the woman reported. "It's fogging the lens. Blurring it."

"Shit," Lofgrin hissed, and glanced once at Boldt with wild eyes. The sergeant saw beads of perspiration covering the man's brow.

"My image is cloudy," the technician reported. "I'm not liking this."

Lofgrin directed her, "Let's retract, clean it off, and try again." He added, "Make note of your distance."

"Thirty-three and one half inches," she reported.

"Copy," Lofgrin said.

"Retracting."

Lofgrin nodded, as if she could see him. He wiped his brow. To Boldt he said, "That's why we use our people instead of bomb squad: She may have been up against the membrane right then.

It may have been the membrane blurring the lens, not water, not condensation. She *knows* that. A different guy, someone who doesn't know this gear intimately—" He left it hanging there, left Boldt with an image of the walls of his house sucked in and white-hot light flooding from the windows.

"The lens is occluded," the woman reported. "I'm cleaning it and trying an application of defogger."

"Condensation," Lofgrin explained to Boldt. "So she was right. Score one for us."

A minute or two passed. Boldt glanced at Bahan and Fidler, who had joined them.

"Well?" Boldt asked.

Bahan answered, "The pressure switch makes sense to me. It allows the victim to actually light off the fire."

Fidler said, "It leaves it a little bit random—a little more exciting."

"Opinions?" Boldt asked.

Bahan said, "We circulated the artist's sketch to every firehouse in the city. Maybe we get lucky."

There was no one standing within fifty yards; a line of uniformed patrol officers was holding back a sea of onlookers, including a group of reporters. Fear is like fire, Boldt thought: It infects randomly, and with great haste.

"All set," the woman said by radio. "We'll give it another try."

She reported when she made the turn into the vertical stack, and again at twenty, and then at thirty inches. She counted off in quarter-inch increments from thirty and one-half. Boldt tensed with each report. Lofgrin inquired about condensation and she answered. "Looking better this time. I've got a good image. . . . Stopping at thirty-three and a half."

"Image?"

"Going to thirty-three and three-quarters . . . thirty-four. Okay. . . . Okay. . . ." Her voice sounded strained over the radio. "I'm picking up a slightly reflective black image. Okay. . . . Okay. . . . This is a foreign object. Repeat"—she was nearly shouting into the radio—"a foreign object obstructing the passage. Black plastic."

Boldt felt heat prickle his scalp. She said, "I'm going a little closer: thirty-four and a half. Copy?"

"Thirty-four and a half," Lofgrin acknowledged.

"Maybe send a bomb boy in to look at this. I've got a rubber O-ring holding it in place. It appears to be a detonator."

"I fuckin' knew it!" Lofgrin exclaimed to Boldt. "They don't pay me the big bucks for nothing."

The joke was not lost on Boldt; the pay was horrible. "What's next?" he asked.

"We send in the bomb man to have a look, and then we attempt to neutralize. We're looking at about eighteen feet of four-inch vent stack packed with hypergolics, Lou. We're talking Apollo Eleven here. If we fuck this up—" He didn't finish the sentence. "We should evacuate a few more houses. I did not expect this kind of volume."

Boldt's knees felt weak. He whispered, "My family was in there. Liz, the kids!"

Thirty minutes passed incredibly slowly. The bomb man confirmed the existence of a detonator. A wet-vac vacuum canister was sent to the roof. Tension filled the air as the top membrane was intentionally punctured and the vent stack's contents carefully removed.

One of Lofgrin's assistants approached him and spoke to him in private, out of earshot from Boldt. Lofgrin returned to Boldt's side and announced proudly, "Silver and blue cotton."

"What?"

"We lifted some fibers from the windows we know he washed. You remember those fibers we found alongside the ladder impressions at Enwright? Muddy. We didn't get a very good look at color, they didn't wash well, but PLM—Polarized Light Microscopy—told us they were a synth/cotton blend. I ruled out window washing at the time because cotton sucks for windows, it leaves itself all over the glass. Newsprint is good, oddly enough, but not cotton. But this guy *was* washing windows—Liz saw that. And a synth/cotton blend is better than pure cotton, at least. But a silver and blue washrag or towel? Mean anything to you?"

"Silver and blue. The Seahawks," Boldt replied. Seattle's failing football team.

"Bingo," said Lofgrin. "And to my knowledge we don't sell
Terrible Towels to our fans the way they do in a place like Pitts-
burgh, right? Do we?"

"I don't follow the Seahawks," Boldt confessed, thinking:
Charles Mingus, Scott Hamilton, Lionel Hampton, Oscar Peterson,
but not the Seahawks.

"What I'm saying is, This is unique evidence, Lou."

"Silver and blue towels," Boldt answered, his heart racing a
little faster, his eyes trained intently on the operation being conducted on the roof of his house.

"That's right." Lofgrin said, "Department stores? A uniform?
How the fuck do I know? That's your job."

Boldt said nothing, images of his house going up in flames
occupying his thoughts. Towels were the farthest things from his
mind.

"We have fiber samples now, Sergeant. We can compare these
to any evidence you might provide us. Understood?"

"We'll search Nicholas Hall's trailer and vehicle again, this
time for blue and silver towels or uniforms or T-shirts," Boldt said,
still watching the house.

"Those fibers can put this boy away, Lou. Are you hearing
me?"

That comment, the way Lofgrin whispered it in a menacing
tone, broke Boldt's attention away from his house. He looked down
into those bulbous eyes, magnified to the point of grotesque. "Blue
and silver fibers," Boldt repeated. "I'm with you, Bernie."

"Found on at least two crime scenes. Just so we understand
each other." Nothing infuriated Lofgrin more than providing a detective with key evidence, only to have it overlooked. Boldt knew
this, and because of that exchange, because of Lofgrin's delivery,
he took the information to heart: Lofgrin believed in those fibers.

"I'm at eight feet, six inches," the man operating the vacuum
reported.

Lofgrin called him off. A decision was made to drill through

Boldt's kitchen wall and drain the Part B chemical from below. As this decision was being relayed, the night sky lit up with a thin column of purple flame that raced up through the clouds and disappeared. It was less than four miles away, in Ballard. Within minutes it was a five alarm fire. Lofgrin's attention remained on the delicate job before him. The distant sound resembled that of a jet taking off. That purple column lasted perhaps ten seconds. Sirens screamed in the distance.

Lofgrin said, "We're okay here, Lou. You go see if your boy's up a tree with a carving knife."

Boldt didn't want to leave his own home, but he did. The crime scene work lasted until three in the morning, at which point he drove to his own home and found it standing.

Another woman was believed dead, another life lost. There was word that all three networks were sending New York crews to shoot the fire remains.

An exhausted Shoswitz reported that despite the cooperation at the field level, the FBI, military CID, ATF, and upper brass of SPD were fighting for control of the investigation. His final comment was, "It's coming apart on us, Lou. Talk about blowing up! Too many cooks, and this thing will die in bureaucratic backstabbing and name calling. We're looking at one giant cluster fuck. And it's you and me bending over, pal."

Boldt did not remember drifting off to sleep but was awakened at his desk at 7 A.M. by an alert and excited John LaMoia. Boldt's neck was stiff and his head dull. LaMoia waited a moment to make sure he had his sergeant's full attention. "You remember Garman telling us his truck was stolen, his Werner ladder in the back?" He continued, "The truck was for real. He owned it, all right. But he's got a little explaining to do. He never reported it stolen to us, Sarge. More incredible, he never claimed the insurance."

Boldt focused on this a moment, allowed his head to clear. "Let's pick him up," he ordered.

LaMoia nodded and beamed. "It's a beautiful morning, isn't it, Sarge?"

It was pouring rain outside.

44

O N the way to Garman's house, LaMoia and Boldt, accompanied by a patrol car following at a close distance, listened not to KPLU, Boldt's jazz station of choice, but rather a random sampling of the AM radio talk shows and all-news stations. The latest victim was identified as Veronica DeLatario. She was the Scholar's fourth known murder victim, and Boldt could describe her before he ever saw her: dark hair, nice figure, mother of a boy between the ages of eight and ten. The radio shows blasted police for arresting the wrong man, in Nicholas Hall, and chastised all city services for the huge display of manpower at a police sergeant's home—"one of their own"—while Veronica De-Latario was "being stalked" and burned to death by a serial arsonist.

It came out that the police had received another poem earlier in the day, accompanied by a melted green piece of plastic, and "had done nothing about it."

There were animated discussions on the talk shows of the "need for new leadership." Federal agencies had made some well-placed leaks about their desire to run the show and take SPD out.

Boldt resented this most of all, because he knew that on the officer level SPD and the agencies were cooperating just fine. It was only at the administrative level that the power plays were under way.

LaMoia, unable to bear it any longer, switched the radio back to Boldt's favorite, KPLU, and they listened to the horn of Wynton Marsalis.

I-5 traffic was unbearably slow in both directions. Even with police lights and sirens, they crawled along.

When Boldt's pager and telephone rang within seconds of each other, he knew there was trouble. Perhaps Shoswitz intended to pull him from the investigation, now that Boldt felt within a few miles of its resolution. Garman's role had nagged at him from the beginning: his being the target of the notes and, later, his Air Force service with its direct connection to missile bases. Their one interrogation had gone poorly, and even now, as they drove to bring him down for another round of questioning, no hard evidence existed against him.

Perhaps the call and page were from Liz, who had told her husband in no uncertain terms that she intended to return to Seattle on that very day, Tuesday. Perhaps Marina was unavailable and he was expected to be father for the day, while his wife did God-knows-what with God-knows-whom. He bristled with anger, even before he connected the call by flipping open the cellular phone. "Boldt," he said sternly, drawing LaMoia's attention.

"Are you near a radio?" It was Daphne.

"In the car."

"Well fasten your seat belt and tune into KOMO AM."

"We were just there."

"Then you heard Garman?" she said heatedly.

"What about Garman?" Boldt asked, at which point LaMoia was nearly leaning onto Boldt trying to hear. Boldt elbowed him away.

"You ready for this?" she asked rhetorically. "Steven Garman, Marshal Five fire inspector, is currently in the process of confessing publicly to being the Scholar, our killer."

Boldt nearly drove the car into a sideswipe. LaMoia snagged the wheel and saved them in a brilliantly timed reaction.

Boldt told his detective, "Garman just confessed." With La-Moia still steering the car, Boldt punched the radio and located the station. It was Garman, all right. And he was well along in describing every last detail of his crimes.

It was fifteen minutes later before they pulled up in front of Garman's residence, and the man was still live on the radio, by that point answering a string of questions offered up by the jock that seemed more an attempt to stall the man. Two local television remotes had beaten Boldt to the scene, and both stations went live with the arrival of the police.

"He's locked in his apartment," a reporter shouted at Boldt, sticking a microphone into his face. "What's the position of the Seattle Police?"

Boldt wanted to issue a "no comment," always the safest decision. But he feared a backlash if he came off as soft or undecided. "We're here to arrest Mr. Garman on a variety of charges stemming from a string of fatal arsons within King County."

A helicopter roared onto the scene and landed incredibly quickly in a vacant lot. Boldt recognized Special Agent Sanders hurrying through the swirling dust and debris.

LaMoia pushed away the reporter's microphone, leaned into Boldt, and said, "We better be first to take him."

They ran up the steps, Sanders shouting from behind. Boldt nodded to his detective, who tried the door, called out a warning, and then reared back and kicked the door twice. It remained locked but broke away from the splintered doorjamb and banged open.

Steven Garman sat peacefully in a recliner, telephone in hand. He spoke into the receiver. "Looks like my ride has arrived."

LaMoia began calling out the Miranda above the roar and chaos and shouts coming up the steps behind them.

Lou Boldt, charged with anger and rage, nonetheless walked

calmly up to Garman, took the phone out of his hand, and cradled the receiver. Under no conditions could he reveal his emotions to the suspect, give himself away. Garman had proven himself cool to the point of cold; Boldt needed all his wits about him.

Meeting Boldt's eyes, Garman said venomously, "If you had caught me sooner, fewer would have died. You have to live with that, Sergeant, not me."

Boldt answered, "I may have to live with it, but you're going to die with it. Given the options, I'd say I got the better deal."

"You think so?" answered Steven Garman. "We'll see."

Within the hour, the Chief of Police held a packed press conference declaring that Garman was in custody and had been among a very small list of suspects all along. He informed his audience that Garman had been interviewed not long before his arrest and that he, the Chief, attributed the man's breakdown and confession in part to that interview. All this was done without ever consulting Boldt, though the sergeant's name was used liberally throughout the briefing.

There was a celebration on the fifth floor, typically reserved for only the most difficult cases—the red balls, the black holes; there were a dozen nicknames. Supermarket carrot cake, fresh milk, a collection of espressos and *lattes* from SBC rather than from the vendor in the lobby.

Boldt did his best to hide his exhaustion and appear cheerful for the sake of the troops, but when he spotted LaMoia and Matthews at different moments during the levity, their eyes showed the same reservations that he felt inside. Garman had invoked the Miranda, turned immediately to silence, and called in one of the city's most notorious defense attorneys. There would be no interrogation. They had the radio confession on tape, but when listened to it was vague and lacked the kind of detail that would make prosecution a no-brainer.

Bernie Lofgrin and his small team of identification technicians missed the festivities because they were combing Garman's home for evidence. They willingly shared that job with an elite team of ATF forensic experts flown up from the Chestnut Grove lab in Sacramento and headed by Dr. Howard Casterstein.

A uniformed officer caught up to Boldt, who was standing off by himself, deep in thought. The officer seemed reluctant to interrupt but finally did so, informing Boldt of a phone call.

The call was from Lofgrin. Boldt took it in his office cubicle.

"I've got bad news, and then I've got bad news," Lofgrin began. "Which do you want first?"

"It's clean," Boldt said, guessing.

"I'm supposed to tell you that," Lofgrin complained. "If we're looking for this guy's lab, we had better start looking somewhere else. Casterstein agrees. This place is not what we're looking for. No hypergolics, no Werner ladder, no blue and silver fibers."

"Is that possible?" Boldt asked, looking up to see Daphne standing nearby. A group of photos in her hand raised Boldt's curiosity, but he couldn't get a good look at them. She caught his eyes and motioned down the hall toward the conference room; she wanted to see him alone. He nodded and she walked off. Boldt watched her backside a little too long for a married man.

"My job is to comb the place, not deal in probability. What I'm telling you is that this guy does not look good from this end. We are not going to deliver the smoking gun. Okay? And quite frankly, Lou, I don't like it. It's *too* clean. Okay? God, we'd expect some kind of connective tissue: tree bark, a penknife, window washing gear."

"He's an investigator," Boldt reminded. "If the lab is off-site, he's smart enough to change clothes and shoes—take precautions not to track evidence home with him. He confessed—if you can call it that. Maybe because he knew we couldn't find enough to make it stick. Maybe it's a game for him."

"Yeah? Well if it is, he's winning. That's all I've got to say. Casterstein knows his shit, Lou, and he's walking around shaking his head, like a kid drawing a blank at an Easter egg hunt. If you were here, you'd see what I mean, and you wouldn't like it, believe me. We're pissing up a rope here, Lou. I'm thinking the best link, the most likely connection, is still this ink. Okay? Connect a pen in the house to the threats he sent. Maybe we can do that. We're rounding up his pens."

"I'd take it, Bernie, don't get me wrong. Gladly. But it's not what I'm looking for. It's not exactly a home run."

"Tell me about it."

"Leads to his lab, that's what I need. Find me something pointing to the location of his shop. You do that, I can go home and go to sleep."

"In that case, I'd start drinking coffee, I was you. It's the fibers, the blue and silver fibers you need to follow. Like you said, he's an investigator. He knows what the fuck he's doing. I wouldn't go counting on much from here." He added quickly, "Save me some cake, if there is any, would you? And not a corner piece— something good. You guys have all the fun."

Boldt hung up the phone thinking about his wife. Amid all the eighteen-hour tours, Liz had come to town for the day and had, as far as Boldt knew, returned to the cabin, having never contacted her husband. He tried her cellular, got her voice mail, and told her, "The coast is clear, love. We're back in the house. I miss you all terribly. Hurry home."

The bulk of the investigation, that rock coming down the hill, had hit bottom and run out of momentum. Lab crews would be busy for several weeks analyzing what little evidence came out of Hall's and Garman's residences. Amid a continued media blitz by city politicians proclaiming the city safe and the guilty parties behind bars, Boldt would watch the investigation be dismantled before his eyes and despite his objections. He had been here before; he felt wrapped in the black cape of depression.

He walked slowly down the long hall to the conference room, attempting to collect his thoughts.

She sat at the table alone under the unforgiving glare of fluorescent light. Her hair was pulled back. She looked tired. She directed him to the city map, into which she had stabbed several pushpins. "Dorothy Enwright, Melissa Heifitz, Veronica DeLatario—red, yellow, and green. All in the same general area of town. Why?''

Boldt studied the map and the location of the pushpins. The simplest things could avoid them, rarely did they fully escape. ''That's the area of service for his battalion. He'd have a firm working knowledge of the area.''

Her lips pursed, and when she spoke her voice was as harsh as the lighting. ''Listen, it's true that psychopaths often restrict their movements to an area a mile or two in radius from their residences, but Steven Garman is so far outside the profile of a psychopath that there's no reason to make the slightest of comparisons. Admittedly, I haven't had time to work with him, but I've listened to that so-called confession more times than the rest of you, and I've got to tell you, there's a clever mind at work here. You listen carefully, most of it is fluff. He's not confessing to anything. And does an intelligent, well-liked man like Garman start killing women in his own back yard? I don't think so, Lou. Maybe across town, maybe in Portland or Spokane, or someplace far, far from home, but down the street?''

''Down the street, he can target them,'' he suggested.

She protested, ''So you know how the Scholar targets them, is that it?''

''You know I don't.''

''Well, neither do I, and I'm willing to bet you that neither does Steven Garman.'' She stared at him through a long silence. ''He's too big and heavy for your boy up the ladder, isn't he?'' she asked rhetorically. ''Same as with Hall. We listen to the evidence, right? Isn't that right, Lou?''

''Shoswitz will cut the team down to nothing. Four of us if I'm lucky: LaMoia, Bahan, Fidler—''

''When do we face we have the wrong man?''

''Facing it and discussing it openly are two different issues,'' he answered. ''Shoswitz will not want to hear it. Period. The brass is crowing all over the airwaves that we caught the big one that got away. We change the story and some heads will roll.''

''I understand that,'' she said. ''But we can't go along with it.

Even if we do it quietly, we push ahead. There's going to be another fire, Lou," she said, voicing his secret fear.

"You had any vacation lately?" he asked, changing the subject, hoping to erase the image of another fire from his thoughts.

"No."

"Where would you go if you did? What kind of places does Owen like?"

"Owen doesn't take vacations."

"I'm thinking about Mexico a lot. Warm. Sunny. Cheap."

"I think I'd ask to borrow your cabin," she said dreamily. "Take a pile of books, a couple of bags of fresh veggies, some really great wine, some CDs. You got a bathtub up there?"

"Of course."

"Candles. Some bath oil. Spoil myself, you know? Indulge."

"Suntan lotion," he proposed. "A Walkman with all of Oscar Peterson. Barefoot on the beach. Long naps."

"The kids?"

"Of course. You bet! Spend time just watching them, just sitting there watching them, you know?"

"Shoswitz suggesting a vacation?" she asked.

Boldt nodded. "Feels like he's ready to shove it down my throat. He mentioned you and John, too."

"He doesn't miss much. He never strikes you that way, but his antenna is always up."

"It would appear so."

"Let's say he's still out there," she said. "You arrested his source when you arrested Hall. Forget Garman for a moment. At this point the Scholar is like a junkie, he's addicted to the power of these arsons. Earlier, there was, more than likely, a justification at work in his mind. Rationalizing his deeds. But somewhere in the course of events there was a transference to where the deed justified itself because it made him feel so good. So all-powerful. The Bible quotes indicate he believes in a Divine Law, and he believes he is the bearer of that flag. But you put a kink in all that. You dried up the source. You put fear into him. His response was to take a big risk by breaking into Chief Joseph and taking the hypergolics for himself. This tells us that he's a planner. He watched Nicholas Hall; he knew what warehouses to hit. We don't know for how long, but he's known the location of those accelerants. He was content to pay for them because it put Hall at risk, not himself; as long as Hall did his job right, the supply was endless. You changed all that.

"Success in such endeavors," she continued, "breeds a lacka-daisical attitude, a complacency. He believed he could go on doing this forever. He felt confident that you would not identify or locate him. But now we have Garman as well—and Garman is trying to cover for him. Why? It's likely the Scholar has stolen more acceler-ant, quite possibly an enormous amount. Why? Some kind of grand finale? Will he just go back to killing these women, content with his stolen fuel? Or will he move away, only to start again in a year or two?"

"You tell me," Boldt suggested.

"He's fooled me from the start, Lou. I don't trust my own judgments. I've been wrong about him time and time again. The point is, neither of us believes Garman set those fires. We'll never convince anyone else until we know why he confessed."

"Protecting someone," Boldt said, repeating what she had suggested.

"Unless it's himself he's protecting," she said, confusing him. "Unless he's two people inside there: the fire inspector and the arsonist. And the fire inspector finally turned in the arsonist." She produced a photograph. "Here's the stumbling block: his ex-wife." She moved her hand out of the way, and Boldt saw a woman's happy face smiling back at him in the photograph.

"Peas in a pod," she said, producing one of the recent family photographs of Dorothy Enwright. The similarities between the Enwright and the ex-wife were astounding. Boldt looked back and forth between them. "Uncanny."

"The problem with fires is they burn the victim, they burn the boxes of photographs, the framed pictures by the bed. We end up with pictures fifteen years out of date. And the thing about women is, we change our look. We move with the fashions. Men? Forget it.

But we're the victims of these fires—you and me, Lou—because we've been working with photos that didn't show us the current look of these women. Here's the photo of Melissa Heifitz *we* have," she said, producing another shot. "Henna-red hair down past her shoulders. But come to find out, the henna was out of a bottle; she went gray in the late eighties and dyed it dark, just like these two. Cut it shorter and left it straight." She used a felt-tip pen to change the look of Heifitz's hair, and all at once the similarity was there as well.

"Damn!" Boldt said. Another piece of his puzzle.

"It's what triggers him, Lou: that particular look."

"So it might be Garman after all?" Boldt questioned uncomfortably. He didn't want to believe this. "He's protecting himself *from* himself? You actually buy that?"

"Not for a minute," said the psychologist who had offered him the theory. "Though one could make the argument fairly strongly."

"You're toying with me," he complained.

"Absolutely." She smiled, though it did nothing to disguise her fatigue. The smile melted from her face as if rinsed off. "There's a third element, a third participant. Someone we don't even know exists—didn't know until now," she corrected herself. "Garman may be a good liar, but he's no killer. We may not have the evidence necessary to prove it, but we both know it's true."

"A third element," Boldt muttered, reaching unsteadily for a chair and sitting himself down.

45

WHEN she looked at him, she wanted to

cry. His pale innocence as he struggled with his homework. The simplicity of movement, unaware of her presence. He had lived so long in a home where he was unwanted that he didn't notice others around him.

In this, as in so many things with Ben, Daphne was wrong. The plain truth was that she had not lived around boys enough to read one correctly. He looked up at her and said, "Why do I have to do this shit?"

"Watch the language!" she scolded.

"Stuff," he substituted.

"It's homework, Ben. We all had to do it."

"So what? That makes it right? I don't think so."

"What's five times twenty-five?" she asked. His face went blank and she explained, "Some guy offers you twenty-five bucks an hour for five hours—"

"I'll take it!" he answered quickly.

"How about five bucks an hour for twenty-five hours?" she fired back.

Confused, Ben scribbled out numbers on a piece of paper. "It's a hundred and twenty-five bucks."

"And how many work days is twenty-five hours if you work eight hours a day?"

"So you need math," he conceded, without doing the numbers.

"Some people will tell you that the difference between not having an education and having one is whether you want to work with your body or with your mind. Whether you want to make a little money or a lot of money. But it goes way beyond that. It's the *way* you enjoy things. The more you know, the more you get out of it."

"Einstein flunked math," he reminded her.

"And PhDs can be the most boring people on earth," she agreed. "I'm not saying it's some kind of cure-all. It just gives you a head start, that's all. You like computers? You like special effects in movies? A computer is no good if you don't know how to run it."

"What about yours?"

"My what?" she asked.

"Your laptop. Will you teach me how to run it?"

She was caught. Stuck. She was protective of her laptop, always keeping it with her, locking it down with password protection when she left it behind at the office for a few hours; she felt it was something personal, not for others. And yet she couldn't deny the boy. "Sure," she said reluctantly, wondering how she had boxed herself in that way.

"Really?" His face brightened in a way she had not yet witnessed, like a kid on Christmas morning.

She nodded. "I'll need to get some games for it. I only have solitaire."

"How about a database?" he asked her, stunning her. "Does it have a database?"

It had one as part of a suite of applications, though Daphne used it only as an address book.

She thought if the definition of love was that you would lay down your life for the other, then she loved Ben. For she would never allow another person, or anything at all, to harm him again. She would wrap her wing around him, pull him close, and protect him from the coldness of the world. He had seen his share and didn't need to see any more.

"Does it have graphs?" he asked.

"I think the spreadsheet does, yes."

"We're doing graphs," he said, tapping his homework.

He scratched at the paper with his eraser. How she wished she could erase those past few years of his life, clean the slate! She had the professional tools within her reach to begin the process, but Ben would have to want it.

"If I show you the laptop," she tested, "will you tell me about Jack and your mother?"

"Like a trade?" he asked. "Are you trying to bribe me?"

"Absolutely," she confessed. "I don't know very much about you, Ben. It bothers me. It's what makes close friends out of people: sharing. You know?"

"Will you tell me about this guy Owen?" he asked, sounding a little jealous.

"How—?" She cut herself off. He had overheard some of her phone conversations. Her crying? He probably knew more about her than she did him. Which one of them was the psychologist? she wondered. "Will you go trick-or-treating with me tonight?" He had not wanted anything to do with Halloween.

He set his pencil down and, facing her with a deadly serious face, asked, "If I agree, does this mean we have a relationship?"

Daphne bit back her grin and, when she felt herself losing it, turned her face away, so he couldn't see. "Yes," she said, and smiled widely, all the way over to the laptop.

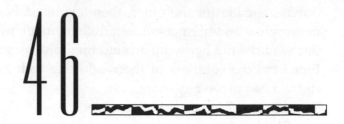

46

THE killer was still out there. Boldt felt certain of it, though as yet he had no conclusive proof.

Bobbie Gaynes had set up her office cubicle as an impromptu task force center. Even though Shoswitz had not allocated her time to Boldt's resources, she refused to be shut out, pulling what amounted to a double shift and looking the worse for wear. On her wall hung several photographs of the early arsons, evidence photographs of the ladder impressions, and magnified close-ups of the cotton fibers mixed into the mud at the Enwright scene. There were photos of all four victims, including Branslonovich. Below these portraits hung a bad photocopy of Garman's wife, eerily similar to the three dead mothers. Gaynes hung up the phone and told him, "Lofgrin has confirmed that the silver fibers are a silver fabric paint; the underlying blue is the actual color of the fabric. Second, commercially available Seahawk jerseys are not a sixty/forty blend—they're twenty/eighty, polyester to cotton, so we can rule them out, which is good because they sell every-where."

"And that leaves?" Boldt asked.

"Silk-screen printers who handle towels or terry cloth," she answered. "The lab is adamant about these being a spiral-twisted cotton-blend fiber typically seen in a towel or a terry-cloth robe. That works in our favor. We tried the jerseys even though they aren't a twisted fiber—they seemed obvious because of the colors—but now we're down to determining what companies produce this particular color in this particular blend and, alternately, which silk-screen companies have purchased that fabric."

"I like it," Boldt said.

"The larger textile mills are in the South and Northeast. I'm on that. The bad news is that there are more printers than you can shake a stick at—you can't believe how many. And though you might think that if it's sold here in Seattle it would also be silk-screened here, it ain't necessarily so. If it's cheaper in Spokane or Portland or Boise, that's where it happens. And most of these silk-screen places are mom-and-pop shops, little independents that crank out sports uniforms, corporate golf shirts, you name it."

"How many?" Boldt asked, dread replacing his flirtation with optimism.

She avoided a direct answer. "Both US West and Pac Bell have their Yellow Pages on CD ROM, which is handy." She laid a hand on her personal computer. Only a few cops had gone to the expense of providing their own hardware.

"How many?" Boldt repeated. He sensed her reluctance to tell him, and that drove his curiosity.

"That's the trouble. Six hundred ninety-seven printers in the Seattle area alone."

Boldt felt the number across his face like a hand slap. When the entire seven-man squad had to make thirty or forty calls, they were stretched to the limit.

She spoke quickly and excitedly. Gaynes was part cheerleader. "We can rule out a whole bunch. The fast-copy places with twenty-five franchises don't do silk-screening or fabric, and that cuts the list literally in half."

It left them making over three hundred calls. Impossible, Boldt thought.

"Needless to say, we're short a little manpower."

Boldt was overwhelmed. He felt choked, as if his collar were too tight. With those numbers, pursuing the fibers was an exercise in futility. "We're stewed," he said.

"Have a little faith, Sergeant. Five years ago we would have needed a couple hundred volunteers to make the calls for us. You've used the university kids a couple of times"—she didn't allow him to interrupt—"but that was *with* the blessing of Shoswitz. This is without. This requires a little Henry Ford," she said, a smile twisting her pallid face. "When in doubt, automate." She continued nonstop, barely taking another breath. "We did it once before, remember? LaMoia has a friend—"

Who else but LaMoia? Boldt wondered, keeping quiet.

"—a woman friend who manages a telephone telemarketing service. You know, those awful prerecorded messages dialed directly into your home, selling aluminum siding. He's checking her out in person, due back here any minute. Thinks he might be able to wangle a few hours of service out of her—her *company*," she corrected, blushing. "We post a message that leads off something like 'This is the Seattle Police, homicide division. Your printing company may have information pertinent to solving a series of homicides in the Seattle area. Your cooperation is critical to our efforts.' Something like that. Grab their attention, ask for their help. He says these machines, with a short enough message, can do a couple hundred calls *an hour* and keep calling until they verify a voice answer. I believe it; I've gotten enough of the calls myself."

"Same," Boldt said.

"So, see? Maybe we reach them all. Maybe one of them hears the message and actually does something about it. The beauty is, if she lets us lease her 800 number, we can do the same for Spokane, Boise, Portland." She lowered her voice to a soft whisper. "We pry a little informant money loose and divert it to this thing— the ultimate informer—and maybe we get lucky."

She had clearly thought this through.

"It makes sense," Boldt agreed, equally quietly. "Maybe that's the direction we go. But let's brainstorm it a minute and see where we get."

He could sense her disappointment as she took up a pen and paper, prepared to jot down each thought. They took alternate turns, Gaynes first. "Cotton fibers," she said.

"Silver paint, blue fabric."

"Seahawk colors."

"Silk-screen paint."

"Sixty/forty blend."

"The textile mills feed the wholesalers, the wholesalers the printers."

"Contract work."

"What's that?" Boldt said.

"Contract work," she repeated.

He nodded slowly. *Contract work.* Why had that interrupted his thoughts? "Let's go on," he said making note of it. "Contract work," he repeated.

"Similar fibers were found on your windows and in the mud by the ladder at Enwright's."

"Window washing," he said.

"A rag maybe, a torn towel."

"Windows," Boldt repeated. It stuck in his thoughts. Why?

LaMoia arrived, clearly worked up.

"Brainstorming," Boldt said, holding up a hand to prevent LaMoia from interrupting.

The detective nodded. His demeanor was serious and contemplative. "With you," he said.

The sergeant said, "Me, then Gaynes, then you. Okay?" LaMoia nodded. Boldt retraced their steps, saying, "Fibers found on the windows and by the ladder."

Gaynes went next. "Window washing. A rag maybe."

"Cotton fibers," LaMoia said, a beat behind in the game.

Boldt hoped he wouldn't hinder them. "A bucket of rags? A rag tucked in a belt?"

"A bucket of soapy water," said Gaynes.

"Window washing," LaMoia said, his voice lower and more ominous than usual.

Boldt sensed the detective's head rise in an attempt to meet eyes, but Boldt wanted this purely stream-of-consciousness communication. His own head slightly bent, Boldt said, "Glass."

"A squeegee."

"Sponge. Rag."

"Ladder," Boldt said.

"Rooftop."

"Glass," LaMoia echoed.

"Windows," Gaynes offered.

"The cars!" LaMoia said more loudly. "The wheels!"

Inadvertently, Boldt snapped his head up.

"The cars," LaMoia repeated. "My assignment, remember? Lab report placed cotton fibers inside the *cars*," he emphasized, his eyes wide, his mustache caught between his teeth as he gnawed.

Boldt wanted to continue the brainstorming but decided to talk it through. "It's a natural fiber, John. It's found everywhere. Every crime scene."

LaMoia appeared too caught up in his own idea to be of any help. Ignoring LaMoia, Boldt asked Gaynes, "What about the Seahawks front office? If we're right about the silver and blue being the Seahawks logo, wouldn't the Seahawks front office license the rights?"

Her eyes brightened. "They'll have a list of anyone authorized to use the colors and logo."

"An agent would handle licensing. An attorney probably."

LaMoia wasn't paying any attention. His eyes were squinted shut tightly.

"I'll get a name," she said. He could see optimism in the brightness of her eyes. He appreciated Gaynes for her can-do attitude. Nothing beat her down.

LaMoia said to no one in particular, "It's the cars. The lab report mentioned an abundance of cotton fibers."

Boldt felt a surge of anger. LaMoia wasn't listening to himself.

It was first-year academy stuff. Attempting to follow natural fibers was like trying to use dust as forensic evidence.

"What about T-shirt *shops?*" Gaynes asked. "They wouldn't necessarily be listed as printers, yet they might have a screen in the back room. Might sell sweat bands, something with a twisted fiber."

"Add them to your phone list as well," Boldt instructed.

LaMoia snapped out of it and said, "The phone deal is on."

"If Bernie says it's a towel or a robe, we go with that."

"Window washing," LaMoia sputtered, annoying Boldt. "The cars."

"What about the silver paint?" Gaynes asked. "The Bureau's crime lab keeps the chemical signature of paints on file. Maybe they could ID the paint manufacturer for us." She continued. "We might narrow the printer field considerably."

"That's good thinking," Boldt told her. "Check it out with Bernie."

"Sarge," LaMoia said, "I need to check something out."

"Go," Boldt told him, happy to be rid of him.

LaMoia took off at a hurried clip. *That* from the man of struts and strides? It caught the attention of Bobbie Gaynes as well. She said, "Well, he's certainly in a strange place."

Boldt checked his watch. He was late to an autopsy that he did not want to attend. Dixie was to go over the skeletal remains of the woman found in the crawl space. He would attempt to confirm it was Ben's mother. If Boldt skipped it, Shoswitz would hear about it; he had no choice but to go.

47

IT was not such a long drive, but for Daphne it felt nearly interminable. Boldt had not been told about the meeting. Susan Prescott did not know. It was the bit of conspiracy between Ben and Daphne that had convinced Ben to cooperate with the video lineup and the police artist: the promise of seeing Emily.

The meeting could not take place at Emily's because Daphne remained concerned about the Scholar's possible whereabouts and media references to the participation of a local psychic and the existence of a twelve-year-old witness. Even without names being mentioned, Daphne was taking no chances; she would protect Ben at every opportunity.

Both Boldt and Susan would have been highly critical of her for arranging such a meeting, but a promise was a promise. Her fears ran far beyond the tongue-lashing she might suffer from Boldt. More important, she might lose her newly formed bond with Ben to this other woman. She wondered if the transition from a possible future with Owen to a present with this boy had resulted in a transference; if, in fact, she was fooling herself, not being honest, using the boy to soften the landing. She had barely thought about Owen over the past few days. He had been gracious enough to give her the distance she requested, and that distance had ended up an emotional abyss, a black hole across which she had not returned. She had rid herself of him. It felt good on many levels. She missed Corky, especially at dinnertime, but much of what she gained from Corky had been easily replaced by her time with Ben. At that point it hit her hard: If she lost Ben the world was going to seem incredibly empty for a time. For the past week, the kid had done more good for her than he would ever know.

She did not trust Emily. The woman was a proven con artist. She played on a person's superstitions, fears, and aspirations. She tricked people. She used the stars and a tarot deck to feed people what they wanted to hear. Worst of all, she owned Ben's heart free and clear; in the eyes of the youngster this woman could do no wrong. If she told Ben to stop talking to Daphne, he would; if she told him to run for her car and lock the doors, he would do this as well. Just the mention of her name drove the boy's eyes wide. Daphne realized that she was in many ways jealous of Emily, just as she was jealous of Liz—envy was too light a word. She didn't like herself much, and that discovery made her wonder if her impending breakup with Owen was a product of his failures, their combined failures, or her own internal dissatisfaction with herself.

Martin Luther King Boulevard was a four-lane road through several miles of an economically patchy black neighborhood kept separate from Lake Washington's upscale white enclaves by a geological formation, a high spine of hill running as a steep ridge, north to south. Daphne marveled how Seattle, like so many U.S. cities, was segregated into dozens of small ethnic and microeconomic communities, villages, and neighborhoods. People moved freely and, for the most part safely, one community to the next, but park a car of blacks in a gated community and a cop or security person would arrive within minutes. A car of whites would not draw the same response. Seattle's various communities consisted of African Americans, Hispanics, Vietnamese, Caucasians, Jews, Scandinavians, yuppies, yaughties, and computer nerds.

Ben pointed out the park before they arrived. A row of cement obelisks loomed in the distance, looking like support piers for a highway overpass. Daphne didn't know this area well and was unfamiliar with the park itself. She followed Ben's directions and pulled over to stop where he indicated.

Ben could not remember feeling this happy, this excited. Emily. He had missed her to the point that he felt his heart might rip from his chest. He had dreamed about her, written in his journal about her, lay awake thinking about her. He had so many questions to ask. More than anything, he wanted a hug—to feel her arms around him.

He walked fast, outpacing Daphne, who chided him for it. "Stay close," she called out to him, and he could hear something wrong in her voice, something different.

To him, the place was out of a *Star Trek* movie: the towering blocks of concrete, the enormous metal cages attached to cement walls, all of it cut into the massive hill like a giant bunker. To Ben it was the tunnel park—eight lanes of I-90 passed beneath it, unheard, unseen. The facility had only recently been completed as a park, and the sidewalks, the flower beds—everything about it— were so new it did not feel inhabited; each time Ben came here it felt as if he were the first person to discover it: the giant slabs of concrete all lined up like blocks, stretching toward the gray sky, all different sizes but topping out at the exact same height.

The sidewalk climbed up a steady grade to reach a wide bike path that ran down the center of the park and served as its focus. A bicyclist sped by, head bent low, legs pumping. Ben said hi to the man, but the cyclist never looked up, never acknowledged him.

Ben's legs began to run underneath him before he managed to say to Daphne, "There she is!" He took off at lightning speed, his eyes welling with tears not because of the wind in his face but because of the ache in his heart. He hadn't realized how much he had missed her until he saw her again. Her silhouette, so unmistakable in the distance, so beautiful, so wonderful. Perhaps it was the sound of his footsteps slapping beneath him, perhaps she had sensed his approach out of thin air as she could sense so much, but something caused her to spin around and face him. As she did, her face lifted in a big moon of a smile, her eyes lighted up, and she opened her arms invitingly.

Daphne let the boy have some distance. She owed the two of them a moment in private, given all she had put them through. A part of her had no desire even to greet Emily, to give the woman a chance to wield her power over the boy and dominate him the way she knew was possible. She would not turn this into an emotional tug-of-war, not for anything. She would not put the boy through that; worse, she would not inflict it upon herself, for she knew this was a game she was certain to lose, and at that point in time she could not afford to lose the boy and his dependence on her. It was a delicate line to walk, and she walked it with one eye glued to the scene before her but with her head turned down in indifference. The human heart is more fragile than one ever expects, she thought.

She strolled the bike path, unfamiliar with it, intrigued by a series of stone posts that rose to knee height on either side. She approached the nearest of these stone posts, admiring the tile work at its base.

The tile held an odd stick-figure drawing, evoking a Native American pictograph. Surrounding the tile's perimeter were words. It took her a moment to discern where the sentence began. But it wasn't a sentence, she realized; it was a quotation: "Crooked is the path of eternity." Nietzsche. She hurried to the next post: more primitive art and a quote from Lao-tsu: "The way that can be told, is not the constant way." Heart pounding, she hurried to the next, reading words emblazoned on her memory: "Suddenly a flash of understanding, a spark that leaps across the soul." Plato. The same quote that had accompanied a melted piece of green plastic. One post to the next, like a bee to flowers. A dozen such quotations and pictographs. She stopped and stared: "He has half the deed done who has made a beginning."

The first of the threats: Dorothy Enwright. She had profiled the suspect as highly educated, a scholar! He was nothing more than a plagiarist who had walked or ridden through this park. The Bible-thumping disturbed man in the trees had not lined up well for her with the poetic intellect, but with this discovery the two melded into one: A plagiarist, with little education and the need to appear smart; a mind steeped in biblical significance; a sociopath intent on burning or disfiguring women.

There on that bike path she found each and every quote mailed to Garman. And then the most important thought of all: The arsonist used this section of bike path—he lived somewhere in the area.

"Quick, Ben!" she shouted from a great distance. "We have to go. Right now!"

48

BOLDT was awaiting a meeting with
King County Medical Examiner Dr. Ronald Dixon, in the basement
of the Harborview Medical Center, when Dr. Roy McClure, a friend
of Dixon's and Liz's internist, approached him and shook hands.

The waiting area was foam couches and three-month-old ce-
lebrity magazines.

The two men shook hands. McClure perched himself on the
edge of the couch.

"How are you taking it?" McClure asked gravely, with great
sympathy in his calming eyes.

"It's unsettling," Boldt admitted.

"I should say it is. The real battle is psychological. Attitude is
ninety percent of the game."

"Yeah," Boldt agreed.

"How about the kids?"

"The kids?"

"Miles and Sarah," McClure answered.

"They're fine, I think," Boldt answered. "I haven't seen them
in a while, quite honestly. Liz has had them."

"Well, I certainly understand that," McClure replied.

"You know, Roy, I get the feeling that we're having two different conversations here."

"You'll feel that way from time to time. The world won't make any sense. The temptation may be to bury yourself in work, but the more prudent course is to talk it out. Sit her down and tell her how much you're rooting for her, give her every ounce of support you can."

"I *was* talking about work," Boldt stated. He felt too tired for any conversation. He wished McClure would go away.

"I'm talking about Elizabeth." It wasn't the doctor's words that jolted Boldt so much as the ominous tone of voice in which they were delivered. Boldt felt a sickening nausea twist his stomach.

"Liz?"

"You're not in denial, are you?"

"Roy, what in bloody hell are you talking about?" the sergeant blurted out. "I'm too tired for this."

"I'm talking about your wife's lymphoma, Lou. I'm talking about your wife's life. Your children. You. How you are all coping with this."

Boldt's ears rang as if someone had detonated an explosive in the room. He felt bloodless and cold. His head swam and he felt dizzy. His eyes stung, and his fingers went numb, and though he struggled to get out some words, nothing happened. He was paralyzed. He could not move, or speak, or even blink his eyes. Tears gushed down his cheeks as if someone had stuck his eyes with a knife. He felt himself swoon. McClure's mouth was moving, but no sound issued from it. No words came forth. The doctor's face twisted into a knot of concern, and it was clear to Boldt that the numbness and the ringing in his ears was his flirtation with unconsciousness—he was passing out.

McClure's strong grip upon his shoulders brought Boldt back just far enough to hear the words, "She didn't tell you." It was a statement. Definitive.

Boldt felt himself shake his head. "Is it . . . ?" He couldn't say the word. To speak it was to cast negative thoughts. He convinced himself that he had heard wrong. "Did you say . . . ?" But Mc-Clure's expression was enough. Boldt pictured her looking so sad in the bathtub, recalled the regular baths that had seemed so out of the place, her request to spend time with one of the children by herself. The pieces of the puzzle suddenly came together like they did occasionally in an investigation.

"It metastasized quickly," McClure answered. "Stage Four by the time we caught it. She must have known, Lou, but she evidently couldn't bring herself to face it. It was the kids, I think."

Tears continued to cascade down his face.

"The surgery is scheduled for next week," McClure said, soberly and dryly. "I'm counting on your support through all this. She needs every bit of strength we can offer her."

Boldt felt trapped inside a small dark box. He could shout as loudly as he wanted, but no one could hear him. He could open his eyes wide, but could not see. It was a dream, he convinced himself, nothing more. A nightmare. He would awaken and find himself at Harborview, on the couch, awaiting his meeting with Dixie. It was guilt playing a nasty trick on his subconscious.

But McClure did not go away.

"The baths?" Boldt mumbled, and somehow McClure understood the question.

"They help with the pain," he said. "She's in a tremendous amount of pain."

There were many shades to gray. There was the gray of forgiveness between the black and white of knowledge, the gray of age at the temples, the gray of a mirror's reflection, the gray of a weathered headstone in a graveyard. Boldt caught a glimpse of himself in the crooked rearview mirror as he drove straight home.

He drove with tears in his eyes, his shoulders shaking, his lips trembling; only the siren filled his ears. Time had stopped, and yet a clock ran inside his head and heart as never before. So many memories, all tangled up in a man's stubborn refusal to let go.

Guilt banged at his chest for distrusting her. He recalled their baby in her arms and at her breast, the two of them in the bath, and he dragged his shirtsleeve over his face to relieve his eyes.

Every second, every moment seemed a lost opportunity. So many had passed while he took their love and their life together for granted. At that point, racing toward the final turn in the road, he wanted it all back, like an athlete with a lost game. It seemed so fast, so quick. They had been building toward something, making a life. In the process their lives had been crossed, lost a few times. They had drifted apart and back together, like boats riding the ebb and flow of the tides. She so private—so unfair. He felt anger, love, fear, and terror all combine in an inescapable emotional avalanche, with him at the bottom looking up. One did not run for cover from such things but steeled the body and soul to face the inescapable. He didn't want to believe it, to buy into it. There was always hope, he reminded himself, always a miracle waiting. Was it too late to pray? Anger surged through him. He didn't want this life alone. He didn't want a world without Liz. It wasn't fair. It wasn't what they had planned.

He pulled to a stop, the siren running down and silenced but the light still flashing on the dash. His terror erupted as a brief sputter of laughter—it was a joke, some kind of mistake, McClure confusing one patient with another.

"They help with the pain." Boldt pressed his hands to his ears. He didn't want McClure's words circulating inside his head. He didn't want to hear his voice. He wanted peace, release. He wanted to awaken, to wash the nightmare from his face with a quick splash of cold water. "Wake me up," he muttered.

Marina opened the door, the smile on her face running off like melted wax, replaced with a troubled look of concern. "Mr. Boldt?"

"She here?"

A shake of the head. "Work."

Was she back at work? He couldn't remember where he had slept last night, what day it was. "The kids?"

On cue, Miles rounded the corner, yelped, "Daddy!" and held

his arms outstretched for his father, who scooped him up and then broke into tears. Marina, arms crossed as if freezing cold, stood in the entranceway, unable to take her eyes off Boldt and his tears. She gasped, "Everything okay?"

Miles cuddled himself around Boldt's neck, clinging tightly. The father's eyes met those of the woman, and she sobered. "I'm right here," the woman told Boldt. He passed Miles back to her and nodded, the tears dripping from his chin. He felt embarrassed, exhausted, terrified. He didn't want a world without Liz; he didn't want to think of her in pain. He wanted to take her away, as if by leaving she might leave the illness behind as well.

His car flew down the road, driven by someone else. Car horns complained behind him as he ran intersections, his vision more occupied by a stream of memories than by the road he traveled. He was a flood of regret, seeing so many chances to be a better person to her, a better husband, a better lover, a better friend. How much of illness is physical, he wondered, and how much a product of one's environment? If he had been more available, less self-absorbed, would she even be sick? His thoughts played tricks on him: self-pity, shame, a bone-numbing fear. He pushed on the accelerator and begged to be released. "Make it not so," he mumbled.

The office building towered over downtown, stretching for a piece of the sky that would offer a glimpse of Elliott Bay and Puget Sound beyond. It had been erected in the mid-seventies at the start of an economic boom that foreshadowed the high-tech revolution and the invasion of the Californians. Boldt parked illegally, pulled his POLICE ON DUTY sign onto the dash to keep the meter readers at bay, and hurried up the long procession of low steps that eventually rose to meet the glass and steel of the lobby.

He turned heads as he marched toward the elevators in long, defiant strides. He rode the elevator alone, which was the first decent thing to happen to him that day.

"Elizabeth Boldt," he informed the receptionist. In all the years of his wife's working here, Boldt had visited the offices only

358

RIDLEY PEARSON

a handful of times. He realized then that he brought his work home almost every night, whereas Liz did so only occasionally. She earned nearly four times his pay and had pleaded with him regularly to give up the badge—or, at a bare minimum, the field work—in part because she couldn't stand the tension resulting from the danger involved. The two years in which he had taken a leave of absence for the arrival and care of Miles had been among their most happy. He'd been seduced back into public service, in part by a bizarre case involving the theft of human organs, in part by the ways and means of Daphne Matthews. But looking back while he awaited the receptionist to notify his wife of his arrival, Boldt thought the return to service a mistake. They had found each other again during those two years, Boldt with late-afternoon happy hour piano gigs, Liz with a husband who wasn't mentally and emotionally preoccupied by his work.

"She's in a meeting. It'll be a few minutes." The woman pointed to the waiting area's three couches. "Can I get you some coffee?"

"No, it'll be now," Boldt told her. "I'm her husband. It can't wait. Where's the meeting?"

The woman said kindly, "I'm sorry, sir—"

"Jenny," Boldt said, naming Liz's assistant. "I need to talk to Jenny." He didn't wait for this woman's approval, but instead charged off with his heavy strides in the direction of Liz's office. As it happened, he passed a conference room immediately, voices chattering inside. He swung open the door without knocking, looked around, and did not see her. "Elizabeth Boldt," he told the gawking faces. They shook their heads nearly in unison, but one of the women pointed farther down the hall. "Thank you." He pulled the door shut quietly.

Jenny was already heading toward him at a run. The two were phone pals but rarely met face-to-face. "Lou?" she called out in a voice of alarm. She apparently knew him well enough to recognize disaster on his face, or perhaps—he thought—it wasn't so difficult to see. "It's not one of the kids, is it?"

"Where is she?"

"A meeting."

"I need to see her now!"

"It's with the president and the chairman. It shouldn't run much longer."

"I don't care who it's with," he snapped. "Now!" he shouted loudly. Looking directly into her brown eyes, he said, "I will make a scene you won't believe, Jenny. Now! Right now. No matter how important that meeting. Is that clear?"

His pager sounded. Jenny looked down at his waist. Boldt moved his jacket aside and looked at the device as well. It seemed attached to a different man, someone else. He glanced down the hall to the corner turn that led to the "hallway of power," as Liz called it. She was down there in one of those rooms. The pager had a sobering effect on him. He switched it off. There he was, once again faced with his job versus his relationship, and despite all the reasoning, all the regret of the last hour, it wasn't as simple as dropping the pager into the trash. The Scholar was out there preparing to kill people. He knew this to his core.

And Liz was in a meeting, and Jenny seemed prepared to put her body between Boldt and the hallway of power.

"How long?" Boldt asked her, pulling the pager off his belt and angling the LCD screen so that it was legible. It was that move that seemed in such violation of everything he had been thinking. An internal voice asked, *How could you?* And there was no immediate answer from the defense. He had responsibilities to his team, to the city, to the innocent, but none of that entered his mind. All he could think was that he knew he was going to call in the page, the summons, and that whatever it was would take him away from there, from her. She would remain in her boardroom and he would be back in his shitheap of a department-issue four-door, racing off to the next emergency.

He looked down at Jenny with sad eyes.

"She called the meeting, Lou," Jenny said. "Whatever it is, it has to be important. I don't dare interrupt it."

Boldt nodded. "It's important, all right," he agreed. She had to be offering her resignation. She wanted time with the kids. He felt his throat constrict with grief. Deciding to spare this woman his bubbling and gushing, he forced out the words. "Tell her I came by. Tell her it's important. I'm on the cellphone," he said, pulling himself back together. Mention of the phone caused him to check it. LO BAT it read. It was dead—just like everything around him. "I don't know," he said to her, feeling beaten. He turned and headed back toward reception.

Jenny followed him the whole way, but she never said a word. She held the door for him and then stepped out into the hall and called an elevator for him, perhaps because he seemed incapable of even the simplest act. Boldt stepped onto the elevator. Their eyes met as the doors closed. Hers were sympathetic and troubled. His were stone-cold dead—and watery, like melting ice.

He reached the office on the radio from the car. The dispatcher put him on hold; he felt it was something of a permanent sentence.

The man came back on the channel and said to Boldt, "Message is from Detective John LaMoia. Would you like me to read it?"

"Go ahead," answered Boldt, driving the car into traffic.

"Message reads, *Must talk immediately. Please notify ASAP.*"

Boldt squeezed the talk button and said, "Tell him I'm on my way."

He felt like a traitor and a cheat.

He stopped at a church on his way downtown. To his surprise, he felt a lot better.

49

AS the elevator doors slid open on the fifth floor of the Public Safety Building, the painful silence inside Boldt's shattered psyche was cracked open by the cacophony of a dozen reporters all shouting at once, boom microphones waving in the air, and the blinding glare of television floodlights. One of the reporters shouted, "Do you have the Scholar in custody or not?" Shoswitz anxiously fought a path through the press, made his way to Boldt, and escorted his sergeant to Homicide's door, shouting, "No comment! No comment!"

As the door opened for the pair, the press remained at bay, stopping at an unmarked line like a dog pulling up short at a buried invisible fence. But the noise of the reporters was not silenced, only replaced by the comments of half as many of his own people. They fell in around him and behind him like the Texas Rangers. Bobbie Gaynes was speaking, but Boldt couldn't hear her. LaMoia was there, Bernie Lofgrin from the lab, and several of the uniformed officers who had previously volunteered on the task force. He noticed a woman name Richert from the prosecuting attorney's office. All spoke at once, some shouting to be heard over others.

Shoswitz joined right in with them. They continued as a group, making for the conference room. There was only one person noticeably absent, and then Boldt caught sight of her standing alongside the briefing room door, arms crossed at her chest, hair impeccably groomed, eyes trained on him, an expression of concern worn like a veil. Only she knew him well enough to take note of his condition; Shoswitz had missed it, too concerned with the media; the others had missed it, more intent on reading from their notes than studying their sergeant. But she saw it. She knew, well before the moment they came face-to-face, and asked him, "What is it?"

He felt himself on the verge of telling her, when an exasperated Shoswitz proclaimed, "You know what it is! It's another poem!"

She informed Boldt privately, as if it hardly mattered, "He's all worked up because a reporter found it in Garman's morning mail. Not us."

"The Scholar is still out there!" Shoswitz declared.

Boldt just looked at him and shook his head. "Everybody out!" he told those gathered. He held Daphne by the elbow, retaining her. "John, you stay." When the room was empty, Boldt closed the door and the three of them were finally alone.

LaMoia explained. "A reporter for the *Times* thought to check Garman's mail each day. He probably had some inside help, but whatever the case, he knew in advance of that latest threat being delivered."

Boldt said, "And of course it's postmarked *after* Garman's arrest."

LaMoia nodded, "You got it."

"What is it, Lou?" she repeated, still showing concern.

His look told her to drop it. That hurt her all the more. She turned away briefly.

"The content of the poem." Boldt asked, "Is it significant?"

She answered with her back to him. "Significant? I fouled up. He's no scholar, Lou. Probably not well read at all. The profile is off." She faced them both. Her confession won LaMoia's undivided attention. Boldt was able to leave his own sorrows briefly and recognize how upset she was. "There's a park built on top of the I-Ninety tunnel coming in from the floating bridge, a bike path running through it." She described her discovery of the various drawings and quotations, though she didn't say she had taken Ben there to meet Emily. She repeated reluctantly, "The profile is all wrong."

An uncomfortable silence was broken by LaMoia. "How wrong?"

"Uneducated. Sociopathic. If I didn't know the facts of the case, I would have put money on there being a revenge issue with Garman."

"That fits with what I've found out," LaMoia said, surprising Boldt, who expected LaMoia to pounce on Daphne's misfortune. The detective continued, "Garman's tax returns for the seventies show *two* dependents."

"Two?" Boldt echoed curiously, marveling at the detective's contacts.

LaMoia said defensively, "I tried calling you on the cellular but you weren't picking up. I wish I could take credit, but Neil"—Neil Bahan, he meant— "has been digging into Garman's past since the arrest, trying to develop a book on the guy. He's got the firehouse connections, so it only made sense. He came to me to dig up the tax records. He had evidently heard something. I know you kicked him out of here just now, along with the others, but you may want to talk to him."

"Get him," Boldt ordered. LaMoia hurried from the room.

They stood facing each other, Boldt and the woman. He didn't see her as beautiful at that moment, not like other times. There was no beauty compared to Liz's. There was only an empty darkness.

"So Garman has a child," Boldt said, voicing what the tax records confirmed. "Does that fit?" he asked.

"You don't want to know," she answered ominously.

"A father would certainly cover for his child," said Boldt, the father.

"And a child would vent anger against the father. Given the right circumstances, a child might symbolically kill the mother, repeatedly kill the mother—or the mother's look-alikes. Send the father threats. Do the kills on the father's turf, using what the child learned from the father: fire."

Boldt felt a chill, not heat. "Why?"

"Anger."

"That's a lot of anger."

She nodded, then shook her head. "Perhaps Garman's only guilty of being a protective father," she whispered. "Probably thought the killings would stop if he took the fall, if he ended up in jail."

"Will he talk to us?" Boldt asked.

"I'd like hear what Bahan has to say," she answered. "The more we hit him with, the better our chances. If we go in fishing, he'll lock up on us. If we go in swinging, it's a whole 'nother matter."

"He's targeted another woman," Boldt said, referring to the latest mailing. He checked his watch; it wasn't getting any earlier. "Jesus God. We've got to do *something*."

"Put someone undercover in the tunnel park. Have them watch the bike path," she advised. "We have the artist's rendering. He visits that park, Lou. He must live nearby."

Boldt reached for the phone. The door swung open: Neil Bahan with LaMoia. Bahan spoke before Boldt had a chance to dial. "It was something that happened in North Dakota," he said. "One hell of a fire."

A decade before, City Jail had expanded out of Public Safety across the street to the basement of the Justice Building. Extreme cases were held there, leaving the group lockups in Public Safety for gangs and the homeless, drunks and druggies, car thieves and burglars. The murders, rapes, robberies, and aggravated assaults were, for the most part, kept separate.

Although it was equipped with four bunks, Steven Garman had his cell to himself. It had a simple sink, a single toilet, an overhead light protected by a wire cage, and graffiti on the walls.

Daphne shivered. She had never liked jails.

Garman wore an orange jumpsuit, usually a humiliating look, but Daphne thought him handsome. His cheeks were florid, his eyes a keen dark brown, and though she didn't care for facial hair, the dark beard and mustache looked good on him.

"I don't see my attorney," he said, as Boldt and Daphne stepped through the cell door and it was closed behind them. La-Moia remained on the other side of the bars, holding them and pressing his face close between the coldness of their steel. "I've got nothing to say without my attorney present," Garman added.

Daphne and Boldt sat down on the bunk opposite. By agreement, no one spoke. Daphne would be the first to break the silence. They would take turns after that; it was arranged.

They remained perfectly still for the better part of five minutes, Garman looking between them and over at LaMoia as well. As the minutes passed, the arrested man looked increasingly nervous. He finally said, "You'd think they would paint the walls, get rid of the graffiti every now and then. It's offensive stuff."

She said, "We can't match a single letter in any of the notes with your handwriting."

Boldt told him, "The individual committing these arsons weighs sixty pounds less than you do."

LaMoia chimed in. "All the quotes used in the threats are collected in a single source. Maybe you might enlighten us as to what that source is."

Garman's eyes continued to tick between them.

LaMoia said, "What is the common source to these quotations you mailed yourself?"

Garman blurted out "Bartlett's," with some authority.

LaMoia made the sound of a game-show buzzer, indicating error.

Garman appeared shaken by his mistake.

Daphne said, "The lab has identified the chemical composition of the ink used in the threats. You don't own a pen that comes close. You don't own the paper. We could only find three stamps in your place, and they aren't the kind the Scholar uses." She studied the man's eye movements and body language. She watched for a busy tongue or other indications of a dry mouth.

"You never reported your pickup truck stolen," Boldt said.

LaMoia added, "You never applied for the insurance money. How is it you lose a seven-thousand-dollar pickup truck and don't apply for insurance?"

"Curious," Daphne said.

A sheen of perspiration glowed on the skin knitted beneath Garman's eyes. He rubbed his index finger against his thumb so tightly that it sounded like crickets chirping.

"My attorney," he mumbled.

"We've called him. We've notified him. He'll be here," Boldt informed the man. It was the truth. What Garman apparently did not know was that his attorney was, at that moment, in court. It would be hours before he made it down to lockup.

"Tell us about the fire," Boldt said, intentionally ambiguous.

"Which fire?" Garman asked, finding room for a slight smile. "I've seen a few."

"But how many have you started?" LaMoia asked.

"Nick Hall sold me the hypergolics," Garman began, repeating his radio performance. "I knew about their destructive power from my work at Grand Forks."

"The North Dakota Air Force base," Daphne said. "Your service record shows you as fire suppression, some demolition work."

"That's right. It was dangerous work."

Boldt began to enjoy the process. Little by little, Garman was talking more than he intended. Coming apart. Little by little, they were zeroing in on the questions they wanted answered. Daphne had devised the order of questioning. "Tell us about the fire," the sergeant said.

Garman's eyes flashed between the three.

"The trailer," LaMoia said. "Your trailer. It burned to the ground, burned down to nothing, according to the reports. Listed as accidental. But Fidler—you know Sidney Fidler—spoke to a couple of folks who remembered that burn quite well. It was extremely unusual in that the water hoses appeared to add fuel to the fire. The thing just got hotter and hotter. That's hypergolic rocket fuel, Garman, the same thing we're seeing here. You understand our curiosity."

This time it was footsteps down the hall, not Garman's nervous fingers. A guard approached, signaled Boldt, and passed a piece of paper through the bars. Another trick of Daphne's. Bahan had come through with the name of Garman's son only moments before the questioning. He had pulled it off of medical insurance records that painted an ugly picture. She had decided some theatrics wouldn't hurt any. There was nothing written on the piece of paper passed to Boldt, but he read it with great interest. He looked up from the note with wide, expressive eyes of pure shock.

Garman leaned a little forward with expectation.

But Daphne spoke, not Boldt. "Was Diana unfaithful? Was that it?"

The suspect's jaw slacked open, and his cheeks lost their color. For a moment he didn't breathe, didn't move. He said vehemently, "You don't know anything about it."

She glanced at Boldt and offered him a faint nod, though Garman's comment churned in the pit of her stomach.

Boldt said softly, "Jonathan Carlyle Garman. He was admitted to the hospital on the Grand Forks base, June 14, 1983. Third-degree burns to the face and upper body. Seven months of reconstructive surgery followed."

"When was the last time you saw him?" LaMoia asked.

Daphne pleaded, "Tell me it was Diana you meant to harm. Tell me you didn't mean for the boy to be hurt."

"Mother of God!" the suspect said, hanging his head into his huge hands, his back shaking violently as he cried.

Daphne took the opportunity to glance over at Boldt. She nodded. But she, unlike LaMoia, was not proud of their accomplishment. A contagious sadness surrounded her and infected Boldt.

Through his sobs the suspect said into his hands, "She took him with her. Kidnapped him. And not out of love, but because of the things he knew, because of the things she had done to him. . . .

What kind of woman is that?" He pulled up from his hands and looked Daphne directly in the eye.

"We're not here to judge you," she whispered. "Only to find out the truth. To help Jonathan. It's the boy who needs our help."

Garman sobbed for five of the longest minutes in Boldt's life. Would he cooperate or demand an attorney? The minutes ticked by, the evening drawing ever closer and the promise of another arson along with it. Another victim.

The phone company had no record of a Jonathan Garman; there was no driver's license or vehicle registration in Motor Vehicle's database. Other sources were being checked, but it appeared that the arsonist either existed outside of the paper shuffle or within an alias.

"I never meant it the way it happened," Garman finally gasped. "She had been selling herself. Made the boy a part of it."

Boldt released a huge sigh and sat back on the bunk. Sometimes he hated the truth.

The footsteps suddenly coming down the hall were not part of the plan, and all three police officers looked in that direction as they drew ever closer, wondering what in the world they could possibly mean. The guard handed Boldt a second message.

Boldt looked up from this second note. "It's a car wash," he said.

The building momentum that captured Boldt's investigation had exercised its influence on Bernie Lofgrin's identification technicians. In the same afternoon, the lab techs determined that the blue and silver cotton fiber evidence collected from the insides of the windshields on the cars of two of the arson victims matched, not only one to the other but to the fibers found on Boldt's kitchen window and those collected at the base of the ladder at the Enwright fire. It was just such evidence that gave a lock on a case, and as Lofgrin was pursuing Boldt to give him the good news, his assistants were tracing the sale of that particular silver ink to a total of only five silk-screen printers in the Northwest.

The fifth printer contacted, Local Color, in Coeur d'Alene, Idaho, recognized the order by its color combination: hand towels ordered by Lux-Wash and Detailing, Inc., Seattle, Washington, printed in silver and green ink on a blue background—Seahawk colors. The towels carried the Lux-Wash logo and the addresses of the chain's three locations. On the reverse side was printed, GO SEAHAWKS! Local Color was on their third printing, of fifteen hundred towels.

Back in the conference room, which was churning with activity at a deafening roar, Boldt sat down heavily into a chair. He said to Detective Bobbie Gaynes, "So it could be any one of fifteen hundred Lux-Wash customers."

"One thousand," the detective corrected. "The last five hundred haven't been shipped yet. And no, I don't think it's a customer. This is a yuppie scrub. Eleven bucks a wash, if you can believe it. Customer gets out and goes inside and drinks espresso while the wheels go down the line. Total vacuum, full wash and optional wax, and windows *inside* and out. The line finishes with a drying crew out the other side—and yeah, the towels the drying crew uses are these promo towels. Hence the fibers found *inside* the windshield."

"Three locations," Gaynes said.

"Two in the city, one in Bellingham," LaMoia informed him, reading a briefing note.

There was so much talk, so much urgent excitement in the room that Boldt felt tempted to stand up and call for a time-out. But better judgment intervened, for he could see the same desire on Shoswitz's face, and he learned from seeing that expression. The team had worked long, hard, unthankful hours, both as individual detectives and combined as a squad. To mute that enthusiasm was to rob them of energy; they were running on vapors as it was. Boldt assessed the situation and contained his impatience, grabbing as much as he could from the words hurled at him.

"We're pulling employment tax records," Gaynes announced.

"He may not be on the payroll," advised Daphne. "He'll work part time, possibly for cash."

Lieutenant Shoswitz, listening in, cautioned, "We run every-thing we have. There's no jumping to conclusions. Acquire and assess. Collect and evaluate. Don't assume anything."

A uniform agreed with Daphne. "If he's drying windshields, he's working for cash and tips. That's the bottom of the food chain at a car wash. Those guys aren't on payroll because they don't last long enough."

LaMoia added his opinion. "Our boy Jonathan has been at this awhile."

Daphne said, "He may have worked part-time at several car washes. The car wash is his trolling phase."

Considering this important, Boldt asked, "Do we have a list of all full-service car washes?"

"We do," called out a uniformed patrol officer. She waved a piece of paper in the air. A hand snatched it away, and it came down a series of passes to reach Boldt. She said, "Seven that we've identified within our jurisdiction, including the two belonging to Lux-Wash."

"He moves around?" Shoswitz asked.

Daphne spoke up. "Not by choice." She met Boldt's eyes. "He carries that face around with him. He's not comfortable meeting new people, establishing himself in a scene. He moved around a lot as a child. It's not his way to move around as an adult." She added, "If it were, he would be gone by now. He's a loner, a man who does what he pleases. He's been getting his way a good long time now. That works for and against us. He was feeling quite confident until we got Hall. That upset him. On the other hand, his father's confession has probably angered him. It's hard for him to punish his father if we've beaten him to it."

Boldt found the way she seemed so familiar with the suspect unsettling. It was as if she had interrogated Jonathan Garman. Boldt told the gathering, "The plastic mask our young witness thought he saw was this guy's skin. No known photos, but the reconstruction was crude. He's believed to be badly disfigured."

"We initiate surveillance of the three Lux-Washes immediately," Shoswitz stated, as if this were an original idea. A couple of the detectives suppressed their smirks.

Boldt said to the gathering, "Special Ops will establish clandestine video surveillance on the two Lux-Wash operations within our turf." He pointed to the young uniform. "You have the addresses," he stated, passing along the sheet containing the information. "Run this down to Special Ops, fill them in. We need a minimum of two teams. I want audio and video, real time and taped. If this guy so much as clears his throat, I want to know about it. Have them contact me when they're ready."

The kid took off at a run. Boldt remembered having that kind of enthusiasm for the job. To LaMoia he said, "Contact Bellingham and ask if we can post this car wash. If not, they cover it for us. But we want that thing under a microscope as soon as possible. Today, not tomorrow, not day after tomorrow."

"Got it," LaMoia answered. He spun in his chair, scooted across the small space, and grabbed for a phone. He wasn't going to leave the room, wasn't going to take a chance he might miss something. Boldt knew then that the man would make a hell of a squad sergeant. He experienced a sense of relief, and this both surprised him and told him something about himself.

The phones in the room rang regularly. Each time one purred, Boldt hoped it was Elizabeth but then realized he had not forwarded his calls to the briefing room. He ordered one of the uniforms to take care of this for him. The guy seemed thrilled to be given a job.

"Meanwhile," he said loudly, in order to win the attention of those at the table and beyond, "just to cover our bases, we need employment records for the other five luxury car washes."

"He's at one of the Lux-Washes," Daphne interrupted, contradicting him.

Boldt overrode her. "All five. The name of every owner, every employee, from the present back six months. No tears," he added, meaning he would take no excuses for failure.

The deputy prosecuting attorney spoke up for the first time. Samantha Richert was in her early fifties, pale, grayish-blond hair thinning, a not unattractive face on a not unattractive body, but the kind of appearance that got lost quickly in a crowd. She wore black leggings under a gray suit. Richert was herself gray in every way; she had succumbed to the skies a decade or two earlier. She had spent fifteen years as a public defender but had switched sides seven years ago after an inmate beat her up badly in a failed attempt to rape her. She had gray eyes and wore a white gold wedding band that she had taken to wearing some months earlier, though to Boldt's knowledge she was unmarried and wasn't even dating.

Richert said, "What evidence do we have against this man?" She looked at Shoswitz, Boldt, and then across the room at Daphne. "I smell a lynching party here. Not these towels, I hope. By your own admission," she said, looking at Gaynes, "over a thousand of these towels have been given away for free."

"He's a suspect is all," Boldt explained. "All we have to do is justify surveillance."

"Agreed, and you're fine there, but we're going to need some positive linkage. If we're going to walk this guy all the way to death row, we're going to need some serious evidence along the way."

"We'll get it," Boldt answered.

Shoswitz watched the events transpiring as would a spectator at a tennis match, his eyes darting left, right, left. Boldt could feel the man's eagerness to enter the debate and knew that, typical of Shoswitz, he would not wade into the water but jump, causing something of a splash. The lieutenant, like everyone else in that room, was clearly feeling the pressure.

"You need him to lead you to this stolen fuel—something like that," Richert suggested. She wasn't being antagonistic, but her questions were probing to the point that Boldt felt uncomfortable.

Daphne drew everyone's attention as she spoke. "A woman is going to die tonight if we don't do something—and I'm *not* saying we should arrest him. We need to find him, *fast*. He may lead us to his cache of fuel or even attempt to rig a fire. Either way, we have a nice strong arrest in place."

Boldt knew her too well. That was not the typical Daphne line. He looked for the point of her statement and he said, "But we might lose another victim if we arrest him—"

Daphne arched her eyebrows and completed for him. "And that's not what we want."

The room's resulting silence was punctuated by several of the phones ringing. Slowly the chaos took over again. Boldt said to her, "You have a plan, don't you?"

She nodded, straight-faced and serious. "Yes. But we'll have to act immediately." She dragged out a copy of the department's personnel directory. Acting as a yearbook, it was divided into two general sections, active personnel and civilian employees, each of which was divided further by rank or classification. It was funded by the union as a means of making the department more familiar with itself. No personal phone numbers, addresses, or information of any sort was given, but internal phone extensions and squad assignments were listed, along with recreational interests and participation in the softball, volleyball, bowling, four-wheeling, and hunting clubs.

Daphne opened the directory to page seven, marked by a Post-it. She produced a photograph of Steven Garman's wife, Diana, and placed it alongside a head-and-shoulders photograph of a patrolwoman named Marianne Martinelli. The similarity between the two faces was impossible to miss, the only difference being Martinelli's hair, which was cut a little longer at the time of the photo. Not looking up from the photo, Daphne called over to LaMoia, busy on the phone, "John? Are you still friends with that cosmetologist over at the Fifth Avenue Theater?"

"The what?" he shouted, cupping the receiver.

"The makeup artist," she answered.

"Geof? That queen? You bet."

Her voice strong with intent and confidence, she explained to Boldt, "The fact that he sent the note means he already has a victim in mind. Maybe we get lucky and we follow him right to that victim. But we both know that kind of surveillance fails more often than it succeeds. We're able to stay with the suspect what, twenty to thirty percent of the time?"

"About that."

"Which means the victim has a seventy-percent chance of going up in flames. Not terribly strong odds."

"Go on."

"We can pull him off the mark," she said, tapping the police directory. As she spoke, the room went increasingly quiet, settling into an eerie hush. "That is, patrol officer Marianne Martinelli can. She's a dead ringer for the mother. A haircut, a little makeup, a band of pale skin where her wedding ring once was, and he'll drop the other mark in a New York minute once his mother comes through that car wash. We can take him by a nose ring and lead him right to the home of our choice. He lifts their addresses off the vehicle registration, right? That's what we're guessing. So we give him an address where we're waiting for him. He shows up with his window-washing gear, prepared to pretend he's got the wrong place, and we have him right where we want him, chemicals and all. Richert gets her evidence; we get our man."

"And Martinelli gets an ulcer," Gaynes said.

Boldt called out loudly, "Anybody here know Marianne Martinelli?" Every eye in the room fell immediately on John LaMoia, whose reputation with women—especially rookie women in their first year—was legendary.

LaMoia looked like the cat caught with the mouse. He shrugged his shoulders and shook his head innocently, but then allowed in an embarrassed voice, "She and her husband were separated for a while. So we had a few dates. So what?"

"Work the charm, John-boy," Boldt ordered. "We need a volunteer."

50

THE events of the next ninety minutes ran like a video in fast-forward. At the peak of the chaos over twenty-one police officers were directly involved in Daphne's plan to subvert the psychology of the suspect. Seven plainclothes officers were dispatched to get their cars washed. At 1:17 P.M., October 24, the radio room alerted Boldt that a possible suspect had been identified at the Lux-Wash on 85th St. N.W. in Greenwood. His description included a slight frame, 130 to 150 pounds, and a face hidden by a sweatshirt and sunglasses.

On the way up to the surveillance, Boldt stopped at home to leave a note for Liz.

As he entered the kitchen, he broke into tears. Everywhere he looked he saw Liz, everything he touched. He could recall their discussions, holidays, birthdays, lovemaking—somehow he couldn't remember any of the bad times, only the good. It was not only for Liz that he wept but, selfishly, for himself as well, both out of self-pity and fear. He begged God for some kind of explanation and apologized for the years he had failed to pray, wondering if prayers could be heard when absent for so long. Did the line go dead like an unpaid telephone?

How would he tell her that he knew? How much of his life was undone by this?

He heard a car pull into the drive. He didn't want to face her; he knew her secret, a secret she had chosen for her own reasons not to share with him. He wondered if he had any right to know or if she needed time to face this for herself first before sharing it, with him or anyone else. The time she had wanted at the cabin, alone with just one child, suddenly made much more sense to him. Perhaps she had wanted a closure with each of the kids, a time to reflect and resolve whatever internal conflicts were raging within her. He had no idea what knowledge of one's own imminent death would inflict upon a person.

He dried his eyes on his shirtsleeve and peered outside. It was Marina and the kids, being dropped off by Marina's husband, not Liz. For a moment, his sentence was commuted. He stepped out into the harshness of sunlight and greeted Miles and Marina. He kissed Sarah. And when the tears flowed again, he walked directly to his car and, without a word, drove off, his little boy waving goodbye with troubled eyes.

51

"WHAT do you think?" Daphne asked him. Boldt and Daphne stood in the far corner of a back parking lot behind an abandoned Super-Sav Market on 85th, four blocks from the Lux-Wash. The suspect remained under surveillance, the radio traffic running in a stream through Boldt's earpiece. The first thing that struck Boldt was how old the Scotch tape looked, used to adhere a school portrait of Ben to the driver's-side visor.

"How did they do that?" he said, touching the tape. It was brittle to the touch. It looked as if it had endured a summer of scorching sunlight.

"That's it?" Daphne asked indignantly. "You look at this, and all you want to know is how we made the tape look so old?"

She was referring to the rest of the car. On the floor of the passenger's side of the front seat were some of Ben's worksheets from school, filled in with his perfectly illegible scrawl and appropriately misspelled words. She had raided her own houseboat for those props. One school worksheet had a dusty imprint of a sneaker across it; next to it, on the floor, was a crushed milkshake cup from McDonald's. On the dash was a Tonka toy dump truck upside down, and in the back seat a G.I. Joe action figure, one arm missing, and a good-sized plastic model of Han Solo's airship from *Star Wars*—all Ben's. On the floor of the back seat was a small fleece pullover and a pair of kid's running shoes, beat-up and held together with silver tape. Resting on the back seat was one of Ben's three backpacks that she had borrowed without asking. A silverplated crucifix hung by a matching chain from the rearview mirror, in case a religious connection was necessary as a trigger.

"It's convincing," Boldt agreed. "I wouldn't have thought of the photo," he admitted.

"We need the direct connection to a child to be made, and yet we sure as hell can't involve one."

"It's very convincing."

"The boy must be a trigger, Lou," she said confidently. "The similarity to his mother, and the existence of a child. One of my mistakes was that I missed the role of the child."

"You sold me," Boldt said. "Now the only thing we have to do," he added, studying the car's exterior, "is get this thing nice and dirty."

At 3:05 P.M., patrol officer Martinelli, dressed in jeans and a sweatshirt, driving a Ford Explorer, entered the inflatable structure leased by Lux-Wash, Incorporated. The mood inside SPD's steamcleaning van was tense but professional, the tiny space crowded by a video tech, a communications pro, and Boldt and Daphne, nearly in one another's laps.

Martinelli's arrival was critically timed to place her car in the proper order so that the suspect—believed to be Jonathan Garman—would be the worker to clean her car's interior. He was one of four such workers, used in rotation; it had required two other plainclothes detectives to determine the order. Jonathon Garman was next up, waiting down that line to do his job.

Inside the van, the video monitor sparkled and sputtered, the image of Martinelli suddenly grainy and cloudy.

"What's up?" Boldt asked.

"There's a lot of metal in a car wash," the tech answered. "The transmitter is hidden under the back seat, the antenna under the vehicle. No system is perfect. That's why we have a camcorder in the car as well. That tape will be clean."

The screen continued to flash and spark; Martinelli's radio channel filled with static. "I'm inside," the detective said. On the screen, all motion was reduced to jerky freeze frames a second or two apart, as black horizontal bars refreshed the screen.

"I'm not liking this," Boldt said.

"Neither am I, Sergeant," the techie whined. "I'm working on it, okay?"

Using her headset's microphone, Daphne asked if Martinelli could hear her.

"Good enough," the woman replied.

The woman's physical resemblance to the photograph of Diana Garman was strikingly convincing, in part due to the efforts and talents of Geof Jeffries of the 5th Avenue Theater.

When it was operating well, the monitor displayed a fish-eye view of the inside of the front seat of the car, from the driver's door clear over to the passenger door.

Dialogue from Martinelli's microphone came through clearly as a male voice told her, "We're not allowed to touch your personal stuff, ma'am. You'll have to pick it up some if we're gonna vacuum for ya. You can take your time."

Daphne instructed into Martinelli's ear, "Leave it." She wanted the triggers in place.

"Do what you can," Martinelli said.

Surveillance, with a view of the far side of the car wash, reported that a worker was vacuuming the car. Garman's participation was still a few steps away.

On-screen, those in the van watched a pair of young black men vacuum the floors.

Martinelli was reported heading toward the reception area.

The car was in the system. Boldt never took his eyes off the monitor as he asked Daphne, "What's your take?"

"I feel good about it. What I wonder is whether Martinelli will hold up."

As she spoke, a man climbed into the front seat, rag in one hand, spray bottle of cleanser in the other. The video signal was worse. For several seconds at a time, the screen went entirely black, followed by a fuzzy freeze-frame of the worker's shoulders or the back of the head as he furiously cleaned the inside front windows, dashboard, and rearview mirror.

"Go!" Daphne told Martinelli, picturing the patrolwoman hurrying back to the car as if she had forgotten something.

"Show us your face, pal," Boldt encouraged the window washer.

"Remember, you're a bitch," Daphne added, sitting forward on the stool. "You're a bitchy mother. And you're just about at wit's end."

Martinelli yanked the earpiece from her ear, as directed, and walked toward Jonny Garman with a forced swagger to her hips, a stuck-up woman from the shoreline who had little time for the lower classes. Inside she was thinking that the next few minutes could propel her from first class patrol officer to a candidate for plainclothes detective work. She hadn't even had time to call her husband and tell him. Where she had pulled off her wedding band was left a pale ring of white flesh that Daphne Matthews had declared perfect. She reminded herself that she was a divorced mother, bitter and overworked. Impatient. Perhaps the college acting classes would pay off, she thought. The highest grade she had gotten was a C. She hadn't told Matthews that.

"Young man," she said loudly, raising her hand derisively and looking into those glasses from a distance. *Intimidate. Provoke*, Matthews had said. "Young man," she repeated, stepping right up to Jonny Garman, her heart feeling as big as melon in her chest.

The skin was not something he had been born with, but had been applied to a face ravaged by fire. The craftsmanship was not good; his nose looked like something made of clay by a first-year art student. That nose and his upper cheeks were all he allowed to be visible; strangely, Martinelli yearned to see the rest of him. She could picture the scar tissue around the hole of a mouth—plastic surgeons had the most trouble with the mouth; the transition, if there was one, between the plastic of his face and the skin of his neck. Did he have hair? she wondered, or were the few strands showing from a wig, as she suspected.

He cowered, painfully shy. And then as he looked at her, as he caught sight of this woman approaching, his body seized as if jolted by an electrical shock. He stiffened and craned forward at the same time.

He wore gloves, she noticed. Thin cowhide gloves, worn small so they held to his hands like a second skin.

In as condescending a tone as she could muster she said, "My little angel has gone and spilled some pop all over the dashboard. It's on the right, in front of the passenger seat. Be a good boy and clean it off for me."

She stepped closer to Garman. "You're not going to make a problem for me, are you? I certainly hope not. It's an easy enough thing to wipe a little pop off the dash." She fumbled in her purse, demonstratively aiming it away from him so that he felt excluded.

"Need a little lunch money, do we? Hmm?" She held up a single dollar bill in her bare left hand so there was no way he could miss the pale line where her ring had been. She stuffed the dollar into his unwilling hand. According to Matthews, it was this contact with him—standing there holding his hand, purposefully a little too long—that would make the connection. He would abhor any physical contact with her whatsoever. He would despise her, for the offer of money, for her condescending tone, and for the uninvited physical contact. "It's not that cold, you know." She let go his hand and lifted hers to her face. "All that wrapping. You're all shuttered up like a house for winter."

She repeated, "The pop on the dash. Let's try again: Did you hear me?"

"Spilled pop on the dash," he uttered, in a voice that sounded like coarse sandpaper on bare metal. She felt a chill pass through her. She didn't want this man stalking her.

She said, "That's better. Thank you. I could have asked my angel to clean it up, I suppose. But then, that's your job, isn't it?" She walked away, working her hips again into a haughty and arrogant gait. She did not glance back; he was too strange. That voice had terrified her. She wanted some air; the warm, humid, soapy choke of the car wash was claustrophobic.

Boldt and Daphne watched as Jonny Garman climbed into the Explorer hurriedly. For a long count of three he stared at Ben's picture taped to the visor and then at the silver cross hanging from the mirror. He cleaned the glass, but at the same time he took in the toys, the fast-food trash, and the clothing. They watched as he dragged his rag across the dash, working his way toward the glove box and the vehicle's registration inside. "Open it," Daphne encouraged, as the car pulled into the pounding storm of the wash, as the water hit the windows in torrents. "Open it," she repeated, her voice slightly alarmed. Inside was the registration from which he would glean the address of the safe house—114 Lakewood Avenue South, a home claimed from drug dealers by the state tax commission.

She felt a long shiver pass through her, a feeling of anticipation registering somewhere between good foreplay and total terror. Go for the glove box! she mentally encouraged. It was inconceivable to her that he might not.

"We've got problems," Boldt said, as the suspect climbed out of the front seat during the drying fans, and into the back.

"Marianne?" Daphne said into the microphone, hoping the woman was inside the ladies' room with the earpiece back in, as instructed.

"Right here," a nervous voice replied.

"Phase two," Daphne said. "And make it *good!*"

Martinelli headed back into the waiting area and watched through the window as the Explorer moved along. Twice she caught sight of Garman inside the car, and both times his rag worked furiously against the glass. It was time. Her legs didn't want to move. A man pushed into the waiting area: Ernie Waitts, a narco undercover cop. *I'm okay*, she told herself. *We're all over this guy*. She pushed through the exit door and paid the man inside the cashier's window with a twenty-dollar bill.

As she approached the Explorer, she saw that the exterior was sparkling clean, from roof to wheels.

She took long strides, for Garman had pushed the far door open and was backing out of the vehicle, still wiping as he went. She called out to him, "Young man! Young man!" as Daphne told her. "Did you get it cleaned up?"

His body language stopped her cold, for he faced her with square shoulders, standing much taller than before. A different person. *He has targeted me*, she thought, knowing this instinctively. His stance was far more aggressive, confident, and inviting. She pointed out a water mark. Jonny Garman's clay nostrils flared. Her bowels churned. As instructed she said, "Lakewood Avenue is no place for water marks."

She did not look again at Jonny Garman; the woman whom she had become for this charade could care less. Instead, she swung open the passenger door and ran an inspecting finger over the dash, satisfying herself that the sticky mess was gone for good.

A moment later she was safe behind the wheel. Safe, but for how long? she wondered, feeling like the guinea pig she was.

Daphne sat transfixed. They would have to wait to study the tape recorded inside the car. But as far as she could tell, Garman had never gone for the glove box and the registration therein. The address. It seemed impossible to her that she had judged him incorrectly. She had failed. A woman—some earlier customer—was going to die that very evening. She mumbled, "I just can't believe it."

Boldt, too, seemed in a daze. "Maybe he has access to DMV

information," Boldt proposed. "Run the tag and lift the address that way. We don't know anything about this guy."

"No, we don't," Daphne agreed. But she did know, and so did he, she suspected.

"Maybe he's a computer hacker. Who knows how he gets these women's addresses?"

He wouldn't look over at her; for Daphne, that said enough.

"Jesus, Lou," she muttered.

Boldt said, "We go ahead as planned. Martinelli did a great job. We watch the place and we wait for him." Radio traffic filled their ears. Boldt responded to none of it. "We watch and see what he does. We follow. We have a huge surveillance team in place. We'll stay with him, Daffy. We can beat the damn odds. This guy is not heading home to read a book tonight. This much we know. This much we made sure of."

"I'm sorry," she apologized in a hushed whisper. But not to him, as he believed. Her apology was to Jonny Garman's targeted victim—the one for whom he had sent the poem. The one she feared was scheduled to die.

52

BEN waited with Susan in the houseboat for an hour before they both became restless. Daphne was late, and despite his pleas Susan would not leave him alone there. Since their visit to the park, he could not stop thinking of Emily. He'd had it with the entire Daphne/Susan program. He wanted out.

Susan, attempting to sound composed, suggested they head down to the police department, where Ben knew he would sit around bored for hours. "She'll call," he said.

"She has been in the same meeting for nearly an hour and a half. I can't stay with you, Ben. You'll have to wait for her there."

"I'll wait here," he suggested, for about the fifth time.

"Don't test me, young man. It's downtown or the center for you."

"The center?" he objected. "You don't mean I have to *sleep* there?" He hadn't slept there yet, and he wasn't going to let any pattern develop in that regard.

"Your choice." Susan stood. "Downtown or the center?"

Ben was terrified at the thought of spending a night in the youth detention center.

"Downtown," he answered.

• • •

Ben and Susan stepped through Homicide's controlled door.

The place was jumping, cops hurrying back and forth like they were in the middle of a fire drill, most of them carrying paperwork, all of them looking tired. Some with their guns showing, which Ben thought was cool.

Susan kept stopping people and asking for Daphne or Boldt, and finally one of them listened long enough to point down a hall and say something about a lieutenant.

Susan pointed to an office chair pushed up against the wall and told Ben to take a seat.

"I want to come," he protested.

"Now!" she directed him, turning his shoulders and giving him a slight push.

Ben headed to the chair.

Susan headed down the hall.

Ben was alone for the first time in ages.

He couldn't get his mind off Emily. If he just got up and walked through that door . . .

If he stayed in that chair, Susan would put him in the youth center for the night. He felt convinced of this. Conversely, their threats to hurt Emily's business rang hollow; they needed him as a witness.

He carefully slipped his hand into his pocket to make sure he still had the five bucks Daphne had given him for emergencies.

He slipped off the chair, glancing around surreptitiously. No one seemed to be taking any notice of him. Susan remained down the hall and out of sight, right where he wanted her. He walked casually toward the exit, through the continuing chaos, a kid looking for the bathroom.

Of the ten or fifteen people in the immediate area, only two women looked over and caught his eye, and they both offered him forced smiles, the way librarians do. He continued walking toward the door, shoulders straight, his back arched—just the way Daphne had told him to carry himself—sure that someone would get in his way and prevent him from leaving.

But no one said a thing.

Ben walked out through the door and broke into a run for the elevators the moment he rounded the corner.

Emily! he thought, his heart swelling to the size of Montana.

53

DAPHNE knew that from the moment Jonny Garman had been identified at the Lux-Wash, he would never spend another moment of his life completely alone. There would always be someone keeping him under surveillance or in the cell next to him. There would be attorneys and counselors and doctors and judges and juries, but he would never be alone.

On the extremely unlikely chance that Garman was not working solo, that an accomplice other than Hall or his father existed, the police could not risk a face-to-face meeting with their decoy, Marianne Martinelli.

Leading Daphne and Boldt's frustrations was that the phone line at 114 Lakewood Avenue was dead, having been out of service since the house had been repossessed by the city. This became of importance as Martinelli's walkie-talkie began to lose battery power. At 4:43 P.M., the reconnected telephone at 114 Lakewood Avenue rang for first time. Martinelli answered, sounding jumpy.

"Hello?" the patrolwoman answered tentatively.

"Boldt and Matthews on a conference call," Boldt announced. "Can you hear me, Marianne?"

"Yes. Go ahead."

It was Boldt, not Matthews who replied. "The suspect is still at the car wash. We expect him to remain there until five P.M. After that, he'll be under constant surveillance, and you'll be notified of his movement as it pertains to your location."

"I copy that," she said. "We're sending you a UPS delivery," Boldt reported. "UPS, Martinelli. You copy that?"

"UPS. Okay."

"Some mace, a fire hood, and a bottle of oxygen."

"And a battery pack," Martinelli reminded him.

"Right," confirmed Matthews.

"If he does watch your place," Boldt informed her, "we'll want you to leave the house, leaving it completely dark, no lights at all."

"To let him know the boy isn't in the house with me. Yes. I understand."

Silence.

Boldt said, "On the off-chance he should follow you, you will need a destination, not just driving around. We're thinking a movie or maybe food shopping."

"He could rig the house while I'm gone."

"We're aware of what he could do," Boldt informed her. "We'll have the house well covered."

"You did real well," Daphne told her, wondering internally why Garman had failed to look for the address in the glove box. Wondering about his other victim.

The UPS truck pulled up in front of 114 Lakewood Avenue at 4:55 P.M., and John LaMoia, dressed in a brown uniform, walked up the steps and knocked on the door. He made Martinelli sign for the package. He whispered to her, "We're all pulling for you, Marianne."

The two of them went through a charade then, for the possible benefit of anyone unknown watching. Martinelli reached inside the door and held up a backpack for LaMoia, as if she wanted to send it. LaMoia returned to the truck and brought her back a collapsible paper box used for express shipments that he quickly built for her, taping it together. While he did this, she quickly filled out the label as well as the shipping air bill. The backpack went into the box, which was then sealed.

Inside Ben's backpack was the video tape recorded directly from the Explorer's hidden camera, a copy that promised a good clean look at Garman's activities while inside the vehicle. Tech Services eagerly awaited this tape for review.

"You gonna be around, John?" Martinelli asked, suddenly appearing quite afraid.

"Right here. You're the most popular girl in town tonight. No sweat."

"He's insane, isn't he?" They both knew to whom she was referring. She said, "I touched his hand. I can't describe it to you."

"I gotta go," LaMoia said. "Hang in there. It's a no-brainer. He shows up; we nab him. Nothing to it." He grabbed the express package and was off.

"Right," she answered, and then thanked the brown back of the delivery man uniform walking away from her. But the cop in her knew differently. LaMoia was himself nervous; he had not spoken that warmly to her since their third date. Had someone coached him to be that way?

She wanted it over with.

Inside the house again, she ripped open the package. Included was a spare battery for her radio, which she replaced just in time for her to receive the surveillance team communication.

Jonny Garman had just left the car wash.

SURVEILLANCE 1: *We got a problem. Suspect is leaving by bicycle, not a car! He's heading east on Eighty-fifth. He's wearing a blue sweatshirt, hood up, jeans, riding a gray mountain bike. Sunglasses. No helmet.*

BOLDT: *A bicycle. East on Eighty-fifth. Copy. Stay with him, One.*

Daphne and Boldt were still inside the steam-cleaner van

parked two blocks away. The dispatcher barked a series of orders, deploying various surveillance teams. But the mood was ugly; a bicycle would be nearly impossible to follow. Garman rode fast, passing cars on the right, crossing on red lights at the pedestrian crosswalks, all the tricks. Dispatch scrambled to keep up, barely able to do so. He rode hard and he rode long, south through the U-District and across Montlake Bridge. The road grew steep and difficult, and had he suspected surveillance he could have lost them. In fact, twice all visual contact was lost, only to have him ride past a surveillance point, legs flailing. At Madison, he turned west toward the city, wreaking havoc with the team that endeavored to keep up with him. The expectation was that he would continue south, and the shift in manpower required to follow spun the radios into a hum of confusion. With no apparent intention on his part, Jonny Garman was giving them hell.

When Boldt called for a helicopter, Daphne realized they were in trouble. The choppers went out at several hundred dollars an hour, and rather than instill confidence in her, the result was quite the opposite: panic seized her chest. The team was desperate.

The order for the chopper came too late. Again without warning, the suspect, heading south on Broadway, turned left at Columbia, entered a short cul-de-sac, and jumped the sidewalk that allowed him through a series of posts installed to stop vehicular traffic. He shot down the hill, crossed 12th Ave. E. and literally vanished.

An unmarked car jumped the grassy knoll at James Way, skidding and spraying mud, but never regained visual contact.

Jonny Garman had disappeared.

A bead of cool sweat trickled down Daphne's rib cage, and she itched it away. Boldt's body odor gave away his own tension. "Shit," he mumbled, as the radio reports confirmed the disappearance.

"He was heading south, Lou. Lakewood is south," she reminded him, naming the street where Martinelli waited as a possible target.

"Then why take Madison? Why that move on Broadway?"

Boldt answered rhetorically, "I'll tell you why: He spotted us. He made us."

"I don't think so," Daphne said. "Not one surveillance report indicated any paranoid behavior on his part. He was riding a route, that's all. To the truck? To his lab? Who knows? A route, is all. To a computer somewhere he can run Martinelli's tags? A route, is all."

Boldt ordered the tunnel park kept under surveillance. He was frantic, not at all himself. Despair paled his skin and glassed his eyes. Two teams were added to the surveillance on Lakewood Avenue. "He burned us!" Boldt said. And then, catching the irony of the statement, he began to laugh. A sick, pathetic laugh.

Daphne felt tempted to reach over and touch him, as much from her own need as his. He had tears in his eyes—again—and she thought he might break, but he recovered as he had a dozen times before, that same afternoon.

She recovered less well, as it turned out, torn by her failure to predict Garman's behavior and her fears over the impending fire she felt certain was to come. But the final straw was neither of these. It was the dispatcher calmly turning around in his chair—the van bumping along the Seattle streets—and saying to Daphne, "Matthews, a message for you from headquarters: They want you to know that someone named Ben has escaped. I didn't get a last name, and I don't know from where he escaped, but they said you would want to hear about it."

Daphne gasped, her body cold with fear. "Pull this thing over!" she shouted.

54

BEN waited across the street from the small purple house with its familiar neon sign, though each passing minute felt more like an hour. Home: There was no other way for him to describe it. There was a Chevrolet truck parked in the driveway, and Ben immediately slipped into his role of detailed scrutiny and analysis, noting the bumper sticker that declared the driver was a proud parent of an honor roll student, the steel toolbox mounted into the bed, probably indicating a construction worker or some other handyman.

Fifteen minutes later the driver of the truck, a lady who looked old enough to have kids, left Emily's, climbed behind the wheel, and drove the truck away.

Ben started out walking but ended up running across the street, up the short driveway, and to the back door. He beat a three-knock summons onto the chipped paint, and when Emily answered, her face lit up, her arms swung open, and he threw himself into that warmth and love, hoping beyond reason that she might never let go.

A few minutes later she was offering him tea, toasting a slice

of sourdough bread, and preparing a string of jams and jellies for
him to choose from. Pouring them both a cup of tea, she delivered
the toast and sat down across from him. She watched him with
tear-pooled eyes as he tore into the toast and slurped down the tea.

"You ran away," said the psychic.

Ben felt a spike of heat flood his cheeks. He forced a shrug, as
if it wasn't anything to get excited about.

"You ran away from the police," she completed.

"They were busy," he said. "Daphne was supposed to meet
me." Emily's face screwed down a little tighter.

"What?" he finally asked her.

"We had a deal, Ben, you and me."

"I know, I know, but—"

"Not buts. We had a deal. The police are looking after you.
They're trying to do their job."

"They threatened you."

"It's not that," she objected. "The police have been on my case
for years. Sometimes they love psychics, like when they need them;
sometimes they want to run them out of town. Believe me, I'm
plenty familiar with the police. I can handle them. It's you I had
the deal with, not them."

"I know."

"And you promised me."

"I missed you," he said honestly, daring to look up at her,
though afraid of her anger with him.

Tears sprang from her eyes. She blinked them away. Black ink
ran down her cheeks, carried by the tears. Her lips were wet and
puckered, and they quivered as she tried to speak. But then she
came out of her chair, and around the table toward him, and took
his head between her hands and drew him into her for another of
those wonderful hugs.

And Ben knew he wasn't going anywhere.

55

LOU Boldt was a tangled knot of emo-
tions. He had gone from the high of a surveillance operation to the
low of losing the suspect amid a light drizzle that turned the air
the same color gray as the sky, and everything in it the same color
gray as the rain, until the world was a blur of gray images that
blended together so that buildings, streetlamps, vehicles, people
on bicycles, formed a homogeneous mass, and Jonathan Garman
vanished into it like something in a magic trick.

The fact that the video tape shot at the car wash did not show
Garman going for the glove box, did not support a subsequent
surveillance operation, meant that when Shoswitz looked for a
scapegoat he did not have to look very far. That Boldt had engaged
the follow-up surveillance operation before studying that video
was at least explainable—he had wanted to protect Martinelli at all
costs. But with nothing more than a psychological profile that
played well, Boldt had only his twelve-year-old witness to connect
Jonathan Garman to any crime whatsoever—and he had lost both
of them, Garman *and* the witness.

Boldt found himself in the unenviable position of preparing to eat crow. They had a fire inspector in lockup who had confessed to the arsons. They had Nicholas Hall's admission that he had sold hypergolic rocket fuel to an unidentified third party. Garman had, under questioning, also confessed to the additional crime of setting fire to his estranged wife's house trailer, a fire that had burned his son to disfigurement, proving in the eyes of many that he was capable of just about anything.

With Garman's first confession firmly in hand, the upper brass and the mayor had put the Scholar's reign of terror to bed, assuring the public the fires were over. This had been done without Boldt's involvement, just as the subsequent surveillance of Jonathan Garman had been done without their involvement. Shoswitz, the middleman, pushed Boldt to a decision the sergeant did not want to make.

The lieutenant's office smelled of foot odor and old coffee. Boldt remained standing despite the lieutenant's repeated offer of a seat. Shoswitz confirmed himself as a pacer, working up a sweat between the back corners of his office. "I don't know what to believe," he finally said, in a tone that Boldt interpreted as his rambling phase. "Believe it or not . . . I mean, you want to know what the real truth of the matter is . . . Your ass, my ass . . . if we want to go upstairs tomorrow morning and try to tell them the fucking Scholar is still out there playing his games, the truth of the matter is we *need* another fire. I'm not shitting you. No fire, no sell. I'm not kidding. We got the note . . . every note meant a fire . . . so if there's no fire tonight they're going to say Garman mailed it to himself before we arrested him—and *don't* go fucking waving the postmark at me, because I know all about it, and my career, your career, is not going to hang on a fucking postmark."

"It's early yet," Boldt reminded.

"Bullshit. These fires go off early. We both know that. Early? Bullshit." He stopped and stared at Boldt. "It's *late* is what it is. We are way fucking late with this Jonny Garman crap and they," he said, pointing overhead, "are not going to buy it. We've got *nada*. Zilch. Zippo. A kid with an applesauce face drying windows in a car wash."

"We've got the towels. The fibers."

"A thousand fucking towels over a six-month period." He began pacing again. "Jesus H. Christ! This Garman shit was a bonehead move, Lou. Strictly bonehead material. We let Matthews wind us up and we marched to her tune, and the only fucking way out of this is to drop it. I mean drop it. Gone. Forgotten. We pull Martinelli and send her home, we say a few thank-yous to all those involved, and we go home to bed. You need it, my friend. You need bed. You look like shit. I feel like shit. I need a Scotch. Two or three would be better. We pull it, we bag it, we bury it in the budget somewhere, and we hope no one asks any questions." He stopped and looked directly at Boldt's pants, of all things. "Where do you buy those khakis?"

"Mail order."

"Not Brooks Brothers? They look like Brooks Brothers."

"Mail order," he said again. "I think we should keep it up and running for tonight—the surveillance. It started to rain. Maybe that was why he took Madison up Broadway and the school. Maybe just to get out of the rain. It doesn't mean he's dropped it."

"Did you watch the same video I did?" the lieutenant asked, perplexed. "Drop what? He never picked up the ball. He never went for that glove box."

Repeating what Daphne had mentioned to him, Boldt said, "Maybe the truck is kept at the university somewhere. Maybe he has access to computers there and can run the tags or something."

"We can't even confirm this guy's name."

"LaMoia, Gaynes, Bahan, and Fidler," Boldt said. "Give me my team for another day. One day. Martinelli too. She stays. Drop the vans, the techies, the overtime payroll."

"No fucking way!" he bellowed. "Bahan and Fidler stay where they are, working up Garman Senior into something we can take to court. Something we can work with. Something I can explain." He pointed to the ceiling for a second time. "You and the others? I turn my back. I don't see. But I don't *hear* about it either. No one hears about it. As far as I'm concerned, you're working on evidence against Garman. You need his son as a possible witness—

there! You hear that? I amaze myself sometimes. A witness. That's all. Someone who can provide the state with damning testimony about Steven Garman setting that arson you were telling me about. Fucking genius, is what I am. Be glad I'm the one looking out for you, Lou. You're in good hands here. I may have just saved your ass with this idea of mine."

"A witness," Boldt repeated.

"Exactly." The lieutenant appeared more his own color. "You eaten anything lately?"

"Not hungry."

"Order some pizza in."

"No, thanks."

"The Scotch sounds better anyway." He looked at Boldt's pants again. "Do they shrink?"

"Jonny Garman is the Scholar, Lieutenant."

"Don't fuck with me, Lou."

"If you'd been there when we spoke with Garman, you'd know it's true. He's covering for him, that's all."

"And doing a fine job of it." He walked over to Boldt and felt the khaki fabric between his fingers. He clearly liked what he felt. "Go find your witness. Bring him in and we'll chat him up and maybe something changes. But until then, not a peep. Not to anybody. No hysterical comments about the Scholar still being out there, no casual talk. No dispatch. No crying wolf. Goes for your people as well. I watch your ass, you watch mine." He looked Boldt directly in the eye. "Don't fuck this up. You do, and you're all alone."

Boldt nodded. He felt the tears coming again. "All alone anyway," he mumbled, heading to the door, thinking of Liz and the life they'd lost. Shoswitz said something about the khakis, but Boldt didn't hear. His ears were ringing, and his right hand had tensed into a solid fist.

56

"WHERE is he?" Daphne demanded.

Ben's eye was trained to the peephole in Emily's kitchen wall, but he couldn't see the front door, where Emily had just gone to answer the doorbell.

He recognized Daphne's voice. His heart sank and he felt desperate. Why was it that, no matter what he did, he disappointed someone?

"Ben? He's not here," Emily said defiantly. "You're supposed to have him!"

"I didn't hear that," Daphne said. "Let's try again, and before we do let me remind you that to shelter him is to harbor a witness. Think carefully. Have you seen Benjamin today?"

"Get out."

Daphne informed her, "I have enough probable cause to search this property, and that is exactly what I intend to do."

That was enough for Ben. He had stepped toward the back door before he remembered Daphne nabbing him there once before.

He used the bathroom window. It was on the side of the house away from the driveway, facing the neighbors.

He hit the ground with his feet running, thinking ahead. They were sure to check his house as well—unless they had already. He could get the sleeping bag from his room and head up to the tree fort. He could spend the night there and come back to Emily's in the morning.

It was raining out, but he barely felt it. He felt as if he ran faster than he had ever run. He splashed along sidewalks, down alleys, and through familiar back yards. He ran as if his life depended on it. He ran for his freedom.

Nothing so sweet.

57

"BELIEVE it or not, we're getting somewhere with this ink," Bernie Lofgrin informed Boldt, stopping him in the hallway. Boldt was on his way to the communications room to initiate the dismantling of the surveillance of 114 Lakewood, where Marianne Martinelli waited as a possible target. He intended to leave LaMoia on that surveillance and move Gaynes to the tunnel park where Daphne had found the quotations, his two best chances at picking up Garman's trail again. He would take the graveyard shift from LaMoia and allow the park to go unwatched from two to six in the morning. Even with this skeleton crew, he believed it possible to keep the surveillance up and running. He wasn't sure what else to do.

Lofgrin's glasses were smudged, obscuring his magnified eyes. Physically, he looked bone-tired, yet he remained animated and enthusiastic. Boldt envied him this.

"It's not a Bic, a Parker, a Paper Mate, a Cross, or any of a dozen other mass-produced pens commonly available. That's good news, believe me. What we do is graph the ink's chemical components—"

"Look, Bernie. I appreciate it, I really do, but Phil has pulled the plug, okay? No more cross-departmental stuff unless it pertains to suspects in custody."

Lofgrin appeared crushed. "So what does he know from what we're talking about?" He whispered, "Fuck Shoswitz. I'm a civilian. You think they're gonna fire me? Do you? No fucking way." He stepped even closer. His breath was sour. Boldt was in no mood for a forensics class. "So we say we're doing this to confirm Steven Garman as the Scholar. Who's to know? Listen, the Bureau has all this shit on file, chromatographs of every goddamn ink manufactured: ballpoint pens, felt tips, typewriter ribbons, computer printer cartridges, you name it. We're downloading a bunch of the graphs now, for comparison purposes." Boldt stiffened; he didn't want a Lofgrin lecture. "We're going to ID this ink, Lou—and I'm telling you, it's significant. Every single one of those notes is written in the same ink. You bring me this guy with a pen in his pocket, and I can tie him to these poems."

"We lost him, Bernie."

"A bicycle. I heard. Yeah."

"No. I mean we lost him. If he shows up at the car wash tomorrow, which he very well may, Shoswitz will call for an interrogation. He'll want a statement from young Garman about his father's prior arson history, I know he will. And that will be that. This guy's too careful. We won't get squat from him if we go at it that way."

"I'm sorry to hear that," Lofgrin confided, his enthusiasm shaken. "Well, then," he said, reconsidering, "Toni and I will just have to work right on through, won't we?" He checked his watch. "You going home?"

"Can't do it," Boldt said. He wanted to go home, yet he didn't want to confront Liz. He wanted to comfort her, but he wanted her to tell him about the illness, not the other way around. He wasn't sure what he wanted.

The evening's twilight was quickly fading. It would be dark soon, which would make surveillance efforts at both sites all the more difficult. Daphne had jumped out of the van forty minutes earlier, and Boldt hadn't heard from her since. If he could talk her into helping, he had a team of four—down from twenty-odd only a few hours earlier. But four people could probably hold it together overnight.

He hurried on toward the communications room to make the necessary arrangements. He willed his pager not to sound, for he feared if it did it would mean another fire, another victim. And though that might prove him right about the Scholar still being at large, it was a price he was unwilling to pay.

At that point in time, failure seemed the best solution of all.

58

DAPHNE

pulled up a chair in the small Tech Services room. Its walls were hidden by metal shelves containing tape recorders and video machines. The room smelled sour like sweat and burned coffee. She plugged in the car wash surveillance tape and hit PLAY.

Ben had not been at Emily's, was not at the houseboat; Emily had threatened to file a complaint. Daphne couldn't believe how quickly the investigation had deteriorated. She felt responsible, having convinced herself that a close look-alike to Garman's mother would distract him. She felt as if all her training and education had failed her. She had been so convinced. She had to see the tape to believe it. She found the taped image considerably clearer than the live transmissions.

Jonny Garman entered the vehicle, took one long look at the photo of Ben, glanced around the front seat and into the back, assessing how dirty it was, and then set about squirting the inside of the windows with his spray bottle and wiping the glass clean with that towel. He conserved his movement within the vehicle, stretching to reach the far window, and performed his duties efficiently and quickly. He cleaned the inside of the windshield, both side windows, the rearview mirror, and the dashboard—in that order. To her surprise, he spent added time working on the sticky stain Martinelli had asked him to clean.

At the gap in the machinery that came ahead of the dryer, Garman climbed out of the front seat and into the back, where he attacked the rear window and both small side windows. He leaned over, nearly vanishing from sight, and then surfaced with an ashtray in his hand, the unseen contents of which he dumped in a plastic trash bag tied to his belt. As the car reached the end of the line, he shuffled out backward and closed the door.

He never looked in the glove box.

She rewound and replayed the tape for a second viewing, resorting to advancing the tape one frame at a time, hoping this might reveal an action overlooked in real time. But there was no such action on the tape. Garman did his job and climbed out of the car. The only brief moment he disappeared was when he was in the back seat, not the front—and that did her no good whatsoever. It seemed impossible.

Over the years she had come to develop certain instincts about her work, her patients. She could sense when a suspect was lying, could feel the truth. She knew when to push and when to pull back, when to work psychological games on an individual and when to talk straight. Jonny Garman would have taken the bait; she felt it to her core. The tape proved her wrong.

She ejected the tape and placed it to the side. The screen was a sky blue. She shut off the gear, the sense of failure a bitter taste in her mouth. Danny Kotch of Tech Services, who had always had a crush on her, caught up to her in the hallway and handed her Ben's backpack, returning it, reminding her of the boy and further disappointment. She carried it to her car and tossed it onto the seat.

Daphne drove with her headlights on through early evening rain that continued to hold the city in a perpetual dusk. She was going a little too fast for conditions when the light changed. She always

drove fast anyway, and her anxiety over Ben only served to in-
crease her speed. Green to yellow: She downshifted and tapped
the brakes. The rear end swerved, but she recovered with a tug on
the wheel. Yellow to red: She downshifted again and gave the
brakes an extra effort. The rubber met the road cleanly and firmly,
and the car slowed hard.

The backpack flew off the front seat and onto the floor mat.

The car lurched to a stop at the red light and rocked on its
springs.

Daphne leaned forward and grabbed for the small backpack
and hoisted it by one of its black straps up onto the seat.

The light changed, but Daphne didn't see it.

A car horn sounded behind her, but Daphne didn't hear it.

Traffic swerved around her, taking advantage of the green
light, and one of the drivers flipped her his middle finger. Daphne
did not see this either. Her full attention was fixed on the backpack.
In her mind's eye she saw Garman briefly glance into the back of
the Explorer as he climbed into the car to wash its windows; she
measured a count of two, as Garman, then in the back seat, dipped
out of sight, coming back up a moment later with an ashtray that
needed dumping.

The backpack had been in the back seat—she had placed it
there herself. The same backpack that was currently in the seat
alongside of her. She stared at it, transfixed. For there on the backpack, slipped into a plastic window designed for just that purpose,
was a small identification tag listing Ben's name and Jackson Street
address. Even the phone number was there, she noted.

Jonny Garman had not needed to open the glove box. The address he sought was available to him in the back seat, something
he had probably determined within seconds of climbing into the
car. She recalled the video tape and Garman's brief disappearance
as he sat up with an ashtray in hand. Ben's backpack had been in
the Explorer's back seat. Garman would have had time to memo-
rize the address.

The police had established an elaborate surveillance operation
at the wrong address. If Garman was watching any house, it was

the Santori house on Jackson, not 114 Lakewood where Martinelli was ensconced.

As she hung a U-turn in the middle of oncoming traffic, Daphne wasn't thinking about Boldt or the investigation; she was thinking about Ben and the fact that she had not bothered to check *his* home, where he clearly might hide in a panic. She would not tell Boldt or the others, not yet. They would want Martinelli, not Daphne, to arrive at the house on Jackson, more worried about their trap than the emotions of a frightened runaway boy.

She owed this to Ben. She would not drive him away again.

It never occurred to her for a minute that at a distance, in the dusk, she and Martinelli did not look so very different.

59

BOLDT was both annoyed with and concerned about Bobbie Gaynes. She had called in to dispatch an hour earlier, explaining she was going to walk Seattle University—the location of Garman's surprise bicycle disappearance—and had not been heard from again. She didn't carry a cellular phone and she was clearly away from her vehicle, because she wasn't answering radio calls. She was one of only two detectives to whom Boldt could turn for his surveillance team, and he felt forced to chase her down.

He drove to the corner of Broadway and Columbia and immediately spotted her department-issue four-door parked a half block down the hill. At that point, his concern gave way to worry.

He parked and walked quickly through the small campus, eyes and ears alert. There was no more daylight left, only a strong twilight glow off the clouds, bouncing back a muted, ambient light that stuck to anything pale in color. Gaynes could have covered the area in no time, he realized, wondering why she had not returned to her car and reported back to dispatch. He had no time to chase detectives around the city. Increasingly impatient, he widened his area of search as he believed she would have. He had been on foot for twenty minutes when he found himself waiting for a car to pass at the intersection of Broadway and James.

He looked up at the many office buildings surrounding him, at first taking in their contrasting brick and concrete architectures, preferring the older brick look, but then assessing their purpose as professional buildings—medical offices. The area was known as Pill Hill. All at once he knew why he had lost Bobbie Gaynes; she too had made this same discovery. Medical offices, and their suspect with a reconstructed face.

Boldt began to run in the direction of Harborview, where he hoped to catch Dixie, still in his offices. As medical examiner Dixie would have access to professional listings. The man often worked late; Boldt felt he had a chance.

Each building he passed had some connection to the medical world. The signs, the names shouted out at him. He couldn't run fast enough. He cut across to Boren and down Boren toward the hospital, out of breath but not slowing his stride.

They had run driver's license and vehicle registration checks on Garman, he recalled. Had LaMoia run credit checks and medical records? He couldn't remember. But then he thought they must have, because they knew the exact date of Jonathan Garman's admission for severe burns in the hospital at Grand Forks. And, if so, they had not discovered any record of medical insurance or they would have had an address to run down, even if only a mail drop.

Think, think! he told himself. And as the idea struck him, Boldt pulled an abrupt about-face, cut back across the street, and ran at a full sprint back toward the school campus.

Less than five minutes later, he burst through the door of the First Hill Medical Clinic, a welfare outpatient service only a block south of the university. It operated out of an old dry-cleaning shop, the rusted mechanized clothes hanger chain still suspended from the ceiling like recovered dinosaur vertebrae.

Bobbie Gaynes was standing at the counter, halfway through a serious pile of paperwork. She viewed a sheet and turned. Viewed and turned. She took no notice of Boldt until he stood panting only a few feet away. Then she glanced over at him and said, "Well, don't just stand there, Sergeant, take a chunk of this." She passed him two inches of paperwork. As if they had been discussing the case together, she said, "Shifts changed at six o'clock, so no one here now saw him come in today. But one of the girls recognized the description. Garman uses the clinic, though she says the name doesn't sound right. She says the plastic surgery was a lousy job—it's always infecting along his ears. They're not so pretty, evidently; he wears the sweatshirt hood up to hide them. And they're real painful. If he was in today, he's in these piles. And if he's in these piles they have some paperwork on him. Everyone has to register here. It's kind of like an uninsured HMO."

A female nurse called another patient's name into the crowded room. A male nurse answered the phone and sat down at a computer terminal.

"You didn't call in," Boldt said. Leafing through the doctors' reports, he asked, "What do I look for?"

"An injection of this." She passed him a Post-it that bore the handwritten name of an antibiotic. "That word will be in this space here," she said, indicating a box on one of the forms. "But doctors can't write, so it's hard to know what you're looking at. How can guys who spend ten years in graduate school write like they never made it through sixth grade?"

"How could you go an hour without checking in?"

She indicated the pay phone. There was someone on it, and a line waiting. "This place has been jumping. I figured, Do the job at hand. I know it's a long shot but—"

"No, Bobbie, it's a stroke of genius." He didn't often hand out that kind of compliment, and it stopped her for a moment.

"When that gal said she knew the disfigured guy with the sweatshirt—well, it kind of felt like Christmas. I wanted to unwrap the present for you. That's all." Suddenly she barked, "Got it!" and tugged one of the forms from the pile. She shouted to the male nurse at the computer terminal. "Jonny *Babcock!* Everything you've got on him!" The man hesitated, having no idea who Bobbie was.

Boldt and his detective both produced their shields nearly in the same movement.

Boldt announced them: "Police!"

The resulting commotion behind them sounded like a stampede. Boldt turned around in time to see four youths already out the door and sprinting down the sidewalk.

Typing the name into the terminal, the male nurse observed, "Well, that's certainly an effective way to thin the waiting room. Thank you. I'll have to remember that." Looking back at his screen he said, "Babcock, Jonathan. No phone. Apartment Two-C, 1704 Washington Street South. You want me to print it for you?"

Not hearing an answer, the man turned around. The two police officers were already out the door.

60

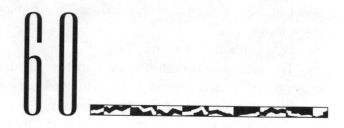

DAPHNE parked a block short of the Santori house on Jackson, where she and Boldt had arrested Nicholas Hall.

She reached for her cellular phone to call for backup, an involuntary action born of the scar on her neck, but reconsidered, both for Ben's sake and, more honestly, because she wanted to avoid making a fool of herself for the second time in the same day. Prudence dictated that she investigate further before calling it in.

Taking her weapon into her hand inside the purse, she hung the purse casually off her right shoulder. She would not go into the driveway because she had the wrong car; Martinelli had driven an Explorer. Instead, she would park where she was and walk, head down. It seemed to her entirely plausible that Garman had gleaned the address off Ben's backpack. If so, the Scholar might be watching the house from a tree or preparing his accelerants in a makeshift lab somewhere. He might be carving a biblical reference into a tree trunk. But she would not look up into the overhead branches, would not risk giving herself away. She would go inside and hope to find Ben. After that, she wasn't sure.

With her sweaty fingers gripping the handgun inside her purse and her heart racing painfully in her chest, she took one final deep breath and left her vehicle. She had things under control, she convinced herself. No reason to panic.

Daphne barely took notice of the light drizzle, of the damp chill in the air. Falling mist was more common than sunshine as winter approached: one day Indian summer, the next a cold drool. Up the hill was a small park. Tall trees, she thought, believing Garman would be found there. She regretted not calling Boldt, not calling for backup, but was again reminded of the fiasco of the failed surveillance.

She walked to the back of the house and climbed the stairs to the landing. A sheet of plastic covered the hole of broken glass where Nicholas Hall had forced his way inside. If she were being watched, she couldn't stand at her own backdoor all day debating whether to enter or not. She tried the door. It was locked. She raised her hand as if using a key and punched through the plastic and let herself in. The door fell open and she stepped inside. It banged shut as she closed it.

Daphne's finger hesitated at the light switch, wondering if it was possibly a trigger. She glanced around the worn kitchen, suddenly thinking of everything as a trigger—the furniture, the faucets, the toilets, the thermostat, the phone—as if any step she took might initiate an explosion or a fire. The place gave her the creeps. She wanted out of there.

She decided to place her faith in Bernie Lofgrin: The trigger was always in the plumbing, not the wiring. She counted to five and threw the light switch. Nothing happened.

She moved through the kitchen and into the living room, slowly and cautiously, step by precious step.

Would he have had time to set his charge? She doubted it. Watch the house for action tonight, wash the windows once Daphne left in the morning.

She switched on several lights and called out Ben's name,

moving room to room. A cold shiver passed through her. She could picture herself as Dorothy Enwright or Melissa Heifitz. Another victim.

Garman was watching the house—she could *feel* it.

61

BEN heard the back door of his own house slam shut and immediately lifted his head to the open window of the crude tree house. Jack Santori was still under arrest, as far as he knew, so who the hell . . . ? The kitchen light came on and, a few seconds later, the living room light.

To avoid any chance of being seen, Ben had been crashed out in his sleeping bag on the tree house floor, basically waiting for tomorrow to come. He would return to Emily and present his plan: They should run away together. No more police. No more Jack Santori. A new beginning. He was too excited by the idea to sleep, so instead he just lay in the dark, listening to the neighborhood, biding his time. And then the back door. Ben recognized that his own curiosity was what had gotten him into all this trouble. It kind of took control of him. Possessed him. He fought the urge to find out who was in his house, reminding himself over and over again that when the sun rose the following morning he was free. All he had to do was cool his jets until then. Sit tight.

A light went on in his bedroom.

He needed a better look. He just had to know what was going on.

He slipped out of the bag but waited before leaving the tree house, because headlights from 31st and 32nd caught the tops of the trees that grew on the western edge of Frink Park, and Ben didn't want to take any chance of his being seen. He still had control of that burning curiosity that boiled away inside him. He didn't want to be too impetuous.

The whitewash of the headlights receded, and Ben crept out onto the main limb, determined to climb higher where he might see down into his own bedroom.

The noise of the city hummed around him, the droning whine of tires, the distant rolling thunder of jets landing and taking off, the moan of ferry horns out on the water. He started up the tree.

Some car doors shut not far away, but he couldn't make out the direction. When a beam of white light spread through the treetops Ben paused briefly, waiting for them to reach him and pass.

That was when he saw the man perched in a nearby tree.

If he had been in better control, he might not have gasped the way he did, but he lacked any such control, and his release of air brought him to the man's attention. The guy was right at the same height, maybe thirty feet off the ground. He was three trees away, braced comfortably in the first main crotch.

Ben recognized him immediately. He wore a sweatshirt pulled up on his head, though he had ditched the sunglasses since the time Ben had seen him at the airport.

Another boy Ben's age might have panicked and frozen in that tree, but Ben had Jack Santori to thank for his ability to move, and move quickly. The headlights swept past. The darkness washed the man out of the tree, and Ben out of his.

Ben moved faster than his legs had ever moved before. He swung like a monkey, one limb to the next, down, down, down. Faster and then faster still. As his eyes readjusted from the headlights, he glanced left and saw the other guy was descending too. And making better time.

Ben moved quickly, but the guy in the sweatshirt was superhuman the way he could climb. He was already halfway down his tree, checking on Ben the entire way.

It wasn't going to be a social call. He had that same look Jack Santori had on a bad night. He intended to get up close to Ben, the way Jack did. To hurt him. To stop him from telling anyone—which was exactly what Ben had in mind.

Down . . . down . . . down. . . .

Ben understood in another flash of headlights that he wasn't going to win this race. And losers paid, as Santori was fond of saying. The guy had only a couple of limbs to go; Ben had fifteen feet.

The decision was not so much conscious thought as an act of survival. Had he reasoned, he would have understood the drop was too great, even given the soft damp earth below. He would not have gone with his instincts but instead would have descended further before jumping. But something propelled him off that limb, threw him right off it, into an open-armed jump, that began with a scream and ended with the solid impact of both legs striking the ground.

He hit hard, but no bones broke; he knew this instantly. And had his glass eye not popped out with the contact before he fully crashed and rolled through the wet leaves, his nose smashed, he might never have thought of what came next. But he had played this game too many times *not* to think of it, had scared the frost out of a dozen of Jack Santori's playmates. He played dead.

He held his breath, popped both eyes wide open, and made no attempt to wipe the trickle of blood that oozed from his nose. Holding his breath was the hardest, but also the most important to the performance. To fool the girls his chest could not move at all.

The man from the tree was already down by the time Ben hit, and he ran to get a look at the boy. He cut through the dense underbrush and reached Ben's silent body just as Daphne's voice cut through the woods, calling, "Ben? Ben?"

The man glanced hotly in the direction of the voice, bent over, and looked directly into Ben's face, wincing as he saw the pulpy red flesh of the open hollow eye socket. He tested Ben with the toe of his running shoe, checking for life. The trick to playing dead was just that: Gross them out with the bad eye, and they never looked at much else.

The two locked eye-to-eye, Ben getting a perfectly clear look at the man, who saw a fallen boy, dead of a broken neck.

The faceless man with eyes like a Halloween pumpkin—carved and artificial—hurried off through the woods as the back door banged shut: Daphne giving up.

Ben waited, hearing the man work back through the woods and up toward the small park, waited as he heard the distinctive sound of a bike chain, the pedals backing up.

As much as Ben tried to convince himself to leave it alone, he couldn't; his system was charged with a small victory, his curiosity pumping like a drug. He sat up, the image of the man a silhouette through the woods as he pedaled away.

Wiping his bloody nose on his sleeve, Ben hurried to the shed behind his house. His bike was there. He had to do it. He had to follow the guy.

He did it for Emily—he told himself—and their chance for a future. He did it to help Daphne. But the truth of the matter was far more simple: He did it to erase the guilt of his earlier crime of climbing into that truck, of taking the money. To be a hero. This was his chance; he knew it instinctively. He would not let the opportunity pass him by.

He jumped onto the bike and went speeding out his driveway, leaving his glass eye far behind and the weight of his past right there along with it.

62

T H E rooming house was one block off
Yesler Way in a racially mixed neighborhood that had both soul-
food kitchens and acupuncture clinics. It was a brown-shingled
two-story structure that looked more like a cheap motel.

In blatant disregard of Shoswitz's orders, Boldt called in the
services of Danny Kotch from the department's Tech Services
squad.

Rule number one, in dealing with a torch or a bomb maker,
was never *but never* kick the apartment. Only experts entered such
a place, and they went in gently and carefully, often through an
opening in a wall they made themselves, rather than a door. Under
no circumstances would Boldt attempt to pick Jonny Garman while
the man was in the apartment. The pick would be on the street,
with Garman out in the open and totally surrounded. But as far as
Boldt was concerned, the pick would come later, and for two reasons: Boldt would need additional manpower, and he wanted another chance to size up the suspect and follow him if possible—to
connect him to hard evidence.

They drove separately, Gaynes parking two blocks west on

Washington but with a clean view of the front of the rooming house, Boldt taking up a position on 18th Avenue South near a battered dumpster, with a slightly obstructed view of what he took to be the building's back door.

Boldt hung up from Kotch, called Domino's Pizza, and placed an order for a medium sausage and mushroom, giving Garman's address—always the easiest way to test if a suspect was home. Kotch and the pizza arrived nearly at the same time, with Kotch first. As ordered, he parked at 19th and Jackson and walked to Boldt's car. He wore blue jeans and an NPR sweatshirt advertising *Morning Edition.*

When the pizza man had come and gone, an incident Kotch watched with great interest through a small pair of binoculars, the Tech Services man detailed his plan. "So no one answered. He's not home or, if he is, not interested. You want me in the back or you would have set this up different. Am I right?"

"The back. Definitely. If you hear my car start, you're out of there."

"It's dark enough that I'm okay with that," the man replied. "I go fishing fiber-optic under that back door. That's all?"

"Booby traps, condition of the interior, anything stored you see. Labels if possible."

"But it's our torch, right? The Scholar? What we're thinking is fire, correct?"

"Correct."

"How many minutes?" he asked. "I can go twenty, twenty-two feet inside. A goddamned nickel tour, Sergeant. How much do you want?"

"If he's in there, you're gone. If not, then three to five minutes. Short and sweet. Can it record?"

"You bet. Camera goes direct to a camcorder with an LCD display. Camera is black-and-white, but it's good quality."

"If his lab isn't in there, and I don't think it is, I'd take any clues you happen upon."

The pizza man tried a second time, apparently having checked his delivery list in the car or used a car phone to call the store. They couldn't see him at the door, but they heard him pounding. He walked around back carrying the pie, gave up, and drove away a few minutes later.

"That's my cue," Kotch said, slipping out of the car.

Boldt wondered what kind of trouble he was in for using the man. Perhaps a case of beer or a bottle of Scotch would buy Kotch's silence. Perhaps Shoswitz would find out and a shouting match would ensue. But he had no choice. For his own safety, for the safety of others in the rooming house, Kotch and the fiber-optic camera were essential.

Boldt looked on as Kotch walked casually across the street, a small backpack slung over one shoulder. In running shoes and jeans, he looked no different from thousands of other Seattlites. There was not a hint of cop about him. This was another area in which they differed. Boldt, with his substantial size and close-cropped hair, couldn't help but reflect his twenty-four years of public service.

Kotch reached the back of the building and hurried up the only fire stairs to the second-story landing that provided egress for each of the rooms. He dropped to one knee, rummaged through the backpack, and in a matter of only seconds was feeding the thin wire attached to the miniature camera under the small gap in the door.

Specialists like Kotch were unique not only in their formidable technical knowledge and expertise but for their ability to appear casual under the most stressful circumstances. From the street, Kotch appeared to be searching out a pair of misplaced keys in his backpack, while in fact he continued to feed additional camera footage into the rented room.

Boldt had been involved in other special ops that had used fiber-optic cameras. In the right hands, the devices could be maneuvered along the floor, room to room, giving a clear fish-eye look at inhabitants and contents. Given the fact that Kotch continued his work, Boldt assumed that not only was the apartment empty but that no booby traps or detonation devices had been spotted. Not seeing them did not mean they did not exist, however. As eager as

Boldt was to sneak a look inside that apartment—warrant or not—he had no desire to die the way Dorothy Enwright had. The Scholar had proved himself a skilled technician. Boldt had no desire to test his abilities.

Kotch packed up, descended the stairs, and walked entirely around the block before joining Boldt again in the car.

He rewound the tape and narrated as it played. The two men huddled around the small three-inch-square screen that was part of the camcorder. The fish-eye image was framed in a large circle, fuzzy at its edges. Seen through this distorted monocular vision, the apartment took on a foreboding, dangerous look. "It's one room. I spend a minute examining the door and frame for triggers or trip wires—nothing there. Bathroom is to our right here. I come back to it. Up here is the bed with a dark blanket, chest of drawers to the left, see? Looks like a coil-element hot plate up on top. Okay. I check the front door—again, no visible triggers or trips." As he narrated, the lone eye snaked around the interior at floor level. Then all of a sudden the screen's image was too jerky to discern. "I retract here and reset the snake to show us waist height. It's a little harder to keep steady when the camera's in the air like that." When the image became clear again, the perspective was from waist height. "Into the bathroom, up on the counter: Crest, Schick, no shaving cream in sight. Back out to the room and that card table—here we go. Oops. Coming up. . . . As you can see, the place is pretty depressing. No TV. No radio. It's kept neat. Your boy is fastidious. It's tricky getting to see the top of the card table. Took me a few tries. You'll notice: No sign whatsoever of any lab gear. No closet. There's a hanging rod in the corner by the bathroom— one raincoat, is all. Not a lot of places to hide shit. I'd say if he's mixing cocktails, it's somewhere else."

"Receipts? Calendars? Matchbooks? Anything pointing to another location?"

"None of that. Oh, here it is. The card table. Seven white envelopes. Eighteen pieces of blank card stock. A tin can full of pens and pencils. A roll of postage stamps—American flag."

"That matches!" Boldt exclaimed. American flag stamps had

been affixed to all the Scholar's notes. It was the stamps that sold Boldt; he knew they had the right place.

"Two books total: a worn Bible on the floor by the bed, and another called *Cruden's Complete Concordance*."

"A biblical concordance." Boldt spit it out quickly. "The Bible citations in the trees. It's definitely him—we've got him!"

The fish-eye view did not hold on the table's contents for long. Kotch lost the precarious balance he had and the camera fell to the floor. It snaked back out of the room, the show over.

Boldt understood immediately that what he had just viewed was convincing enough to warrant a legal look inside the room. The video tape would never be admissible evidence, but it had showed him enough. He thought he might be able to secure a search warrant by telephone using the fibers as evidence. He and Gaynes would await Garman's return and sit on him, probably clear through work the following day. Two or three days if necessary, with LaMoia and Matthews in rotation. Boldt felt convinced that eventually Garman would lead them to some evidence. His big problem was maintaining the patience required to wait the man out.

His other problem was time, he thought, as he checked his watch. Eight o'clock and still no fire announced over the police radio. It broke with the Scholar's established pattern—always a bad sign. Worse, it *fit* with what Daphne had been insisting all along: Jonny Garman had taken the bait, Martinelli now next on his list.

"I want to review that tape back downtown," Boldt told Kotch, who made for the car door. "A bigger monitor. See what we see."

"Sure thing."

"You got the time?" Boldt asked.

"No problem." He stopped, his hand on the door handle. "Listen, I heard Shoswitz is squeezing your stones over manpower, Sergeant. My involvement? No big deal. It never happened."

"I appreciate that," Boldt replied. "I was wondering how to approach you."

"Never happened," Kotch repeated. "See you downtown."

Boldt used the cellular to ring LaMoia because he wanted to keep it off the radios. He told them they had located Garman's residence and there was no sign of a lab. "It could be in the basement; it could be ten miles away." He warned the detective that Marianne Martinelli might be the target after all. He told him, "Heads up. And call me for backup at a moment's notice. No heroics."

LaMoia mocked him, as the detective was fond of doing. LaMoia would do anything macho, just to get a story out of it. He loved to tell stories, especially those involving himself.

"Is Matthews in position?" Boldt asked.

"Matthews? I haven't heard a peep."

Boldt had left a message on her voice mail, explaining Shoswitz's imposed curbs and asking if she would help LaMoia with the Lakewood surveillance. It was unlike her to leave John in the lurch, especially since she had instigated the operation. Boldt mumbled, "We don't know if she found the kid or not. That's probably what's going on."

"She's touchy about this kid, you know? Have you picked up on that? A little close for my taste."

"She's responsible for him, John. The kid blew us off. Walked right out of the unit." She had her reputation to defend, he thought, suddenly more worried. It had not been a good day for her.

Daphne Matthews did not take failure well.

To call her was only to force her to admit she had still not found their witness. Boldt wanted none of that. He would give her another hour before inviting that wrath upon himself.

He left Gaynes to watch the rooming house without him and headed downtown to get a better look at the video.

He was halfway back to the Public Safety Building when a nearly hysterical Bernie Lofgrin called him with the latest on the ink used in the notes.

The boulder that was the investigation was suddenly rolling downhill again, and this time, Boldt thought, Jonny Garman was directly in its path.

63

THE man with the dead face rode fast. Ben was in his highest gear, riding as hard as he could and losing ground. It was like trying to chase a phantom.

The police artist had called it a hockey mask, but that was no mask. It wasn't skin either. Ben wasn't sure what it was, but it was ugly. A monster was more like it. Way worse than a glass eye. A person could hardly feel sorry for himself after seeing something like that.

They rode Yesler under the highway and turned into the International District. The guy knew how to time the lights. If he hit a red, he went with the pedestrian lights, the white marching man in the box on the lamppost. If Ben could have ridden faster he might have hung back intentionally, but as it was, the distance between them only increased, and rather than worry about being seen, Ben's concern was keeping up. The Face, as Ben thought of him, shot across Dearborn, connected up with Airport Way, and started pumping like he was in some kind of race, growing smaller and smaller in the distance.

Ben felt all hope ride away with the guy.

And then he heard the truck coming up fast from behind.

It was a stunt he had wanted to do a hundred times but had never had the belly to try. And suddenly there was no question in his mind as to *if* he would try but whether or not he could pull it off.

He pedaled hard, rising up off his seat, glancing once over his left shoulder, a slight smirk as he twisted his head fully around so his right eye could see back there. A good-sized truck, bigger than a pickup but smaller than a dump truck. Picking up speed after the last light. Gaining on Ben.

His legs pushed hard; he needed to match that speed.

Gaining . . . gaining . . .

Another look, a huge swivel of the head: Only a few yards back, the engine louder than a locomotive, the gears singing. Ben inched the bike to his left, swerving, the truck looming closer.

Closer still. Legs flailing then to match the speed. It had to be exact. He knew. He had heard stories. If you timed it wrong, the truck pulled you right off the seat or, worse, folded the bike underneath the twin rubber tires, bearing down like a steamroller.

He had never tried because it took nerves and timing and depth perception. And like so many things—catching a ball, swinging a bat, even patty-cake as a little kid—Ben had given up before he had tried, because others had told him he couldn't.

He reached out and took hold of the truck.

The feeling was like the only time he'd been in a sailboat, when a gust of wind had caught them and tipped them so hard that everyone slid inside the boat. One minute Ben was riding. The next, he was launched down the road, a passenger in a sidecar.

The truck picked up speed. Ben held on for dear life. Up ahead, the tiny image of the Face on the bike grew larger as the truck closed the distance. He felt the wind in his smiling face and wanted to cheer, to shout, to show everybody what he'd done. The poor little boy with one eye. The kid doing thirty-five, one-handed, on a bicycle. He felt as if he were riding a rocket, as if it were strapped right onto his bike.

The Face was in plain sight again and, if Ben had it right, was slowing down. They had come a mile, maybe two. Green lights the whole way. He felt empowered. He felt like a grown-up. A hero.

They closed fast on the other bike, and suddenly Ben lacked the nerve to let go and release the truck. The idea terrified him. He had grabbed on okay, but he wasn't so sure about letting go. Those wheels were *right there*, grabbing the pavement, bumping, bouncing. Ben could just see himself squashed under them.

Let go! a voice inside him announced. But his hand wouldn't do it. It just couldn't do it.

Worse, the Face was getting closer by the second, by the yard. He had slowed down to nothing.

At once, without a hand signal, the Face turned right and the bike pulled to a stop and the guy jumped off. The truck, and Ben along with it, went whizzing right by—Ben looking back quickly to mark the location.

U-STOR-IT—SELF-STORAGE UNITS AVAILABLE

He looked ahead then, the road conditions worsening, potholes everywhere. Just like that! One minute smooth asphalt; the next, land mines. He swung the wheel left and right, dodging the holes, slaloming between them.

The light up ahead was green.

"Turn red," Ben begged, repeating it like a mantra. "Red," he pleaded.

The light changed to yellow. The gears ground as the driver downshifted; the truck slowed noticeably. Ben dodged one last pothole, pulling the bike too far to the right and breaking his grip. Without intending to, he let go.

He snapped his other hand onto the handlebars and hung on tight as he squeezed the back brake, the front wheel vibrating and dancing with a life of its own. He pulled, but the front wheel would hardly move. The truck lumbered on up ahead. Ben lost control, hit the curb, and was launched through the air onto a patch of grass and a pile of dog shit that smeared all the way down his back. He came to a stop sitting up, facing backward, dizzy and unable to focus. He sat there for a long time waiting for his vision to return, his head to stop swimming.

The bike looked okay. He felt his arms and legs. Nothing broken, he decided, for the second time in the same night. He glanced around at his surroundings: Spiro Aviation, Glyde Avionics and Engineering. Not a pay phone in sight.

U-Stor-It was only a half mile behind him.

64

DAPHNE found herself sitting in the Santori home doing nothing, wondering why she was there. Fifteen minutes had passed since she had heard one of the neighborhood boys scream out from the woods. Kids! She had actually allowed herself to believe it had been Ben. How paranoid can a psychologist get? she wondered.

Her biggest mistake was leaving her cellular phone in her car, plugged into the cigarette lighter. She had debated walking the one block to get it but worried that it might attract Jonny Garman's attention to her red Honda; Martinelli had been driving an Explorer. This car difference was what had kept her grounded in the house. If Garman was watching the place—and she believed he could be—and she returned to the wrong car or he got a good look at her, the game was up. They were back to square one.

For the last quarter hour she had been attempting to develop the nerve to call Boldt and tell him her latest theory—that Garman had lifted the wrong address off the backpack. But Boldt had been cut back to one or two detectives, and she didn't want to be the one to screw things up again, to pull LaMoia off Martinelli just in time for Garman to fry the woman.

But she had to check in. Officially off-duty, she knew Boldt was nonetheless counting on her. She called her voice mail, to check messages, with one eye on her car, wondering how she had been so stupid as to park directly under a streetlight. When things went wrong, she decided, they went wrong in a big way.

There were six messages: one from Owen, two from Susan, two from Boldt, and one from Emily Richland. Of all the calls, it was Emily Richland's she returned; the woman had sounded half out of her mind.

"Daphne Matthews," she announced when the woman said hello.

"He was here," Emily Richland confessed immediately, without introduction or small talk. "When you came looking for him, he was here. I hid him. I lied, and I know now that was stupid."

Daphne felt her heart racing away from her. She tried to calm herself, but the woman's agitation was contagious.

Emily continued, "He ran away. Left the house while we were talking, I imagine. But of course I expected him back, and he never returned. He hasn't returned. A long time now, and he hasn't returned."

"Probably doesn't trust either of us," Daphne allowed, trying to calm the other.

"No, it's not that," said Emily nervously.

"Then what?"

"Listen. I don't expect you to believe this. . . . I know you *don't* believe this. Maybe it's impossible for you to. But I beg you to believe just this one time. At least hear what it is I have to say."

"Go on." Daphne fought against her own desire to shout, to scold the woman. Get on with it! she wanted to say.

"I *do* have visions. I really do. You must believe me. And I've had one tonight. Several times. The first time . . ."

Daphne could hear the woman's voice falter, and the tears begin. She struggled with her own emotions to keep from giving in to the other's. Tricks! she reminded herself. Emily Richland was a professional liar, nothing more.

"He was dead. On the ground, his eyes open." Emily broke down crying—sobbing—into the phone. If it was an act, it was a damn good one. "Ben," she muttered, "lying there on the ground. Oh, God. . . . And then, just now—right before you called—a second image. All dark and a fence, and Ben's face pressed up against it. He's in trouble, I know he is! I know this. I've seen it! And I don't know what to do about it!"

Daphne did not want to reveal the terror she was experiencing. The images of the boy were fixed in her head. To give the woman some encouragement seemed the best route. "Anything else you can tell me? Anything at all?" As a psychologist she simply could not allow herself to believe in paranormal activity; as a woman who loved this boy herself, she believed every word.

"A fence . . . darkness . . . chain link, you know? Looking through it. Boxes. Blue boxes."

"Train cars?"

"I don't know."

"Containers. Ship containers?"

"I can't see it clearly. Blue boxes. . . . fence . . . darkness."

"I'll call," Daphne said. "If we find out anything, I'll call."

Emily Richland was still crying as Daphne hung up the phone. One hell of an act indeed, if that's what it was.

She needed no more courage than that call. She lifted the receiver and dialed Boldt's cellular.

65

"CHECK it out," Lofgrin said proudly, hoisting a pair of graphs up for Boldt to compare. "The one on the left was downloaded from the FBI database I told you about, every goddamn kind of ink manufactured. The one on the right is the chromatograph of the ink used on the Scholar's threats." The match, though not perfect, was unmistakable.

Boldt said, in a voice that sounded more like a prayer, "Tell me that two hundred thousand people in Seattle don't own this same pen."

"They don't, not by a long shot. Maybe it helps us locate him. It's from a company in St. Louis that specializes in cheap custom pens: giveaways. The kind that advertises in the back of magazines: *Your logo here!*" Lofgrin was so excited he was shouting. "You've seen 'em: golf clubs, hardware stores, rental shops. You name it."

"No, *you* name it," Boldt said, turning the man's phrase and sobering him some. "How big a field, Bernie?"

"We're a long way from St. Louis, Lou. It's not like a company like this would be flooded with Seattle orders."

"How many Seattle clients?"

"How many? How should I know? That's *your* job. I match the fucking graphs. That's *my* job. It's your phone call to make, not mine. And don't expect miracles. Firms like this make a lot of models, you know? And it's not like we know the model."

"The shape, you mean?"

"Shape, size, color. All that would narrow the field."

"*You* make the call, Bernie. Wake someone up if you have to. Threaten them. I don't care what you do. But get someone down to their records—tonight—right now! Every Seattle client, every customer." Boldt took off quickly down the hallway.

"And what the fuck are you going to do?" the man called out indignantly. "I am *not* a detective!"

Without looking back, Boldt broke into a jog and shouted into the hallway, "I'm going to get a description of the pen for you. I'm going to get you the model."

Kotch was already at work at the video monitor when Boldt entered the smoke-filled room. The big man waved the air. "Hasn't anybody here heard that this building has been no smoking for about seven years?"

The offending cigarette dangled from Kotch's pinched lips. "So arrest me." He exhaled.

On the large monitor, Boldt saw a portion of the grainy video shot inside Garman's rooming house. "Fast-forward," Boldt ordered.

"I was just—"

Boldt interrupted, repeating the order. He steered him to the section of tape where the contents of the desktop were revealed. First the envelopes, then the cards. In the background, Boldt saw the tin can filled with pens and pencils. He directed the man to freeze-frame.

"Can you enlarge this?" Boldt asked.

"We've got some cool toys, Sergeant. We can enlarge anything, though we'll lose resolution pretty fast on a tape this small."

"Give me the pens and pencils," Boldt said, pointing to the

screen. Static sparked off the tip of his finger, and Boldt jumped back with the spark.

"A little tense, are we?" Kotch inquired.

The can of pens and pencils grew ever larger on the screen. What writing may have been on the pens was lost immediately, but it became quickly apparent that of the few items in the can, three of the pens were the same—button-operated ball points, short and thick. Cheap pens. Just what Lofgrin needed.

"Can you print that?"

"It's not a very clear image. I can doctor it up some."

"No time. Print it. It's gorgeous. It's exactly what we need."

"The pens?" Kotch questioned earnestly. "You're interested in a bunch of junk pens?"

"Interested? With those pens, the Scholar just signed his own death warrant."

The printer began to sing.

Boldt smiled for the first time in days.

66

BEN pressed his face closer to the chain link fence outside the automated gate to the U-Stor-It facility, his fingers laced through the metal webbing. The Face had evidently used the keypad to open the gate, which was now closed. And although Ben was curious to find out where the guy had gone to, once inside, his eye was not on the endless rows of storage units but on the pay phone outside the door marked OFFICE.

That pay phone called to him. Up and over the fence, a quick run across the open pavement (that to Ben seemed a mile wide), and over to that phone. Call Daphne. Tell her the Face was here at the U-Stor-It on Airport Way. A hero. Back over the fence. Ride like hell. A plan. Pretty simple at that. Hardest part would be the climb over, and again on the way back, but he could climb sixty-foot trees so why not a ten-foot-high chain link fence?

He looked around for some options. Airport Way seemed about a thousand miles long in both directions, and with virtually no traffic. The industrial businesses that lined the street were closed, every one of them. He remembered passing an old run-down hotel way back there, but it looked a lot scarier than that telephone only twenty yards away.

The thing that tore at him was he knew it was wrong. He could feel it clear down in his stomach. Climbing the fence was no different from climbing into that blue pickup truck. He wondered where to draw the line between just doing something wrong and doing it in order to do good. He didn't need any more trouble. He had plenty. He was all through with trouble.

He checked for traffic and began to climb.

It surprised him how loud the fence was. It rattled like a bunch of cans. Scared the life out of him the way it made so much noise. The more noise, the faster he climbed; the faster he climbed, the more noise. His brain told him to slow down, take his time. His legs went like mad. But the faster he went, the worse his toeholds; his feet kept slipping out from under him, leaving him dangling and scraping for purchase, his toes attempting to run up the fence, his fingers pinched against the wire and hurting badly.

Finally, he reached the very top and threw a leg over, but the fence was cut ragged along the top edge. His pants caught and the wire bit into his thigh, stabbing him, and before he could stop himself he let out a shout that cut off halfway out when his brain kicked in and told him to shut up. He threw himself over to the other side, clawed his way down a few feet, and then bailed out, letting go and dropping to the blacktop.

What a mess, he thought, sprinting for the phone. A person would have to be deaf not to have heard that. What a stupid jerk! What a mess.

It was one of those things he knew without needing anyone to tell him: He'd screwed up big time. He'd screwed up so badly that halfway across the vast sea of blacktop separating the fence from the phone, he chickened out and froze, feeling the urgency to get back over that fence and flee. But then his legs moved again and the phone drew ever closer, looking to him like an oasis to a man too long in the desert.

He scooped a hungry hand down into his pocket and came up empty. No quarter. No way to make the phone call. He punched in 911—a number he was getting kind of used to.

"Emergency Services," a man's voice said.

"This is Ben . . . Ben Santori." He hated using that last name; his father's name had been Rice, and it seemed more right to him. "You gotta get a message to Daphne Matthews. She's a cop."

"I'm sorry, fella, we don't—"

"She's a cop. Listen to me!" he hissed in a whisper. "She's at my house: S-A-N-T-O-R-I." Ben spelled it for him. "Call her. Tell her I followed the guy with the face. The *face*—remember that. It's an emergency—" He broke off. It sounded like a garage door. The Face! he thought. There it was again, the same sound, the door closing maybe. He dumped the phone into the cradle and debated sprinting for the fence. The Face had heard him come over that fence; he was coming around to check it out.

The storage units were built in long rows, Ben closest to the end near the gate. He spied more fence at the far end of the units and wondered if it wouldn't be safer to try getting over down there, somewhere away from the entrance. He sneaked off along the side of the building, in the building's shadow, more scared than he had ever been of Jack Santori. He moved a few feet and paused, listening, looking, his heart hurting in his chest.

And then he saw a man's long thin shadow stretch across the pavement to his right. It was the Face, out prowling the grounds.

Out looking for him.

67

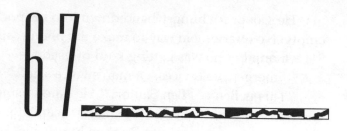

BERNIE Lofgrin came through. An 800 number for the St. Louis pen company's twenty-four-hour catalog had in their possession a phone number for the manager. Marv Caldwell kept his client information on a laptop computer that he took with him everywhere, even home at night. Along with relevant contact information, the client list also showed what product had been ordered and the quantity and date of the last order.

Within fifteen minutes of Lofgrin's first call, the printout from the rooming house video that showed a close-up of three similar pens had been faxed to Caldwell's laptop and the manager had identified the product as most closely resembling their model AL-440 ballpoint. His client list showed eleven Washington State customers as having ordered AL-440s, four of them in the Seattle area: a golf course north of town, a dry cleaner in Ballard, a self-storage company on Airport Way, and a Japanese restaurant on 5th Avenue.

Without hesitation, Boldt, sitting at Lofgrin's side, took the self-storage company. Marv Caldwell had three phone numbers on his client list for U-Stor-It, including the supervisor's home number. Boldt telephoned that number but got a message machine.

He double-checked with both of his detectives on surveillance, LaMoia and Gaynes. Neither reported any activity at their locations. He filled them in on the most recent lead and left them both with the address of the storage facility, a nagging sense of urgency getting the better of him. He couldn't free LaMoia from his post, because he couldn't put Martinelli at risk. Likewise, he wanted Gaynes to keep an eye on the rooming house in case Garman returned. He debated calling Shoswitz at home and requesting additional manpower, but knew in advance the lieutenant would want some confirmation of Garman renting at the site before committing any additional manpower or resources. He could practically hear the man saying, "Scout the place and let me know. We'll reassess at that time."

He decided to place the storage facility under surveillance for a few hours, though he didn't want to drive too close without a first look. He stopped three blocks short on Airport Way and shut down the car's radio and turned off his cellular phone so it wouldn't suddenly ring and announce his whereabouts in the middle of his poking around. He left his pager on but switched it to vibrate.

He parked in a parking lot for a helicopter maintenance company, locked the car, and headed off on foot, the U-Stor-It sign dimly visible a hundred yards ahead. The optimism that had begun with the discovery of the rooming house, and then spread to Lofgrin's identification of the ink, built to a drumming of adrenaline through his system. He experienced an increasing sense of certainty with each step that brought him closer to the storage facility. Garman could keep his father's stolen pickup truck there, could have his lab there, or both. Self-store units were the perfect anonymous address. Used in drug deals, as chop shops, and even as body storage in homicides, they proved to be fertile ground for criminal activity of every sort. That Garman might have an unknown quantity of rocket fuel stored there did little to settle Boldt's nerves.

He moved along fence lines and detoured into parking lots whenever possible, in an attempt to avoid being seen by traffic on Airport Way on the off-chance Garman was in the area. As distant as it seemed, he couldn't completely rule out the possibility that Garman was at the facility. The man had not been home in several hours. Without a fire reported, Boldt believed that Daphne might have been right after all: Garman could have taken the bait offered at the car wash. That suggested the possibility—however remote— that he might be preparing for another arson. And where better, Boldt wondered, than at a self-storage facility late at night?

The telephone rang, filling Daphne with anxiety. Her hand hovered above the cradle. At last, on the fourth ring, she answered. "Hello?"

"Daphne Matthews, please."

She wasn't sure how to answer. She was playing the roll of Marianne Martinelli, and it occurred to her that Garman might verify his victims by placing a call. How he might know that she was here was beyond her, but she wasn't going to fall prey to a ruse.

"My name's Marianne," she answered. "May I help you?"

"Listen, I'm calling for a Daphne Matthews. This is Seattle Communications Center. My name's Victor." He gave her the number.

She knew the number. She cut him off. "This is Matthews," she answered, her system charged with expectation.

"Is it or isn't it? I got a weird message for a Daphne Matthews. And I gotta tell you, I'm not in the habit of playing receptionist, okay?"

"Lieutenant Matthews, Seattle Police. You can verify that with the department, if you want."

"The message was from some kid named Ben San—"

"Go ahead." She sat down, her legs no longer capable of supporting her.

The man read her Ben's exact words. "We've got it on tape, of course," he added.

"An address? Do you have an address?" she called out hysterically.

"Sure do." He read her the address.

"Airport Way?" she asked, writing the address onto the table with the only thing available to her: red lipstick. "Is that a business of some sort?"

"We only show physical locations," he informed her. He repeated the address for a second time.

She scribbled the name Victor on the table as well.

She went out of the Santori home at a full run, not caring who might be watching. The car started effortlessly and her cellular phone engaged. The tires cried out as she shoved the accelerator to the floor. She dialed the number she knew by heart. She wouldn't request backup from a patrol car, wouldn't put the boy at risk until she knew what was going on. She needed to talk to *him*.

For once she was going to do something right.

The more Boldt looked at the possibilities, the more adrenaline filled him, the more convinced he was that Garman could very well be at the U-Stor-It. He increased his pace, removed his weapon from its holster, checked its load, and returned it to the leather.

It was that inspection of the gun that rattled him. With Liz's illness, the importance of his own health, for the sake of their children, suddenly loomed large. He understood clearly, for the first time, why Liz was urging him to drop the field work. How long had she known about the cancer? How long had she sensed it? Given that his children were home in bed, what was he doing on a deserted stretch of industrial roadway, alone, sneaking up on a storage facility that could be the laboratory of a serial arsonist? Seen in this light, his present situation seemed an act of foolishness. Shoswitz be damned, he thought. Regulations called for backup and Boldt wanted it.

He pulled into shadow, flipped open his phone, and turned it on. It was the graveyard shift; there was certain to be a number of detectives bored at their desks, counting the minutes. He wanted two pair of plainclothes backup in unmarked cars. He wanted them now—right this minute.

If he was going to do this, he was going to do it right.

He closed the phone, feeling better about his decision.

At that moment, a red Honda blurred past, slowed, and pulled to a stop a quarter mile past the U-Stor-It. Daphne had a red Honda, but for once he uncomfortably had to acknowledge the role of coincidence.

When a female form hurried from the car, Boldt, recognizing that particular female form even from a hundred yards away, realized his plans had changed again.

Backup be damned. What the hell was she up to?

Boldt began to run toward her.

68

BEN had cowered in his hiding place while the Face walked over to the fence, grabbed hold, and shook it. It rattled loudly, at which point he glanced around the facility, surveying it. He seemed to know.

He patrolled the place then like a soldier, walking along the first row of storage units, occasionally leaning an ear against one of the doors, passing not twenty feet from Ben, who held his breath, his one good eye fixed on the man in full concentration. The man with the strange face walked on by, his attention seemingly attached to the storage units. A few minutes later he rounded the far corner, and Ben guessed he was going to check each and every row of units—there had to be ten or fifteen of them total.

He didn't dare make his break for the fence with the Face out patrolling. It wasn't until several minutes later, when he heard the same sound of a garage door opening and shutting, that he decided the man had gone back inside his unit. Ben waited another several minutes, every pore of his skin alert for the slightest activity. Nothing. But then a feeling of dread came over him. What if the garage door opening and shutting for the second time was a trick? What if the man had done it to fool Ben into *thinking* it was safe to make for the fence? What if that was exactly what he wanted?

The possibility froze Ben where he was, about dead center between the two fences, both feeling miles away.

It was only as Daphne's red Honda pulled past out front— missed the place!—that Ben realized it was time to do something. He ran toward the fence, but only about fifteen feet before stopping, hiding once again in shadow.

Where was the army of cop cars like in the movies? he wondered. The helicopters? One car? Daphne, alone? Had 911 screwed up the message?

And what if the man with the Face was in fact in hiding, waiting for whoever had climbed the fence? What if he saw *her*? What then?

There was only one thing to do, Ben decided: He had to make his move right away, before the whole thing came apart.

He couldn't see her car, but he cut to his right, away from the gate, as far away from his last sighting of the man as possible, around the office, past an unmarked building, around that corner—and straight into a pair of arms that gripped him like a vise. Daphne! he thought. But then his brain quickly adjusted to the strength of those arms, and he looked up into the white, shiny skin and hollow eyes of that face and his world began to spin. A deep blue haze crept in from the edges of his vision, like the end of a cartoon where the screen collapses to a center speck of light. For Ben, the end of that light, the beginning of total darkness, came as a dry wind issued from the throat of the man who held him. "You?" the voice gasped, as if he too had seen a ghost.

69

WHEN Boldt crept up on Daphne, he scared her half to death. She lifted off the ground from a squatting position ten yards away from the southeast corner of the storage lot where she hid behind a beat-up U-Haul trailer with two flat tires.

It took her a full fifteen seconds to recover. She hissed at him angrily, "I might have shot you."

Boldt disregarded the comment, his attention fixed on the facility. "I didn't use the radio," he said, "so you didn't pick it up there."

"It was Ben," she explained, solving the puzzle for him. She told him about the call from Emergency Services.

"He's *in* there?" Boldt asked incredulously. The kid seemed to have a knack for trouble, especially where Jonny Garman was concerned.

She pointed off into the darkness. It took Boldt a moment to spot the bicycle on its side, tucked under another decrepit trailer. He had seen that same bicycle in the shed behind Santori's. "The metal on the wheels is still warm," she said, reminding him that she had a lot of cop in her to go along with the psychologist. "He claimed in his message that he had followed Garman here," she whispered angrily. She seemed ready to cry. Boldt knew that feeling.

"In there?"

"Nine-one-one ID'd the call location as a pay phone at this address." After a long silence, she said, "Tell me he didn't do this, Lou. Why would he do this?"

Boldt, staying focused, tried to follow the logic. "If he had come back out, he'd have taken his bike, which means he's in there somewhere. And if Garman is in there too, who knows what we've got going?"

"I'm going in."

"Ridiculous," Boldt snapped. The look she gave him could have stopped traffic. "Come on! This is textbook. We don't make the pick on his turf. We wait him out, put up a net, take him on neutral ground."

"Who cares about *him*?" Daphne asked. "I'm talking about Ben. Are we going to wait for Ben too? Is that in the textbook? He's in there—either playing hero or afraid to come back out. Either way, for his safety, we have to get him out of there. And right now! Anything less than that and we invite a hostage situation. Anything less than that and Phil Shoswitz will *never* glue this back together."

"This isn't about Shoswitz."

"With the mind-set of a Jonny Garman, we do not want a hostage situation, believe me." She added spitefully, "And I will not have Ben at the mercy of an ERT rescue attempt."

The battle lines had long since been drawn between the department's psychologist, who believed in talking through an incident, and ERT, which believed in quick, efficient strikes. There were marks on both sides of the scoreboard; each solution had its place. But Daphne Matthews was outspoken and one-sided on the issue. Boldt was not about to debate it with her.

She worked his paternal emotions, like a potter with clay. "If that were Miles in there, what would you do?"

"I've called for backup," he informed her, dodging the question.

"How many?" she asked, panic seizing her.

Boldt told her. "Two pair. Unmarked. No ERT."

That seemed to both relieve her and disgust her at the same time. He saw her in a different light. Was she too far invested in Ben to remain even partially objective? He feared she was, which left him alone in his decision making. As if to confirm this, she admitted, "I don't know that I can make it over that fence." She paused, studying it. "But I'm going to try."

He grabbed her by the arm; she looked down at his handhold with disdain. "If it were Miles, I'd go in," he answered honestly. "I wouldn't let ERT within a mile of the place."

A faint smile found her eyes.

"But I'd do it smart," he continued. "And I'd have as much information available as possible."

"Yes, you would," she agreed, knowing him well.

"We don't know for a fact that the boy is in there. We certainly cannot confirm that Garman is. What Ben reported seeing and what actually is the case are two different animals. He doesn't know Garman."

"He saw him at the airport," Daphne corrected. "He *does* know him. Of all of us, he's the only one who does."

Boldt felt the wind knocked out of him. He had forgotten that connection, and the reminder of it blanked his mind momentarily. He tried to regain his thoughts. Either you stayed ahead of Daphne Matthews, or you played catch-up from then on.

"If you're suggesting reconnaissance," she encouraged, "I'm in."

"He's under the name Babcock at a rooming house over on Washington," he informed her, stunning her with the news. "If he used the same name here, it would be in the files in the office. We'd know which unit is his."

"Forget him," she repeated. "We get Ben out, then we worry about him."

"No way," he said.

"You know I'm sorry to do this," she said, turning her head slowly to face him. Their eyes met. And then, all at once, she shoved him—struck him with open palms, sending him off-balance from where he crouched and skidding back through the loose stone and gravel.

She took several long strides with that athletic body of hers and leapt up onto the chain link like a cat, vaulting it as if it were a regular exercise. Both legs cleared the top and she was on the other side and down with a minimum of effort. She did not look back, did not give him a chance to wield power over her.

She stole into the dark and was gone.

70

"I never had me a little brother," Garman said to Ben, as the boy came awake from unconsciousness. "I'm Jonny."

Ben found himself on the storage unit's cement floor, sitting in a corner away from the large garage door. His wrists were stuck together, as were his sneakers, sole to sole. He tried to speak, but his lips wouldn't open.

"Super Glue," Jonny explained. "I only had a little tape left, and I needed it. Now don't go fighting it," he said, as Ben struggled with his wrists. "At best you'll only tear your skin open, and I'll have to reglue you. You'll make a mess and it'll hurt. Just sit still."

The sweatshirt hood was off his head and hanging down his back. The skin on his face looked strange, like smooth white clay, but his ear looked like a big scab, yellow and rust colored, like puss and dried blood. It took Ben a few minutes to adjust to not breathing out of his mouth. Every time he became too scared, he got dizzy. Things would go soft and fuzzy, but when he awakened everything was clear again. He realized it all had to with his breathing. If he kept himself from getting scared, he'd stay awake.

Jonny was soldering something, using what to Ben looked like an oversized butane lighter. There was a Coleman lantern going, making a loud hissing sound and throwing off a tremendous amount of bright light.

"I ain't going to hurt you," Jonny said, reading Ben's thoughts accurately. "You shouldn'ta followed me here, you know that."

Ben nodded, as terrified as he'd ever been. It looked like the guy was making some kind of bomb, all those wires coming out of a piece of plastic tubing.

"But what's done is done." He raised a finger to Ben. "You fucked with my head back there at the tree. I thought you was dead."

He didn't sound like other grown-ups to Ben. Besides having a voice that was like a cat's hiss, he seemed more like a kid than an adult—someone who hadn't aged, like a movie where the kid is trapped in an older guy's body.

"Why the hell did you follow me?" he asked the boy who couldn't answer. "My face?"

Ben shook his head violently no. He dared to look into those eyes and felt light-headed again. He was going to passout. He heard the words "You can admit it" but only faintly. "And now, 'cause of you, I gotta pack up and leave. Leave you here. Never killed no kid." Ben's world went woozy—he hyperventilated—and he lost several minutes to the blue darkness.

When Ben came to again, Jonny was through soldering. Ben endeavored to keep his eyes off the man, because every time he looked at him he felt queasy. The area was occupied nearly entirely by a large pickup truck, with just enough room left over for a pair of oil drums marked USAF, lots of black plastic pipe, and a green metal trunk unlocked but not open. Jonny sat on the trunk, working off the truck's tailgate. There was a car jack and a pair of beach chairs stacked along the wall and a couple of cardboard boxes that were taped shut. There were boxes from Radio Shack that had once contained radio-controlled four-wheel-drive cars.

There were only two pictures in the place, a postcard of Jesus and a slightly larger image of a woman being burned at the stake.

Ben thought about God. He believed in him. He prayed to him. He made all sorts of promises about how he would live his life, how he would obey Emily or whoever ended up taking care of him; he would even spend the night at the detention center, if that were asked of him. He promised not to run away. To listen. To learn respect. The prayers gushed out of him.

In his mind's eye, he saw Daphne's red car driving past. He wanted so badly to believe it had been her car. Although he didn't know exactly how long he had been held captive, he guessed at least ten minutes, maybe more. His hope of being rescued waned, and he returned to his prayers.

The man who called himself Jonny spoke to the wall but intended it for Ben. "You and I aren't so different." A half minute later he added, "I ain't never had no little brother."

Ben hung his head to the floor. He didn't want the man to see he was crying.

71

BOLDT climbed the chain link fence quickly, tearing his coat sleeve and slicing his right forearm on the sharp spikes at the top, but he was up and over more easily than he had expected. He landed at a run, pursuing Daphne as if she were the suspect.

She had crossed over an extremely rare threshold for her: operating from her emotions rather than her intellect. It was one of the most dangerous transitions a cop can make, and Boldt had no choice but to stop her before she got herself, or the boy, or all three of them into what Boldt thought of as the "red zone"—that place from which there was no out other than confrontation or violence.

She hesitated at the pay phone, as if it might answer some questions for her, sensed Boldt's approach, and took off around the side of the office building.

Boldt took his weapon in both hands, training it down to his side, an automatic response born of some sixth sense that had responded to an internal alarm. He didn't believe in such responses, but he trusted them when they happened.

Daphne was athletic, a daily runner, and she was fast. If she had chosen to outrun Boldt it would have been no contest, but her focus was on locating Ben, and she moved slowly alongside the building, checking the shadows. Boldt bumped her from behind and whispered, "Move, move!" as he herded her to the end of the building, his attention spread in too many directions: behind him, along the storage units, along the wall of the building. He urged her on with his left shoulder, stopped her, peered around the corner of the building, and then indicated her on ahead. She glared at him but allowed him to guide her. He drove them into a recessed brick corner that felt protected and hissed, "Stupid move."

"He's here, goddammit. You may not believe that but—"

"We'll find him," he said, to reassure her. "If he's here, we'll find him. He's a *kid*. A curious kid, at that. Precocious. Our job is to keep him—and us—out of trouble. Not *make* trouble." He scanned the area as he spoke, rarely meeting her eyes. It didn't escape him that he was suddenly playing the psychologist and she the renegade cop. "We'll check the rows, but we'll do it organized, not running around on our own. If we work together, side-to-side, we can net him. Listen, it's like a giant supermarket, these rows. We'll miss him if we don't do it in an organized way." She looked a little dazed. "You hearing me?"

She nodded faintly.

"We both want him to be okay," he reminded her. He was hoping that by pinning her here he might buy time for the arrival of the backup, but to utilize them would either mean returning to the radio in his car or spending time on the cellular phone relaying messages—and Daphne's patience was running low. He could sense her about to make another break. He felt rushed, hurried; he knew that was when he made mistakes. He had to get her involved, engaged in a plan, focused. If she went running through the facility she might get them all killed. He decided to hit her with the truth. "May I remind you," he said, still scanning the immediate area, "that Garman has an undetermined amount of this rocket fuel? Just consider that for a moment." He stared at her.

"Point taken."

"An undetermined amount."

"I get it, *Sergeant*. Let's get on with it."

"Okay," Boldt said, forming a plan, wishing for the backup. "Right up against this first row. Weapons at the ready. We walk quietly—super quietly—slowly. Patiently. We hold position at the end of the first row. Round the corner, cover the side. Round the next corner and make eye contact. We hold to the wall and meet in the center. We cross to the next row and start it all over. If we need cover, we press ourselves into the recesses at the garage doors. We walk quietly because we're listening—for voices, for movement, a radio. We're interested in light and sound. Those are our signals." He paused, hoping some of it might sink in. "If this is his lab, his storage area—and we have every reason to believe it is—it's a second home to this creep. It's familiar turf for him." He released the gun with one hand and tapped his forehead. "Keep that right in here: his turf. Expect the unexpected. We watch for things like trip wires, sensors maybe, who knows? He has surprised us too many times to count. He prides himself on it. No surprises. Expect anything. Everything."

He had talked long enough to calm her. Or perhaps his words had sunk in. Her eyes trained on his, she thanked him and followed it with an apology. Then she said desperately, "I just want to find him."

He nodded. There were a dozen things he wanted to tell her—about Liz, about the change in his thoughts on field work, about feeling as if he were tempting fate. But the look on her face wouldn't allow him to back out of his plans, and he realized that she loved little Ben Santori.

If that were Miles in there. . . . The words rang inside his head like bells.

"Okay?" she asked.

"Okay," he answered. But it didn't feel okay. As they crossed the blacktop toward the first row of units, an increasing sense of foreboding filled him. Daphne's intuition was right; Ben was in trouble.

• • •

They moved methodically through the rows of storage units, and much to Boldt's surprise Daphne stayed in lockstep, following Boldt's plan to the letter. The sound of traffic on I-5 was oppressive, interrupted only by the drumming in Boldt's ears. He rolled his shoes across the blacktop to avoid being heard, keeping himself alert for the unexpected.

Beyond the third set of blue units, all doubts concerning Garman's whereabouts were suspended. A wash of pale light illuminated the fronts of the units that Boldt and Daphne faced; the source of that light, the unit immediately to Boldt's right. At the far end of the row of units, Daphne's face appeared. Boldt signaled her. Together, they moved toward each other, ducking from one doorway to the next, moving toward the center of the row. Less than a minute later, they stood on opposite sides of the garage door that was leaking light, ten feet apart. Boldt's heart pounded heavily in his chest and clouded his hearing as he tried to discern the sounds coming from within. It sounded like a fan. Like a cat hissing, or water just beginning to boil. But it was none of these, he realized; it was a gas lantern and the voice of Jonny Garman, coming from a throat burned in a fire in North Dakota, a voice trying to make itself heard.

When Boldt signaled Daphne to withdraw from their positions by Garman's storage unit, her first temptation was to disobey— allow him to take a few steps back and then throw open the garage door and face whatever Garman had to offer. But intelligence, training, and discipline won out, leaving her feeling a victim of her profession.

Step by step they pulled away from the unit, back to the far corners, and finally retreated until they caught sight of each other once again in the second aisle. Boldt motioned toward the office, where they met outside a few minutes later.

"We're going to assume it's Garman"—Boldt led off at a fraction of a whisper—"and work from there. If Gaynes or LaMoia spot a suspect, we'll reconsider, but buying this as coincidence is too great a stretch for me. Garman came here to prepare—"

"For Martinelli," Daphne informed him, mouthing her words more than speaking them. She explained to him her discovery of the backpack with the Santori address and how, in her opinion, the bait of a woman so close in appearance to his mother had overridden the other arson he had planned. She admitted reluctantly, "I have no idea how Ben became involved." And those were the last words she could manage, her emotions winning out.

"If Ben isn't in hiding—"

"—then he's inside that storage unit," she completed for him. "Garman won't harm a child—especially not a young boy. He won't even use him as a hostage, Lou. He won't risk the boy's life."

"We don't know that."

"Yes, we do," she contradicted. "We know the great lengths he went to in order to avoid harming the offspring of his victims. He stayed in those trees to make sure the young boys were out of the house. He knows Ben's face, Lou, it's the face he saw on the sun visor. That will have an effect on him; he will empathize with Ben. He will think he's doing him a favor by burning up his mother, which is exactly what he has planned. He will not harm him in any way. If anything," she suggested, "Ben's presence *reduces* the chance that Garman will resist arrest."

"No, no, no," Boldt objected, sensing where she intended to take that line of argument. "We are not confronting the suspect."

"Of course we are!" she protested. "What we are *not* going to do is turn this thing into a circus. He's an introvert, a paranoid, a man afraid of society because of society's reaction to his disfigurement. He's angry. He blames his father. You surround a person like that with flashing lights, bullhorns and armed men in uniforms and he'll lose it. Reality will blur for him. Who knows what he'll do?"

"Daffy—"

"We confront him, Lou. You and I. We stand outside that door, our weapons put away, and we talk to him. We reinforce that he doesn't want the boy hurt and that he doesn't want to contend with an army of trigger-happy cops. We make, and we keep, a promise to bring him in quietly. He's not a headline hunter, Lou, not this one. This is a family matter—between him and his father, him and his mother. We can resolve this right here, you and I."

"And if you're wrong, the place we're standing will look like ground zero by tomorrow morning."

"I'm not wrong," she stated bluntly. "Work with me here, Lou. There's a right way and a wrong way to a Jonny Garman. You know that's right; you know I know what I'm talking about. You bring the circus, and he'll join it. You bring a show, and he'll outdo your show. We offer him a way out, and he'll take it."

Boldt shook his head no. She wanted to take him by the shoulders and shake him. He looked exhausted. She convinced herself he wasn't thinking clearly. He said, "We wait him out. It's the long route to discovery, admittedly, but it's the safe way. We may wait only to find out that it's not Garman, but we will not corner him in a place where he may be storing that kind of firepower."

She was ready to interrupt, vehemently, but she held her tongue, sensing his own difficulties. Perhaps he wanted to do exactly what she had just described. Perhaps it was better to allow him to talk his way through it and reach the same conclusion.

"If he comes out on his bicycle, without a backpack, say, we pick him. If he comes out with the boy, we watch but we don't pick. If his father's truck is in the storage area—and I'm betting it is—we've got big problems, because he's going to leave here some-time before tomorrow morning, ready to do a little window wash-ing and set up the Santori house, believing it to be Martinelli's. Once he's in that truck, he's too dangerous—"

"You see," she objected, "we should do it now." She heard him explaining their situation and knew he was right, but the ob-jection came out anyway.

"No, the point is *not* to do it now," Boldt countered, "but to find a way to separate Garman from his truck, if that's what it comes to. We're going to need a way to distance him from his mate-rials. Once we accomplish that, we pick him and it's over." He added, "And it isn't a matter of simply waiting for him to do his thing at Santori's, because he'll have the accelerant with him, on his person. We cannot move on him until he's away from that fuel—with or without Ben involved."

It was no place to argue, standing in shadow less than a hundred yards from the assumed location of their suspect. Nonetheless, she heard herself say, "You won't get him away from that truck."

"No," Boldt agreed—too quickly, she thought, sensing she had been tricked. "That's *your* job. You know him so well," he suggested, "you figure it out." He added, "And don't move from this spot. I'm going to check on the bicycle and see about the backup."

Her loyalty to Lou Boldt, her love for him, was far too great. She would not willfully corrupt the investigation. She nodded, though with great disappointment written on her face.

"Promise me, Daffy. Nothing stupid."

"We'll wait," she agreed reluctantly. "But you won't get him out of that truck. We'd be smarter to do this now." Her eyes pleaded with him. *Listen to me*, they said.

But Boldt walked off into the darkness.

By the time the inspiration came to her, she had settled down onto the blacktop, knees into her chest, hidden in shadow. Boldt walked right past her, and she could feel him thinking that she had gone ahead without him.

"Right here," she whispered.

He pulled her up by the hand and led her around to the far side of the office, where they could talk a little more normally.

"Bike is still there," he announced gravely. "We have two north," he said, pointing, "and one south—five of us on the ground. I put Richardson up high," he said, indicating the interstate, a good distance away, "with a set of glasses. He's got a clean line of sight on the storage unit. He'll page me if there's any activity."

"He's there for the night," she speculated.

"Yes," Boldt agreed. "Until morning." He wanted to encourage her. "The car wash, the baiting worked. You saved a life last night."

"And put another at risk," she said, meaning Ben.

"If we shoot out a tire," he said, speculating, "or somehow cause a flat, he'd be forced out of the truck. But if we blow it, or if the truck goes off the road or into traffic, we could cause a disaster. If he picks up on what we're up to, who knows what he might do? Surrender? I don't see that."

"Not once he's out there," she said, indicating beyond the fence. "The time to do this is now, Lou." She wanted one last try at him, for she believed herself right; if coaxed properly, Garman would give it up. "The wild card is his father," she explained. "We bring Steven Garman down here and him in front of that storage unit. The son is doing this to prove something to his father. They *both* hate the mother. Jonny Garman never for a moment sided with his mother. If we believe the husband, and we have no reason not to, she had sex with strangers on a regular basis, sometimes in the presence of her son, possibly even in the company of her son. Jonny Garman is trying to one-up his father, show he can do what the father failed to do—kill the mother. Burn her to death. If we get Steven Garman down here, Jonny will walk right out of that storage unit."

"The father is an arrested felon," Boldt reminded her. "And no one but the bomb squad is going anywhere near that storage unit until Jonny Garman is a mile away from here. This isn't productive," he said. "We're supposed to be focusing on how the hell to get him out of that truck."

She felt a confusion of emotions—knowing she had the answer and knowing Boldt, for whatever reasons, felt obligated to lessen the risk for all involved. She couldn't blame him; she wanted to do the same thing.

"We need to focus on Garman and that truck, Daffy. You asked what I would do if it were Miles. What I know is, if Miles came out of that storage area inside a truck containing that kind of volatile fuel, I would want Jonny Garman as far away from the truck as possible.''

In the silence a corporate jet came in low and loud overhead. It felt to her as if the ground actually shook. She thought again about raiding the storage unit, how they could use the cover of a jet landing to make their move. But then she considered the idea of Ben caught in an inferno of purple flame rising thousands of feet in the air. If it was her plan, and it failed, could she ever find her way out? In that same instant, she wondered how Boldt could live with the pressure of such decisions. She had an immediate out: She could leave it up to him.

"I know how to get him out of the truck," she announced proudly, surrendering to his plan, prepared to share her moment of inspiration with him.

His face filled both with excitement and doubt. He too had given it much thought but had come up blank.

She answered his expression with a single word. "Fire," she said. Then, explaining quickly, "The one thing irresistible to Jonny Garman is a fire."

72

IN the hours between 2 A.M. and 5 A.M., sixty-seven on-call patrol officers from seven policing districts, and twenty-four regular-duty firemen, along with four Marshal Fives, organized into an instant task force whose sole mission was to burn an abandoned machine shop to the ground and divert morning traffic south of the International District so that it was required to pass within a city block of the fire. This involved a staged vehicular accident, a road construction crew, and six dozen pink Day-Glo traffic cones.

The building was one of seventeen on various lists for demolition, some of which had been offered to the city—in lieu of tax breaks—for fire training.

For Lieutenant Phil Shoswitz, it was a bout of heartburn and temper tantrums. From the moment Boldt proposed the operation, the lieutenant objected, claiming Boldt had yet to confirm the identity of the individual inside the storage unit. This hurdle was overcome at 2:20 A.M. when Boldt, under advisement of the facility's manager, entered the U-Stor-It offices, disabled the security device, and confirmed not only that Jonny Babcock—aka Garman—was a paying customer but that he rented unit 311, the very same unit from which the light had come and the voice had been heard. That same unit, 311, went dark at 1:15 A.M., but the door never opened and no one ever left the property. At that point in time, seven different sets of eyes and a video camera using infrared night-sight technology had all aspects of unit 3, as the row was called, under surveillance.

Boldt never experienced a moment of feeling tired. To the contrary, he had to slow himself down on several different occasions, simply to be understood. The nearly one hundred participants engaged in Operation Inferno were his orchestra; Lou Boldt was the conductor. Neil Bahan and Sidney Fidler were his first chairs, for only Bahan and Fidler understood both the fire and the police sides of the planned incident. Shoswitz, Bahan, Fidler, two Marshal Fives, an ATF man named Byrant, and three FBI special agents, along with two dispatchers, worked out of the conference room in the Seattle Field Office of the FBI, whose communications capabilities dwarfed any resources owned or operated by the city. Dozens of radios and cellular phones were all tied into a central dispatch, coordinated by the team assembled there.

The Santori house was under full surveillance. A part of ERT was in position to move on Garman if the ruse failed. With that considered a last resort, the emphasis of the police side of the operation was on field coverage. By 6 A.M., there were police officers and federal agents in place posing as telephone linemen, street people, construction workers, garbage collectors, electric company meter readers, a variety of delivery men, and assorted other occupations. Every major intersection between Airport Way and the Santori house had some degree of representation by armed law enforcement. It was a virtual gauntlet—with Jonny Garman its sole target.

At 8 A.M. the U-Stor-It office was opened by an FBI special agent, who took his place behind the desk inside and went about his work as if it had been part of his daily routine for years. At 8:12 A.M., the first report of activity at storage unit 311 was verified by three separate scouts and delivered to Boldt over a radio earpiece. At 8:15 A.M. a light rain began to fall. Lou Boldt felt it a bad omen.

To have driven Airport Way on that morning would have seemed no different than any other, except for a few detours that required different routes. But in Seattle, as in any major city, construction was a daily part of urban life and traffic accidents were a regular part of morning delays. Heading north into the city was not discernibly different from any other day: hurry up and wait.

A white pickup truck bearing Nevada plates pulled out of unit 311 and stopped. A man with a disfigured face, wearing a sweatshirt hood drawn tightly around his head and a pair of sunglasses, was seen climbing out of the truck and returning to shut and lock the unit's door. For approximately fifteen seconds, Jonny Garman was nearby but out of his truck. This possibility—which some viewed as an opportunity—had been discussed in great depth among various factions of the operation's coordinators. In the end it was decided that he would be too close to both his lab and his truck to attempt any kind of pick at that location. A suggestion had been made to use a sharpshooter on Garman, but with the boy's life at stake it had been quickly dismissed. The suspect climbed back behind the wheel of his truck and drove out through the facility's automatic gate, joining the slow-moving traffic, hindered by detours more than a mile ahead.

"This is Birdman," reported a voice in Boldt's ear. The helicopter was owned by KING radio and used for traffic reports. On that day, it was being used for surveillance. "Looking down through the windshield, I'm not showing a hostage. Contents in the back of the truck don't look as promising. There appear to be two fifty-five-gallon drums, a variety of boxes, and assorted other items. No tarp in place."

Fifty-five-gallon drums, Boldt thought. Enough to burn a hotel or a shopping mall to the ground. Either Garman had packed up shop or was planning an enormous hit. A flurry of radio traffic passed along the Birdman's observations. Traffic moved slowly, Garman's position reported every fifteen to thirty seconds.

At the Santori house, Marianne Martinelli prepared to make herself seen leaving the home, if it came to that.

At the abandoned machine shop, three ladder trucks and two pumpers stood by, lights flashing, hoses ready. Inside, last-minute preparations were made as the incendiary charges and detonator wire were checked and double-checked.

Dressed in coveralls, Lou Boldt threw a pickax into a dirt hole in a vacant lot across from the machine shop. The three men around him, including Detective John LaMoia, also wore coveralls but were working shovels. Boldt didn't understand why he always got the pickax.

"Dig," Boldt said. "He's a half mile and closing."

LaMoia jumped on the shovel and dug into the wet earth. Boldt's hands were wet on the pickax's handle, but it had little to do with the rain. His weapon weighed down the coverall's right pocket, within easy reach.

"Hey," LaMoia said, sensing everyone's sudden tension. "This is a damn good-looking hole. Listen, if we fuck this up, Sarge, maybe we've found ourselves a second occupation."

"Gravediggers?" one of the shovelers asked.

The three other workers stared this man down.

"Sorry," he said.

73

WHEN Garman's vehicle crossed an imaginary line one mile from the U-Stor-It facility, two members of the SPD bomb squad moved into place, accompanied by Tech Service Officer Danny Kotch and psychologist Daphne Matthews.

Kotch worked flawlessly with the fiber-optic camera, Daphne immediately alongside. The thin black wire was fed under the gap in the garage door and the first images of the unit's contents were revealed.

Daphne leaned onto Danny Kotch in order to get a good look at the tiny screen. She gasped aloud and began to cry as she saw Ben tucked into a ball in the corner, a single piece of rope binding him. There was no gag in place, and she wondered why he hadn't called out. The screen was too small to show his eyes.

Let him be alive! she prayed.

The space was empty except for some black PVC pipe, a pair of beach chairs, and some cardboard boxes from Radio Shack.

Attempting to sound professional, Daphne sniffed back her tears and said to the bomb squad team. "He's inside. We want him out as quickly as possible."

"With a torch like this, we're going to move slowly," the man wearing the thick vest informed her.

She had been warned of this already, but she found the thought of even a minute longer too long.

"Ben, can you hear me?" she shouted.

The little head rocked up, and a single eye angled to look for her. She felt herself burst into tears. Through a blur she told the others, "Shit, hurry it up, would you? I want him out of there."

A plainclothes detective ran toward them, a radio held in his hand. He shouted, "Matthews, Garman is a half mile and closing. They need you for the count." He met up with her and passed her the radio.

The decision of when to light the house was hers and hers alone. Boldt had insisted that, of all those involved, she understood the dynamics of the psychology best of all and the call should be hers. This had offended Bahan and others, especially several of the Marshal Fives.

She grabbed the radio, repeating what she had told Boldt several times. "Is the suspect within full visual range of the structure?" she inquired.

"A half mile and closing," a deep male voice informed her.

"But can he see the building?" she repeated, amazed how so simple a question could become so complicated an issue.

"No. He wouldn't have a visual at this time."

Speak English, she wanted to shout.

"When he's got the building fully in sight," she informed the dispatcher, "torch it. But he has to see it ignite if he's to get off on it. He has to *participate* in it. If he sees it go off, he'll stay to see them fight it. Do you copy?"

"Another hundred yards," the dispatcher told her. "I'm told he'll have full visual in another hundred yards."

"Let's go with full visual, shall we?" she said sarcastically.

Releasing the radio's button, she told the bomb team, "Hurry it up. I want the boy out of there. And I want it now."

74

"**WE'RE** thirty seconds to ignition," Boldt heard in his earpiece. "Suspect is a quarter mile off and closing." With each detour, each intersection, Garman's position had been carefully reported, and it was deeper and deeper in Inferno's hastily crafted web.

"Thirty seconds," Boldt told the others.

"We been here before, Sarge," LaMoia reminded. "It's a grounder."

Boldt glared at his detective. It was no grounder.

The four cars in front of Garman's truck were all being driven by members of the operation, exactly as planned. The same had been intended for the traffic following the suspect's vehicle, but the first glitch in the operation occurred when a Chevrolet four door, driven by a white male in his late thirties, ran a red light and cut into the line immediately behind the pickup.

The ensuing radio traffic was heated.

CAR 1: *Dispatch, we have a visitor. Some asshole just cut into our line.*
SHOSWITZ: *We need him out of there. Now.*
DISPATCH: *All vehicles maintain position. Let us jaw on this a moment.*

Less than twenty seconds later, the dispatcher came back on line.

DISPATCH: *Okay. It's a bump-and-run by you, One. Copy that?*
CAR 1: *Bump-and-run.*
DISPATCH: *Make it a good collision, one he has to stop for. Williamson,
     we want you to assist at the moment of impact. Get the civilian to
     safe cover. Copy?*

All parties copied correctly.

    This man's safety was now the joint assignment of the driver
immediately behind him and the detective in the work crew to
Boldt's right. His existence was a sticking point of the operation.
They could not knowingly place a civilian at such close risk. The
decision was for a synchronized, coordinated effort. The plainclothes undercover officer driving behind the Chevy was to ram
the car at the moment of the fire's ignition. He would then rush
this driver, apologizing over the accident, as one of the workmen
went over as a "witness" to the fender bender. Exactly how it
would play out was anybody's guess. Shoswitz had clearly made
the decision not to abort the operation over this one civilian. They
would do their best.

    "Twenty seconds," the dispatcher announced.

    Boldt relayed the timing. He glanced up. The white pickup
was advancing slowly in the bumper-to-bumper traffic. Into his
radio, Boldt announced visual contact.

    LaMoia, not turning around to look, not stopping his shovel-
ing, repeated, "It's a grounder, Sarge. If he moves back toward the
truck, we're gonna drop him. And as far as him getting out of that
truck? My money's on Matthews any day. Ain't a head she can't
shrink."

    "Ten seconds," Boldt echoed. He set down the pickax.
"Five . . ."

Three miles south of Garman's pickup truck, a bolt cutter on the
end of a remote-controlled robot that looked like a lawnmower
severed the padlock under the direction of the bomb squad ex-

perts. The remote claw removed the lock, dropped it to the side, and exerted an upward pressure on the garage door.

Despite the reassurances that the unit was not wired, a collective breath was held as the robot lifted the door.

It came open without an explosion.

A fully padded man rolled under the door's opening and inside the storage unit. Against all rules, Daphne Matthews broke under the restraining tape and ran at full sprint toward the unit, a chorus of protest arising behind her. She rolled under the partially open door right behind the bomb man.

At the first sound of a series of dull explosions to the north, she pulled Ben into her arms and cradled him. She tasted his tears on her lips and spilled her own into his hair as the rope came off and the two were forcibly encouraged toward the opening of daylight by the man in the padded suit.

"Paramedics!" Daphne shouted, knowing an ambulance was waiting to the south.

The boy's lips were glued shut, and in all the excitement he seemed on the verge of passing out.

The charges went off in a string of five, sounding to Boldt like a burial salute. Six, counting the crunch of metal and glass as the Chevy was struck from behind.

The flames were instantaneous: huge blue and orange and black tongues licking up toward the sky. Whoever had set it knew his stuff, reminding Boldt how close a fireman was to an arsonist. If Jonny Garman had not been behind the wheel of that pickup truck, Boldt wouldn't have been able to take his eyes off the inferno. Everyone's attention was glued to the spectacle. It was as if, for a moment, the world blinked. The traffic braked and came to a stop in unison, any and all conversation ceased, and a giant plume of heat rose dramatically into the sky, a pillar of subterfuge.

The bright flash and subsequent roar was seen and heard over twenty-five miles away as the core fire reached over four hundred feet into the air and the resulting column of smoke over ten times that.

Boldt leaned on his pickax, his head angled toward the fire, his eyes on the driver of that pickup truck. *Stay and watch it,* Boldt encouraged the man silently. *Get out of the truck and watch.* The burning building was a block and a half away from traffic, but firemen were deliberately allowing pedestrians a closer look, having roped off a spot only half a block away from the event. Of the seven people standing there watching, all were from law enforcement.

Get out of the truck, Boldt encouraged for a second time, the dispatcher's voice listing Garman's location in that inhuman monotone. Daphne had been convinced that a spectacular fire would lure him out of his vehicle. "He can't resist a fire," she had said. Boldt was taking that to the bank, right or wrong.

As part of the ruse, one of the four cars preceding Garman pulled over and the driver climbed out and hurried toward the fire for a better look. *Lead by example,* Boldt thought. But to the sergeant's horror, Garman did not get out, electing to watch from the front seat of the truck. Worse, some cars farther behind launched into a protest chorus of honking. The driver of the Chevy was nursed back, away from the truck, but wasn't liking the manhandling.

The truck's wheels crept forward, as if Garman was to drive on.

Out of the truck! Boldt begged. He could feel the man drawn to the fire, but—concerned over his cargo and the job at hand, Martinelli—he seemed reluctant to stay and watch. Boldt pleaded silently for him to stay. The fire roared loudly as the first hose was trained onto it. Firemen, bearing hose, charged the structure.

Jonny Garman pulled his truck over to the shoulder. Traffic moved around the minor accident in the road and drivers rubbernecked as they passed the blaze. Boldt reached into the pocket of the coveralls and felt the grip of the gun's stock. He locked eyes with LaMoia and then across the street with the officer closest to Garman, a woman dressed as a street person.

As the truck's cab door came open, Boldt's world crawled into slow motion. His elation surfaced as a clarity of thought, vision, and hearing. Garman appeared to be as much interested in the firemen as the fire itself. Perhaps it had to do with memories of his father; perhaps it would never be explained.

One leg dangled out of the cab, followed by the other—he was getting out! Garman slipped down onto the pavement and, still holding the door, spun his head forward and back, assessing his situation. Worried about the parking? Boldt wondered. Feeling the presence of something wrong, something misplaced, something staged? The suspect pushed the cab door shut and walked toward the front of his truck, toward a better view of the burn and the action.

The street woman, near the back of the truck, took several long strides to close the distance, her hand slipping into her torn shopping bag. LaMoia, carrying his shovel—a worker fascinated by the fire—ran past Boldt, as if going for a better look.

Garman took no notice of any of them. His neck craned back and his head lifted up in that eerie slow motion, and he drank in the power of the fire. The magnificence. He stepped several feet in front of, and away from, the truck, just far enough to pick him.

In Boldt's ear, the drone of radio communication sounded slowed down as well, the words impossible to discern. The sergeant's hand gripped the pistol. The investigation came down to that moment: a truck loaded with volatile fuel and a disturbed, disfigured man just out of reach.

Garman, his synthetic face filled with a childish glee as he drank in the fire, rocked his head back and forth in joy, spraying rainwater off his sweatshirt like a dog shaking, glancing around him, attempting to share the thrill of that moment with others. The fire erupted into a shower of flame, spark, and ash, and Boldt thought he saw the suspect's body convulse; his awkward mouth seemed shaped into the curve of a laugh.

Garman's excited eyes swept briefly over the scene behind him, where, in a failed attempt to convince the driver of the Chevy to retreat, the undercover cop had resorted to dragging and shoving the bystander to the ground, anticipating a fire fight. In the process, the man's coat flew open and his gun, holster, and harness showed.

Garman's elation collapsed. Realization stung him. His eyes registered each of the fifteen people immediately in his vicinity, and he seemed to acknowledge that each and every one was law enforcement personnel. He was trapped. He identified LaMoia, and then the street woman, and backed up two steps toward the truck and the fuel it contained.

LaMoia changed direction too quickly, slipped, and fell. The street woman was blocked by the truck itself.

Boldt and his fellow construction worker, the closest officers to Garman, launched themselves in the direction of the suspect. Over the radio a sharpshooter announced a line-of-sight shot. Shoswitz's voice gave the order to take him.

The shot went straight through his shoulder and sprayed blood onto the truck, but Garman never felt it. He swung open the truck door, which absorbed the sniper's next two attempts, and jumped in behind the wheel.

Boldt's slow-motion world continued—all action, all sound misplaced.

The pickup truck lurched ahead, smashing into the car parked in front of it. LaMoia was back on his feet, and Garman looked just quickly enough to see him. Boldt was three strides from the truck, as Garman cut the wheel and, rather than turn into traffic, rather than face LaMoia, jumped the sidewalk. The driver's side window blew out behind the power of another sniper attempt. Boldt jumped for the truck, his toes catching the running board, his right hand losing hold of his gun as he clawed to hold on.

Garman shoved down the accelerator.

The pickup's back tires squealed over the curb, and Garman drove through the weedy vacant lot toward the street ahead and that raging fire.

Boldt did not know nor did he think that the fuel in the truck was enough to consume over three city blocks; he knew only that Miles and Sarah needed a father, now more than ever, and that their father was riding a pickup truck toward Hell.

Whether Garman was attempting an escape or a suicide didn't

matter, because the present course of the truck predetermined the destination.

The driver aimed his blank white face at the sergeant, brown eyes recessed behind sculpted plastic skin. For that instant, something exchanged between them, something sparked. Boldt reached for the gear shift, but Garman struck him hard. The sergeant shoved himself deeper into the window, pushing the driver across the seat. He reached for balance, and his arm pushed through and stuck inside the steering wheel, making it impossible to turn the wheel. They bounced through the lot, and Boldt's head struck the ceiling and the pickup altered its course just far enough to crash into one of the pumpers. It was like hitting a brick wall. They careened off to the right, heading once again for the burning building, and thumped over the swollen fire hoses. Boldt felt his arm snap. His head swam with the pain, and for an instant he slipped toward unconsciousness. He couldn't catch his breath.

They were headed straight for the missing front door of the burning building—straight for Hell.

I don't belong here, Boldt thought. It's not my time.

Garman clawed at Boldt's face, trying to drive him back out the window. His foot found the accelerator and the truck surged forward.

Overcoming the pain, Boldt heaved his broken arm farther through the wheel, his fingers fishing for the key. Garman's attention was fixed on the white bucket on the floor. It registered in Boldt that this bucket would have been the one to use in window washing; Garman's rocket fuel was inside it. The driver craned forward to reach for it, but Boldt grabbed the sweatshirt hood, pulled hard, and held him up short.

Those ears are painful, he remembered the nurse explaining.

Still clinging to the sweatshirt hood, Boldt swung the man's head on the end of the sweatshirt's tether, back and forth, Garman resisting, but Boldt with the better angle. The man's right ear pounded into the rear panel of glass. Garman cried out and grabbed for the pain.

Boldt heaved his broken left arm forward; his fingers groped and found the key and he twisted.

The engine died.

The truck grumbled to a stop, fifteen yards from the burning building's brick wall. The paint on the truck's hood bubbled and blistered from the heat. The inside of the truck was instantly an oven.

Fire hoses trained on Boldt and Garman, and the truck was swamped in hundreds of gallons of water with a force so powerful that Boldt was lifted up and driven further into the cab, fully atop Garman.

They were too close. The truck would catch fire and blow.

Boldt felt his feet and legs grabbed by strong hands. "Hold tight!" a voice called out. The pickup rocked onto two wheels and then slid sideways as a fire truck collided with the pickup and drove it away from the fire, the man holding Boldt never letting go.

The truck stopped, now twenty yards from the inferno. Loud voices shouted orders simultaneously in a language all their own— what sounded to Boldt like total chaos. Boldt felt Garman dragged out from underneath him. "Hold him!" Boldt shouted, his voice buried by the others. He realized that few of the firefighters would be aware of the ultimate purpose of the operation, would not know the threat Garman represented. "Hold on to him!"

As Garman hit the ground, dragged from the wreckage, he left his rescuers with only his zippered sweatshirt in their heavily gloved hands. He rolled twice. Boldt counted the revolutions and would later swear to Daphne that he and the suspect locked glances in the midst of one of them. He would swear there was nothing in those eyes: no remorse, no fear, no life.

Jonny Garman came to his feet, and faced a team of police rushing toward him. Boldt recalled Daphne's comments about an asocial's reaction to crowds.

"No!" Boldt shouted at the group of cops, closing at a run.

Garman looked once at that wall of armed men rushing him, glanced once toward Boldt, turned, and ran at a full sprint into the burning building. Already engulfed in flames before his screams ripped toward the sky, he disappeared into the pulsing orange light.

75

APPROPRIATELY, it was
raining. Daphne was glad for that because it would disguise her
tears.

"You don't need to come in or anything," Ben said, meaning
he didn't want her to.

"I'll just see you to the door," she said.

"Whatever."

It hurt her to see him so excited to be reunited with Emily.
How she wished he might change his mind at the last minute and
beg to find a way to stay with her. But the finest things pass
through your life, she thought, like migratory birds. They do not
light. They leave you with a glimpse of beauty and pass on.

This was not the death of a friendship, it was the beginning of
a young man's life.

Reading her thoughts, as they sat in the dull glare of a red
light, the windshield wipers working like a metronome, he said,
"It's not like we won't see each other."

She didn't answer. Perhaps they *would* see each other from
time to time; she wanted to support him, to be there for him. She

reached out and took his hand in hers. It was the first time she had dared to do so, but not from lack of want. Of need. Her heart wanted to burst. Her throat was tight. His small fist was hot. Her hand was cold. He looked down at their hands, and when the light changed, she pulled away from him and drove on, her moist eyes focused on the moist road, but she felt his intense gaze fixed upon her. Perhaps he had felt it too. Perhaps.

"You know, Ben, sometimes a person comes along in your life, a special person, and without knowing it they show you something about yourself, they point you in a particular direction that maybe you didn't see until they came along. You know?" She was talking like him now. She could hardly believe it. A smile sprang onto her face.

"I guess so," he answered.

"What I mean to say is, you are that person for me. You helped me in ways I can't explain, I guess, but profoundly and forever. Good stuff," she said.

"That guy Owen. Is that what you mean? Look out, it's yellow."

She slowed the car, realizing she had better pay closer attention. "Thanks."

"You mean him?" he asked, not letting it go the way an adult might have.

"I mean you," she answered.

"I don't see what I did, except screw everything up."

"Watch the language."

"It's the next right."

"I know."

He bit away a sly grin. "You're okay, D. I know you did a ton of stuff for me—to make this happen with Emily and all. You and Susan. And, well, it's really cool, is all. You know?"

"If you ever, *ever*, need *anything*, you had better call me," she said, trying to avoid crying, which only made it worse.

"We'll see each other," he repeated, a little more desperately. She wanted to believe that only then was their separation registering in him.

"You have a lot of love in you, Ben. Don't be afraid to share it." The rain did her no good, for she hadn't held off the tears until outside as she had hoped to do. She finally dared look at him, and he was crying too, and selfishly this made her happy.

She pulled to a stop in front of the purple house.

"I don't normally do this," he said. He reached into the back seat for his backpack and books. "You and Susan are going to help me move, right?"

"Right."

"So we'll see each other."

"Maybe I won't get out," she said, seeing Emily open the door and wave. She couldn't stop the tears now. She abandoned any effort to do so. The wipers sounded peaceful, their rhythm soothing. She was heading back to the houseboat alone to listen to the rain fall on the dock and beat on her roof. To a log fire and a glass of wine and more tears. It was good. It was what she wanted.

"Well," he said. He leaned forward and kissed her on the cheek, his excitement over seeing Emily already winning out.

Daphne nodded and sniffled, unable at first to get any words out. He popped open the door and jumped out.

"Ben!" she called out sharply, sounding like a wire breaking.

Out in the rain, Ben leaned his head down and into the car.

"Tell her to paint the damn house," Daphne said. She found a smile at last.

"Watch your language," Ben replied. But his expression said it all. She would remember that look for a lifetime. Cherish it.

He pushed the door shut and hurried off through the falling rain.

76

THE Dahlia Lounge was crowded. Boldt and Liz owned two stools up by the receptionist as they waited for a table. She was drinking fruit juice. Boldt, uncharacteristically, was drinking straight vodka. She looked like a million dollars. His cast itched.

"He had moved all his stuff out, probably because if the kid talked we could locate him, and he had no desire to hurt the kid."

"It was two weeks ago." She studied him. For two weeks he had lain awake petting her hair as she slept. For two weeks they had said things they had always wanted to say, shared things they had always wanted to share. They had talked about why it took something so severe to bring two people to such rich honesty. He believed it unfair. She believed it a blessing.

The pain was worse. They were taking an evening out while they still had one to take.

"What about the boy?" she asked.

"Daphne pushed hard. He gets to be with the psychic short-term, maybe long term. It's a good thing."

"Yes," she agreed. They clinked glasses.

"What's this dinner about?" she asked.

"Can't we just go out to dinner?"

"No. Not here. Not like this. What's it about?"

He snorted and looked to the drink for courage. "I'm going to put in for lieutenant."

"Seriously?"

"Would I joke?"

She studied her husband, leaned over, and kissed his cheek. She reached up to take off the lipstick, but Boldt leaned away.

"No," he said. "I want to keep it."

"It looks kind of silly."

"Good," he said. He lifted his glass and ordered another vodka.

"I'm driving," she said.

"You're driving," he agreed. Then he said, "Hell, you've been driving us for years."

They looked into each other's eyes a few times, but neither said a word. Liz eventually couldn't fight off the smile, and Boldt joined her.

"Crazy, huh?" she said.

"Yeah. Weird," Boldt agreed. He felt tears at the back of his throat. He fought against them.

"You never know," she offered. Her eyes were glassy.

"No. You never know."

"We'll help each other through it." She reached down and took his hand in hers and squeezed hard—she squeezed the way he'd wanted her to squeeze for years. Where had that squeeze gone? he wondered. How had they lost that squeeze until such a moment? She squeezed again and squeezed tears from both their eyes.

But Boldt managed the smile that time. He realized that was how it was going to be, trading back and forth, the both of them. "A lot of this lately," he confessed.

"Yeah. Good for the tear ducts," she offered, blinking through her own.

"Scared?" he asked, his voice trembling.

"Yes," she answered. "You bet I am." Her lips quivered and she looked to him for some answer that he didn't have.

"Me, too," he whispered, to the most beautiful wife in the world.